2011年
考研英语(一)阅读
分阶训练

考研英语阅读研究组 编著

U0140923

北京航空航天大学出版社

图书在版编目(CIP)数据

2011 年考研英语(一)阅读分阶训练 / 考研英语阅读研究组编著.
-- 北京：北京航空航天大学出版社,2010.3
ISBN 978-7-5124-0020-7

Ⅰ.①2… Ⅱ.①考… Ⅲ.①英语—阅读教学—研究
生—入学考试—习题 Ⅳ.①H319.4-44

中国版本图书馆 CIP 数据核字(2010)第 022515 号

2011 年考研英语(一)阅读分阶训练
考研英语阅读研究组 编著
责任编辑 潘 静

*

北京航空航天大学出版社出版发行
北京市海淀区学院路 37 号 (100191) 发行部电话：010-82317024 传真：010-82328026
http:// www.buaapress.com.cn Email: bhpress@263.net
北京市松源印刷有限公司印装 各地书店经销

*

开本：787×1092 1/16 印张：15.5 字数：397 千字
2010 年 3 月第 1 版 2010 年 3 月第 1 次印刷
ISBN 978-7-5124-0020-7 定价：29.80 元

前 言

本书编写的目的与要达到的预期效果

本书旨在帮助立志考研者迅速提高阅读能力,直通考研英语的内部,所以从某种意义上来讲这本书的价值和意义并不完全在于其内容上,更重要的是它在编排体制上所体现出来的考研英语学习思路给考生所带来的启发。其实真正拥有语言天赋的人并不多,每个人只要有正确的方法,都能把英语学好。虽然本书的目的不在于讨论英语学习这个大问题,而在于帮助考生战胜考研英语,但方法的重要性却是不言而喻的。

那什么才是最好的方法?对这个问题的回答似乎因人而异,但是,须知任何一种考试,无论是四、六级还是考研,或者是托福、雅思等都因为考试性质的不同而有其不同于其他考试的规律,因此首先要明白所要参加考试的目的、结构和难度等等各个方面。直接的切入要比在外围做准备更有效率。但考试毕竟需要一定的基础和积累。以考研英语为例,做真题似乎成了一个众所周知的秘诀,但许多考生却很难坚持下来,原因就在于真题难度太大,直接切入很困难,并且经常打击学习英语的信心和兴趣。因此词汇、句法等各方面的基础也是非常重要的准备工作。而按部就班地从头学起又来不及,本书编写的目的就是要解决这一个困难,让考生先从相对容易的文章入手进行学习,循序渐进地进入到考研英语之中。

考研英语阅读理解部分共分三节,其实是三种题型。A 节属于对文章的深度理解,B 节类似于完形填空,考查的主要是对文章逻辑结构的理解,C 节是精读翻译。针对不同的题型,要有不同的策略和方法。本书试图以简洁明了的方式对考研英语的阅读进行全方位的介绍和训练,达到事半功倍的效果。

本书的内容与章节安排

学习英语最重要也不过有几点内容,首先是词汇量的多少。然而大的词汇量并不一定能保证英语能力可以有相应的水平,有的人词汇量虽然很大,但是遇到一定难度的文章还是读不懂,这就涉及到第二方面的内容——对英语句子的读解能力。第三点就是对西方人的文化背景不了解,这样理解起来就存在一定困难,因此了解西方尤其是英语国家概况是很必要的。第四点是思维方式的问题,对英语文章的篇章构成不了解,读起来不知所云。

本书的目的就是试图解决这些问题。考研英语阅读的文章大都来自英美国家一些知名的书刊杂志,除去个别难度上的改动之外基本上都是原汁原味的英语,因此在真正进入到考研英语真题之前要先解决语言和文化差异等各方面的问题。而作者编写这本书很难在如此有限的篇幅内完成这个任务,但作者精选了几十篇这方面的文章供大家阅读,既提高阅读能力,扩大词汇量,同时又对英语国家的背景有所了解。

希望可以帮助考生提高阅读水平,顺利通过考研英语大关!

目　录

第一章　基础与巩固 ……………………………………………………… 1

第一节　地理常识 ……………………………………………………… 2

第二节　经济金融 ……………………………………………………… 12

第三节　政治制度 ……………………………………………………… 25

第四节　文化教育 ……………………………………………………… 38

第二章　提高与拓展 ……………………………………………………… 52

第一节　政治经济 ……………………………………………………… 53

第二节　文化教育 ……………………………………………………… 69

第三节　社会法制 ……………………………………………………… 87

第四节　科技发展 ……………………………………………………… 101

第三章　真经与实战 ……………………………………………………… 116

2005 年考研英语全真试题（阅读理解部分）……………………………… 119

2005 年考研英语全真试题（阅读理解部分)解析 ………………………… 128

2006 年考研英语全真试题（阅读理解部分）……………………………… 140

2006 年考研英语全真试题（阅读理解部分)解析 ………………………… 149

2007 年考研英语全真试题（阅读理解部分）……………………………… 161

2007 年考研英语全真试题（阅读理解部分)解析 ………………………… 170

2008 年考研英语全真试题（阅读理解部分）……………………………… 182

2008 年考研英语全真试题（阅读理解部分)解析 ………………………… 191

2009 年考研英语全真试题（阅读理解部分）……………………………… 202

2009 年考研英语全真试题（阅读理解部分)解析 ………………………… 210

2010 年考研英语(一)全真试题（阅读理解部分）………………………… 222

2010 年考研英语(一)全真试题（阅读理解部分)解析 …………………… 231

第一章

基础与巩固

1. 本部分的目标和内容

这部分内容的基本目标有三个,第一是扩大词汇量,第二是了解西方文化背景知识,第三是提高阅读英语文章的能力。因此,这部分也有助于那些英语基础薄弱的考生提高学习英语的积极性,快速入门。从体例上来讲,也是三者兼顾的,首先文章右面的方框内有词汇的注解,目的是节约查词时间,更快地扩大词汇量。其次,每篇文章都有"长难句分析",主要目的是降低文章难度,便于学习者掌握重要的句型,学会分析长难句。最后是参考译文,目的是方便读者检查自己的理解是否正确。

为了便于读者了解西方社会的知识背景,提高阅读能力,在内容方面特别选取与主要英语国家的政治、经济、法律、文化、教育、科技相关的文章,内容丰富多彩,不限于说明性文章,还有评论性、记叙性文章入选。这样既在文章题材方面又在文章类型方面都能对读者有所裨益。

2. 如何使用本章

第一步:熟悉文章内容,在不借助任何帮助的情况下完成对文章的理解。不认识的单词也不需要看右边的注释, 可以先自己根据上下文对词义进行猜测。了解文章大意是初步工作,也是对阅读能力的基本要求。

第二步:词汇记忆。一是要注意词汇的积累,把新学习到的单词都记在纸上,随身携带,随时随地都可以进行复习。

第三步:精读文章,解决文章中的长难句。在学习时尤其重要的是分析长难句的思路是什么,不是仅就句子看句子,而是要逐渐理解英语句子的构成特点,如何能抓住句子的核心部分进行简化等等。

第四步:对文章内容进行深化理解,要求读懂所有句子,不放过任何一个疑难点,可以"参考译文"作为对照,检查自己的理解是否正确。当然,我们所列出的单词和句子不可能解决不同读者的所有问题,面对疑难一定要勤于动手查阅资料和辞典。

第五步:复习回顾。这仍然是重复的问题,但如何重复是一个问题。在完成了上述环节之后,并不要求读者一口气把这些文章读上几十遍,而是要不断循环。建议在学习完一个单元的内容后再进行复习和整理。

第一节　地理常识

Passage 1

The United States is a land of great differences—differences in climate (you can find every kind of climate here, though the country lies mostly in the temperate zone); in landscape (you'll see high mountains, plateaus, plains, water-falls etc.); in altitude (that is, differences in the height above sea level). The continental United States, the country's territory on the North American continent, stretches about 4,500 kilometers from the eastern coast, that is, the Atlantic Coast, to the Pacific Ocean on the West; and it extends 2,557 kilometers from the northern boundary to the southern tip of Texas. The country borders Canada on the north and goes down south to Mexico and the Gulf of Mexico. Including the States of Alaska and Hawaii, the United States covers an area of nine million square kilometers, or to be more exact, 9,191,843 sq. km., a little less than the area of the People's Republic of China, which is 9,600,000 sq. km..

There are altogether 50 states in the United States, the largest of which is Alaska. It borders on the northwestern Canada and is 82 km away from Russia across the Bering Strait. It was known as Russian America until purchased by the United States from Russia in 1867. It was linked to the United States by the Alaska Highway in 1942, and became the 49th state of the USA in 1959.

Texas is the second in size, which is larger than France, but is only a little less than half of the area of Chinese Xin Jiang Uighur Autonomous Region.

Hawaii lies in the tropical zone of the Pacific, 3,200 km away from the North American Continent. It is a group of islands, which became the 50th state of the United States in

temperate *a.* (气候)温和的
plateau *n.* 高原
altitude *n.* 海拔
territory *n.* 领土;疆域
stretch *v.* 延伸;伸展

boundary *n.* 边界
border *v.* 接壤

Bering Strait *n.* 白令海峡
purchase *v.* 购买

autonomous *a.* 自治的,自动的
tropical *a.* 热带的

1959. Hawaii, was made very famous by the Japanese attack, on December 7, 1941, on one of its islands—Pearl Harbor which is situated near Honolulu, the capital of Hawaii.

A jet plan can fly over the continental United States from the east coast to the Pacific Ocean on the west in about five hours; it will take a little more than two days to travel by train from Los Angeles on the west to New York City on the east coast. However, by driving along the highways and super-highways, which crisscross the country, you'll get a better bird's-eye view of the mainland of the United States.

crisscross *v.* 纵横交错

重点词组

lie in	位于	get a bird's-eye view of	鸟瞰
that is	也就是		

长难句分析

However, by driving along the highways and super-highways, which crisscross the country, you'll get a better bird's-eye view of the mainland of the United States.

该句中 by 引出的介词短语 by driving along the highways and super-highways 作全句的方式状语。此外,句中还有一个"which"引导的非限制性定语从句,先行词为 the highways and super-highways。

参考译文

美国的差异很大,体现在气候上,这里有各种气候,虽然大部分地区位于温带;地形有高山、高原、平原、瀑布;海拔也各不相同。美国大陆部分从东部大西洋海岸到西部太平洋海岸有 4,500 公里;由北部到南部的田纳西有 2,557 公里长。北部与加拿大接壤,南部毗邻墨西哥与墨西哥湾。美国国土面积,包括阿拉斯加州和夏威夷岛在内为 9,191,843 平方公里,仅次于面积为 9,600,000 平方公里的中国。

美国有 50 个州,最大的州是阿拉斯加。它与加拿大西北部相邻,与俄罗斯隔着白令海峡相距82公里。它曾被叫做"俄罗斯的美洲",直到1867年被美国购得。1942年修建的阿拉斯加公路将它与美国大陆连接在一起。1959年阿拉斯加成为美国的第41个州。

田纳西州为美国第二大州,比法国大,但还不到新疆维吾尔自治区面积的一半。

夏威夷位于太平洋的热带地区,距北美大陆3,200公里。它由群岛构成,1959年成为美国的第50个州。夏威夷因1941年7月的日本偷袭珍珠港事件而闻名。珍珠港位于夏威夷州火奴鲁鲁附近的一个岛上。

坐喷气式飞机从东海岸到太平洋西岸穿越美国大陆需要大约5小时;乘火车从西部的洛杉矶到东海岸的纽约需要两天多。<u>但是,驾车行驶在纵横交织的公路与高速公路上,可以更好地欣赏整个美国大陆的全景。</u>

Passage 2

Britain comprises Great Britain (England, Wales and Scotland) and Northern Ireland, and is one of the member states of the European Union. Its full name is the United Kingdom of Great Britain and Northern Ireland.

comprise *a.* 构成;由…构成

Britain constitutes the greater part of the British Isles. The largest of the islands is Great Britain. The next largest comprises Northern Ireland and the Irish Republic.

constitute *v.* 构成;组成

With an area of some 242, 500 sq. km., Britain is just less than 1,000 km. from the south coast to the extreme north of Scotland and just less than 500 km. across in the widest part.

According to preliminary result of the April 1991 census, Britain's population is 55.5 million. It ranks 17th in the world in terms of population. The British population is expected, on mid-1989 based projections, to be 59.2 million in 2001 and 60 million in 2011.

preliminary *a.* 初步的;起始的

In the later 18th and 19th centuries Britain became the first industrialized country, basing its wealth on coal-mining, on the manufacture of iron and steel, heavy machinery and textiles, on shipbuilding and on trade.

industrialized *a.* 工业化的
machinery *n.* 机械
textile *n.* 纺织品

In the 20th century a second period of industrialization

changed the broad pattern of development in Britain. In the 1920s and 1930s the northern industrial centers saw their traditional manufactures weakened owing to fluctuations in the world trade and competition from other industrializing countries.

fluctuation *n.* 波动

Tourism and the leisure industries have expanded considerably in recent years. Over half of expenditure by overseas visitors in Britain takes place in London, and areas elsewhere, encouraged by government policies to expand tourism in the regions, are becoming increasingly popular with overseas tourists.

leisure *n.* 休闲；空闲
expenditure *n.* 花费

Of the many tourist attractions in Britain, for instance, are Madame Tussaud's waxworks in London, the Tower of London and Alton Towers, with more than millions of visitors per year respectively.

respectively *ad.* 各自地
association *n.* 联系；联想

Many regions and towns have associations with great English writes an artists, such as William Shakespeare (Stratford-upon-Avon), William Wordsworth (lake District), the Bronte sisters (York-shire).

重点词组

according to	依据	have association with	与…有联系
owing to	由于		

长难句分析

In the 1920s and 1930s the northern industrial centers saw their traditional manufactures weakened owing to fluctuations in the world trade and competition from other industrializing countries.

该句的谓语动词为 saw，意为"为（某事）的现场或背景"，主语为地点名词；see 还可指"某事发生之时，目睹"，此时其主语为时间名词。另外，weakened 是 weaken 的过去分词，表示被动，意为"被削弱"。

参考译文

英国包括大不列颠(英格兰、威尔士和苏格兰)和北爱尔兰,是欧盟成员国之一。全称为大不列颠及北爱尔兰联合王国。

英国是由不列颠群岛中的大部分岛屿组成的,其中第一大岛是大不列颠,第二大岛上有北爱尔兰和爱尔兰共和国。

英国的面积大约是 242,500 平方公里,从南部海岸到苏格兰的最北部不到 1,000 公里,横向最宽只有 500 公里。根据 1991 年 4 月的人口普查的初步结果,英国人口有 5,500 万,在世界上名列第 17 位。

根据 1989 年中期的人口为依据所做的预测,英国的人口预计在 2001 年将达到 5,920 万,2011 年将达到 6,000 万。

在 18 世纪后期和 19 世纪,英国成为第一个工业化国家,其财富主要来自采煤、钢铁制造、重型机械制造、纺织工业、造船业和商业。

在 20 世纪,第二阶段的工业化使得英国的发展模式发生了变化。在 20 年代和 30 年代,由于世界贸易的波动,以及其他正在进行工业化的国家的竞争,北部工业中心传统的制造业出现了衰退。

旅游业和娱乐业近年来发展得相当快速。外国游客在英国总的开支中有一半以上用在伦敦,其他地区在政府政策的鼓励下也在扩大各自的旅游业,并且吸引着越来越的外国旅游者。

英国有很多的旅游胜地,比如图索德夫人蜡像馆、伦敦塔、奥尔顿堡,每年都有百万以上的参观者。

许多地区和城镇与一些英国伟大的作家的名字联系在一起,如威廉·莎士比亚(艾冯河畔斯特拉特福),威廉·华兹华斯(湖畔地区)、勃朗特姐妹(约克郡)。

Passage 3

Canada is situated in the northern half of the North American Continent. It occupies an area of 9,976,139 sq. km.. It is a bit larger than China. Thus, in area it is the second largest country in the world, being exceeded only by Russia. In comparison, Canada is more than forty times the sizes of Britain.

occupy v. 占据;占用

exceed v. 超过;超出

The only country that is adjacent to Canada on land is the United States. It is to the south of Canada. On the other sides, Canada is surrounded by water. To the east of Canada is the Atlantic Ocean. To the west is the Pacific Ocean. And to the north is the Arctic Ocean. The borderline shared by the U.S. and Canada is as long as 5,524.5 km. It is called the longest undefended borderline in the world. Citizens of both countries can cross the border without a visa.

People tend to think that as Canada is a northern country its winters must be harsh and long. But contrary to popular belief, on the whole, Canada is a very sunny land with a distinctive change of seasons. Since Canada is a vast country, its climate varies greatly from region to region. When it comes to Canada's climate, people usually divide it into six climate regions, the Arctic Region, the Northern Region, the Prairie Region, the Cordillera Region, the Pacific Region, and the Southeastern Region.

It is estimated that one eighth of the land is suitable for agricultural production. However, as Canada is a sparsely populated country, only eight percent of the land is presently used for farming. Agriculture plays a very important role in Canada's economy. It accounts for more than a quarter of the country's economy. Farm exports alone amount to 20 percent of the country's foreign exchange. Other major industries of Canada include forest industry, fisheries, mining and metallurgical industry, electric power generating industries and manufacturing industries.

adjacent *a.* 毗邻的

visa *n.* 签证

harsh *a.* 严酷的；严厉的

distinctive *a.* 有特色的

arctic *a.* 北极的
prairie *n.* 大草原
cordillera *n.* 山脉

sparsely *ad.* 稀少地；
　零散地

metallurgical *a.* 冶金的

重点词组

be situated in	位于	be suitable for	适合于
be adjacent to	与…毗邻	account for	(数量等)占…
when it comes to	当涉及…时	amount to	总计

长难句分析

Thus, in area it is the second largest country in the world, being exceeded only by Russia.

句中 thus 是连词，意为"因此，所以"。短语 in area，其中 in 表示在某一方面；being exceeded 是由现在分词引出的独立主格结构，省略了主语"it"。

参考译文

加拿大位于北美大陆的北半部。面积 9,976,139 平方公里，比中国稍大。其为世界第二国土大国，仅次于俄罗斯，是英国面积的 40 多倍。

美国是加拿大惟一的陆上邻国，位于其南部。加拿大其余三面皆环水，东部是大西洋；西部是太平洋。加美两国边界长达 5,524.5 公里，是世界上最长的不设防国界线。两国居民可以不持签证自由穿梭。

人们倾向于认为，加拿大因位于北部，冬季会严寒而漫长。恰恰相反，加拿大阳光充足、四季分明。由于加拿大很大，地区间的气候差别也很大。其气候可分为 6 个气候带：北极带、北部带、大草原带、山脉地带、太平洋地带和东南部地带。

据估计，加拿大八分之一的土地适合于农业生产。然而人口稀少，目前只有 8% 的土地用于农耕。农业在加拿大经济中很重要，占到全国经济总量的四分之一。农业出口额达到国家外贸交易总额的 20%。加拿大其他的主要产业还包括林业、渔业、矿产、冶金业、发电业和制造业。

Passage 4

Australia is the smallest continent and the largest island in the world. It is the sixth largest country in the area after Russia, Canada, China, the United States and Brazil and also the only nation that occupies an entire continent. It is about 25 times larger than Britain and Ireland.

With an area of 7,682,300 sq. km., Australia is situated in the Southern Hemisphere entirely below the

Brazil *n.* 巴西
occupy *v.* 占据；占用
Ireland *n.* 爱尔兰

hemisphere *n.* 半球

equator. Almost 40 percent of the land lies within the tropics, and a larger part of the country stands within the driest area of latitude.

Roughly a rectangular shape, Australia has the shallow Great Australia Bight in the south and the Gulf of Carpentaria in the northeast. Its coastline is as long as 36,735 km. Numerous islands, mostly small, surround the continent.

The Australian climate ranges from tropical in the north to temperate in the south. Summer is from December to February, autumn from March to May, winter from June to August and spring from September to November. A notable feature of the climate is the low rain fall in the most parts. Over much of the north seasonal droughts occur, and throughout Australia flooding is fairly common.

Australia is the flattest of the seven continents. The average elevation in Australia is less than 300 meters, with the world's mean of about 700 meters. Only about one-twentieth of the continent is more than 600 meters above sea level. The Australian Alps in the southeastern area contain Australia's highest area with the highest point at Mount Kosciusko (2,228 meters).

tropics *n.* 热带
latitude *n.* 纬度;回旋余地
rectangular *a.* 长方形的

drought *n.* 干旱

elevation *n.* 海拔;举起;抬高

重点词组

be situated in 位于

range from... to 在…之间变化

长难句分析

It is the sixth largest country in the area after Russia, Canada, China, the United States and Brazil and also the only nation that occupies an entire continent.

该句中 after,在此是介词,表示"(在顺序、排列或重要性上)仅次于…"。而 "... and also the only nation that occupies an entire continent."是 it is 的另一个表语,后面是一个定语从句,先行词由 the only 加以界定,故引导词必须是 that。

参考译文

澳大利亚是世界上最小的大陆也是最大的岛屿。<u>澳大利亚国土面积居世界第六位,仅次于俄国、加拿大、中国、美国及巴西,也是世界上惟一占据一个大陆的国家</u>。是英国与爱尔兰面积总和的 25 倍。

澳大利亚国土面积为 7,682,300 平方公里,位于赤道下方的南半球,大约 40% 的国土处于热带地区,大部分处于最干旱的纬度。

澳大利亚大致像一个长方形,南部有澳大利亚大海湾,东北部是卡奔塔利亚湾。其海岸线长达 36,735 公里。大大小小的岛屿环绕在其周围。

澳大利亚北部为热带气候,南部为温带气候。夏季从 12 月至 2 月,秋季从 3 月到 5 月,冬季从 7 月到 8 月,春季从 9 月到 11 月。气候的一个显著特点是大部分地区降雨量低。北部大部地区都出现季节性干旱,而澳洲各地时有洪水泛滥。

澳洲在七大洲中最为平坦,平均海拔不到 300 米,而世界平均海拔大约为 700 米。整个大陆只有二十分之一的地区海拔超过 600 米。澳大利亚山脉位于东南部地区,这里有澳洲最高的地区,其中科西阿斯科山(2,228 米)是全国最高点。

Passage 5

Australia is a continent with a landscape consisting mainly of low plateaus, which are sectioned off by rugged mountain ranges.

landscape *n.* 景观;风景

The Great Dividing Range is the biggest mountain range, and starts in central Victoria and ends in Northern Queens land some several thousand kilometers in length. An area on the Victoria and New South Wales border receives more snow than the country of Switzerland.

Switzerland *n.* 瑞士

Other prominent mountain ranges include The Hammersley Ranges, the Flinders Ranges, the Macdonell Ranges, the Darling Ranges and the King Leopold Ranges.

Northern Australia is located in the tropics and the landscape consists of rainforest, which leads into large areas of grasslands, which eventually merge into the central deserts. These deserts are the largest in the world outside of the Sahara. This part of Australia's is called the Red Centre because of the unusual red color in the sand.

grassland *n.* 草原

The Southwest corner of Australia is populated by Karri Forests, which is rated as some of the tallest trees on earth.

Tasmania to the south is a mountainous island about the same size as Ireland or Sri Lanka located in the temperate climatic zone immediately below the Australian continent. One quarter of this island is protected wilderness and is similar in appearance to nearby New Zealand.

mountainous *a.* 多山的；巨大的

wilderness *n.* 荒原
New Zealand *n.* 新西兰

重点词组

consist of	由…组成	the same as	与…相同
be located in	位于		

长难句分析

Australia is a continent with a landscape consisting mainly of low plateaus, which are sectioned off by rugged mountain ranges.

句中 consisting 是现在分词，作 landscape 的定语。which 引导非限制性定语从句，先行词为 low plateaus；词组 section off 的意为"将某物切成部分"。

参考译文

澳大利亚主要由低矮的高原构成，这些低矮的高原被高低不平的山脉分隔开。

大分水岭是最大的山脉，起于维多利亚州中部、绵延至北昆士兰州约数千公里。在维多利亚州和新南威尔士州交界的一个地区的降雪量超过了瑞士。

其他著名的山脉还有哈默斯利山脉、弗林德斯山脉、麦克德纳尔山脉、达令山脉和国王利奥波德山脉。

澳大利亚北部位于热带，拥有大片雨林，雨林延伸至大面积的草原，最终融入到中部沙漠。这些沙漠是撒哈拉沙漠以外世界上最大的沙漠。澳大利亚的这一地区被称为"红色中心"，正是得名于该地区不寻常的红色沙子。

澳大利亚的西南角是卡里森林，有地球上最高的树木。

南部的塔斯马尼亚州，是一个多山的岛屿，面积相当于爱尔兰或斯里兰卡，处于温带气候区，海拔略低于澳大利亚大陆。这个岛的四分之一是受保护的荒野，地貌与附近的新西兰相似。

第二节　经济金融

Passage 1

Federal Reserve Chairman Ben Bernanke says the dollar is strong, but investors quite literally aren't buying it.

Just hours after Bernanke told an audience in the southern state of Georgia that one can count on a strong dollar because the Fed is committed to making sure we have price stability in this country, the dollar on Tuesday plunged to multi-week lows against rival currencies.

That's because saying the Fed is committed to price stability and enacting measures to ensure such an outcome are two different things. Investors seem to be fairly certain the measures taken thus far by the U.S.. The Fed has lowered interest rates to virtually zero and appears content to keep them that way for a good while to encourage economic growth. It has also been printing money like crazy to bail out the banking industry, which is pushing the deficit of U.S..

The fear is that such heavy deficit spending will lead to high inflation that depreciates the value of a currency. And the Fed won't be able to fight by raising interest rates if it is still trying to promote growth.

That's not to say the dollar is about to fall off a cliff. Preventing a dollar rout will likely be the realization that global economic recovery isn't coming as soon as many hope.

"We continue to expect more losses in the U.S. dollar," says Kathy Lien, director of currency research at Global Forex Trading. "But with growth still expected to be below trend and the U.S. economy facing more job losses, a 'V'- shaped recovery or a strong rebound is a bit too optimistic."

---

literally *ad.* 此处无实意，用以加强语气

plunge *v.* 猛跌；使突然陷入

enact *v.* 制定；通过
ensure *v.* 确保；保证

virtually *ad.* 几乎

deficit *n.* 赤字
depreciate *v.* 贬值

rout *n.* 溃败；动荡

rebound *v.* 反弹
optimistic *a.* 乐观的

重点词组

count on	指望	bail out	救市
be committed to doing	保证做	fall off	下降

长难句分析

That's because saying the Fed is committed to price stability and enacting measures to ensure such an outcome are two different things.

整句为 because 引导的表语从句。从句中有两个并列主语,分别为 saying 和 enacting measures。此外,句中出现的 commit... to...意为"向…保证…",句子为省略引导词的定语从句:saying（which）the Fed is committed to price stability。

参考译文

美国联邦储备委员会(Federal Reserve, 简称美联储)主席贝南克(Ben Bernanke)认为美元走势坚挺,但投资者对此根本不买账。

贝南克周一晚间在佐治亚州发表讲话时指出,美元会保持强劲,因为美联储将努力确保美国物价稳定。而就在贝南克发表上述讲话几小时后,美元兑其他主要货币却于周二滑落至数周最低点。

原因在于美联储口头承诺确保物价稳定与采取实际行动履行其诺言完全是两码事。鉴于人们期待已久的经济复苏已经显现萌芽迹象, 投资者看似十分肯定美联储迄今为止采取的各项措施只会削弱美元走势。

美联储已将利率下调至实际的零水平, 而且甘愿在未来较长一段时间内将利率保持在低位,以刺激经济增长。与此同时,为帮助银行业摆脱困境,美联储还在大量发行货币,从而导致美国联邦政府的财政赤字。

人们担心的是,如此巨大的赤字开支将引发高通货膨胀进而会导致美元贬值。而且若美联储仍继续致力于刺激经济增长的话,那么将无法通过加息来应对通货膨胀。

不过,这并不是说美元将一落千丈。如果全球经济复苏并非像诸多人预计的那样很快到来,那么美元或许就能避免贬值。

纽约全球外汇交易的外汇研究部门主管凯西·利恩称,"我们仍预计美元会进一步下跌,不过,鉴于经济增长仍将低于趋势水平,而且美国失业现象还会加剧,市场对经济实现 V 型复苏或强劲反弹的预期可能有些过于乐观。"

Passage 2

International stock markets have long taken their cues from the U.S., but as it became clear that emerging-market economies would hold up best and rebound first from the downturn, the U.S. has in some ways moved over to the passenger seat.

cue *n.* 榜样;提示

Money managers that invest in U.S. and other big developed markets are paying more attention than ever to what's going on in places like China and Brazil and are putting their investments in areas that are most heavily exposed to overseas economic growth.

The resilience of emerging-market economies, particularly China, is helping drive a strong rebound in crude-oil prices to north of $66 a barrel, as well as big gains in other commodity prices. That in turn has fueled a rally in many U.S. energy and materials stocks. Some also see emerging-market strength helping battered consumer companies.

resilience *n.* 迅速恢复的
  能力
commodity *n.* 商品
fuel *v.* 供给燃料
rally *n.* 回升
battered *a.* 破旧的,此处
  指经营困难的

Even beyond their borders, "what happens in those countries is clearly very important," says Virginie Maison-neuve, head of global equities at Schroders Investment Management in London.

Certainly, emerging markets have been the place to be this year. The MSCI Emerging markets index is up 36%, while the Dow Jones Industrial Average and the Standard & Poor's 500-stock index are both basically flat despite a strong rebound from 12-year lows hit on March 9.

index *n.* 指数

But the ripples have spread beyond emerging-market stocks. In the energy markets, China is a major focus.

ripple *n.* 波纹

重点词组

take the cue from 照…的样子去做   be exposed to 显露或暴露于…

长难句分析

Money managers that invest in U.S. and other big developed markets are paying more attention than ever to what's going on in places like China and Brazil and are ratcheting up their investments in areas that are most heavily exposed to overseas economic growth.

该句主语为 money managers，后接由 that 引导定语从句。money mangers 有两个并列谓语 paying more attention 和 ratcheting up their investments。在后一谓语中，又包含有一个 that 引导的定语从句，先行词为 areas。短语 exposed to 意为"暴露于…"。

参考译文

全球股市长期以来一直以美国股市为榜样，但由于新兴市场经济体表现抢眼，并可能率先从低迷中反弹，美国在某些方面已退居次位了。

投资于美国等发达国家市场的基金经理对中国和巴西等国发生的事情给予了比以往更多的关注，并将更多资金投向了同海外经济增长关系最为密切的领域中。

中国等新兴经济体的坚挺推动原油价格强劲反弹至每桶 66 美元之上，其中大宗商品价格也大幅上扬。这反过来又推动美国许多能源和材料类股票出现反弹。有些人还预计，新兴市场走强会助那些身陷困境的消费品公司一臂之力。

施罗德投资管理公司驻伦敦的全球股票部门负责人麦森纽(Virginie Maisonneuve)说，即使对身处异国的人来说，"这些国家发生的事情也非常重要。"

的确，新兴市场今年的表现出类拔萃。摩根斯坦利资本国际新兴市场指数上涨了 36%，而道琼斯工业股票平均价格指数和标准普尔 500 指数尽管从 3 月 9 日的 12 年低点强劲反弹，但今年仍是基本持平。

不过新兴市场之外的股票也感受到了这种扩散效应。在能源市场，中国成了主要关注点。

Passage 3

How did the American economy get in danger? When the economy was strong a few years ago, many people wanted to buy houses. Banks gave people mortgages, or

mortgage *n.* 抵押，借款

loans to buy house. That resulted in a housing "boom", when many people bought homes. The prices of homes increased because so many people wanted to buy. At the height of the housing boom, many banks gave mortgages to people who, a few years before, could not get a mortgage because of low income.

boom *n.* 繁荣期

That all changed in 2006, when gas and food prices rose. As costs increased, many people found they could no longer afford their monthly mortgage payment. When those people told the banks they could not pay back their loans, the banks took back their homes to sell them. But the houses were worth less than the mortgages were worth. Banks found they were losing money fast.

loan *n.* 贷款

In September 2008, some of the nation's biggest financial companies hit rock bottom. The government helped some banks by loaning money to them. Others had to file for bankruptcy. That means they are unable to pay off their debts. The remaining banks worried about ending up with more bad loans, so they stopped lending money.

bankruptcy *n.* 破产

The effects were felt beyond the housing industry. Without loans, business had trouble paying their employees. People were afraid to spend money on expensive items such as cars. Others could not get loans to pay for big purchases.

item *n.* 条款,项目
purchase *n.* 购买的东西

重点词组

result in	导致	end up with	以…方式结束
pay back	偿还	rock bottom	最低点
take back	收回		

长难句分析

At the height of the housing boom, many banks gave mortgages to people who, a few years before, could not get a mortgage because of low income.

该句式为非限定性定语从句,先行词为引导词,其中" a few years before"为插入语。because of 为介词短语,后接名词或动名词。

参考译文

美国经济是如何陷入泥潭的？几年前经济形势大好时，很多人想买房。银行给想买房的人提供抵押或贷款。结果导致了房地产业的迅速繁荣。买房的人多，所以房价飙升。楼市火爆的时候，很多银行给低收入者也提供抵押或贷款，早些年，这些人是申请不到贷款的。

在 2006 年，随着汽油和食品价格的上涨，一切都变了。生活成本增加，很多人无法偿还每月的抵押贷款。他们告知银行无法还贷，银行就收回并变卖他们的房产。但这些房子的价值低于它们的抵押贷款。银行发现他们的资产正在大量流失。

2008 年 9 月，美国几家最大的金融公司相继"触底"。政府向一些银行发放的贷款以帮助其度过难关，部分银行因无力偿还债务而不得不申请破产。其他银行担心摊上更多的不良贷款，于是就停止放贷。

遭受影响的不只房地产业。没有贷款，企业就没法开工资。人们不敢去购买像汽车那样的昂贵产品，有些人则无法贷款消费大件商品。

Passage 4

For the last month or two, the U.K. currency has been on the rise, with the hopes that the worst of the U.K. recession is over.

recession *n.* 衰退；倒退

This has ensured that investors kept on supporting the pound, despite grave concerns about the U.K. government's attempts to spend its way out of the recession.

However, last week's announcement by the Bank of England that it is extending its quantitative easing by another GBP 50 billion appears to have shaken the market out of its torpor.

extend *v.* 扩展；延伸
quantitative *a.* 数量的
torpor *n.* 迟缓；麻木
tacit *a.* 暗含的

The central bank's move is being interpreted as a tacit admission that all is far from well with the U.K. economy and that even the highly expensive bailout of U.K. banks hasn't worked.

bailout *n.* 救市

Evidence of the BOE's concerns are expected in the growth and inflation projections in its latest quarterly Inflation Report on Wednesday.

Data has already shown that the 4.1% economic contraction in the first quarter was much worse than expected and that any recovery starting in 2010 will be only very slow and very gradual.

contraction *n.* 萎缩

Analysts now fear that the *Inflation Report* will show that the bank's inflation projections remain similarly subdued. If so, this would suggest that the quantitative easing the bank has enacted so far has failed to stimulate prices and leaves the country at risk from disinflation.

subdue *a.* 抑制的

Hopes that the recent slowdown in the fall in house prices might herald a recovery also have been shattered.

herald *v.* 宣告…的到来

重点词组

on the rise　　　上升　　　　　　　at risk　　　冒风险

长难句分析

The central bank's move is being interpreted as a tacit admission that all is far from well with the U.K. economy and that even the highly expensive bailout of U.K. banks hasn't worked.

该句谓语动词 is being interpreted 为动词 interpret 现在进行时的被动语态形式,意为"被理解为";另外,tacit admission that... and that...句中包含两个 that 引导的定语从句,先行词均为 tacit admission。

参考译文

过去一两个月,英镑一直处于上升状态,因当时市场沉浸在英国经济衰退最严重的时期已经过去的憧憬之中。

这能确保投资者继续支持英磅,尽管他们对英国政策走出经济萧条的尝试仍深感忧虑。

然而,英国央行(Bank of England)上周宣布将定量宽松政策规模扩大 500 亿英镑后,市场似乎如梦初醒。

市场认为,英国央行此举等于默认英国经济离恢复正常还相距甚远,甚至英国政府耗巨资对国内银行业展开的救助也未见成效。

预计英国央行所考虑的不利因素会在周三最新季度通货膨胀报告中对经济增长和通货

膨胀的预期中体现出来。

数据显示第一季度经济下滑 4.1%，比预计更糟。2010 年经济将开始复苏，但增幅平缓。

分析师们目前担心季度《通货膨胀报告》将显示出英国央行的通货膨胀预期仍像之前一样温和。如果事实如此，则说明央行采取的定量宽松政策至今仍未能刺激物价增长，英国仍面临通货膨胀下降的风险。

有关近期住房价格降幅放缓可能预示着经济将实现复苏的希望也已被打破。

Passage 5

Schroeder's Ms. Maisonneuve agrees that oil and materials benefit from an emerging-markets growth story. During the pullback earlier this year, she bought mining and steel stocks. As the global economy collapsed, those firms slashed production capacity, she says. "All we need to see is a little more normalization of demand and you will see continued strong reaction in those prices," she says.

But she's also looking for consumer companies with growing businesses in those nations, such as Nestle, Tesco and L'Oreal.

"It's not just a story about industrials," she says. When it comes to consumer demand, "the dynamic out of this recession is going to come from emerging markets."

Jonathan Masse, a senior portfolio manager at Alpha Shares LLC, also sees an emerging-markets play in some consumer companies. For example, fast-food chain operator Yum! Brands saw its first-quarter same-store sales grow 1% globally, thanks to a 2% increase from China, which now accounts for 20% of total revenue. He also sees positives for otherwise struggling luxury brands and casino operators that have a bigger presence in China, such as Wynn Resorts or LVMH Moet Hennessy Louis Vuitton.

Of course, the emerging-markets story isn't without caveats. Many of these stocks have had a big run, and may be due for a short-run pause. Some critics say China's economic success is built on a shaky foundation excessively reliant on exports.

collapse v. 坍塌；倒塌
slash v. 削减；砍

reaction n. 反应

chain n. 连锁；锁链

revenue n. 收入
casino n. 赌场

caveat n. 局限性

excessively ad. 过度地

And to some degree, the gains in emerging markets reflect "what goes down the most, goes back up the most," says Robert Buckland, chief global equity strategist at Citi Investment Research & Analysis in London. Emerging-market stocks dropped in the second half of 2008, losing 55% for the year. That was far worse than the 39% drop in the S & P 500.

strategist *n.* 策略师

重点词组

when it comes to	谈到,论及	be reliant on	依赖于…
account for	(数量)构成		

长难句分析

All we need to see is a little more normalization of demand and you will see continued strong reaction in those price.

整句话的前半句 All (that) we need to see is a little more normalization of demand 是一个省略引导词 that 的定语从句,先行词为 all。后半句 you will see continued strong reaction in those price 中 continued 是动词的过去分词形式,修饰 reaction。

参考译文

施罗德公司的麦森纽也认为,石油和原材料类股票受到了新兴市场增长的提振。在今年早些时候股市回调期间,她买进了矿业和钢铁类股。麦森纽说,随着全球经济的崩溃,这些企业大幅减产。她说,"需求只需要更加正常化一点,你就将看到这类股票的价格出现持续强劲反应。不过,她也看好在新兴市场国家的业务不断增长的消费品公司,比如雀巢公司、特易购和欧莱雅。

她说,"这不仅与行业有关,"在消费需求方面,"走出这场衰退的活力将来自新兴市场。"

Alpha Shares LLC 的高级投资经理马斯看到了新兴市场对一些消费品公司的重要意义。举例来讲,快餐连锁运营商百胜餐饮集团(Yum! Brands)一季度全球同店销售额增长 1%,由于其中国业务增长了 2%,如今在中国的收入占了该公司总收入的 20%。他还认为,其他一些奢侈品品牌和赌场运营商也出现了积极的迹象,比如永利度假村(Wynn Resorts)、酩悦轩尼诗-路易威登集团(LVMH Moet Hennessy Louis Vuitton)——若不是在中国有着更多业务,这些公司就会陷入困境。

当然,新兴市场的作用并非没有局限性。上述这些股票中有很多已经大幅飙升,其涨势可能短期内要暂告一段落。一些批评人士说,中国的经济成功是建立在过度依赖出口这一不稳定的基础上的。

花旗投资研究驻伦敦的首席全球股票策略师罗伯特·巴克兰德(Robert Buckland)说,从某种程度上讲,新兴市场的上涨正应了"跌得最惨的也是反弹最大的"那句话。新兴市场股票在 2008 年下半年触底,当年跌了 55%,远远超过标准普尔 500 指数 39%的跌幅。

Passage 6

Rising confidence in a global recovery, the recent rally in commodity prices, optimism over growth in China and hopes that the Australian economy itself will soon bounce are all encouraging a feeding frenzy. Even though the Australian dollar has bounced nearly 20% from its recent low in February, there is little sign that investor appetite is fading.

If anything, the rally has sparked fresh interest from asset allocators and real money players — suggesting the Aussie could yet make it back up as far as $0.8, a level last seen before Lehman Brothers collapsed last September.

A measure of the currency's underlying strength came late last week when the market took the RBA's growth downgrade on the chin.

Instead of being put off by the news that the central bank is now looking for a 1% contraction this year instead of only the 0.5% decline it has seen previously and that it is still contemplating further rate cuts if needed, the investment community focused on the RBA's confidence that the growth in China, and the economic stabilization in Asia and the U.S., is here to stay.

The fact that earlier data showed unemployment had fallen unexpectedly to 5.4% from 5.7% has also helped sentiment, as this could translate into better consumer confidence.

The sheer appetite for risky assets — of which the

rally n. 恢复;集会

frenzy n. 狂热
bounce v. 反弹;弹回

allocator n. 管理者

contemplate v.打算;沉思

sheer a. 纯粹的

Australian dollar is probably the prime example—was also lifted late last week as monetary easing by the European Central Bank and the Bank of England helped to reassure investors that major central banks are still prepared to keep on pumping more money in an effort to boost liquidity and secure a global upturn.

boost *v.* 增强
liquidity *n.* 流动性
release *v.* 发布；释放
obstacle *n.* 困难

The final release of the results of the U.S. bank stress tests also removed a major obstacle to the recovery by removing the threat of more banking problems in the world's largest economy.

重点词组

take... on the chin	失败,忍受	the obstacle to	有关…的困难
stress test	压力测试		

长难句分析

The fact that earlier data showed unemployment had fallen unexpectedly to 5.4% from 5.7% has also helped sentiment, as this could translate into better consumer confidence.

该句中前半句是一个主语从句，主语为 The fact that earlier data showed unemployment had fallen...，谓语为 has also helped。后半句中短语 fall from... to... 的意思是"从…降到…"。translate into 意思为"把…用另外一种形式表现出来"。

参考译文

目前市场对全球经济复苏的信心日益增强,近期大宗商品价格出现上扬,投资者对中国经济增长持乐观态度,而且澳大利亚经济也有望很快实现反弹,这些因素引发了投资者对澳元的投资热潮。澳元现已从 2 月份低点累计上涨了近 20%,但仍无多少迹象表明投资者的风险偏好有降温之势。

此轮涨势还引发了资产管理者和长线投资者新的投资兴趣，预示着澳元或将回升至去年 9 月雷曼兄弟(Lehman Brothers)倒闭前的 0.8 美元的高点。

上周晚些时候,市场对澳大利亚央行(RBA)下调本国经济增长预期并未有强烈反应,澳元潜在的强势由此可见一斑。

澳大利亚央行把澳大利亚今年经济增长预期由先前预计的下滑 0.5% 下调至萎缩 1%，而且还表示会在必要情况下进一步减息。不过澳元投资者们似乎并没有将关注重点放在该消息上，而是更侧重于澳大利亚央行对中国经济将保持增长的信心、亚洲和美国经济能够稳定等诸多因素。

此前有关澳大利亚失业率已从 5.7% 意外降至 5.4% 的消息也对澳元人气带来提振，因为失业率下降将有助于消费者信心的增强。

上周晚些时候投资者对高风险资产的偏好大幅升温(澳元可能是最明显的例子)还因为，欧洲央行(European Central Bank)和英国央行(Bank of England)上周四采取的宽松性货币政策使投资者们进一步确信，全球主要央行仍随时准备向市场注入更多资金，以提振流动性并确保全球经济的复苏。

美国银行业压力测试结果的最终公布解除了美国这一全球最大经济体将曝出更多银行业问题的威胁，从而也就消除了市场风险回升的一大障碍。

Passage 7

Teasury Secretary Timothy Geithner Monday continued U.S. efforts to assuage Beijing's concerns over the safety of its U.S. assets, saying China's dollar assets are "very safe" and repeating that the U.S. believes in a strong dollar.

When Geithner was replying to questions at Peking University, where he spoke as part of his first visit to China since he took office earlier this year. China is the biggest creditor nation to the U.S., and Premier Wen Jiabao in March expressed worries about the safety of China's assets in the U.S.

Asked about the U.S. government's approach to investing in U.S. automakers, Geithner said, "We want to have a quick, clear exit."

Rising long-term rates in the U.S. bond market reflect "an improvement in confidence," he said, adding "that's something we should welcome."

Geithner's visit comes as long-term interest rates have

assuage *v.* 减轻；平息

creditor *n.* 债权人

automaker *n.* 汽车制造商
exit *n.* 退出；出口
bond *n.* 国债

begun to rise. The rise in yields on U.S. Treasury bond could signal that the recession is easing and investors no longer feel the need to rush to safety in the form of U.S. bonds. But it also means higher borrowing costs, at a time when federal officials hope to keep rates low to boost the economy and thaw credit markets.

thaw *v.* 解冻;融化

重点词组

believe in	相信	in the form of	以…的方式
take office	上任		

长难句分析

But it also means higher borrowing costs, at a time when federal officials hope to keep rates low to boost the economy and thaw credit markets.

该句中 borrowing costs 指的是"借债成本",该句的时间状语 at a time when federal officials hope to keep rates low to boost the economy and thaw credit markets 中包含一个 when 引导的定语从句,先行词为时间名词 a time;hope to do 意为"希望做";to boost the economy...表示目的。

参考译文

美国财政部长蒂莫西·盖特纳(Timothy Geithner)周一继续努力减轻中国政府对美元资产安全性的担忧情绪,称中国持有的美元资产非常安全,并重申美国坚持强势美元的立场。

盖特纳是在北京大学回答问题时做出上述表述的。这是他今年年初上任后首次访华。中国是美国最大的债权国,中国总理温家宝3月份时曾表达了对中国持有美国资产安全性的担忧。

当有人问道美国政府将如何投资美国汽车制造商时,盖特纳说,"政府希望能尽快地完全退出。"

他说,长期美国国债收益率走高反映出"投资者信心有所改善"。他还补充道,"这应当是他们乐于见到的。"

盖特纳此次访华正值长期美国国债收益率上扬之际。美国国债收益率走高可能表明经济衰退的情况正在缓解,因而投资者不再急需投资美国国债等避险资产。但这也意味着借款成本上涨,而此刻正是联邦政府官员希望将利率持低位,从而提振经济并促使信贷市场解冻之时。

第三节　政治制度

Passage 1

British Government consists of the Prime Minister and other ministers, all of whom are collectively responsible for every part of the Government's administration. The Queen appoints all the ministers, formally, but she makes the appointment entirely on the Prime Minister's advice. The Prime Minister effectively appoints the other ministers and may also require them to resign, though in fact the resignation of ministers are always arranged so as to appear to be voluntary. All the ministers must be members of either the House of Commons or the House of Lords. Some of the ministers are entitled, for example, Minister of Agriculture, but other offices have special titles, such as the Chancellors of Exchequer, the President of the Board of the Trade and the Lord Chancellor. Some archaic offices survive: Lord President of the Council, Lord Privy Seal, Chancellor of the Duchy of Lancaster and Paymaster-General. Their duties are nominal, but the Prime Minister uses these posts to give positions in the Government to people whom he wants to perform special tasks. Some changes were made in the structure of the Cabinet in 1963—1970. And as a result of the changes, all the Secretaries of State were in some way super ministers. Before the changes some Ministers were more important than some Secretaries of State; the new rationalization of names of offices makes things a little less confusing, but it may not be permanent. In 1962—1970 there was a First Secretary of State. For a time this title indicated that its holder was the second man in the Government, but in 1970 Mr. Heath formed his team without it.

appointment *n.* 任命

resign *v.* 辞职；放弃

voluntary *a.* 主动的；义务的

entitle *v.* 命名；使有资格

archaic *a.* 古代的

nominal *a.* 名义上的

rationalization *n.* 理性化

permanent *a.* 永久的；经常的

indicate *v.* 表示；表明

The cabinet consists of the heads of the most important departments together with a few ministers without departments. The Prime Minister decides which ministers will be included, but there are some, like the Foreign Secretary, whom he could not easily leave out. The numbers has varied in the peaceful times between fifteen and twenty-three. All these are paid salaries varying between the Prime Minister's 20,000 pounds a year and 8,500 pounds for a junior minister.

重点词组

consist of	由某事物组成	perform special tasks	执行特殊任务
as a result of	由于…	leave out	排除在外

长难句分析

The Prime Minister effectively appoints the other ministers and may also require them to resign, though in fact the resignation of ministers are always arranged so as to appear to be voluntary.

该句前半句是主句,后半句是由 though 引导的让步状语从句,从句 though in fact the resignation of ministers are always arranged so as to appear to be voluntary 又由 so as to 引导的结果状语从句构成。

参考译文

英国政府由首相和其他大臣组成,他们共同负责政府行政的一切事务。所有的大臣,在形式上由女王任命,事实上女王完全依据首相的意思来任命。首相可以任命其他大臣,也可以要求他们辞职。只是大臣的辞职是安排的,所以看上去像是主动要求辞职的。所有大臣都必须是下议院或上议院的成员。有些大臣是被任命的,比如农业大臣,而有的则有特别的称号,如财政大臣、贸易大臣、大法官。有些古老的官职依然存在,如枢密院长、掌玺大臣、兰开斯特公爵郡大臣和主计长。这些职务都是有名无实的,但首相会利用这些职位,让那些他打算用来为自己执行特殊任务的人充当。1963—1970 年,内阁在结构上做了一些变动,结果是,所有的国务卿都在某种程度上成了超级大臣。在变动前,有些大臣比某些国务卿要重要些。对职务名称重新做出合理的变更减少了一些混淆,但新的名称或许也不会一成不变。在1962—1970 年间,曾一度有过"第一国务卿",这个头衔曾表明这位大臣是政府里第二号人物。但是,1970 年希斯先生组成班子的时候就没有这一职位。

内阁由政府各主要部门的领导和几位不隶属于任何部门的大臣组成。首相决定哪些大臣将进入内阁,但也有些大臣,如外交大臣,不大可能被轻易排除在内阁之外。在和平时期,内阁成员的人数在15—23 名之间。内阁成员的年薪从副大臣每年 8,500 英镑到首相的 2 万英镑不等。

Passage 2

Elections are the lifeblood of a democracy. The word democracy literally means "the people rule", an important concept in America's history. In the mid-1700s, England began passing laws that made the American colonies angry. The colonists had to pay more and more taxes and enjoyed less and less freedom. They felt the government of England didn't represent their interests. On July 4, 1776, the colonies declared their independence from England. They wanted to establish a democracy where people could have a voice in government.

colony *n.* 殖民地

represent *v.* 代表
declare *v.* 宣布

An effective democracy holds regular elections. In America, elections are held every two years for members of Congress. In these elections, all seats in the House of Representatives and one-third of the Senate seats are up for grabs. In addition, every four years, voters go to the polls to elect the nation's president and vice-president. Voters also regularly cast their ballots for state and city government leaders and local school board members. Sometimes they also have to vote on a proposed law.

effective *a.* 有效的;有力的

In the American electoral system, people don't really vote for presidential candidates. Instead, voters cast their

candidate *n.* 候选人

ballots for "electors" who support each candidate. Each state has as many electors as the total number of its representatives in Congress. This equals two senators per state plus the number of its representatives in the House (which is based on the state's population). The candidate who has the most votes in a state wins all of the state's electors. To win the presidential election, a candidate must gain at least 270 of the 538 total electoral votes.

representative n. 代表（指人）

senator n. 参议员；上院议员

presidential a. 总统的

重点词组

| have a voice | 有发言权 | vote on | 投票决定… |
| cast ballots | 投票 | | |

长难句分析

The candidate who has the most votes in a state wins all of the state's electors.

该句的主干为 The candidate... wins all of...。主语为 who 引导的定语从句，in a state 介词短语作地点状语。

参考译文

选举是民主的原动力。民主这个字照字面的意思是"人民自主"，是美国历史中一个重要的观念。18 世纪中期，英国开始通过一些使美国殖民地愤怒的法律。殖民地人民必须付愈来愈多的税，享有愈来愈少的自由。他们感到英国政府没有代表他们的权益。1776 年 7 月 4 日，殖民地宣布脱离英国独立。他们想要建立民主制度，使人们在政府中有发言权。

有效的民主制度会定期举行选举。在美国，每两年选一次国会议员。在这些选举中，人们可以争取所有众议院的席位和三分之一的参议院席位。除此以外，选民每四年去投票所选出国家的总统和副总统。选民也定期投票选出州长、市长及当地学校的董事会成员。有时他们也必须投票决定提议的法律。

在美国的选举制度中，人们并不直接投票给总统候选人，而是由选民投票给支持各个候选人的"选举人"。每一州的选举人人数和代表此州的国会议员人数相同，等于每一州有两位参议员，加上众议院的众议员人数(以各州的人口为基准)。在一个州里拥有最多票数的候选人就赢得了那一州所有选举人的票数。要赢得总统大选,候选人必须至少获得总共 538 个选举人中的 270 张票。

Passage 3

Over the years, the U.S. has made a number of election reforms. Some early reforms outlawed cheating, giving bribes and threatening voters. They also limited the amount of money candidates could receive from donors and spend on their campaigns. In 1870, black people gained the right to vote, and in 1920, that right was extended to women. In recent decades, laws against unfair rules for voting have been passed. No longer do people have to pay a special tax or pass a test in order to vote. In 1971, the voting age was lowered to 18. Other reforms made voting easier for the blind, the disabled and people who couldn't read. In some areas, ballots had to be printed in languages besides English.

"Of the people, by the people, and for the people." That's how Abraham Lincoln described the American government in his Gettysburg Address. These simple phrases capture the essence of American democracy. Instead of ruling over U.S. citizens, the government is ruled by them. Elected officials are known as public servants who represent their constituents. Americans can get involved in government by voting, by writing letters to their representatives and even by organizing peaceful demonstrations to make their voices heard. Each American citizen has a vested interest in how he or she is governed. Former President Theodore Roosevelt expressed the American view of government well: "The government is us."

outlawed *a.* 非法的
bribe *n.* 贿赂
donor *n.* 捐赠者

address *n.* 演讲

constituent *n.* 选民

demonstration *n.* 游行;
演示
vested *a.* 既得的

重点词组

give bribes　　　行贿　　　　　　vested interest　　　既得利益
the view of　　　关于…的观点

长难句分析

No longer do people have to pay a special tax or pass a test in order to vote.

这是一个倒装句,no longer 在句首使谓语动词 do 提前,表示强调。in order to 是介词短语,后跟动词不定式,意为"为了",表示目的。

参考译文

多年来,美国在选举方面做了一些改革。早期有些改革禁止作弊、收受贿赂或威胁选民。他们也限制候选人从捐赠者那儿获得的金额数目及花在竞选宣传上的费用。1870 年,黑人获得选举权。1920 年,权利延伸至妇女。近几十年来,通过了反对不公平选举规则的法律。人们不再需要付特殊的税或通过测验才能选举。1971 年,投票的年龄降至 18 岁。其他的改革减轻了盲人、残障者及文盲投票的困难。在某些地区,选票上面除了英文以外,还必须印上别的文字。

"民有、民治、民享",这是亚伯拉罕·林肯在盖特斯堡演说时,描绘的美国政府。这简短的几个字道出了美国民主的真谛。美国政府不是统治人民而是受人民所统治。民选的官员被认为是人民的公仆,他们代表的是他们的选民。美国人可通过投票,向他们的代表陈情,甚至于组织和平的示威活动,来发表心声,参与政事。每一个美国公民都有一份保护自身利益的权利与义务,来决定他们的政府该如何执政,前总统泰迪·罗斯福深刻地表达了美国人对政府的看法:"政府就是我们"。

Passage 4

At first glance, it might seem that the U.S. president, as "leader of the free world," is the "ruler" of America. On Inauguration Day, the swearing in of President will reflect the pomp and circumstance of a coronation ceremony, with dignitaries from around the world in attendance. Even as far back as George Washington, who once rejected a suggestion to become "King of America," people have sought to ascribe far-reaching powers to the president. But the Constitution ensures that the president will not become an all-powerful ruler.

inauguration *n.* 就职

dignitary *n.* 要员；显贵

constitution *n.* 宪法

The U.S. government, as outlined by the Constitution, is divided into three branches: legislative, executive and judicial. The legislative branch passes the laws, the executive enforces the laws and the judicial interprets the laws. The legislative branch is comprised of the two houses of Congress, the Senate and the House of Representatives. Thanks to CNN, C/SPAN and the nightly news, many lawmakers have almost become celebrities in their own right. The president, who is called the chief executive or chief of state, represents the executive branch. Besides that, as commander in chief of the armed forces, the president carries more than a little clout in world affairs. The judicial branch is made up of the Supreme Court and about 100 other federal courts. The nine Supreme Court justices hold office for life.

legislative *a.* 立法的
executive *a.* 行政的
judicial *a.* 司法的

重点词组

at first glance	乍一看	ascribe to	赋予
in attendance	出席	be comprised of	由…组成

长难句分析

The U.S. government, as outlined by the Constitution, is divided into three branches: legislative, executive and judicial.

此句讲的是美国政府的三权分立。句中 as outlined by the Constitution 是插入语，is divided 是动词谓语的被动语态。be divided into 意为"被分成若干部分"。

参考译文

乍看之下，身为"自由世界领袖"的美国总统似乎是美国的"统治者"。在就职日当天，来自世界各地的达官显要都将出席。总统的就职宣誓仪式，如同国王加冕典礼一般的华丽与隆重。即使远溯至华盛顿总统，他曾经拒绝了成为"美国国王"的建议，人们还是想要把无比的权力赋予总统。但是美国宪法确保了总统不会成为一个集权的统治者。

美国宪法概略地将政府分为三部分：立法部门、行政部门及司法部门。立法部门通过法律，行政部门执行法律而司法部门解释法律。立法部门由国会的参议院及众议院组成。由于 CNN 及 C/SPAN 和夜间新闻的传播作用，这些议员们都因个人的论调、举止成了名人。行政部门由总统代表，他被称为最高行政长官，或是国家元首。除此之外，身为三军司令，美国总统在世界局势所有的影响力也是不小的。司法部门是由最高法院及大约 100 个其他的联邦法院组成。九位最高法院的法官是终身制的。

Passage 5

In many countries, power rests with a strong centralized government. In contrast, under the American federal system, the national government shares its power with the state governments. The federal government possesses only those powers clearly delineated in the Constitution; all remaining powers are reserved for the states.

federal *a.* 联邦的

delineate *v.* 刻画；描写

The English political theorist Thomas Paine wrote in 1776, "Government, even in its best state, is but a necessary evil; in its worst state, an intolerable one." The American government, like every government, has its share of thorny problems. An increasing number of governmental agencies

intolerable *a.* 无法忍受的
thorny *a.* 棘手的

and government workers has created the problem of bureaucracy, where a mountain of paperwork stifles efficiency. Lobbyists make appeals to Congress on behalf of special interest groups. As a result, those with the biggest lobby — and the most money — tend to have the loudest voice in Washington.

bureaucracy n.官僚体制

Americans harbor mixed feelings about their own government. They recognize the need for it, but they remain suspicious of it. To some Americans, the government is Big Brother, an oppressive organization which delights in taxing its people and meddling in their affairs. To others, the government is a rich Uncle Sam who provides for the poor and protects his people from bullies at home and abroad. But no matter how they view their government, Americans wouldn't trade it for any other on the face of the earth.

harbor v. 怀有;收容

oppressive a. 压迫的

bully n. 恃强凌弱者; 欺侮

重点词组

| in contrast | 对比 | meddle in | 干预 |
| on behalf of | 代表 | | |

长难句分析

The English political theorist Thomas Paine wrote in 1776, "Government, even in its best state, is but a necessary evil; in its worst state, an intolerable one."

这是英国政治理论家托马斯·潘尼对政府的一句著名言论,此处 state 指的是 "状态",短语为 in the state 意为 "出于某种状态"。is but a necessary evil 中的 but 在此用于加强语气,表示 "仅仅、只不过"。

参考译文

在许多国家,权力集中于中央政府。相对之下,在美国联邦制度下,国家政府与州政府分摊权力。联邦政府只拥有宪法中明确陈述的权力,其他所有的权力都保留在州政府。

英国政治理论家托马斯·潘在 1776 年写道,"政府,即使在其最好的状态,也不过是一个无可避免的恶魔;在它最坏的状态,就是一个无法忍受的恶魔。"美国政府就像每一个政府一样,也有棘手的问题。不断增加的政府机构及公务员造成了官僚政治的问题,使堆积如山的纸上作业扼杀了效率。游说者为特定利益团体向国会上诉请愿。结果,说客人数最多,即钱最多的团体,在华盛顿就有最大的声音。

美国人对他们自己的政府怀有复杂的情感。他们知道它存在的必要性,但还是对它存疑。对某些美国人来说,政府是一个压迫人民的组织,是以向人民征税为乐,并干预人民隐私的"老大哥"。对其他人来说,政府是一个富有的"山姆大叔",它供养穷人并保护它的人民在国内外免受欺凌。不管他们怎样看待他们的政府,美国人都不会将它与地球上任何一个政府交换的。

Passage 6

There are two major political parties in Britain: the Conservative Party and the Labor Party. The Conservative was evolved from Tory, a political group which appeared under King Charles the second. After the Restoration in 1660, Charls the second ruled Britain. He wanted his brother James, Duke of York, to succeed him. Some people were against his arrangement because James was a Catholic and these people favored Protestantism. They were derisively called "Whigs", a nickname once given to the rebelling Scottish drovers. The Whigs represented the interests of the then landed aristocracy and big merchants of the towns. Many of them were opposed to the Church of England. To amass more wealth, the Whigs wanted more social changes and greater freedom of exploitation and expansion. Towards the middle of the 19th century, they began to use another name, the Liberal Party. After the First World War the Liberal Party began to disintegrate and soon disappeared. The opponents of the Whig Party were called Tories, a word from the Irish term for robbers. The Tories represented the interests of the tradesmen. They feared disturbance and wanted a stable social order for development. They were afraid that sudden social changes might result in crises, which in turn would cause them to suffer. During the middle of the 19th century the Tory Party changed its name into the Conservative Party. After the disintegration of the Liberal Party, some of its members joined the Conservative Party.

The Conservative are supported by most landowners and businessmen, and generally speaking the older and

conservative *a.* 保守的	
evolve *v.* 演变;进化	
succeed *v.* 接替;成功	
nickname *n.* 绰号;外号	
aristocracy *n.* 贵族	
amass *v.* 积蓄;积累	
disintegrate *v.* 解体	

more successful you are, the more likely you are to be a Conservative. Farmers too, are businessmen of a sort, self-employed, independent, owners of land; and they too are mostly Conservative. Thus the party is particularly associated with the middle class.

self-employed *a.* 自雇的

The party of the left is the Labor Party, whom their opponents prefer to call the Socialists. This is a comparatively new party, having formed its first government in 1924. The Labor Party is strongest in the areas of heavy population. For these are the industrial areas, full of the most typical members of the working class.

opponent *n.* 对手；竞争者

重点词组

be evolved from	来自于	result in	导致
be opposed to	反对		

长难句分析

They were afraid that sudden social changes might result in crises, which in turn would cause them to suffer.

该句是一个由 that 引出的宾语从句，在宾语从句中又由一个 which 引导的非限制性定语从句，定语从句的先行词是 crises。短语 cause sb to do 意思是"使某人做某事"。

参考译文

在英国有两大政党，即保守党与工党。保守党由托利党演变而来，最初是查理二世时期的一个政治团体。1660 年复辟后英国进入查理二世统治时期。他有意让兄弟约克公爵詹姆斯做他的继承人。这一安排遭到了一些人的反对，因为詹姆斯信奉天主教，而这些人则拥护新教。他们被讥讽为"辉格党"，这曾是给反叛国王的苏格兰牛贩子起的绰号。辉格党代表当时拥有土地的贵族和城镇的大商人的利益，他们中有很多人反对英国国教。为了积累更多的财富，辉格党希望进行个别更多的社会变革和获得更大的自由来进行剥削和扩张。在 19 世纪中期，辉格党改名为自由党。一战后，自由党开始解体并消失。辉格党的反对派叫托利党，这是爱尔兰语，意为歹徒。托利党代表商人的利益，这些人害怕社会动荡，想有一个稳定的社会秩序以利于发展。他们担心急剧的社会变革可能引发危机，最终会使他们遭受损失。19 世纪中期，托利党改名为保守党。自由党解体之后，其部分成员加入了保守党。

保守党受到大多数土地拥有者的支持。一般说来，在英国一个人年纪越大，或者成就越大,就越可能是个保守党人。农场主也算商人的一种,他们不受雇于别人,独立自主,拥有土地,他们大多也是保守党人。所以说,这一党派与中产阶级有着特别的联系。

左翼派为工党,反对派倾向于称其为社会主义政党。这个党派比较年轻,1924 年才首次执政。其在人口最密集的地区最有影响,因为这些地区是工业区,聚集着最为典型的工人阶级成员。

Passage 7

Australia's political system follows the western democratic tradition, especially the British and American models. Generally, the Australian Federation has a three-tier system of government: the Australian Parliament and Government; six states governments and their legislatures; and about 900 local government bodies at the city, town and shire level.

The Australian Federal Parliament has two chambers: the House of Representatives and the Senate. Australia is a pioneer in voting by secret ballot in parliamentary elections. By 1879, the system operated in all six of the colonies and became known as the Australian ballot. Australian federal and state electoral laws require compulsory voting for Australian citizens aged or over 18. These people who fail to vote without good reason are liable to a fine ranging from A$4 to A$10. However, voting is not always compulsory at local government elections; and the practice varies from state to state. The Australian Federal Government, each state government and the Northern Territory Government have permanent agencies to conduct elections, carry out the electoral laws.

Electoral rolls are brought up to date once every 12 months. Election dates are widely made known by election officers and by candidates as well. A candidate in elections to either house of the Federal Parliament must be at least 21 yeas of age and must have been a resident in Australia for three years.

three-tier a. 三层的

legislature n. 立法机构

shire n. 郡
chamber n. 议院;卧室

ballot n. 投票;投票选举

compulsory a. 必须的;
义务的

permanent a. 经常的;
永久的

resident n. 常住居民

重点词组

become known as　　以…著称　　up to date　　赶时髦
liable to　　　　　倾向于

长难句分析

These people who fail to vote without good reason are liable to a fine ranging from A$4 to A$10. However, voting is not always compulsory at local government elections; and the practice varies from state to state.

句子里有 who 引导的定语从句,注意几个词组如:liable to sth.,意为"可能遭到某事",rang from... to...,vary from... to... 意思相近,表示变化范围,意为"从…到…"。

参考译文

澳大利亚的政治制度沿袭了西方的民主传统,尤其是英国与美国的模式。澳大利亚联邦政府系统一般分为 3 个层面:澳大利亚议会和政府;6 大州政府及其立法机构;以及大约 900 个城市城镇和郡一级的地方政府。

澳大利亚联邦国会分为两院:众议院和参议院。澳大利亚是在议会选举中采取无记名投票方式的先行者。到 1879 年为止,此制度就已经在 6 个殖民地全面实行了,并被誉为澳大利亚式投票。澳大利亚联邦和州的选举法要求每个年满 18 周岁的澳大利亚公民都必须参加选举。那些没有充分理由退出选举的人要被处以 2 至 10 澳元的罚款。但是,地方政府的选举却并不是强制性的。选举方式在各州也各不相同。澳大利亚联邦政府、各个州政府以及北部的地区政府都有常设机构来指导选举工作,实施选举法。

选举人的名册每隔 12 个月要更新一次。选举日期由选举官员和候选人广泛加以宣传,使其家喻户晓。竞选联邦国会两院的候选人必须年满 21 岁,并在澳大利亚居住 3 年以上。

第四节 文化教育

Passage 1

There are more than forty universities in Britain. They are all private institutions. Each has its own governing council, including some local businessmen and local politicians as well as a few academics. Each university has its own syllabuses, and there are some quite important differences between one and another. In general the Bachelor's degree is given to students who pass exams at the end of three or four years of study. Bachelor's degrees are at two levels, Honor and Pass. In some cases the Honors degree is given for intensive study and exam in one, two or three related subjects while the Pass degree may be somewhat broader.

The first post-graduate degree is normally that of the Master, conferred for a thesis based on at least one year's fulltime work; the time actually taken is usually more than a year. Oxford and Cambridge are peculiar in that they give the Master of Arts degree automatically to any Bachelor who pays the necessary fees at any time after the seventh year from his first admission to the university.

Oxford and Cambridge resemble each other quite closely. They have a special preeminence, but they two no longer belong to the upper and upper-middle classes as the public schools do. They based on colleges. These colleges are parallel and equal institutions, and none of them is connected with any particular field of study. In order to become a member of the university, a student must first accept as a member of a college.

It is easy to see advantages of an education at Oxford.

institution *n.* 机构
council *n.* 委员会

syllabus *n.* 教学大纲

bachelor *n.* 学士;单身汉

intensive *a.* 集中的;密集的

confer *v.* 授予;协商

resemble *v.* 相像
preeminence *n.* 卓越,杰出

The surroundings of the ancient buildings are *infinitely* pleasing. The teaching varies between good and bad, but the whole effect is highly stimulating. The libraries and bookshops are probably unequalled anywhere.

infinitely ad. 无限地

Oxford is more tolerant than Cambridge; and except Churchill, every Prime Minister from 1945 to 1974 was an Oxford graduate. But Cambridge is more developed than Oxford in scientific studies. The *rivalry* between the universities at sports is a part of the national life.

rivalry n. 竞赛

重点词组

in some cases　　在某些情况下　　be based on　　以某事物为根据

长难句分析

In some cases the Honors degree is given for intensive study and exam in one, two or three related subjects while the Pass degree may be somewhat broader.

该句是由 while 引导的并列句,while 具有转折、对比的意味。句中的Honors degree 指"荣誉学位,优等成绩"。Pass degree 指"及格"。

参考译文

英国有四十多所大学,均属私立高校。每个大学都有一个自己的管理委员会,它由当地的商人、政治家和一些学者组成。每一所大学会有自己的教学大纲,而且有时会极不相同。一般来说,学生经过3到4年的学习并通过考试后,就可以拿到学士学位。而学士学位又分为两种:优秀与及格,前者一般授予在一门或二三门课程中进行集中学习并通过考试的学生,而及格学位的涉及范围则更广泛些。

本科以后的第一个学位是硕士学位。学生要经过至少一年的学习,写出一篇论文以后,方可拿到学位,而实际上,它一般都会超过一年。在这方面,牛津和剑桥显得与众不同,任何一个学士进入大学7年以后,只要交清所需费用都可以获得文科的硕士学位。

牛津和剑桥大学两者非常相似。它们都非常杰出,不过如今已不像公立学校那样只属于上流和中上流社会。这两所大学都是建立在学院的基础上的,而这些学院是互相平行和平等的机构,而且都不局限于某个特定的领域。一个学生想成为大学的一员,必须先进入一所学院。

在牛津教育的优势是明显的,光是其古老的建筑环境就给人一种无限的享受。虽然它在各个教学领域参差不齐,但总体水平还是令人振奋的。此外,其图书馆和书店的规模之大在别的地方也是罕见的。

相比之下,牛津大学比剑桥大学显得更为开放一些。除了丘吉尔以外,1945 至 1974 年间所有的英国首相都出自牛津。但剑桥在科学研究方面比牛津发展得更好。两个学校之间的体育比赛已成为英国社会公众生活的一部分。

Passage 2

Australians are all required to go to school from the time they are six until they finish junior high school at the age of 15. However, the pressure of a specialized technological society means that Australians commonly continue formal education well into young adulthood.

junior a. 初级的

At the age of 12 or 13, children are transferred to a local government high school. Pupils entering government high schools are not subject to streaming in academic or technically oriented institutions, as in some countries. However, Victoria does provide a choice between university-oriented school and technical high school, slanted towards preparing pupils for careers in skilled trades or sub professional courses by placing greater emphasis on practical and craft subjects.

transfer v. 转移;调动

stream v. 将学童分班

slant v. 使有倾向性

craft n. 手艺

Universities in Australia take in some 200,000 new students each year. There are at least two universities in every State and Territory, except for the Northern Territory, which has none. Universities were first established in Sydney and Melbourne in the 1850s. Today many still tend to follow British or American traditions, and responsibility for academic matters is vested in university boards and committees. The more old-fashioned establishment are run by professorial boards, comprising professors, deans and

tend v. 倾向于

heads of department. And the structure of courses varies, depending on the university and field of study. In general Australians are not as keen on gaining education and job skills as other western countries. Nevertheless, Australia still manages to make big news with its breakthroughs in everything. The Australians write 2 percent of the world's scientific papers win 1.3 percent of Nobel prizes and make 0.7 percent of the world's patent applications.

vary *v.* 多样

breakthrough *n.* 突破

重点词组

be subject to	从属于…	be keen on	热衷于…
take in	吸收,吸纳		

长难句分析

However, Victoria does provide a choice between university-oriented school and technical high school, slanted towards preparing pupils for careers in skilled trades or sub professional courses by placing greater emphasis on practical and craft subjects.

句子中 does 用于谓语动词前,是强调用法。slanted towards preparing pupils for... by placing greater emphasis on practical and craft subjects 是形容词引出的状语从句,其中 slanted towards 指的是"倾向于",句中 by 表示方式,意为"通过…途径"。短语 place great emphasis on... 意为"强调…"。

参考译文

澳大利亚的法定上学年龄为 6—15 岁(即完成初中的学业)。但是,生活在这样一个高技术的社会里,各种压力使得澳洲人的正规教育通常都延续到早期成年时期。

儿童在 12 至 13 岁时转入当地政府办的中学学习。此类中学是文理不分科的,这一点与一些国家不同。但在维多利亚州,学生们面临着大学预备科与技校科的选择,技校强调一些实践和技艺型的功课,倾向于让学生学习技术职业与次职业性的课程以便为将来从事的职业做准备。

澳大利亚每年招收大约 200,000 名大学新生。每一个州和地区都至少有两所大学,北部省例外,没有大学。大学最早是在 19 世纪 50 年代的悉尼和墨尔本建立的。很多大学依然承袭英国或美国的传统,学校董事会和委员会负责学术事务。更为古老的组织由教授董事会来管理,包括教授、系主任以及其他系领导。课程的结构也因大学与研究领域的不同而各异。总之,澳大利亚人并不像其他西方人那样热衷于教育和工作技能的获得。然而,澳大利亚却总能在各领域做出突破性成绩。澳大利亚这占全球2%的科技论文写作量,1.3%的诺贝尔奖和0.7%的专利权。

Passage 3

As a country, Australia is the sixth largest in the world. Its many and diverse cultures provide also a great variety of education. Among Asians, Australia has been one of the most popular places to study. The Australian government and schools have provided a standard and quality of education, which is equal to the best in the world. However, Australian has higher standard for its education because they believe that education is part of their children's birthright.

diverse a. 多样的

There is no discrimination between boys and girls. The girls are even encouraged to reach the same educational level as the boys. The children must have and are learning by finding out and asking questions. Their interest and enthusiasm are encouraged for learning. In addition, they are also actively involved in school organizations.

discrimination n. 区别,歧视

enthusiasm n. 热情

Not only are the students taking part in extra activities, but also their parents. Most schools encourage parent involvement and wish to help newcomers. They have parent and teacher associations, which play an active part in school life, such as raising funds for many school needs and helping to decide what is taught and done at school. This situation helps both the children and the school.

involvement n. 参与
association n. 协会;联系

Education at public schools is free in most states, although the schools also have to cover extra activities. Items, such as books or uniforms, and extra activities such as summer or youth camps are the parents' responsibility.

responsibility n. 责任

重点词组

be equal to	等同于	in addition	此外
be involved in	参与		

长难句分析

Not only are the students taking part in extra activities, but also their parents. 该句为倒装句。有 not only... but also 引导的并列句，其中 not only 前置，故而该句的前半句要倒装，即将谓语动词 are 提前。后半句不倒装，依然是陈述语序，其中谓语 are taking part in extra activities 为避免重复而省略掉了。

参考译文

　　作为一个国家，澳大利亚国土面积在世界上排第六位。它的多元的文化也提供各种各样的教育。在亚洲，澳大利亚一直是学子们出国留学最受欢迎的国家之一。澳大利亚政府和学校提供了与世界上最好的教育相当的教育标准和教育质量。然而，澳大利亚有着更高的教育标准，因为他们认为，接受教育是孩子们天生人权的一部分。

　　没有男孩和女孩的区别对待。女孩们甚至被鼓励达到与男孩相同的教育水平。孩子们必须自律，通过发现并提出问题来学习。他们的兴趣和热情将被调动起来促进学习。此外，他们还积极参与学校组织。

　　不仅学生参加课外活动，而且他们的父母也参加。大多数学校鼓励家长参与，并愿意帮助新来者。他们有家长会和教师协会，在学校生活中非常活跃，如为学校筹集资金，并帮助决定学校应该教授的课程和该做的事情。这种情况有利于孩子和学校。

　　大多数州的公立学校教育是免费的，尽管这些学校还必须支付额外的活动费用。但如书籍、校服等物品，夏令营或青年营等支出由家长负责。

Passage 4

Imitation, then, is one instinct of our nature. Next, there is the instinct for "harmony" and rhythm, meters being manifestly sections of rhythm. Persons, therefore, starting with this natural gift developed by degrees their special aptitudes, till their rude improvisations gave birth to poetry.

Poetry now diverged in two directions, according to the individual character of the writers. The graver spirits imitated noble actions, and the actions of good men. The more trivial sort imitated the actions of the meaner men, at first composing satires, as the former did hymns to the gods and the praises of famous men.

A poem of the satirical kind cannot indeed be put down to any author earlier than Homer; though many such writers probably there were. But from Homer onward, instances can be cited — his own *Margites*, for example, and other similar compositions. The appropriate meter was also here introduced; hence the measure is still called the iambic or lampooning measure, being that in which people lampoon on another. Thus the older poets were distinguished as writers of heroic or of lampooning verse.

As, in the serious style, Homer is preeminent among poets, for he alone combined dramatic form with excellence of imitation, so he too first laid down the main lines of comedy, by dramatizing the ludicrous instead of writing personal satire.

instinct *n.* 本能；天赋
rhythm *n.* 节奏
meter *n.* 格律；米

aptitude *n.* 天赋
improvisation *n.* 即兴

satire *n.* 讽刺；反讽
hymn *n.* 赞美诗

iambic *n.* 抑扬格
lampoon *v.* 嘲笑

ludicrous *a.* 可笑的

重点词组

give birth to　生育　　　　lay down　制定
put down to　归因于

长难句分析

The appropriate meter was also here introduced; hence the measure is still called the iambic or lampooning measure, being that in which people lampoon on another.

句中"hence the measure is still called..., being that in which..."的前半部分由副词 hence 引出结果,意思为"所以这种格律至今仍被叫做抑扬格律或讽刺格。"后半部分 being that in which people lampoon on another 是以 being 独立主格的形式表原因,句中 which 引导定语从句,先行词为 the iambic or lampooning measure,意为"由于人们在相互嘲讽时喜用抑扬格。"

参考译文

摹仿是我们的一种天性。和谐与节奏也是一种天性,格律显然是节奏的一部分。所以,具有这种天赋的人,通过点滴的积累,在即兴口述的基础上促成了诗的诞生。

诗的发展依据作者性格的不同而形成了两大类型。较稳重者摹仿高尚的行动,即好人的行动。而较浅俗者则摹仿低劣小人的行动,最初创作的是讽刺诗,而前者则创作颂神诗与赞美诗。

我们举不出一首由荷马以前的作者所作的此类诗,虽然在那个时候可能已经有过许多讽刺诗作者。但是从荷马及其以前的作者的作品中,我们却可以找出一些例子,例如荷马的《马尔吉忒斯》和其他类似的作品。适合于此类作品的诗格也应运而生。由于人们在相互嘲讽时喜用短长格,这种格律至今仍被叫做抑扬格或讽刺格。这样,在早期的诗人中,有的成了英雄诗诗人,另一些则成了讽刺诗人。

荷马不仅是严肃作品的最杰出的大师,也是第一位勾勒出喜剧轮廓的诗人。他将戏剧化的表现形式与卓越的摹仿结合在了一起,把滑稽可笑的事物戏剧化,而不是进行人身讽刺。

Passage 5

Feminists have recently begun to recognize and explore the problems facing those women from the poorer and less developed parts of the world who travel to the affluent western countries to work. Women from Mexico and Latin America move to the United States; women from Russia and Eastern Europe look for jobs in Western Europe and in Britain. South East Asian girls often seek work in the Middle East. Some are legal immigrants; those who are not are particularly vulnerable. Many women work as maids, nannies, cleaners, do unskilled jobs in old people's homes and hospitals, or take low-waged work in restaurants; but many others, inevitably, drift into prostitution.

Some western women, having fought for women's right to take jobs outside the home, and struggled to achieve their own liberation from domestic drudgery, look for not-too-expensive help with domestic work. For some foreign women — the lucky ones — migration is a way of improving their lives. But more often, migrant workers — often unqualified, sometimes barely speaking the language of their new home — get poorly paid, insecure jobs, that leave them isolated and unprotected in all kinds of ways. They often have no ideas of what their rights might be or how to demand them if they do. They rarely have any kind of support network, though in America some campaigning groups have sprung up to their defense. Their very existence poses western feminists with a painful paradox; they challenge us to look more closely at how we may be silent in the oppression of other women.

affluent a. 富裕的;繁荣的	
immigrant n. 移民	
vulnerable a. 易受伤害的	
prostitution n. 卖淫;滥用某事物	
drudgery n. 繁重,单调的工作	
paradox n. 悖论	
oppression n. 压迫	

重点词组

drift into	无意间成为…	spring up	迅速出现;发展

长难句分析

Some western women, having fought for women's right to take jobs outside the home, and struggled to achieve their own liberation from domestic drudgery, look for not-too-expensive help with domestic work.

该句主语为 some western women，having 分词结构作状语，struggled 在该句中是表示过去动作的谓语，这样前半部分意思是"曾经为妇女外出工作权而战、并且积极斗争把自己从繁重的家务劳动中解放出来"，而 look for 用一般现在时指的是主语现在的动作状态，即"现在寻找起廉价的家庭帮手"。

参考译文

女权主义者近年来开始意识到那些从世界上贫穷以及欠发达地区到西方富裕国家工作的妇女所面临的问题，并且已经着手研究这些问题。墨西哥和拉丁美洲的妇女前往美国；俄罗斯和东欧的妇女到西欧和英国寻找工作。东南亚的女孩往往跑到中东。她们中有些是合法移民，而那些非法移民则非常容易受到伤害。许多妇女做女佣、保姆、清洁工，在老人家或医院里干些不需要什么技术的活儿，或是在餐厅里做些工资微薄的工作。但是还有很多妇女不可避免地沦为妓女。

曾经为了妇女外出工作权而战，为了把自己从繁重的家务劳动中解放出来的一些西方妇女，现在寻找起廉价的家庭帮手来。对一些外国妇女来说——那些幸运儿——移民是改善自身生活的一种方式。但是更多的情况是，移民工人往往资质不高，有时几乎不会说自己新家的语言。收入微薄，工作没有保障，使得她们在各方面都孤立无援，得不到保护。她们往往连自己有哪些权利都不知道——要么即使知道也不清楚如何主张这些权利。她们几乎没有任何支持网络。不过在美国，一些团体已经挺身而出，维护她们的权利。她们的存在对西方女权主义者构成了一个痛苦的悖论；促使我们更加仔细地审视自身，也许我们正在纵容这些对其他妇女的压迫。

Passage 6

In the contention of the best picture of the 67th Oscar Award in 1995, the film *Forrest Gump* have got six Grand Prizes, such as the best picture, the best actor, the best achievement in directing, adapting drama, the best achievement in film editing and the best visual effect, etc. at one blow.

The film was passed to a intellectual disturbance person the description of life has reflected every aspect of U.S.'s life, important incident of social political life make and represent to these decades such as U.S. from one unique angle.

The film adapt Winston's novel of the same name. Only the original work is that one is full of fantastic novels with a satiric flavor, but the film modifies and beautifies the story, have abandoned the absurdity of the original work and revealed that satirizes meaning, have added a kind of tender feeling for the film. In the film, Forrest Gump who is unfortunately to be born with a lower IQ and the muscle problem, usually, people always think this kind of person can't be successful in doing anything. But, instead, this unlucky man has achieved lots of incredible success, he is a football star, a war hero, and later a millionaire! This undoubtedly makes the film suit audience and judging panel's taste even more, but has sacrificed the struggle spirit of the rebel of the original work, make the film become one kind and idealized ethical symbol.

Tom Hanks has obtained the laurel of the best actor of Oscar for the behavior in this film. Success of *Forrest Gump*, makes Tom Hanks become one of the most popular movie stars in Hollywood too. To Tom Hanks, those two years are the luckiest period of time in his performing art careers.

Oscar *n.* 奥斯卡金像奖

intellectual *a.* 智力的

decade *n.* 十年

satiric *a.* 讽刺的

rebel *n.* 叛逆者,造反者
ethical *a.* 道德的
laurel *n.* 月桂树,桂冠

重点词组

at one blow　　　一下子　　　　　　be born with　　　天生…

suit one's taste　适合某人的趣味

长难句分析

This undoubtedly makes the film suit audience and judging panel's taste even more, but has sacrificed the struggle spirit of the rebel of the original work, makes the film become one kind and idealized ethical symbol.

该句由三个并列分句构成，主语都是 this，三个并列谓语动词分别的 makes，has sacrificed，makes。其中 idealized 为动词 idealize 的过去分词形式，意思为"理想化的"。

参考译文

1995 年的第 67 届奥斯卡金像奖最佳影片的角逐中，影片《阿甘正传》一举获得了最佳影片、最佳男主角、最佳导演、最佳改编剧本、最佳剪辑和最佳视觉效果等六项大奖。

影片通过对一个智障者生活的描述反映了美国生活的方方面面，从一个独特的角度对美国几十年来社会政治生活中的重要事件做了展现。

影片改编自温斯顿·格鲁姆的同名小说。只不过原著是一本充满了讽刺意味的荒诞小说，而影片则对故事进行了修饰和美化。摒弃了原著的荒诞和揭露讽刺意味，为影片增添了一种温情。影片中，阿甘是一个出生很不幸的人，他智力低下并有肌肉运动障碍，通常人们总是认为这种人做任何事情都不能成功。但是，相反的，这个不幸的人却取得了许多难以置信的成功，他是一个橄榄球明星，一名战斗英雄和一位百万富翁。这无疑使影片更符合观众和评委的口味，但却牺牲了原著的反叛精神，使影片成为了一种理想化道德的象征。

汤姆·汉克斯以其在此片中的表现获得了奥斯卡最佳男主角的桂冠。《阿甘正传》的成功，也使汤姆·汉克斯成为了好莱坞最受欢迎的影星之一。对于汤姆·汉克斯来说，那两年是他演艺生涯中最为幸运的一段日子。

Passage 7

Dr. Spencer Johnson is an internationally respected speaker and author whose insights have helped millions of people discover simple truths they can use to have healthier lives with more success and less stress.

He has often been referred to as the best there is at taking complex subjects and presenting simple solutions that work.

He has written many bestsellers, including *The Precious Present*, a great favorite; *Yes or No*, a guide to better decisions; *Value Tales*, the popular children's books; and five other books in the One Minute series: *The One Minute Sales Person*, *The One Minute Mother*, *The One Minute Father*, *The One Minute Teacher and One Minute for Yourself*.

His education includes a B.A. in psychology from the University of Southern California, a M.D. degree from the Royal College of Surgeons, and medical clerkships at Harvard Medical School and The Mayo Clinic.

Dr. Johnson was Medical Director of Communications for Medtronic, the inventors of cardiac pacemakers; Research Physician at The Institute for Inter-disciplinary Studies, a think tank; and Consultant to the Center for the Study of the Person, and the School of Medicine, University of California.

His books have been featured often in the media, including CNN, The Today Show, The Larry King Show, *Time Magazine*, *Business Week*, *The New York Times*, *The Wall Street Journal*, *USA Today*, the Associated Press, and United Press International.

stress *n.* 压力;重要性

complex *a.* 复杂的;复合的

series *n.* 一系列的事物

psychology *n.* 心理学

royal *a.* 皇家的;皇室的
surgeon *n.* 外科医生

cardiac *a.* 有关心脏的
inter-disciplinary *a.* 跨学科的

重点词组

cardiac pacemaker　　心脏起搏器　　　a thinking tank　　　思想库

长难句分析

　　Dr. Spencer Johnson is an internationally respected speaker and author whose insights have helped millions of people discover simple truths they can use to have healthier lives with more success and less stress.

　　该句是由 whose 引导的定语从句，后半句中...simple truth （that）they can use to have healthier lives with more success and less stress 是一个省略引导词 that 的定语从句，其中先行词为 simple truth。

参考译文

　　斯宾塞·约翰逊博士是享誉全球的演说家和作家。他的许多见解，使成千上万的人发现了许多生活中的简单真理，这些真理使他们的生活更为健康、成功与轻松。

　　在对复杂的问题提出简单有效的解决办法方面，他被认为是最出色的专家。

　　他还写了许多畅销书，包括备受欢迎的《珍贵的礼物》；作为决策指南的《是或否》，最受欢迎的儿童德育读物《道德故事》，还有"一分钟系列"里的其他五本书：《一分种销售》、《一分钟母亲》、《一分钟父亲》、《一分钟老师》和《给你自己一分钟》。

　　他所受的教育包括：南加州大学心理学学士、皇家医学院医学博士、哈佛大学医学院及梅奥诊所的医生临床实习。

　　约翰逊博士是梅特罗尼克交流(研究)机构的医疗主任，是心脏起搏器的发明人；他还是"跨学科研究机构"智囊团的医学研究人员，以及加州大学医学院人格研究中心的顾问。

　　他的书成为许多媒体特别介绍的对象，这些媒体包括：美国有线新闻网、"今日秀"、"赖瑞·金访谈"、《时代杂志》、《商业周刊》、《纽约时报》、《华尔街日报》、《今日美国》、联合出版社和合众国际社。

○ 第二章　提高与拓展

1. 本章的目标和内容

本章是"提高与拓展"，和第一章相比最主要的差别在于文章的难度上。提高指的是英语运用能力的提高，主要还是表现在词汇句子与篇章结构等方面。拓展是学习内容的拓展，所选文章仍然以西方主要英语国家的政治、经济、文化、教育、科技等为主，但内容更复杂，语言也更接近考研真题的水平，是基础与真题之间的过渡。本章的目标是在第一章学习的基础上，词汇、语言分析能力和西方背景知识三方面都能有所提高和突破。在内容编排上和第一章相似，可以参见第一章的详细说明。

2. 如何使用本章

第一步：扫读。扫读是阅读英语文章的最基本技能之一，指的是快速浏览，抓住文章的大意。它是什么性质的文章？主要内容是什么？作者有什么样的观点？文章基本的结构是怎么样的？扫读的主要目的是掌握整个文章的大致情况而不讲求细节，一般的文章可以在两三分钟内就读完。

第二步：精读并解决词汇。扫读是浏览，是对全文大意和文章的结构的一种把握。精读是学习英语文章最重要的一个阶段，逐字逐行地阅读，并排除词汇方面的障碍。不懂的句子可参照后面的"长难句分析"或"参考译文"进行对比学习。

第三步：重复阅读。在精读之后应该带着问题返回再看一遍文章，通过反复阅读找寻答案。

希望读者能在完成这一章的内容之后顺利进入到考研真题的环节！

第一节 政治经济

Passage 1

Tesco is preparing a legal battle to clear its name of involvement in the dairy price-fixing scandal that has cost consumers £270 million. Failure to prove that it had no part in collusion with other supermarkets and dairy processors may land it with a fine of at least £80 million. The Office of Fair Trading (OFT) said yesterday that Asda, Sainsbury's and the former Safeway, plus the dairy companies Wiseman, Dairy Crest and Cheese Company, had admitted being in a cartel to fix prices for milk, butter and cheese. They were fined a total of just over £116 million as part of a leniency deal offered by the watchdog to companies that owned up quickly to anti-competitive behavior.

Officials at the OFT admitted privately that they did not think they would ever discover which company or individual had initiated the pricing formula. But the watchdog recognises that at the time supermarkets were under pressure from politicians and farmers to raise the cost of milk to save dairy farming, though it is not certain that money found its way to farmers. The OFT claimed in September that it had found evidence that the retail chains had passed future milk prices to dairy companies, which then reached a fixed price among themselves.

The average cost to each household is thought to be £11.25 over 2002 and 2003. Prices went up an extra 3 p on a pint of milk, 15 p on a quarter of a pound of butter and 15 p on a half pound of cheese. There is no direct recompense for consumers, however, and the money will go to the Treasury. The National Consumer Council gave warning that the admissions would dent consumer confidence in leading high street names and that people would become sceptical of their

involvement *n.* 牵涉, 纠缠	
scandal *n.* 丑闻	
collusion *n.* 勾结	
admit *v.* 承认	
leniency *n.* 宽大, 仁慈	
watchdog *n.* 看门狗, 观察员	
initiate *v.* 开始, 加入	
retail *n.* 零售	
recompense *n.* 补偿	
sceptical *a.* 怀疑的	

claims. Farmers For Action, the group of farmers that has led protests over low milk prices since 2000, is seeking legal advice on whether it can now bring a claim for compensation.

> protest *n.* 抗议

The OFT investigation is continuing, however, in relation to Tesco, Morrisons and the dairy group Lactalis McLelland, and any legal action is expected to be delayed until that is completed.

Tesco was defiant and said that it was preparing a robust defence of its actions. Lucy Neville-Rolfe, its executive director, said: "As we have always said, we acted independently and we did not collude with anyone. Our position is different from our competitors and we are defending our own case vigorously. Our philosophy is to give a good deal to customers."

> defiant *a.* 反抗的,挑衅的

> vigorously *ad.* 有力地,强健地

Morrisons has supported the OFT in inquiries into the former Safeway business that it took over, but in a statement said that it was still making "strong representations" in its defence. A spokeswoman for Lactalis McLelland said that the company was "co-operating" with the OFT. Industry insiders suggested that the three companies were deliberately stalling the OFT investigation.

> stall *v.* 使停止,使陷入故障

Sainsbury's admitted yesterday that it had agreed to pay £26 million in fines, but denied that it had sought to profiteer. Justin King, the chief executive, said he was disappointed that the company had been penalised for actions meant to help farmers but recognised the benefit of a speedy settlement. Asda declined to say how much it would pay in fines and also said that its intention had been to help farmers under severe financial pressure.

> profiteer *n.* 谋取暴利者

> penalise *v.* 处罚

> decline *v.* 拒绝,跌落

长难句分析

1. **They were fined a total of just over £116 million as part of a leniency deal offered by the watchdog to companies that owned up quickly to anti-competitive behavior.**

❖ 结构分析 该句主干为They were fined a total of just over £116 million as part of a leniency deal... 这是一个复合句,其成分比较复杂。offered by the watchdog to companies 作为一个分词短语来修饰前面的 deal，而后面 that 引导的定语从句又修饰 companies。own up 是一个词组，意为"坦白的承认，供认"。

2. The National Consumer Council gave warning that the admissions would dent consumer confidence in leading high street names and that people would become sceptical of their claims.

❖结构分析　该句主干为 The National Consumer Council gave warning... 这是一个复合句，句子的宾语 warning 带着两个由 that 引导的同位语从句；第一个同位语从句中，confidence in 后面是一个分词短语作介词的宾语。这种句子看似复杂，如果仔细分析，问题自然会迎刃而解。

参考译文

　　特易购公司为了摆脱限定奶制品价格风波，正在准备一场大官司。奶制品事件已经给消费者带来了 2 亿 7 千万的损失。如果不能证明自己并未和其他超市、奶制品加工商串通一气的话，特易购就得接受至少 8 千万的罚单。昨天，公平交易办事处(OFT)声称艾斯达超市和前塞夫韦超市，还有奶制品公司怀斯曼、克雷斯特乳品公司都已承认它们联合设定了牛奶、黄油及奶酪的价格。他们总共的罚金只有 1 亿 1 千 6 百万左右，这是监察部门对积极坦白反竞争行为公司的一种宽大处理。

　　OFT 官员私下声称，他们并非一定要找出到底是哪家公司或哪个人发起这次价格行动的，但是监察部门承认这次超市受到政治家和农民的双重压力，要求提高牛奶成本以拯救乳品业，但是最终钱还不一定能落到农民手中。OFT 9 月份称他们已经发现证据证明零售链已经将未来的牛奶价格告知奶制品公司，然后奶制品公司自己内部设定了固定价格。

　　2002 年和 2003 年间平均每户损失为 11.25 英镑。每品脱牛奶价格上涨 3 便士，每 0.25 磅黄油上涨 15 便士，每半磅奶酪上涨 15 便士。但是消费者却没有任何的补偿，利润全部到了国库。全国消费者委员会警告说长此以往会损害消费者的信心，人们也会逐渐怀疑委员会的声明。Farmers For Action 2002 年以来一直领导农民抗议牛奶价格过低，目前正在就是否可以申请补偿寻求法律意见。

　　不过 OFT 还在继续对特易购、莫里森超市和 Lactalis McLelland 奶制品集团进行调查，任何法律行为都将推迟到调查结束。

　　特易购对此不屑一顾，声称在为自己的行为准备最坚决的辩护。执行理事露西说："正如我们一贯宣称的，我们行动完全独立，和谁都没有联合。我们的立场和我们的对手不一样，我们在尽力保护我们的事业。我们的理念就是为消费者更好地服务。"

　　莫里森超市协助 OFT 调查它所管理的前塞夫韦超市的交易，但是在一次声明中还称自已依然会在辩护中进行强烈抗议。Lactalis McLelland 的一个代言人说公司在与 OFT "合作"，而企业内部人士暗示这三家公司在蓄意拖延 OFT 调查。

昨天塞恩斯伯里超市承认已经同意支付 2 千 6 百万的罚金，但是却否认它在牟取暴利。执行董事贾斯廷·金说本来是要帮助农民却因此受到惩罚，非常失望，但他也承认，尽快解决问题才是当务之急。艾斯达超市不愿意透露要赔付多少，并声称其初衷是要帮助那些有沉重经济压力的农民。

Passage 2

Controlled bleeding or cauterisation? That was the unappealing choice facing UBS, a Swiss bank which has been badly hurt by the carnage in America's mortgage market. The bank opted for the latter. First it opened the wound, by announcing a hefty $10 billion write-down on its exposure to subprime-infected debt. UBS now expects a loss for the fourth quarter, which ends this month. Then came the hot iron: news of a series of measures to shore up the bank's capital base, among them investments from sovereign-wealth funds in Singapore and the Middle East.

Bad news had been expected. UBS's third-quarter write-down of over SFr 4 billionin October looked overly optimistic compared with more aggressive markdowns at other banks such as Citigroup and Merrill Lynch. Steep falls in the market value of subprime debt since the end of the third quarter made it certain that UBS would take more pain, given its sizeable exposure to toxic collateralised-debt obligations(CDOs). Analysts at Citigroup were predicting in November that write-downs of up to SFr 14 billion were possible.

Why then did this new batch of red ink still come as a shock? The answer lies not in the scale of the overall loss, more in UBS's decision to take the hit in one go. The bank's mark-to-model approach to valuing its subprime-related holdings had been based on payments data from the underlying mortgage loans. Although these data show a

unappealing *a.* 不能让人满意的

mortgage *n.* 抵押

exposure *n.* 暴露，揭发

shore *v.* 支持

sovereign *n.* 主权，君主

aggressive *a.* 挑衅的，强势的

subprime *n.* 次贷

underlying *a.* 潜在的

worsening in credit quality, the deterioration is slower than mark-to-market valuations, which have the effect of instantly crystallizing all expected future losses.

Thanks to this gradualist approach, UBS had been expected to take write-downs in managed increments of SFr 2 billion — 3 billion over a period of several quarters. It now appears that the bank has incorporated market values into its model, sending its fourth-quarter write-downs into orbit. The change of approach may be on the advice of auditors and regulators but it is more likely to reflect a desire by UBS's bosses to avoid months of speculation about the bank's exposure, something that Marcel Rohner, the chief executive, described as "distracting".

In a particular indignity for a bank long associated with conservatism, concerns about the level of UBS's capital ratio had even started to surface. Hence the moves to strengthen its tier — one capital, an important measure of bank solidity, by SFr 19.4 billion, a great deal more than the write-down. The majority of that money will come from sovereign-wealth funds, the white knights of choice for today's bank in distress. Singapore's GIC, which manages the city-state's foreign reserves, has pledged to buy SFr 11 billion-worth of convertible bonds in UBS; an unnamed Middle Eastern investor will put in a further SFr 2 billion. UBS will also raise money by selling treasury shares, and save cash by issuing its 2007 dividend in the form of shares. Its capital ratio is expected to end up above 12% in the fourth quarter, a strong position.

Hopeful talk of lines being drawn under the subprime crisis has been a feature of banks' quarterly reporting since September. Marrying bigger-than-expected write-downs with bigger-than-expected boosts to capital looks like the right treatment in this environment. But UBS still cannot be sure that its problems are over. Further deterioration in its subprime asset values is possible; the broader economic impact of the credit crunch is unclear; and the damage to the bank's reputation cannot yet be quantified. The patient still needs watching.

deterioration *n.* 恶化

crystallize *v.* 使明朗

increment *n.* 增值，增加

incorporate *v.* 吸收，包含

auditor *n.* 审计员

distracting *a.* 让人分心的

surface *v.* 浮出水面

convertible *a.* 可转变的

quantified *a.* 量化的

长难句分析

1. Then came the hot iron: news of a series of measures to shore up the bank's capital base, among them investments from sovereign-wealth funds in Singapore and the Middle East.

❖结构分析 该句主干为Then came the hot iron... 这是一个有复杂同位语的简单句。news of... 是前面the hot iron 的同位语,to shore up the bank's capital base 是不定式短语作定语修饰前面的 measures, 而后面 among them... 也是用来修饰 measures,具体介绍其中的一些措施。

2. The change of approach may be on the advice of auditors and regulators but it is more likely to reflect a desire by UBS's bosses to avoid months of speculation about the bank's exposure, something that Marcel Rohner, the chief executive, described as "distracting".

❖结构分析 该句主干为The change of approach may be... but... 这是一个并列句,but 引导的分句比较复杂,to avoide...不定式短语作前面 a desire 的定语,而 something that... 是 a desire 的同位语,该同位语中又包含了一个定语从句。

参考译文

　　有控制地流血还是灼伤?这是瑞士联合银行,一家因美国抵押信贷市场受到重挫的瑞士银行,所要面对的尴尬选择。而这家银行选择了后者——先是在公开次级感染债务之际宣布高达100亿资产价值缩水,从而暴露出伤口。瑞士联合银行目前预计第四季度也将亏损,本月就能见分晓。紧接着就传来了热点议题:报道说将有一系列的措施来支持银行的资本基础,其中就有新加坡和中东的主权财富基金。

　　也应该会有些坏消息。10月,瑞士联合银行四分之三的资产价值缩水超过40亿瑞士法郎,这与其他银行(如花旗银行和美林证券)更为严重的状况相比而言,还是较为乐观的。第三季度末次级债市场价值的急剧下落使得瑞士联合银行将会面临更多的苦痛,尤其是它相当大的一部分资产都受到抵押的影响。花旗银行分析师在11月预言可能会有140亿瑞士法郎的损失。

　　那么为什么这次新的一组赤字还是让人们大吃一惊呢?答案并不是因为总亏损的规模,而是瑞士联合银行决定一次性地承担损失。银行估量其与次级债相关的股票所用的按模型定价方法是基于第一担保抵押贷款的支付数据上的。尽管这些数据显示信用有所降低,但比起用按市值计价的估量方式其恶化速度要慢一些,具有迅速明确所有未来损失的作用。

正是由于采取了这个缓和的方式，瑞士联合银行可望在几个季度内将资产账面价值增长控制在 20 亿到 30 亿瑞士法郎。目前显示出该银行已经将市场价值纳入其模式中，从而将第四季度的资产账面价值控制在一定范围内。方法可能是审计员或调节员的建议，但更反映了瑞士联合银行高层要避免数月来对银行曝光的猜测——首席执行官马塞尔·罗纳将其形容为"转移注意力(的方案)"。

一个长期以保守见称的银行如今却受到这种侮辱，对于瑞士联合银行的资本比率的担心也就逐渐出现了。于是就采取措施加强第一层资金约 194 亿瑞士法郎，该数额比资产账面损失要多许多，这是增加银行信用的重要方法。资金大部分来源于主权财富基金，这是当今处于困境的银行的白衣骑士。新加坡 GIC 掌握着这个城市国家的外汇储备，它承诺要购买瑞士联合银行 110 亿瑞士法郎的可转换债券。一个匿名的中东投资者又投入了 20 亿瑞士法郎。瑞士联合银行也会出售债券，以股票的形式发行 2007 年的红利来募集现金。其资本比率有望在第四季度超过 12%，这样处境就很不错了。

9 月份以来，银行季度报告会的一大特色就是讨论将额度控制在次贷危机之下。把比预期大的资产账面降低程度和比预期大的资本增加相结合，这好像是这种氛围下的一个正确处理方案。但是瑞士联合银行还是不能确保问题都已解决。有可能出现次级资产价值的继续恶化，而且信用危机引起的更广阔范围内的经济冲击也不是很明确，还有对公司名誉的损害程度也还没有确定。病情还有待观察。

Passage 3

The bride and groom, a guitar-wielding rock girl and a muscle-rippling dragon-slayer, make an odd couple — so it is hardly surprising that nobody expected their marriage. But on December 2nd the video-game companies behind "Guitar Hero" and "World of Warcraft", Activision and Vivendi Games respectively, announced plans for an elaborate merger. Vivendi, a French media group, will pool its games unit, plus \$ 1.7 billion in cash, with Activision; the combined entity will then offer to buy back shares from Activision shareholders, raising Vivendi's stake in the resulting firm to as much as 68%.

elaborate *a.* 详细的，复杂的

Activision's boss, Bobby Kotick, will remain at the helm of the new company, to be known as Activision

helm *n.* 舵，驾驶盘

Blizzard in recognition of Vivendi's main gaming asset: its subsidiary Blizzard Entertainment, the firm behind "World of Warcraft", an online swords-and-sorcery game with 9.3 million subscribers. The deal was unexpected, but makes excellent strategic sense, says Piers Harding-Rolls of *Screen Digest*, a consultancy. Activision has long coveted "World of Warcraft", and Vivendi gets a bigger games division and Activision's talented management team to run it. As well as making sense for both parties, the $18.9 billion deal — the biggest ever in the video-games industry — says a lot about the trends now shaping the business.

The first is a push into new markets, especially online multiplayer games, which are particularly popular in Asia, and "casual" games that appeal to people who do not regard themselves as gamers. "World of Warcraft" is the world's most popular online subscription-based game and is hugely lucrative. Blizzard will have revenues of $1.1 billion this year and operating profits of $520 million. "World of Warcraft" is really "a social network with many entertainment components," says Mr. Kotick.

Similarly, he argues, "Guitar Hero" and other games that use new kinds of controller, rather than the usual buttons and joysticks, are broadening the appeal of gaming by emphasising its social aspects, since they are easy to pick up and can be played with friends. Social gaming, says Mr. Kotick, is "the most powerful trend" building new audiences for the industry. He is clearly excited at the prospect of using Blizzard's expertise to launch an online version of "Guitar Hero" for Asian markets. Online music games such as "Audition Online", which started in South Korea, are "massive in Asia," says Mr. Harding-Rolls.

A second trend is media groups' increasing interest in gaming. Vivendi owns Universal Music, one of the "big four" record labels. As the record industry's sales decline, it makes sense to move into gaming, a younger, faster-growing medium with plenty of cross-marketing

---

subsidiary *a.* 辅助的; *n.* 子公司

covet *v.* 觊觎

multiplayer *n.* 多人

lucrative *a.* 赚钱的,可获利的

prospect *n.* 前景,希望

decline *v.* 衰落,下降

opportunities. (Activision might raid Universal's back catalogue for material for its music games, for example, which might in turn boost music sales.) Other media groups are going the same way. Last year Viacom, an American media giant, acquired Harmonix, the company that originally created "Guitar Hero". It has been promoting its new game, "Rock Band", using its MTV music channel. Viacom has also created online virtual worlds that tie in with several of its television programmes, such as "Laguna Beach" and "Pimp My Ride". Disney bought Club Penguin, a virtual world for children, in August. And Time Warner is involved in gaming via its Warner Bros Home Entertainment division, which publishes its own titles and last month bought TT Games, the British firm behind the "Lego Star Wars" games.

长难句分析

1. Activision's boss, Bobby Kotick, will remain at the helm of the new company, to be known as Activision Blizzard in recognition of Vivendi's main gaming asset: its subsidiary Blizzard Entertainment, the firm behind "World of Warcraft", an online swords-and-sorcery game with 9.3 million subscribers.

❖ 结构分析 该句主干为 Activision's boss will remain at the helm. 这个句子看似复杂,其实是一个简单句。to be known 是一个省略的定语从句,来修饰 new company,其完整形式是 which is to be known。冒号后面的内容则是对 new company 的进一步说明。

2. Similarly, he argues, "Guitar Hero" and other games that use new kinds of controller, rather than the usual buttons and joysticks, are broadening the appeal of gaming by emphasising its social aspects, since they are easy to pick up and can be played with friends.

❖ 结构分析 该句主干为 He argues, "Guitar Hero" and other games are broadening the appeal... since... 这同样也是一个简单句。argues 后面跟的是宾语从句,rather than 表示否定的意思,other games 后面跟的是定语从句,are broadening 是该从句的谓语部分,而 since 所引导的句子则表示原因。

参考译文

    新娘是挥舞着吉他的摇滚悍妇,新郎是浑身肌肉的屠龙勇士,这一对实在古怪,也怪不得没人相信他们居然可以走到一起。但是 12 月 2 日,"吉他英雄"和"魔兽争霸"所属的两个视频游戏公司——美国动视(Activision)和维旺迪(Vivendi)公司宣布了他们的精心策划的联姻。维旺迪是一家法国媒体公司,它准备将自己的游戏单元以及 17 亿美元现金注入到美国动视公司。联合体之后再从美国动视股东那里买回股份,维旺迪在联合公司的股份提升到 68%。

    <u>新公司仍由美国动视公司老总博比·科蒂克来掌舵,更名为"美国动视暴风雪",取这个名字是为了酬谢维旺迪注入的主要游戏资产——</u>子公司"暴风雪娱乐",该公司拥有"战舰世界",这个拥有 930 万注册者的在线游戏"剑与巫术"。这笔生意出乎大家意料,但却有非凡的战略意义,《银幕文摘》的顾问皮尔斯·哈丁·罗尔斯这样说。美国动视对"战舰世界"已经觊觎很久,而维旺迪公司也因此获得了更大的游戏份额,拥有美国动视公司优秀的管理团队来为之运营。同样对双方有利的是,189 亿美元的交易是视频游戏产业中最大的,因此其决策将对未来该产业的发展趋势起着举足轻重的作用。

    第一个趋势是推进新的市场,尤其在风靡于亚洲的在线多人游戏领域吸引那些不把自己当游戏玩家的人的"休闲游戏"。"战舰世界"是全球最流行的在线注册游戏,盈利巨大。"暴风雪"今年收入将达 11 亿美元,操作利润就有 5.2 亿美元。科蒂克先生评价说,"战舰世界"是真正的"拥有众多娱乐成分的交际性网络游戏"。

    同样的,他说,<u>"吉他英雄"和其他游戏没有用普通的按钮和操作杆,而是使用了新式控制器,通过强调其交际性的特点来增加游戏的吸引力,因为这些游戏很容易上手,而且可以和朋友一起玩。</u>科蒂克先生说,交际游戏是为这个产业创造新玩家的"最强大的趋势"。很明显,他谈到利用"暴风雪"的技术来向亚洲市场推行"吉他英雄"在线版的前景时十分兴奋。哈丁·罗尔斯说,像最先开始于韩国的"在线试听"这样的在线音乐游戏"在亚洲占有相当大的份额"。

    第二种趋势就是媒体集团在游戏方面兴趣不断增加。美国动视拥有"四大"唱片之一的"全球音乐"。由于唱片行业销售衰退,它就转向游戏,这是更为年轻且成长迅速的一种媒介,拥有很多跨市场型的机遇。(比如维旺迪可能就要从"全球音乐"曲目中为自己的音乐游戏搜索一些素材,而这样反过来又促进了唱片的销售。)其他的媒体集团也大体一样。去年,美国媒体巨头维亚康姆(Viacom)收购了 Harmonix 公司——"吉他巨人"最初就是由该公司创造出来的。目前它利用自己的 MTV 音乐频道推广新游戏——摇滚乐队。维亚康姆还创造了在线虚拟世界,这个游戏和几个电视频道如"Laguna Beach"、"Pimp My Ride"取得了联合。迪斯尼也于 8 月份购买了"企鹅俱乐部",这是专门为孩子创造的虚拟世界。华纳时代通过其华纳兄弟家庭娱乐公司也涉足游戏业,该公司以自己的名称进行出版活动,并于上个月收购了 TT 游戏公司(该公司为"Lego 星际争霸"游戏所属的英国公司)。

Passage 4

Berkeley seems like a fitting place to find the godfather of the open-innovation movement basking in glory. The Californian village was, after all, at the very heart of the anti-establishment movement of the 1960s and has spawned plenty of radical thinkers. One of them, Henry Chesbrough, a business professor at the University of California at Berkeley, observes with a smile that "this is the 40th anniversary of the Summer of Love."

Mr. Chesbrough's two books *Open Innovation* and *Open Business Models* have popularised the notion of looking for bright ideas outside of an organisation. As the concept of open innovation has become ever more fashionable, the corporate R&D lab has become decreasingly relevant. Most ideas don't come from there.

To see why travel to Cincinnati, Ohio — which is about as far removed culturally from Berkeley as one can get in America. The conservative mid-western city is home to P&G, historically one of the most traditional firms in America. For decades, the company that brought the world Ivory soap, Crest toothpaste and Ariel detergent had a closed innovation process, centred around its own secretive R&D operations.

No longer. P&G has radically altered the way it comes up with new ideas and products. It now welcomes and works with universities, suppliers and outside inventors. It also offers them a share in the rewards. In less than a decade, P&G has increased the proportion of new-product ideas originating from outside of the firm from less than a fifth to around half. That has boosted innovation and, says its boss, Mr. Lafley, is the main reason why P&G has been able to grow at 6% a year between 2001 and 2006, tripling annual profits to $8.6 billion. The company now has a market capitalisation of over $200 billion.

---

open-innovation *a.* 开放式创新

bask *v.* 晒太阳

spawn *v.* 产卵，造成

Summer of Love 指 1967 年的旧金山夏天，是 60 年代嬉皮文化的高潮。

decreasingly *ad.* 渐渐减少地

conservative *a.* 保守的

detergent *n.* 清洁剂，洗涤剂

radically *ad.* 根本地，完全地

supplier *n.* 供应商

proportion *n.* 比例

boost *v.* 提高，推动

triple *vt.& vi.* (使) 增至三倍，三重

IBM is another iconic firm that has jumped on the open-innovation bandwagon. The once-secretive company has done a sharp U-turn and embraced Linux, an open-source software language. IBM now gushes about being part of the "open-innovation community", yielding hundreds of software patents to the "creative commons" rather than registering them for itself. However, it also continues to take out patents at a record pace in other areas, such as advanced materials, and in the process racks up some $1 billion a year in licensing fees.

bandwagon *n.* 势力,流行

yield *v.* 产出
common *n.* 大众

Since an army of programmers around the world work on developing Linux essentially at no cost, IBM now has an extremely cheap and robust operating system. It makes money by providing its clients with services that support the use of Linux — and charging them for it. Using open-source software saves IBM a whopping $ 400 million a year, according to Paul Horn, until recently the firm's head of research. The company is so committed to openness that it now carries out occasional "online jam sessions" during which tens of thousands of its employees exchange ideas in a mass form of brainstorming.

commit *v.* 献身

brainstorm *n.* 集思广益

Mr. Chesbrough, of course, heartily approves. He gives dozens of other examples of firms doing similar things, ranging from Clorax, a household products firm to Air Products, an industrial gases company. Mr. Chesbrough reckons that "IBM and P&G have timed their shift to a high-volume open-business model very well" and that if their competitors do not do the same they will be in trouble.

reckon *v.* 认为,估计

长难句分析

1. For decades, the company that brought the world Ivory soap, Crest toothpaste and Ariel detergent had a closed innovation process, centred around its own secretive R&D operations.

❖结构分析 该句主干为 The company had a closed innovation process. 这是一个复合句,that 引导的是 company 的定语,centred… 分词结构作前面 process 的定语。

2. IBM **now gushes about being part of the "open-innovation community", yielding hundreds of software patents to the "creative commons" rather than registering them for itself.**

❖ 结构分析 该句主干为 IBM now gushes about being... 这是一个简单句, yielding... rather than registering... 是作前面 community 的定语。

参考译文

伯克利似乎是备受瞩目的开放创新运动教父的故乡。毕竟这个加利福尼亚村庄是 20 世纪 90 年代反固化运动的中心,在这里诞生了许多激进的思想者。其中有一位名叫亨利·切斯布洛的加利福尼亚大学商业学教授,他笑着说,"这是'爱之夏'的 40 周年庆典"。

切斯布洛先生的两本书《开放创新》与《开放商业模式》使得在组织向外部寻找好主意的理念开始流行起来。随着开放式创新的理念越来越流行,公司的研发实验室就显得越来越不重要了。大多数的新主意都并不是从那些实验室里产生的。

为什么要到俄亥俄州的辛辛那提去呢? 因为那里是全美与伯克利文化差异最大的地方了。这个保守的中西部城市是宝洁公司的发源地,宝洁是美国历史上最传统的公司之一。几十年来,该公司为世界制造了象牙牌香皂、佳洁士牙膏和 Ariel 清洁剂,它拥有封闭的创新程序,以其秘密的研发部为核心。

但这些都已经成为历史了。宝洁公司已大幅度改变了其获取新想法,发明新产品的模式。公司现在欢迎与大学、供应商以及外面的发明家合作,甚至还将奖金分给他们一份。10年之内宝洁公司就大幅增加了公司外新产品研发的比例,从不到 1/5 的比例升到了现在的1/2。公司老总拉弗利先生说这大大推进了创新,也是宝洁从 2001 年到 2006 年保持每年 6%增长的主要原因,现在年利润已是原来的三倍,达到 86 亿美元。目前该公司的市场资本总额为两千亿美元。

IBM 是另外一家跳上开放式创新流行花车的传统公司。这家曾经非常秘密的公司进行了 U 型反转,开始欢迎一种资源公开的软件语言 Linux。IBM 现在总说自己是"开放创新社团"的一员,将大量的软件专利权给了"创造性的公众"而不是由公司自己注册。但是,IBM 在其他领域继续以创纪录的速度取得专利,比如高级材料,在这个过程中许可费用就达到了每年 10 亿美元。

由于在全世界有大批程序师以几乎零成本的方式开发 Linux,因此 IBM 现在拥有非常廉价且强健的操作系统。它通过为户提供支持 Linux 系统的服务来收取费用。据该公司研发主任保罗·霍恩称,使用开放式资源的软件一年就为 IBM 节约了 4 亿美元。该公司如此致力于开放的态度,以至于它有时会召开一些"在线会议",使得成千上万的员工可以通过自由讨论来交流想法。

切斯布洛先生当然赞同这点,他还举出许多其他公司相似的情况,其中就有一家居用品公司 Clorax,还有一家工业汽油公司"空气产品"。切斯布洛先生承认"IBM 和宝洁公司成功转变为高度开放的商业模式,而如果他们的竞争对手不这样做的话,可能就麻烦了。"

Passage 5

With technology leased from the German company Tronical, Gibson has modified its classic Les Paul design to create a guitar that adjusts itself to one of six preset tunings. This is no instrument for beginners. Retailing for between \$ 2,200 and \$ 2,500, the Robot Guitar is courting serious hobbyists and professionals who demand precision tuning, or frequently switch between different tunings and don't want the hassle of lugging multiple instruments around. "It's a cool idea. Nobody likes tuning," concedes Dinosaur Jr. frontman J. Mascis. "But I have to wait for the drummer to rest anyway between songs." Another company, called TransPerformance, sells a similar tuning device that it will install in your nonrobotic guitar for you. But Gibson's is the first out-of-the-box self-tuning ax.

It sounds like a minor development in guitar technology, even rather gimmicky. But for an instrument that has barely evolved since the 1950s, the Robot Guitar is nothing short of magic: simply pull out the "master control knob" and strum the guitar. The knob lights up as a computer embedded in the back of the guitar measures each string's pitch. The tuning pegs turn by themselves, making a robotic whirring sound that enhances the wow. The control knob's lights flash blue when your instrument is locked into the tuning you select. If you're so inclined you can override the device and tune manually. But why would you? It takes all of 10 seconds for the Robot Guitar to do its thing—and blow your mind as it hasn't been blown since the first time you heard "Eruption."

In an industry that has been flat to sagging, the Robot

lease *n. & v.* 出租	
adjust *v.* 校正,调整	
retailing *n.* 零售业	
hobbyist *n.* 业余爱好者	
hassle *n.* 辩论,争吵	
concede *v.* 承认,让步	
self-tuning *a.* 自我调节的	
gimmicky *a.* 巧妙手法的	
strum *n.* 弹奏	
knob *n.* 把手	
whir *n.* 呼呼作响	
eruption *n.* 爆发	
sag *v.* 下垂,下弯	

Guitar could provide a welcome boost to retailers. After 10 years of brisk growth, guitar sales headed south in 2006, according to the April 2007 *Music Trades Magazine* industry census. Low-end beginner acoustic guitar sales dropped 24.4 percent last year; electric guitars fell 19.1 percent. Certainly there is a dearth of righteous shredding on today's Top 40 radio. And the wildly popular videogame "Guitar Hero" allows even the most tone-deaf nonmusician to simulate the experience of rocking out. Professional musicians account for 15 percent of instrument purchases in the country, according to George Van Horn, a senior analyst at IBISWorld. "Gibson is obviously aiming high, but it's worth chasing" the pros, he says.

census *n.* 人口普查，统计

dearth *n.* 缺乏

simulate *v.* 模仿

Judging by all the buzz the Robot Guitar has generated, Gibson won't have a hard time chasing down anyone. "You don't see this kind of excitement often," says Norman Hajjar, the chief marketing officer at Guitar Center, which has stocked 1,000 of the 4,000 Robot Guitars hitting the market nationwide Dec. 7. "They're quite a draw. We let people touch and play with the guitars — they're putting them through their paces. It really charms people." As of Thursday morning, Guitar Center had already taken deposits on roughly a third of the 1,000 Robot Guitars they have in stock.

chase *v.* 追逐，追赶

deposit *n.* 定金，存款

The very fact that "Guitar Hero" and now "Rock Band" are power-chording their way off store shelves this holiday season proves that the dream is alive. The reason that the odious song "Rock Star" is currently ubiquitous has nothing to do with quality songwriting. Truth is, we all want to be rock stars; the videogames and Nickelback's opus get us all a little closer to living the fantasy. But with the Robot Guitar, it's the musicians themselves who have gotten a long overdue leg up.

chord *n.* 弦，和音

ubiquitous *a.* 无所不在的

overdue *a.* 过期的

长难句分析

The very fact that "Guitar Hero" and now "Rock Band" are power-chording their way off store shelves this holiday season proves that the dream is alive.

◆结构分析 该句主干为 The very fact that... proves that... 这是一个复合句，fact 后面 that 引导的是同位语从句；后面 that 引导的是宾语从句。

参考译文

吉布森利用从德国公司 Tronical 租借来的技术改造了经典圣保罗-莱迪朗斯(Les Paul) 的设计，从而创造出一把可以自动调节到事先设好的 6 个调的吉他。这可不是给那些初学者用的吉他。自动吉他售价为 2,200 美元至 2,500 美元，其对象为真正的吉他爱好者或者专业人士，他们往往对音准有比较高的要求，或是那些要不停在各个调音间变化的人，他们不希望把那么多的工具拖来拖去。"这个主意太妙了，没有人喜欢调音"，"恐龙青年乐队"领唱 J. 马希斯肯定了这一点，"但是我必须得等鼓手在两首歌之间休息的时候才能调音"。另外一个名为 TransPerformance 的乐队也在出售类似的一种调音器，可以安装在非自动吉他上。但是吉布森发明的是第一个盒外自动调音的吉他。

听起来这好像是吉他技术的一个小小的进展，甚至可以说是个小发明。但是对于这种从上世纪 50 年代后就再没有改进过的乐器来说，自动吉他绝对是个奇迹：只要把"大师控制的旋钮"拽出，然后就可以弹吉他了。这个按钮是发光的，好像是嵌在吉他背后的计算机一样，可以调节每根弦的音。调音栓会自己转动，发出自动运行的声音，从而增加了颤音。如果吉他被锁定在自己选择的调音上，控制按钮就发出蓝光。如果你愿意，也可以不管这个装置而手动调节。但是为什么不用呢？只需要 10 秒钟自动吉他就设置好了，你第一次听到了"爆发"时会受到很大的震动。

对于这么一个濒临衰败的产业，自动吉他能给销售商带来一定的增长。根据 2007 年 4 月《音乐商业杂志》进行的行业调查，在经历了 10 年快速成长后，吉他销售开始于 2006 年一路滑坡。低端的初学者原声吉他的销售去年下滑了 24.4%，电子吉他销售则下滑了 19.1%。当然当今排名前 40 位的电台缺乏优秀的吉他音乐，而流行的视频游戏"吉他英雄"可以让最五音不全的人模拟弹奏摇滚乐。IBIS World 公司资深分析家乔治·温·霍思说，专业音乐人占到本国乐器购买的 15%。他谈道"吉布森意在高远，但值得去争取"更多支持者。

从自动吉他引发的广泛影响来看，吉布森公司要找到支持者不是件困难的事。"不可能经常看到这种令人兴奋的事情"，吉他中心市场部门负责人 Norman Hajjar 说道，他已经囤积了 4,000 把自动吉他中的 1,000 把，计划于 12 月 7 日推向市场。"这确实挺吸引人的，我们让人们触摸并弹奏吉他，让人们感受节拍。这真的很吸引人。"自从周四早上开始，吉他中心已经接受了库存的 1,000 把吉他中 1/3 的定金了。

而"吉他英雄"们和现在的"摇滚乐队"有望在这个假期从货架上买到这种新吉他，从而实现其梦想。现今难听的"摇滚之星"随处可见的原因与有品质的作曲扯不上关系。实际上我们都希望成为摇滚明星，视频游戏和"五分钱乐队"的作品把我们与幻想拉近了一点。而自动吉他的发明是音乐人开始追赶自己长期以来落下的路的表现。

第二节 文化教育

Passage 1

He emerged, all of a sudden, in 1957: the most explosive new poetic talent of the English post-war era. Poetry specialised, at that moment, in the wry chronicling of the everyday. The poetry of Yorkshire-born Ted Hughes, first published in a book called *The Hawk in the Rain* when he was 27, was unlike anything written by his immediate predecessors. Driven by an almost Jacobean rhetoric, it had a visionary fervour. Its most eye-catching characteristic was Hughes's ability to get beneath the skins of animals: foxes, otters, pigs. These animals were the real thing all right, but they were also armorial devices — symbols of the countryside and lifeblood of the earth in which they were rooted. It gave his work a raw, primal stink.

raw *a.* 自然状态的,生的

It was not only England that thought so either. Hughes's book was also published in America, where it won the Galbraith prize, a major literary award. But then, in 1963, Sylvia Plath, a young American poet whom he had first met at Cambridge University in 1956, and who became his wife in the summer of that year, committed suicide. Hughes was vilified for long after that, especially by feminists in America. In 1998, the year he died, Hughes broke his own self-imposed public silence about their relationship in a book of loose-weave poems called *Birthday Letters*. In this new and exhilarating collection of real letters, Hughes returns to the issue of his first wife's death, which he calls his "big and unmanageable event". He felt his talent muffled by the perpetual eavesdropping upon his every move. Not until he decided to publish his own account of their relationship did the burden begin to lighten.

major *a.* 主要的,重要的

vilify *v.* 诽谤,辱骂

impose *v.* 强加,征税

weave *v.* 编,织

exhilarating *a.* 让人兴奋的

muffle *v.* 捂住,听不清

The analysis is raw, pained and ruthlessly self-aware.

ruthlessly *a.* 无情地

For all the moral torment, the writing itself has the same rush and vigour that possessed Hughes's early poetry. Some books of letters serve as a personalised historical chronicle. Poets' letters are seldom like that, and Hughes's are no exception. His are about a life of literary engagement: almost all of them include some musing on the state or the nature of writing, both Hughes's own or other people's. The trajectory of Hughes's literary career had him moving from obscurity to fame, and then, in the eyes of many, to life-long notoriety. These letters are filled with his wrestling with the consequences of being the part-private, part-public creature that he became, desperate to devote himself to his writing, and yet subject to endless invasions of his privacy.

Hughes is an absorbing and intricate commentator upon his own poetry, even when he is standing back from it and good-humouredly condemning himself for "its fantasticalia, its pretticisms and its infinite verballifications". He also believed, from first to last, that poetry had a special place in the education of children. "What kids need", he wrote in a 1988 letter to the secretary of state for education in the Conservative government, "is a headfull [sic] of songs that are not songs but blocks of refined and achieved and exemplary language." When that happens, children have "the guardian angel installed behind the tongue".

engagement *n.* 约会,誓言

trajectory *n.* 轨道
obscurity *n.* 费解,身份低微
notoriety *n.* 臭名昭著

intricate *a.* 复杂的,难懂的

condemn *v.* 批判,谴责

长难句分析

1. **But then, in 1963, Sylvia Plath, a young American poet whom he had first met at Cambridge University in 1956, and who became his wife in the summer of that year, committed suicide.**

   ❖结构分析 该句主干为 But then Sylvia Plath committed suicide... 这是一个同位语带有定语从句的复合句。whom 和 who 引导的两个定语从句修饰 a young American poet,整体作为 Sylvia Plath 的同位语。

2. **These letters are filled with his wrestling with the consequences of being the part-private, part-public creature that he became, desperate to devote himself to his writing, and yet subject to endless invasions of his privacy.**

   ❖结构分析 该句主干为 These letters are filled with his wrestling... 这是一个简单句,难点

在于最后两个形容词词组的成分（desperate to devote himself to his writing, and yet subject to endless invasions of his privacy）。这两个形容词词组用来修饰前面的名词 creature，而 creature 后面紧跟着的 that 引导的从句也是修饰它的定语从句。

参考译文

1957 年,他横空出世,成为英国战后最具影响力的诗坛天才。当时,诗歌的主要题材是对日常生活的扭曲记录。特德·休斯出生在约克郡,在其 27 岁时出版了名为《雨中鹰》的诗集,这本诗集所收入的诗与前辈的作品风格大相径庭。受詹姆士一世时代风格的影响,其诗歌呈现出幻觉式的激情, 其最显著的特点是休斯可以描述动物外表以下的东西,无论是狐狸、水獭还是猪。这些动物的确是真实的,但同时又是象征性的,代表着乡村,代表着它们植根的地球的生命之源。正是这一点赋予了其作品一种野性、原始的气息。

他的作品不仅仅在英国得到认同。休斯的书也在美国出版,并且赢得了一项重要的文学奖——加尔布雷思奖。但是在 1963 年,西尔维亚·普拉斯自杀了,这个年轻的美国诗人与他第一次见面是在 1956 年的剑桥大学,当年夏天成为了他妻子。之后很长的时间里休斯都受到人们的谴责,尤其是美国的女权主义者。1998 年,也就是休斯去世的那一年,他在自己一本名为《生日信札》的结构松散的诗集中公开了他俩的关系,打破了他自己一直以来的缄默。在这本令人兴奋的书信集中,休斯回忆说他第一个妻子的死是"难以处理的大事情"。他感觉自己的一举一动都受到监视,他的天赋因而受到了制约。直到他出版了自己的这本有关他们关系的书时,他身上的负担才得以减轻。

他对自然的剖析饱含痛苦, 具有强烈的自我意识。尽管书中极致地表达了其精神的苦痛,但文字本身却具有休斯早期诗歌的激情和活力。一般书信集只是个人的经历记录而已,但是诗人的书信集却不同,休斯的也不例外。他的书信集描写了其文学生涯;几乎所有的书信都是关于写作状态或写作性质的思考。休斯的文学生命轨迹是从无名到闻名,而后,在众人看来又经历了漫长的名誉扫地的阶段。这些信中处处都显现出休斯和自己成为半私人、半公开人物这样一个结果反复挣扎的心理,他渴望将自己奉献给文字,但又时时受到私人空间被侵袭的威胁。

有意思且令人费解的是,休斯还对自己的诗歌进行评论,他甚至还以局外人的身份来看待自己的作品,很幽默地批评自己的诗歌"有空想色彩、唯美化且一直咬文嚼字"。他还从始至终坚信诗歌在教育孩子方面有特殊的作用。1988 年他在给保守党政府国家教育部长的一封信中这样写道:"孩子们需要的是满脑子的歌曲,其实不是歌曲,而是精致、优秀,具有代表性的语言。"如果真能这样,那么孩子们"舌头后面就会有守护天使了"。

Passage 2

The haunting paintings of Helene Schjerfbeck, on show in the final leg of a traveling tour that has already attracted thousands of visitors in Hamburg and The Hague, may come as a surprise to many. Few outside the Nordic world would recognise the work of this Finnish artist who died in 1946. More people should. The 120 works have at their core 20 self-portraits, half the number she painted in all. The first, dated 1880, is of a wide-eyed teenager eager to absorb everything. The last is a sighting of the artist's ghost-to-be; Schjerfbeck died the year after it was made. Together this series is among the most moving and accomplished autobiographies-in-paint.

Precociously gifted, Schjerfbeck was 11 when she entered the Finnish Art Society's drawing school. "The Wounded Warrior in the Snow", a history painting, was bought by a private collector and won her a state travel grant when she was 17. Schjerfbeck studied in Paris, went on to Pont-Aven, Brittany, where she painted for a year, then to Tuscany, Cornwall and St Petersburg. During her 1887 visit to St Ives, Cornwall, Schjerfbeck painted "The Convalescent". A child wrapped in a blanket sits propped up in a large wicker chair, toying with a sprig. The picture won a bronze medal at the 1889 Paris World Fair and was bought by the Finnish Art Society. To a modern eye it seems almost sentimental and is redeemed only by the somewhat stunned, melancholy expression on the child's face, which may have been inspired by Schjerfbeck's early experiences. At four, she fell down a flight of steps and never fully recovered.

In 1890, Schjerfbeck settled in Finland. Teaching exhausted her, she did not like the work of other local painters, and she was further isolated when she took on the care of her mother(who lived until 1923). "If I allow myself the freedom to live a secluded life", she wrote, "then it is because it has to be that way." In 1902, Schjerfbeck and

recognise v.认出,承认

absorb v.吸收,吸引注意力

precociously a. 早熟的,过早的

grant n. 拨款,同意

convalescent n. 恢复期
sprig n. 小枝,嫩枝

melancholy a. 忧郁的

exhauste v.耗尽,费尽

secluded a. 与世隔绝的

her mother settled in the small, industrial town of Hyvinkaa, 50 kilometres north of Helsinki. Isolation had one desired effect for it was there that Schjerfbeck became a modern painter. She produced still lives and landscapes but above all moody yet incisive portraits of her mother, local school girls, women workers in town(profiles of a pensive, aristocratic looking seamstress dressed in black stand out). And of course she painted herself. Comparisons have been made with James McNeill Whistler and Edvard Munch. But from 1905, her pictures became pure Schjerfbeck.

> moody *a.* 情绪低落的
>
> seamstress *n.* 女裁缝

"I have always searched for the dense depths of the soul, that have not yet discovered themselves", she wrote, "where everything is still unconscious — there one can make the greatest discoveries." She experimented with different kinds of underpainting, scraped and rubbed, made bright rosy red spots; doing whatever had to be done to capture the subconscious — her own and that of her models. In 1913, Schjerfbeck was rediscovered by an art dealer and journalist, Gosta Stenman. Once again she was a success. Retrospectives, touring exhibitions and a biography followed, yet Schjerfbeck remained little known outside Scandinavia. That may have had something to do with her indifference to her renown. "I am nothing, absolutely nothing", she wrote. "All I want to do is paint". Schjerfbeck was possessed of a unique vision, and it is time the world recognised that.

> unconscious *a* 无意识的，大胆的
> underpaint *n.* 画底色
> scrape *v.* 刮,擦
> capture *v.* 俘获,捕获
>
> retrospective *a.* 追溯的,回想的

长难句分析

1. **The haunting paintings of Helene Schjerfbeck, on show in the final leg of a traveling tour that has already attracted thousands of visitors in Hamburg and The Hague, may come as a surprise to many.**

   ❖结构分析 该句主干为 The haunting paintings may come as a surprise to many...这是一个简单句,介词短语 on show...作为插入语,修饰 the haunting paintings,that 引导的定语从句修饰 the final leg of a traveling tour。

2. **To a modern eye it seems almost sentimental and is redeemed only by the somewhat stunned, melancholy expression on the child's face, which may have been inspired by Schjerfbeck's early experiences.**

   ❖结构分析 该句主干为 It seems almost sentimental and is redeemed only by...这是一个并列句,第二个分句的状语比较复杂,介词短语的宾语 expression 由 which 引导的非限定性定语从句来进行修饰。

参考译文

海伦·谢夫贝克那些让人难以忘怀的作品在这次巡展最后的展出已经在汉堡和海牙吸引了成千上万的参观者,但这一次可能依然能让很多人大吃一惊。北欧民族之外很少有人会知道这位于 1946 年去世的芬兰艺术家,但更多的人应该了解她的作品。在这 120 幅作品中有 20 幅是她的自画像,这是她所有自画像的一半。第一幅创作于 1880 年,那是渴望一切的一个大眼睛少女,而最后一幅是艺术家即将成为鬼魂的一幕,而她正是在这幅作品创作完成后的那年去世的。这个系列是最生动、最完美的自画像之一。

谢夫贝克少年时就天赋显露,11 岁就进入了芬兰艺术协会的绘画学校。"受伤战士在雪中"是一幅历史画,由一位私人收藏家买走,这使得她在 17 岁就赢得了可以环游全国的资金。她在巴黎学习,后来又到布列塔尼的阿旺桥,在那里进行了一年的创作,随后又去了托斯卡纳区、康沃尔和圣彼得堡。1887 年在访问康沃尔的圣艾夫斯期间,她创作了"康复的病人"——裹着毯子的一个孩子靠着一把大柳条椅坐着,手里摆弄着一根小树枝。这幅作品在 1889 年巴黎世界展览上赢得了铜牌,并被芬兰艺术协会买走。在现代人看来这幅画是十分感伤的,只有孩子那略显惊恐、忧郁的表情算是一点缓和,这可能是谢夫贝克根据自己小时候的经历而创作的。她 4 岁时曾从楼梯上摔了下来,后来再没有完全康复。

1890 年,谢夫贝克在芬兰定居。她厌倦了教学生涯,她不喜欢其他当地画家的作品,而后来当她开始照顾她母亲(活到 1923 年)时就变得更加孤独了。"如果我自己选择了一种隐居生活"她写道,"那是因为我别无他选。"1902 年,谢夫贝克和她母亲定居在工业小镇许温凯(Hyvinkaa),在赫尔辛基以北 50 公里的地方。

不过与世隔绝的生活倒是产生了一种意外的效果,因为就是在那里谢夫贝克转变为一位现代著名画家。她依然画了许多静物和人物,但最重要的是,她刻画了她那忧郁、尖刻的母亲,还有在当地上学的女孩,小镇上的女工(其中一位身着黑衣的、沉思的,具有贵族气质的女裁缝师的侧面像最为突出)。当然她还画了自己。人们将她的画和詹姆斯·麦克尼尔·惠斯勒、爱德华·蒙克进行比较,但从 1905 年开始,她的作品拥有了纯粹的谢夫贝克风格。

"我一直在探索灵魂的最深处,但是还是一无所获,"她这样写道,"哪里有无意识的东西,哪里就有最伟大的发现。"她尝试着使用不同的底色,采用不同的技巧,画出了明亮的玫瑰红点;她用尽全力,去捕捉潜意识——她自己的,还有她那些模特的。1913 年,谢夫贝克被一位艺术商人兼记者哥斯塔·斯滕曼重新发现。这一次她又成功了。作品回顾展、巡回展,接着是一部传记,但是在斯堪的纳维亚半岛之外很少有人知道她。这也许和她对声望的不予理会有关。"我不是什么名人,绝对不是,"她这样写道,"我需要的只是绘画。"谢夫贝克有独特的眼光,现在该是全世界认识她的时候了。

Passage 3

It was a brief, shining moment in Egypt's history — a time of epochal change presided over by a Pharaoh named Akhenaten and his beautiful wife Nefertiti. During his 17-year reign the old gods were cast aside, monotheism was introduced, and the arts liberated from their stifling rigidity. Even Egypt's capital was moved to a new city along the Nile called Akhetaten (modern Amarna). But like Camelot, it was short-lived, and its legacy was buried in the desert sands.

Now Akhenaten's 3,400-year-old world has been brilliantly recalled in an exhibit titled "Pharaohs of the Sun: Akhenaten, Nefertiti, Tutankhamen," which opens this week at Boston's Museum of Fine Arts. Part of the city's eight-month tribute to ancient Egypt (operas, ballet and an IMAX film), it is a unique assemblage of more than 250 objects from Egypt's 18th dynasty, some of which have languished unseen in storerooms and private collections for decades. They range from larger-than-life statues of Akhenaten to exquisitely sculpted reliefs and dazzling jewelry to such poignant reminders of everyday life as a perfectly preserved child's sandal.

The exhibit illuminates a murky period in Egyptian history that curator Rita Freed describes as having "all the elements of a soap opera." When Amenhotep Ⅳ, as he was originally called, ascended the throne in 1353 B.C., Egypt was a flourishing empire, at peace with its neighbors. Yet there were troubling signs. His father Amenhotep Ⅲ had already challenged the powerful priesthood by proclaiming the sun god Aten as foremost among Egyptian deities and himself as his living incarnation.

His son shook things up even more, not only changing his name to honor the new god(Akhenaten means "one who serves Aten") but also banishing the older gods, especially

preside	v. 住持,主管
monotheism	n. 一神论
stifling	a. 令人窒息的
tribute	n. 称赞,礼物
assemblage	n. 集合
languish	v. 凋萎,凋零
larger-than-life	a. 英雄色彩的
poignant	a.令人痛苦的,心酸的
illuminate	v. 阐释
ascend	v. 上升
foremost	a. 最初的,首要的
banish	v. 驱逐,排除

the priestly favorite Amen. Some scholars believe Akhenaten"s monotheism, a historic first, inspired the Hebrew prophets, but it had the more immediate effect of freeing Egypt's artists. They could now portray the Pharaoh and the voluptuous Nefertiti (who may have shared the throne with him) in a far more casual, realistic way. Akhenaten's cone-shaped head, elongated face, fingers and toes, pot belly and flaring hips have led some scholars to suggest that he had hydrocephalus or Marfan's syndrome.

voluptuous *a.* 沉溺酒色的

elongate *vt.* 拉长
flaring *a.* 闪耀的，华丽的
syndrome *n.* 综合症

He was certainly a revolutionary, propelled either by madness or by great vision. Still, his changes did not endure. After his death, his son-in-law (and perhaps son) Tutankhamen moved the political and religious capitals back to Memphis and Thebes respectively and reinstated the old gods. Egyptian art returned to its classic, ritualized style. And like Camelot, Akhenaten's once bustling capital became only a mythic memory. "Pharaohs of the Sun" will remain in Boston until February, then travel to Los Angeles, Chicago and Leiden, the Netherlands.

endure *v.* 忍受，持久

respectively *ad.* 各自地
ritualize *v.* 使仪式化

◎长难句分析◎

1. **Part of the city's eight-month tribute to ancient Egypt (operas, ballet and an IMAX film), it is a unique assemblage of more than 250 objects from Egypt's 18th dynasty, some of which have languished unseen in storerooms and private collections for decades.**

   ❖结构分析 该句主干为 It is a unique assemblage...这是一个包含同位语和定语从句的长简单句。其中 "Part of the city's..." 是主语 it(指展览)的同位语,定语从句 "some of which have..." 修饰名词 objects。

2. **They range from large-than-life statues of Akhenaten to exquisitely sculpted reliefs and dazzling jewelry to such poignant reminders of everyday life as a perfectly preserved child's sandal.**

   ❖结构分析 该句主干为 They range from... to... and... to such... as...虽然句子成分比较多,但这仍是一个简单句,其中最后一个 to 接的是"such... as"短语。

参考译文

这是埃及历史上短暂辉煌的时期，是法老阿肯纳顿和他美丽的妻子纳费提提统治下发生划时代变革的时期。在他 17 年的统治期间，以往的多神论被摒弃，一神论被引入，艺术也从令人窒息的一成不变中解脱了出来，甚至埃及的首都也迁到尼罗河边的新城市阿肯纳顿（现为阿玛纳）。不过同卡姆洛特的结局一样，这个时期持续时间并不长，其遗迹也淹没于漫漫黄沙之中。

现在，3,400 年前阿肯纳顿时代的辉煌将在波士顿美术馆等待人们的瞻仰。这里正举办"太阳神法老：阿肯纳顿、纳费提提、图坦卡蒙"展览。这次展览只是波士顿为期 8 个月的纪念古埃及活动中的一部分（其他形式还有歌剧、芭蕾、一部 IMAX 电影）。这次独特的展览展出了埃及第 18 个王朝的 250 多件文物，其中有些物品几十年来一直深藏于博物馆或为私人所藏，人们一直无缘一见。展品包罗万象，既有阿肯纳顿的大型雕像，做工精致的浮雕，又有令人眼花缭乱的珠宝首饰，甚至还有日常生活的起居用品，如一只保存完好的童鞋。

这次展览向世人展示了埃及历史上一段不为人知的时期，一段被馆长丽塔·弗里德称为"充满肥皂剧色彩"的时期。当阿蒙霍特普四世（阿肯纳顿原本的名字）公元 1353 年上台执政时，埃及国运昌盛，同邻国友好相处。但也有征兆表明要出乱子。他的父王阿蒙霍特普三世已经对势力强大的教会进行了挑战。他宣称太阳神阿吞（Aten）是埃及诸神中最具威力的神灵，而他本人则是太阳神的转世化身。

他的儿子更是变本加厉。他不仅把自己的名字改为阿肯纳顿（意为阿坦的仆人）以表示对太阳神的敬意，而且不许人们崇拜过去的神灵，特别是教会至爱的阿门神。有些学者认为阿肯纳顿所倡导的一神论——历史上前无古人的做法——启发了希伯来先知，但它对埃及艺术的发展有着更为直接的影响。一神论解放了埃及艺术家。现在他们可以更为真实随意地描画法老和妖艳性感的纳费提提（或许曾和阿肯纳顿共同执政过）。阿肯纳顿的头呈圆锥形，脸、手指和脚趾较常人略长，大腹便便，臀部肥大，这使得某些学者推测他曾得过脑积水。

不管他的所作所为是疯狂所致还是出于远见卓识，他都称得上是一位变革者。但这变革却未能持久。在他死后，他的女婿（或许也是儿子）图坦卡蒙把政治中心迁回孟斐斯，宗教中心移回了底比斯。那些被摒弃的旧神重新归位，埃及艺术又回到拘泥呆板的古典风格。正如卡姆洛特一样，阿肯纳顿时曾经繁华熙攘的首都现在只是神话中的记忆罢了。"太阳神法老"展览在波士顿持续到二月份，然后再前往洛杉矶、芝加哥、荷兰的莱顿。

Passage 4

Amy High is decked out in the traditional pink dress and golden stole of ancient Rome. She bursts into a third-grade classroom and greets her students: "Salvete, omnes! " (Hello, everyone!) The kids respond in kind, and soon they are studying derivatives. "How many people are in a duet? " High asks. All the kids know the answer, and when she asks how they know, a boy responds, "Because duo is 'two' in Latin." High replies, "Plaudite! " and the 14 kids erupt in applause. They learn the Latin root later, or side, and construct such English words as bilateral and quadrilateral. "Latin's going to open up so many doors for you," High says. "You're going to be able to figure out the meaning of words you've never seen before."

High teaches at Providence Elementary School in Fairfax City, Va., which has a lot riding on the success of her efforts. As part of Virginia's high-stakes testing program, schools that don't boost their scores by the year 2007 could lose state funding. So Fairfax City, just 18 miles southwest of the White House, has upgraded its two crumbling elementary schools with new high-tech television studios, computer labs and one very old feature — mandatory Latin.

Here lies one of the more counterintuitive developments of the standardized-testing movement: Though some critics complain that teachers are forced to dumb down their lessons and "teach to the test," some schools are offering more challenging course work as a way of engaging students. In the past three years, scores of elementary schools in high-stakes testing states such as Texas, Virginia and Massachusetts have added Latin programs. Says Allen Griffith, a member of the Fairfax City school board: "If we're trying to improve English skills, teaching Latin is an awfully effective, proved method."

deck *n.* 甲板
burst *v.* 爆炸,挤满

boost *v.* 提高,激励

upgrade *v.* 提升,使升级

mandatory *a.* 命令的,强制的

counterintuitive *a.* 违反直觉的

awfully *ad.* 十分,很

This is not your father's Latin, which was taught to elite college-bound high schoolers and drilled into them through memorization. Its tedium and perceived irrelevance almost drove Latin from public schools. Today's growth in elementary school Latin has been spurred by new, interactive oral curriculums, enlivened by lessons in Roman mythology and culture. "One thing that makes it engaging for kids is the goofy fun of investigating these guys in togas," says Marion Polsky, author of *First Latin: A Language Discovery Program*, the textbook used in Fairfax City.

Latin enthusiasts believe that if young students learn word roots, they will be able to decipher unfamiliar words. (By some estimates, 65% of all English words have Latin roots.) Latin is an almost purely phonetic language. There are no silent letters, and each letter represents a single sound. That makes it useful in teaching reading. And once kids master the grammatical structure of Latin — which is simple, logical and consistent — they will more easily grasp the many grammatical exceptions in English.

drill *v.* 操练，钻孔

enliven *v.* 使活跃

goofy *a.* 愚笨的，傻的

decipher *v.* 破译

consistent *a.* 一致的，一贯的

长难句分析

So Fairfax City, just 18 miles southwest of the White house, has upgraded its two crumbling elementary schools with new high-tech television studios, computer labs and one very old feature — mandatory Latin.

❖ 结构分析　这是一个包含同位语的简单句。句子主干是 Fairfax City... has upgraded its... schools with... just 18 miles... 是同位语，表示所处方位。

参考译文

　　艾米·海身着古罗马传统的粉色外套，金色披肩，冲进三年级教室和学生打招呼："Salvete, omnes！"（大家好！）学生们也用同样的语言向她问好，然后他们开始学习派生词。

"Duet 指几个人？"海问道。孩子们都知道答案,海问他们是怎么知道的。一个男孩答道:"因为拉丁语 duo 意思是'两个'。""真棒！"海赞美道。14 个孩子使劲鼓掌。他们又学了拉丁词根 later(意思是"边"),并且组成了英语单词 bilateral(双边的)和 quadrilateral(四边的)。"拉丁语会为你们打开许多扇门",海说,"即使你碰到从未见过的词,你也能猜出它的意思。"

海在弗吉尼亚州费尔法克斯市的天佑小学任教。由于她的努力,这所学校学生的成绩有了明显提高。弗吉尼亚州制订了非常关键的测试计划,其中一条是,任何在 2007 年成绩不能提高的学校将无法得到州政府的资助。所以白宫西南方 18 英里的费尔法克斯市更新了两所破落小学的设备,新添了高科技的视听室、电脑实验室,还有非常老套的一招——强制学习拉丁语。

标准化考试运动违背天性的一面即在于此:虽然有批评家抱怨说,老师被迫简化讲课内容以求人人都能听懂,"只为考试而教学",可有些学校却教授更难的课程来吸引学生。过去三年里,一些对州内学校实行关键评价的州,比如得克萨斯州、弗吉尼亚州、马萨诸塞州,他们的小学总评里已经把拉丁语成绩包括在内。费尔法克斯市的学校董事艾伦·格里菲思说,"要想提高英语水平,学习拉丁语是一种非常奏效的方法。"

这当然不是你父辈那时的拉丁语。那时学拉丁语的都是些想上大学、学习拔尖的高中生,通过死记硬背、反复操练来学习。这门语言学起来枯燥乏味,学的人又觉得即便学了也没多大意义,结果是公立学校几乎都不开拉丁语课了。现在开拉丁语课的小学又多了起来,主要是由于新颖互动,着重口语的授课模式以及精彩的罗马神话及文化吸引了学生。"孩子们觉得对那些穿长袍的人进行了解,有着无穷的乐趣,这一点使他们对拉丁语非常着迷。"马里昂·波尔斯基说。他是目前费尔法克斯市使用的拉丁语教科书《第一拉丁语:语言探索项目》的作者。

热衷学习拉丁语的人认为,如果学生学习掌握词根,认识生词就不成问题。(据估计,65%的英语单词包含拉丁词根。)拉丁语几乎是纯粹的语音语言,即单词中没有不发音的字母,每个字母都有固定的发音。这在教学生阅读时非常有用。而且,一旦孩子们掌握了拉丁语的语法结构——简单,逻辑性强,前后一致,再学习英语的语法就容易多了。

Passage 5

Largely for "spiritual reasons", Nancy Manos started home-schooling her children five years ago and has studiously avoided public schools ever since. Yet last week, she was enthusiastically enrolling her 8-year-old daughter, Olivia, in sign language and modern dance classes at Eagleridge Enrichment — a program run by the Mesa, Ariz., public schools and taught by district teachers. Manos still wants to handle the basics, but likes that Eagleridge offers the extras, "things I couldn't teach." One doubt, though, lingers in her mind: why would the public school system want to offer home-school families anything?

A big part of the answer is economics. The number of home-schooled kids nationwide has risen to as many as 1.9 million from an estimated 345,000 in 1994. And school districts that get state and local dollars per child are beginning to suffer. In Maricopa County, which includes Mesa, the number of home-schooled kids has more than doubled during that period to 7,526; at about $4,500 a child, that's nearly $34 million a year in lost revenue.

Not everyone's happy with these innovations. Some states have taken the opposite tack. Like about half the states, West Virginia refuses to allow home-schooled kids to play public-school sports. And in Arizona, some complain that their tax dollars are being used to create programs for families who, essentially, eschew participation in public life. "That makes my teeth grit," says Daphne Atkeson, whose 10-year-old son attends public school in Paradise Valley. Even some committed home-schoolers question the new programs, given their central irony: they turn home-schoolers into public-school students, says Bob Parsons, president of the Alaska Private and Home Educators Association. "We've lost about one third of our members to those programs. They're so enticing."

Mesa started Eagleridge four years ago, when it saw

studiously *ad.* 故意地, 谨慎地	
enrichment *n.* 丰富, 改进	
linger *v.* 逗留, 徘徊	
double *v.* 使加倍	
innovation *n.* 革新, 创新	
complain *v.* 抱怨, 埋怨	
eschew *v.* 避开, 远避	
enticing *a.* 引诱的, 迷人的	

how much money it was losing from home-schoolers—and how unprepared some students were when they re-entered the schools. Since it began, the program's enrollment has nearly doubled to 397. and last year the district moved Eagleridge to a strip mall (between a pizza joint and a laser-tag arcade). Parents typically drop off their kids once a week; because most of the children qualify as quarter-time students, the district collects $ 911 per child. "It's like getting a taste of what real school is like," says 10-year-old Chad Lucas, who's learning computer animation and creative writing.

Other school districts are also experimenting with novel ways to court home schoolers. The town of Galena, Alaska, (pop. 600) has just 178 students. But in 1997, its school administrators figured they could reach beyond their borders. Under the program, the district gives home-schooling families free computers and Internet service for correspondence classes. In return, the district gets $ 3,100 per student enrolled in the program — $ 9.6 million a year, which it has used partly for a new vocational school. Such alternatives just might appeal to other districts. Ernest Felty, head of Hardin County schools in southern Illinois, has 10 home-schooled pupils. That may not sound like much — except that he has a staff of 68, and at $ 4,500 a child, "that's probably a teacher's salary," Felty says. With the right robotics or art class, though, he could take the home out of home schooling.

enrollment n. 登记,注册	
arcade n. 拱廊	
novel a. 新颖的	
correspondence n.通信	
vocational a. 职业的	

◎ 长难句分析 ◎

Yet last week, she was enthusiastically enrolling her 8-year-old daughter, Olivia, in sign language and modern dance classes at Eagleridge Enrichment—a program run by the Mesa, Ariz., public schools and taught by district teachers.

❖ 结构分析 该句的主干为 She was... enrolling her 8-year-old daughter... in sign language and modern dance classes. 这是个简单句。其中 enroll in 意为"注册,报名"; Olivia 是 daughter 的同位语;a program 是 Eagleridge Enrichment 的同位语,过去分词 run 和 taught 作定语来修饰 program。

参考译文

由于"灵性方面的原因",南希·马诺斯 5 年前开始自己在家里教育孩子,从此以后有意避开公立学校。然而上周, 她却急切地给她 8 岁的女儿奥利维娅报名, 让她参加在 Eagleridge Enrichment 举办的手语课和现代舞蹈课的学习。Eagleridge Enrichment 项目是由亚利桑那州的梅萨公立学校举办的,并由社区教师授课。马诺斯还想继续教基础课,但她希望 Eagleridge 教授"我教不了的东西"。但是她思想里一直有一个疑问:为什么公立学校愿意为家庭教育提供他们所需要的一切呢?

这主要是出于经济方面的原因。全国在家受教育孩子的数量已经从 1994 年的 34.5 万人上升到了 190 万人。那些靠按孩子人数从州政府和当地政府获得财政支持的学区正在受到亏损。在梅萨所在的马利科帕县,在家受教育孩子的数量在这期间增长了两倍,达到了 7,526 人。按一个孩子 4,500 美元的学费来计算,这意味着学校一年所流失的收入将达到近 3.4 亿美元。

并非人人都对这些举措感到满意。有些州采取了与之相反的策略。同其他州的做法一样,西弗吉尼亚拒绝在家受教育的孩子参加公立学校的运动比赛。在亚利桑那州,有人抱怨,政府使用他们缴纳的税金, 去设立一些专门为那些实际上在逃避社会责任的家庭参加的项目。"这真让我恨得咬牙切齿。"达夫妮·阿特基森这样说。他 10 岁的儿子在帕拉代斯瓦利公立学校上学。甚至那些坚持在家进行教育的人也对新计划嗤之以鼻,他们表示疑问说,这些项目旨在把在家学习的人变成公立学校的学生,阿拉斯加个人和家庭教育者协会会长鲍勃·帕森斯说,"这些计划已挖走了我们三分之一的会员。这些计划实在是太诱人了。"

四年前,当意识到从那些在家学习的人身上损失了那么多的钱,并且当这些人重新入学时他们又毫无准备时,梅萨便率先发起了 Eagleridge 项目。从成立之日起,前来注册的人数几乎翻了一番,达到 397 人。去年,学区将 Eagleridge 项目转移到一家商铺云集的商业广场(在一家比萨饼店与一个带巨大标记的拱廊之间)。孩子的父母一般每周只需接送一次。由于大多数孩子只取得普通学生四分之一学时的资格,所以学区只收 911 美元的学费。"这只是让你体会一下,去真正的学校上学是什么滋味。"10 岁的查德·卢卡斯这样说道。他正在学习电脑动画制作和写作。

其他学区也在尝试新办法,来吸引那些在家接受教育的人。阿拉斯加州的加利纳镇(人口 600)只有 178 名学生。但是在 1997 年,学校负责人认为他们可以(使学生人数)超过这个数。按照学校计划,学区为在家学习的家庭免费提供函授课程所使用的电脑和互连网业务。作为报酬, 学区在这个项目中对每个注册的学生收取 3,100 美元的费用——一年合计 960 万。学区把其中的一部分资金用来再建一所新的职业学校。这样的方案对其他学区还是很有吸引力的。欧内斯特·费尔蒂是伊利诺斯州南部哈丁县县属学校的负责人。他负责 10 个在家接受教育的小学生。这听起来没什么大不了的——除了他有 68 名员工。每个学生 4,500 美元的学费,费尔提说:"那差不多相当于一个老师的工资"。凭借合适的机器人技术或美术课,他能够让那些在家学习的人离开家庭了。

Passage 6

As long as her parents can remember, 13-year-old Katie Hart has been talking about going to college. Her mother, Tally, a financial-aid officer at an Ohio university, knows all too well the daunting calculus of paying for a college education. Last year the average yearly tuition at a private, four-year school climbed 5.5 percent to more than $17,000. The Harts have started saving, and figure they can afford a public university without a problem. But what if Katie applies to Princeton (she's threatening), where one year's tuition, room and board — almost $34,000 in 2002 — will cost more than some luxury cars? Even a number cruncher like Tally admits it's a little scary, especially since she'll retire and Katie will go to college at around the same time.

Paying for college has always been a humbling endeavor. The good news: last year students collected $74 billion in financial aid, the most ever. Most families pay less than full freight. Sixty percent of public-university students and three quarters of those at private colleges receive some form of financial aid — mostly, these days, in the form of loans. But those numbers are not as encouraging as they appear for lower-income families, because schools are changing their formulas for distributing aid. Eager to boost their magazine rankings, which are based in part on the test scores of entering freshmen, they're throwing more aid at smarter kids — whether they need it or not.

The best way to prepare is to start saving early. A new law passed last year makes that easier for some families. So-called 529 plans allow parents to sock away funds in federal-tax-free-investment accounts, as long as the money is used for "qualified education expenses" like tuition, room and board. The plans aren't for everyone. For tax reasons, some lower-and-middle-income families may be better off

Vocabulary	
financial-aid	*a.* 财政资助的
calculus	*n.* 微积分
tuition	*n.* 学费
cruncher	*n.* 嚼食发出声音
humbling	*a.* 谦逊的,卑贱的
freight	*n.* 货物,运费
distribute	*v.* 分配,分发
freshman	*n.* 大一新生
federal-tax-free-investment	联邦免税投资

choosing other investments. But saving is vital. When's the best time to start? "Sometime," says Jack Joyce of the College Board, "between the maternity ward and middle school."

> ward *n.* 病房，守卫

Aid packages usually come in some combination of grants, loans and jobs. These days 60 percent of all aid comes in the form of low-interest loans. All students are eligible for "unsubsidized" federal Stafford loans, which let them defer interest payments until after graduation. Students who can demonstrate need can also qualify for federal Perkins loans or "subsidized" Staffords, where the government pays the interest during school. Fortunately, this is a borrower's market. "Interest rates are at their lowest level in the history of student loans," says Mark Kantrowitz, publisher of *Finaid*. Kantrowitz expects rates to fall even further when they're reviewed this summer.

> grant *n.* 补助金
>
> eligible *a.* 有资格的
>
> subsidize *v.* 津贴，资助

Traditional scholarships, academic or athletic, are still a part of many families' planning. Mack Reiter, a 17-year-old national wrestling champion, gets so many recruiting letters he throws most away. He'll almost certainly get a free ride. Without it, "we would really be in a bind," says his mother, Janet. For everyone else, it's worth the effort to pick through local and national scholarship offerings, which can be found on Web sites like *collegeboard.com*.

长难句分析

So-called 529 plans allow parents to sock away funds in federal-tax-free-investment accounts, as long as the money is used for "qualified education expenses" like tuition, room and board.

❖ 结构分析　本句是个有一个条件从句的复合句。主句是 529 plans allow parents to sock away funds... federal-tax-free-investment 是一个复合名词；as long as 引导条件从句，be used for 意为"用做某一目的"，like 是介词，后跟名词，共同来修饰 qualified education expenses。

参考译文

　　卡蒂的父母记得,13 岁的卡蒂·哈特就一直在谈论上大学的事。她的母亲塔利是俄亥俄大学的一名负责给学生贷款的工作人员,她对大学教育费用是一个多么令人心跳畏缩的数字再熟悉不过了。去年,私立四年制大学的年平均学费增长了 5.5%,超过 17,000 美元。哈特家已经开始存钱了,估计支付公立大学的费用不成问题。但是,如果卡蒂要申请普林斯顿大学的话(她是这样威胁的),那该怎么办呢? 上这样的大学一年的学费和食宿费在 2002 年大约是 34,000 美元,这比买几辆豪华轿车还贵。就连塔利这样搞数字工作的人也承认这真有点让人恐慌,尤其是她即将面临退休,卡蒂又要上大学这两件事几乎在同时发生。

　　支付大学费用一直都是让人难以启齿的尴尬事。有条好消息:去年学生获得的财政资助达 740 亿美元,这比以往获得的都多。大多数家庭都不是一次全部付清学费。60% 的公立大学学生和四分之三的私立大学的学生要接受某种形式的财政资助——现在大多是以贷款的形式发放。但是这些数字对于那些低收入家庭来说,并不像它表面上看起来那样令人鼓舞,因为学校正在改变它们的资助发放方案。那些想急于提高其杂志排名的学校(学校排名在一定程度上取决于入学新生的成绩)把更多的资助给了成绩较好的学生,不管他们是否需要这种资助。

　　最好的准备办法就是早点开始存钱。去年通过的一项新的法律使一些家庭存钱的方法变得容易了一些。这就是所谓的"529 方案"。该方案准许父母把钱存在联邦免税投资账户上,但他们所存的钱只能用于支付类似学费、食宿费等"符合资格的教育费用"。这一方案并不是对每一个人都适合。由于税收原因,对于那些低收入和中等收入家庭来说,如果选择其他的投资方向,他们会生活得更富裕些。但是存钱是头等大事。那么什么时候开始存钱最合适呢? 大学委员会的杰克·乔伊斯说,"从孩子出生开始到上中学这个阶段的任何时候都行。"

　　一揽子资助计划通常以助学金、贷款和兼职相结合的形式提供。现在有 60% 的资助项目是以低息贷款形式提供的。所有学生都有资格获得联邦"非补贴性"斯塔福德贷款。这种贷款可以使学生把利息支付推迟到毕业以后。确实能证明经济上有困难的学生还有资格申请联邦珀金斯贷款或联邦"补贴性"斯塔福德贷款,这种贷款的利息在学生就读期间由政府偿付。所幸的是,现在是借方的市场。《资助》杂志出版商马克·坎特罗威茨说:"现在的利率是学生贷款史上最低的。"坎特罗威茨认为,今年夏天进行回顾评论时,利率可能还要降低。

　　争取获得学术或体育等传统奖学金仍然是很多家庭计划的一部分。17 岁的迈克·赖特是全国摔跤冠军,他收到了很多招收信,但大部分信都被他扔到了一边。他几乎肯定会获得全额免费。他的母亲珍妮特说,要不是这样的话,"我们真的就陷入困境了。"对于其他人来说,值得费些工夫去搜寻地方和国家提供的奖学金。这类奖学金可以在 *collegeboard.com* 这样的网站上找到。

第三节 社会法制

Passage 1

When Catholic clergy or "pro-life" politicians argue that abortion laws should be tightened, they do so in the belief that this will reduce the number of terminations. Yet the largest global study of abortion ever undertaken casts doubt on that simple proposition. Restricting abortions, the study says, has little effect on the number of pregnancies terminated. Rather, it drives women to seek illegal, often unsafe backstreet abortions leading to an estimated 67,000 deaths a year. A further 5 million women require hospital treatment as a result of botched procedures.

In Africa and Asia, where abortion is generally either illegal or restricted, the abortion rate in 2003(the latest year for which figures are available) was 29 per 1,000 women aged 15—44. This is almost identical to the rate in Europe (28), where legal abortions are widely available. Latin America, which has some of the world's most restrictive abortion laws, is the region with the highest abortion rate (31), while western Europe, which has some of the most liberal laws, has the lowest (12).

The study, carried out by the Guttmacher Institute in New York in collaboration with the World Health Organisation (WHO) and published in a British medical journal, the *Lancet*, found that most abortions occur in developing countries — 35 million a year, compared with just 7 m in rich countries. But this was largely a reflection of population size. A woman's likelihood of having an abortion is similar whether she lives in a rich country(26 per 1,000) or a poor or middle-income one (29).

Lest it be thought that these sweeping continental numbers hide as much as they reveal, the same point can be made by looking at those countries which have changed

---

clergy *n.* 神职人员

termination *n.* 终止，结束

cast *v.* 投，丢

pregnancy *n.* 怀孕

botch *v.* 弄坏，搞砸

available *a.* 可利用的

collaboration *n.* 合作

reflection *n.* 反映

likelihood *n.* 可能性

sweeping *a.* 全面的，大规模的

their laws. Between 1995 and 2005, 17 nations liberalised abortion legislation, while three tightened restrictions. The number of induced abortions nevertheless declined from nearly 46 million in 1995 to 42 million in 2003, resulting in a fall in the worldwide abortion rate from 35 to 29. The most dramatic drop — from 90 to 44 — was in former communist Eastern Europe, where abortion is generally legal, safe and cheap. This coincided with a big increase in contraceptive use in the region which still has the world's highest abortion rate, with more terminations than live births.

induce *v.* 引起,导致

coincide *v.* 同时发生,相符

contraceptive *a.* 避孕的

The risk of dying in a botched abortion is only part of a broader problem of maternal health in poor countries. Of all the inequalities of development, this is arguably the worst. According to a report published this week by Population Action International, a Washington-based lobby group, women in poor countries are 250 times more likely to die in pregnancy or childbirth than women in rich ones. Of the 535,000 women who died in childbirth or from pregnancy-related complications in 2005, 99% were in developing countries, according to another report by a group of UN agencies, including WHO, also out this week. Africa accounted for more than half such deaths. As the UN report noted, countries with the highest levels of maternal mortality have made the least progress towards reducing it. A woman in Africa has a one in 16 chance of dying in pregnancy or childbirth, compared with one in 3,800 for a woman in the rich world.

complication *n.* 困难,并发症

长难句分析

1. The study, carried out by the Guttmacher Institute in New York in collaboration with the World Health Organisation(WHO) and published in a British medical journal, the *Lancet*, found that most abortions occur in developing countries — 35 million a year, compared with just 7 m in rich countries.

❖ 结构分析 该句主干为 The study found that... 这是一个简单句,其主语的定语为两个并列的分词短语:carried out by... 和 published in...。破折号后面的成分可以看

做是补语,compared with 作状语，这里是将发达国家的堕胎率与发展中国家进行对比。

2. **Of the 535,000 women who died in childbirth or from pregnancy-related complications in 2005, 99% were in developing countries, according to another report by a group of UN agencies, including WHO, also out this week.**

❖ 结构分析 该句主干为 99% of the 535,000 women were in developing country... 这里是成分提前，其一般形式是 99% of the 535,000 women were in... 而 who 引导的定语从句则修饰 women, including 的意思是在这些 agencies 中包括 WTO 这一机构。

参考译文

天主教牧师或反对堕胎的政治家们要求对堕胎进行立法禁止，他们这样做是因为他们相信,这样就可以降低堕胎的数量。然而迄今为止最权威的全球堕胎调查却让人们对这种主张产生了怀疑。该研究表明,限制堕胎对降低怀孕几率影响甚微,这样反而使得妇女不得不寻求一些非法的、危险的秘密堕胎手段,而每年因此死亡的妇女高达 67,000 人,还有另外 500 万妇女因为手术失败而不得不住院治疗。

一般来说,堕胎在非洲和亚洲或是非法的,或是受到制约的,2003 年(有调查数据的最近年份)每 1,000 名 15 岁至 44 岁的妇女中就有 29 名经历过堕胎。这个数字和欧洲堕胎率几乎持平(欧洲为 28 名),而在欧洲堕胎的方式却非常安全。而拥有世界上最严厉的堕胎法的拉丁美洲却有着最高的堕胎率(31 人),在世界上拥有最宽松的堕胎法的西欧,其堕胎率却最低(12 人)。

这项研究由纽约的古特马赫研究所和世界卫生组织合作进行,发表于英国医学期刊《柳叶刀》上,该研究发现,大多数堕胎都发生在发展中国家,一年大约有 3,500 万例,而在富裕国家则只有 700 万例。不过这在很大程度上也反映了人口规模。一名妇女不论在哪里,堕胎的可能性大致相同,在富裕国家是 26‰,而在贫穷或中等收入国家则有 29‰。

为了让人们对这些数字有着更深入的了解,只要看看那些改革法律的国家的情况,问题也同样可以得到证实。1995 年至 2005 年期间,有 17 个国家放宽了堕胎法律,有 3 个国家加强了对于堕胎的限制,然而堕胎数量却从 1995 年的近 4600 万例下降到 2003 年的 4200 万例,使得全世界堕胎率由 35‰ 下降到 29‰。而最大的降幅(从 90‰ 降到 44‰)发生在共产主义时代的东欧,在这些国家中,堕胎一般是合法的、安全的,而且价格也非常便宜。而在同一时期,世界上堕胎率最高的地区(堕胎数比出生人数多),其避孕措施的使用则进展迅速。

在贫穷国家,因落后的堕胎技术而死亡,不过是妇女健康问题的一个组成部分而已。但在所有的发展不平衡问题中,这可以说是最糟糕的。一个游说组织"国际人口行动组织"(该组织总部设在华盛顿)本周发表的一篇报道中声称,贫困国家妇女在怀孕或生产过程中的死亡率是发达国家妇女的 250 倍。而根据本周联合国诸多机构(其中包括世界卫生组织)的报道,2005 年死于生产或怀孕所造成的并发症的 53 万 5 千名妇女中,99% 来自于发展中国家。非洲妇女占了多半。正如联合国报道所指出的,产妇死亡率最高的国家,其为了降低该死亡率进行的行动进展也最慢。一个非洲妇女因怀孕或生产的死亡率是 1/16,而在富裕国家这个数字则为 1/3800。

Passage 2

After receiving a six-year prison sentence on July 31st, Sanjay Dutt, an Indian film star, begged for bail while he appealed against it. "Sir, I made a mistake," he said. But the judge said no. Mr. Dutt's crime—to have procured two guns from Muslim mobsters who were responsible for bomb attacks in Mumbai in 1993—was serious. Yet he urged Mr. Dutt, 48. to return to the silver screen after serving his sentence. "Don't get perturbed," he said. "You have many years to go and work, like the *Mackenna's Gold* actor Gregory Peck."

Thus ended one of the longest song-and-dances in India's criminal legal history. Mr. Dutt was convicted last year, having already spent 16 months in jail. He was acquitted of direct involvement in the bombings, which killed 257 people. They were carried out in 1993 in revenge for the demolition of an ancient mosque in the Hindu holy city of Ayodhya by Hindu fanatics, and subsequent Hindu-Muslim rioting. Some 100 people have been found guilty of the bombing. They have all been sentenced in the past three months, including a dozen to death and 20 to life-imprisonment. But the alleged masterminds of the attacks are still at large. One of them, a Mumbai gangster called Dawood Ibrahim, is alleged by Indian officials to be linked to al-Qaeda and to be hiding in Pakistan.

Despite the bleak immediate outlook, Mr. Dutt, who made his name playing tough-guy anti-heroes, is unlikely to

词汇
appeal v. 呼吁,上诉
procure v. 获得
perturb v. 烦扰
convict v. 证明…有罪
acquit v. 宣判无罪
demolition n. 破坏,毁坏
fanatic n. 狂人分子,疯子
sentence v. 判罪
despite prep. 尽管

find his career much damaged. The son of two of Bollywood's biggest stars, a Hindu-Muslim couple, he has garnered enormous sympathy for his suffering. Many Indians believe his claim that he wanted the guns to protect his family during the riots. Other Bollywood stars express support for Mr. Dutt as passionately as their Hollywood peers worry about global warming.

garnere *v.* 收藏，积累

Then again, Bollywood is rather shady. Gangsters and crooked politicians have long laundered ill-gotten money through film productions. Indeed Mr. Dutt was investigated over money-laundering allegations in 2001. Other recent Bollywood stars to grace the courts include Monica Bedi, an actress convicted of dealing in fake passports. Her accomplice was another Mumbai gangster, Abu Salem, who delivered the guns to Mr. Dutt, and is currently awaiting trial for his alleged part in the 1993 bombings.

shady *a.* 可疑的

money-laundering 洗钱

accomplice *n.* 共犯，从犯
currently *ad.* 目前，当下

An even bigger Bollywood star, Salman Khan, is appealing against two prison sentences of five years and one year for poaching respectively an endangered antelope and two gazelles. A Bollywood film about the case has been scheduled. Mr. Khan has also had to battle a four-year-old charge that he recklessly drove his car over five people sleeping on a pavement in Mumbai, killing one of them.

poach *v.* 偷猎
gazelle *n.* 瞪羚

Bollywood's biggest star, Amitabh Bachchan, also known as "the Big B", is, in contrast, venerated. Where Mr. Khan is vain and brash, he has a reputation for humility and Hindu piety. But even this has been imperilled of late by revelations that Mr. Bachchan and his film-star son, Abhishek, bought valuable plots of land reserved for farmers. They registered themselves thus after being allotted farmland by a former government of the state of Uttar Pradesh, led by the Samajwadi party. Mr. Bachchan is close to one of the party's leading lights, Amar Singh, a famed socialite. Mr. Bachchan's wife, Jaya, an actress, is now also a Samajwadi politician.

venerate *v.* 尊敬

imperil *v.* 危害，损害

allot *v.* 分配，分派

◎ 长难句分析 ◎

1. **They were carried out in 1993 in revenge for the demolition of an ancient mosque in the Hindu holy city of Ayodhya by Hindu fanatics, and subsequent Hindu-Muslim rioting.**

   ❖结构分析 该句主干为 They were carried out... 这是一个简单句,具有比较复杂的状语,有一个时间状语,一个以 in revenge for 引导的目的状语;在该目的状语中,有两个介词宾语,the demolition 和 subsequent rioting;而在第一个宾语中,in the Hindu holy city of Ayodhya 和 by Hindu fanatics 都用来修饰前面的 the demolition。

2. **They registered themselves thus after being allotted farmland by a former government of the state of Uttar Pradesh, led by the Samajwadi party.**

   ❖结构分析 该句主干为 They registered themselves...这是一个简单句,after 后面跟的是时间状语,led by 是对 government 的修饰。

参考译文

7 月 31 日,印度影星桑贾伊·杜特被判处六年监禁,他提起上诉同时要求保释。"先生,我犯了个错,"他这样说道。但法官驳回了。杜特先生的罪行比较严重,他从穆斯林匪徒那里得到两支枪,而这些匪徒是 1993 年孟买爆炸袭击的主犯。不过,法官劝说 48 岁的杜特服完刑后重返银屏。"别烦恼,"他说,"你前面的路还长着呢,就像《麦肯纳淘金记》里的演员格雷戈里·佩克一样。"

这样就结束了印度刑事史上最长的审理。去年杜特被宣判有罪,已经在监狱服刑 16 个月。他被赦免直接参与爆炸事件的罪名,这些爆炸事件炸死了 257 人。爆炸事件发生于 1993 年,是为了报复印度教狂热教徒毁坏了印度圣城阿约提亚一座古老的清真寺以及随后的印度-穆斯林暴乱。到目前已有 100 人因该爆炸事件被判有罪,并且已在过去三个月里进行了量刑,其中十几人被判处死刑,20 人终身监禁。但是这些袭击的主要策划者仍然逍遥法外,印度官员断言其中一个名叫达乌德·易卜拉欣的孟买歹徒与基地组织有关系,目前藏匿在巴基斯坦。

尽管杜特先生目前的前景看起来比较黯淡,但他已经因扮演硬汉式的平凡角色而出名,自己的事业会因此而走向终结。作为宝莱坞最大的影星,一对印度-穆斯林夫妻的儿子,他已经为自己的遭遇攒够了同情。许多印度人都相信他所说的,即他是为了在暴乱中保护自己的家庭才购买枪支的。其他宝莱坞明星也对杜特表示支持,其程度不亚于他们好莱坞同行对全球变暖问题的关心。

不过,宝莱坞却是问题重重。长时间以来许多匪徒和无耻的政客一直在通过电影工业洗钱。实际上,2001 年杜特就因洗钱受到过调查,其他在法庭出现的宝莱坞明星还有莫妮卡·贝迪,她被指控从事假护照买卖。其同伙是也是一个孟买匪徒叫阿布萨利姆, 就是此人将枪支卖给了杜特,目前他因被指控参加了 1993 年的爆炸事件而在等待审判。

一位更著名的宝莱坞明星萨尔曼·汗目前正在提起上诉,他因偷猎濒临灭绝的羚羊和瞪羚分别被判 5 年监禁和 1 年监禁。目前已有一部宝莱坞电影打算以此为题材,搬上大银幕。萨尔曼·汗还要为自己进行了四年的另一项上诉奔走。他因鲁莽驾驶将躺孟买一处人行道上的人碾死。

相反,宝莱坞最著名的明星阿半塔布·伯昌,人称"大 B",他却受人尊敬。汗自负而又无礼,而他但却因谦虚和对印度教的虔诚而出名。但是目前有人揭发伯昌和他的影星儿子阿比谢克购买了本来预留给农民的宝贵土地,因此他们的境地也不妙。<u>印度社会主义党领导的前北方州政府分配给他们这些土地后, 他们就进行了注册。</u>伯昌和该党一位著名的领袖阿马尔·辛格,一位前社交名流交往甚密。而伯昌先生的演员妻子贾亚现在也是印度社会主义党政治家。

Passage 3

It was a ruling that had consumers seething with anger and many a free trader crying foul. On November 20th the European Court of Justice decided that Tesco, a British supermarket chain, should not be allowed to import jeans made by America's Levi Strauss from outside the European Union and sell them at cut-rate prices without getting permission first from the jeans maker. Ironically, the ruling is based on an EU trademark directive that was designed to protect local, not American, manufacturers from price dumping. The idea is that any brand-owning firm should be allowed to position its goods and segment its markets as it sees fit: Levi's jeans, just like Gucci handbags, must be allowed to be expensive.

Levi Strauss persuaded the court that, by selling its jeans cheaply alongside soap powder and bananas, Tesco was destroying the image and so the value of its brands — which could only lead to less innovation and, in the long

cut-rate *a.* 打折的,二流的
ruling *n.* 判决
directive *n.* 指令,指示

segment *n.* 部分

run, would reduce consumer choice. Consumer groups and Tesco say that Levi's case is specious. The supermarket argues that it was just arbitraging the price differential between Levi's jeans sold in America and Europe — a service performed a million times a day in financial markets, and one that has led to real benefits for consumers. Tesco has been selling some 15,000 pairs of Levi's jeans a week, for about half the price they command in specialist stores approved by Levi Strauss. Christine Cross, Tesco's head of global non-food sourcing, says the ruling risks "creating a Fortress Europe with a vengeance".

specious *a.* 似是而非的

fortress *n.* 堡垒

The debate will rage on, and has implications well beyond casual clothes(Levi Strauss was joined in its lawsuit by Zino Davidoff, a perfume maker). The question at its heart is not whether brands need to control how they are sold to protect their image, but whether it is the job of the courts to help them do this. Gucci, an Italian clothes label whose image was being destroyed by loose licensing and over-exposure in discount stores, saved itself not by resorting to the courts but by ending contracts with third-party suppliers, controlling its distribution better and opening its own stores. It is now hard to find cut-price Gucci anywhere.

resort *v.* 求助,采用
distribution *n.* 分配,分布

Brand experts argue that Levi Strauss, which has been losing market share to hipper rivals such as Diesel, is no longer strong enough to command premium prices. Left to market forces, so-so brands such as Levi's might well fade away and be replaced by fresher labels. With the courts protecting its prices, Levi Strauss may hang on for longer. But no court can help to make it a great brand again.

premium *a.* 高级的

长难句分析

Levi Strauss persuaded the court that, by selling its jeans cheaply alongside soap powder and bananas, Tesco was destroying the image and so the value of its brands — which could only lead to less innovation and, in the long run, would reduce consumer choice.

❖结构分析　该句主干为 Levi Strauss persuaded that... that 后面接的是一个宾语从句；by 之后的句子作伴随状语来修饰宾语从句；宾语从句中 which 又引导了一个非限制性定语从句。

参考译文

　　法庭的裁决使消费者感到义愤填膺，也使很多人认为，这对自由贸易者来说显然是一桩不公正裁决。11 月 20 日，欧洲法庭对特易购(Tesco)这家英国连锁超市做出了如下判决：特易购不能从欧盟之外的国家进口利维·斯特劳斯公司生产的牛仔裤；未经制造商许可，不得打折销售。具有讽刺意味的是，这项裁决是根据一条欧盟商标指令做出的。该指令的目的在于保护本地而非美国制造商免受价格倾销造成的损害。其意思是，任何一家拥有自己品牌的公司都可对自己的产品进行定位，并以适当的方式分割市场，比如利维牛仔裤，它必须像古奇手提包一样高价销售。

　　利维·斯特劳斯公司使法庭相信，特易购把利维牛仔服与肥皂粉、香蕉等放在一起廉价销售这一做法对其形象造成了损害，因而也影响到其品牌价位，这势必会使产品缺乏新意，最终导致消费者选择范围大大缩小。消费者团体和特易购却认为，利维公司一案(的判决)貌似有理，实则不然。特易购争辩说，它只是从美国和欧洲利维牛仔服装销售的差价中获利。这是一种在金融市场极其常见、并使消费者真正受益的商业行为。特易购一直以低于利维·斯特劳斯公司授权专卖店一半的价格进行销售，每周销售 15,000 条牛仔裤。特易购公司全球非食品类商品采购主管克里斯廷·克罗斯认为，这一裁决会让欧洲产生贸易壁垒。

　　这场激烈的争论还将继续进行下去，涉及范围将远远超出休闲服装业(季诺·大卫多夫香水制造商也和利维·斯特劳斯联手起诉)。核心问题不在于品牌是否需要通过控制销售方式来维护其形象，而在于法院是否有责任来帮助其达到这一目的。意大利品牌服饰公司古奇公司由于许可经营管理松懈和商品折扣过多，其形象正在受到损害，但它并没有依靠法庭，而是通过中止与第三方供应商的合同，更好地控制商品销售、以及开专卖店等方式挽救了自己的命运。现在已经很难找到打折销售古奇产品的地方了。

　　品牌专家认为，利维·斯特劳斯公司正在逐步丧失其市场占有率，而像迪赛(Diesel)这样市场信息颇为灵通的竞争对手则后来居上。利维·斯特劳斯公司已无力控制品牌溢价。在市场机制的作用下，像利维这样的一般品牌很有可能逐渐消失，进而被新的品牌所取代。由于其价格受到法庭保护，利维·斯特劳斯公司可能会继续维持一段时间，但是没有任何一个法庭会使它起死回生，再度成为知名品牌。

Passage 4

A white kid sells a bag of cocaine at his suburban high school. A Latino kid does the same in his inner-city neighborhood. Both get caught. Both are first-time offenders The white kid walks into juvenile court with his parents, his priest, a good lawyer — and medical coverage. The Latino kid walks into court with his mom, no legal resources and no insurance. The judge lets the white kid go with his family; he's placed in a private treatment program. The minority kid has no such option. He's detained

There, in a nutshell, is what happens more and more often in the juvenile-court system. Minority youths arrested on violent felony charges in California are more than twice as likely as their white counterparts to be transferred out of the juvenile-justice system and tried as adults, according to a study released last week by the Justice Policy Institute, a research center in San Francisco. Once they are in adult courts, young black offenders are 18 times more likely to be jailed — and Hispanics seven times more likely-than are young white offenders. "Discrimination against kids of color accumulates at every stage of the justice system and skyrockets when juveniles are, tried as adults," says Dan Macallair, a co-author of the new study. "California has a double standard: throw kids of color behind bars, but rehabilitate white kids who commit comparable crimes."

Even as juvenile crime has declined from its peak in the early 1990s, headline grabbing violence by minors has intensified a get-tough attitude. Over the past six years, 43 states have passed laws that make it easier to try juveniles as adults. In Texas and Connecticut in 1996, the latest year for which figures are available, all the juveniles in jails were minorities. Vincent Schiraldi, the Justice Policy Institute's director, concedes that "some kids need to be tried as adults. But most can be rehabilitated."

cocaine *n.* 可卡因	
Latino *n.* 拉丁裔	
offender *n.* 罪犯	
insurance *n.* 保险	
detain *v.* 拘留	
nutshell *n.* 果核,陋室	
felony *n.* 重罪	
transfer *v.* 转移,转让	
Hispanics *a.* 西班牙的	
accumulate *v.* 累积,增加	
skyrocket *v.* 迅速上升	
rehabilitate *v.* 改造,恢复	
headline *n.* 新闻提要,头条	
intensify *v.* 加剧	
juvenile *n.* 少年	
concede *v.* 承认,让步	

Instead, adult prisons tend to brutalize juveniles. They are eight times more likely to commit suicide and five times more likely to be sexually abused than offenders held in juvenile detention. "Once they get out, they tend to commit more crimes and more violent crimes," says Jenni Gainsborough, a spokeswoman for the Sentencing Project, a reform group in Washington. The system, in essence, is training career criminals. And it's doing its worst work among minorities.

brutalize v. 残酷对待

detention n. 滞留,拘留

essence n. 本质

长难句分析

Minority youths arrested on violent felony charges in California are more than twice as likely as their white counterparts to be transferred out of the juvenile-justice system and tried as adults, according to a study released last week by the Justice Policy Institute, a research center in San Francisco.

◆ 结构分析 该句主干为 Minority youths are more than... 这是一个比较长的简单句。more than twice as likely as their white counterparts 是一种倍数的表达方式;to be transferred out of the juvenile-justice system and tried as adults 不定式短语来修饰 white counterparts; according to a study released last week by the Justice Policy Institute 是现在分词作伴随状语;a research center in San Francisco 是 the Justice Policy Institute 的同位语。

参考译文

　　一名白人少年在他就读的郊区中学贩卖一袋可卡因。一名拉丁美洲少年在其居住的市内社区也做同样的事情。两人都被抓。两人都是初犯。白人少年在其父母、牧师、知名律师陪伴下走进少年法庭——他还有医疗保险;而那个拉丁美洲少年却只在他母亲陪伴下来到法庭,没有任何法律援助,也没有什么保险。法官让白人少年随家人回家,判他接受私下处理计划监管。而那位少数族裔少年则别无选择。他被拘留了。

　　简而言之,这样的事情在少年法庭上越来越常见。根据旧金山一家司法政策研究中心上周发表的一项研究结果, 在加州因暴力重罪嫌疑被捕进而移交到少年法庭系统作为成人被审判的少数族裔青少年的数量可能是白人少年的两倍。一旦被移交成人法庭,那些青少年黑人犯法者被送进监狱的可能性是白人的 18 倍,美籍西班牙人是白人的 8 倍。"司法系统对有色人种青少年的歧视每升一级都加一次码,而这些年轻人一旦以成人的身份被审判的话,这种歧视便被极度升级,达到无以复加的地步。" 这项研究的合作者丹·麦卡莱尔(Dan Macallair)说,"加利福尼亚历来奉行双重标准:把犯罪的有色人种青少年投进监狱,但对犯有同等罪行的白人少年却实行教育感化。"

正当青少年犯罪率从 20 世纪 90 年代初期的高峰开始下降的时候,常常成为报刊头条新闻的少数民族未成年人暴力犯罪强化了公众的强硬态度。在过去 6 年中,43 个州通过的法律使青少年以成人的身份受审变得更加易如反掌。1996 年,美国得克萨斯州和康涅狄格州(这两个州是唯一能收集到最近一年青少年犯罪记录的州)的资料表明,在监狱服刑的所有青少年都是有色人种。司法政策研究所所长文森特·斯基拉尔迪(Vincent Schiraldi)承认,"有些青少年需要作为成人进行审判,但是他们中大多数人是可以教育感化的。"

成人犯人经常虐待这些青少年。这些人自杀的可能性是少管所的罪犯的 8 倍,遭到性虐待的可能性是他们的 5 倍。华盛顿的一个改革团体——"审判项目组织"的女发言人珍妮·盖恩斯伯勒(Jenni Gainsborough)认为,"这些人一旦被释放,他们往往会疯狂作案,实施更多的暴力犯罪。"这种体系实质上是在培养职业罪犯。对有色人种而言,它起的作用更糟。

Passage 5

By almost every measure, Paul Pfingst is an unsentimental prosecutor. Last week the San Diego County district attorney said he fully intends to try suspect Charles Andrew Williams, 15, as an adult for the Santana High School shootings. Even before the tragedy, Pfingst had stood behind the controversial California law that mandates treating murder suspects as young as 14 as adults.

So nobody would have wagered that Pfingst would also be the first D.A. in the U.S. to launch his very own Innocence Project. Yet last June, Pfingst told his attorneys to go back over old murder and rape convictions and see if any unravel with newly developed DNA-testing tools. In other words, he wanted to revisit past victories — this time playing for the other team. "I think people misunderstand being conservative for being biased," says Pfingst. "I

prosecutor n. 起诉人
attorney n. 律师

controversial a. 有争议的
mandate v. 强制执行
wager v. 打赌,保证
launch v. 开始

unravel v. 阐明,解释

biased a. 有偏见的

consider myself a pragmatic guy, and I have no interest in putting innocent people in jail."

Around the U.S., flabbergasted defense attorneys and their jailed clients cheered his move. Among prosecutors, however, there was an awkward pause. After all, each DNA test costs as much as $5,000. Then there's the unspoken risk: if dozens of innocents turn up, the D.A. will have indicted his shop.

But nine months later, no budgets have been busted or prosecutors ousted. Only the rare case merits review. Pfingst's team considers convictions before 1993, when the city started routine DNA testing. They discard cases if the defendant has been released. Of the 560 remaining files, they have re-examined 200, looking for cases with biological evidence and defendants who still claim innocence.

They have identified three so far. The most compelling involves a man serving 12 years for molesting a girl who was playing in his apartment. But others were there at the time. Police found a small drop of saliva on the victim's shirt — too small a sample to test in 1991. Today that spot could free a man. Test results are due any day. Inspired by San Diego, 10 other counties in the U.S. are starting DNA audits.

flabbergaste *v.* 使大吃一惊

unspoken *a.* 未明言的

indict *v.* 控告
bust *v.* 破产
merit *v.* 值得,价值

discard *v.* 抛弃
release *v.* 释放

compelling *a.* 强制的,引人注意的
molest *v.* 干扰,调戏

长难句分析

Even before the tragedy, Pfingst had stood behind the controversial California law that mandates treating murder suspects as young as 14 as adults.

❖结构分析　该句主干为 ... Pfingst had stood behind...。even before the tragedy 是本句的时间状语;主句是 Pfingst had stood behind...; that 引导的宾语从句修饰 law; 在从句中,as... as 意思是"和…一样";出现的第三个 as 是介词,意思是"作为"。

参考译文

用任何标准衡量,保罗·芬斯特都不是位感情用事的检察官。上周,圣地亚哥县地方检察官说,他决意对桑塔纳高中枪杀案疑犯——15 岁的查尔斯·安德鲁·威廉斯——作为成人进行审讯。甚至在这场悲剧发生之前芬斯特就支持加利福尼亚州的一项颇有争议的法律。这项法律规定,以成人身份受审的谋杀嫌疑犯的最低年龄可以降到 14 岁。

谁也不能保证芬斯特会成为美国第一个实施自己"清白计划"的地方检察官。然而,去年6 月,芬斯特告诉手下的律师对过去的谋杀罪和强奸罪重新进行审理,看是否有能用最新的DNA 检验工具揭开的无头案件。换句话说,他想重新回顾过去的胜利——这回是为了另一方。"我想人们把保守错误地理解成了心存偏见。"芬斯特说,"我认为我自己是一个讲究实际的人。我并无意把无辜的人送进监狱。"

在美国,那些哑然失色的辩护律师及其被收监的当事人为他的举动感到欢欣鼓舞。然而,在检察官当中却出现了令人尴尬的沉默。毕竟每一次 DNA 检测的费用都高达 5,000 美元。这其中还存在隐含的风险——如果出现众多的无罪受害者,地方检察官肯定会自砸饭碗。

9 个月后,并没有出现资金短缺或检察官被罢免的情况。只有极少数案件需要重新审理。该市是从 1993 年开始进行常规 DNA 检测的,因此芬斯特的手下只考虑 1993 年前宣判的案件,并排除了那些被告已被释放的案例。在 560 份现存档案中,他们重新审理了 200 份,主要是寻找那些留有生物证据的案件和被告人仍声明无罪的案件。

到目前为止,他们只确定了三起案件。其中有一起案件最引人注意。案件的当事人因被控调戏一名在他的公寓玩耍的女孩而被判服刑 12 年。案发时还有他人在场。警方在受害人的衬衣上发现了一小滴唾液——这个样本太小,无法在 1991 年检验。但在今天,那滴唾液却能使一个人获释。检验结果什么时候都可以拿到。受圣地亚哥的影响,美国又有 10 个县开始用 DNA 对案件进行审核。

第四节　科技发展

Passage 1

"The creation of the PC is the best thing that ever happened," said Bill Gates at a conference on "digital dividends" in 2000. He even wondered if it might be possible to make computers for the poor in countries without an electric power grid. The answer is yes, and things are going even further. Villagers in a remote region of Laos that has neither electricity nor telephone connections are being wired up to the Internet.

grid *n.* 格子,电网

Lee. Thorn, the head of the Jhai Foundation, an American-Lao organisation, has been working for nearly five years in the Hin Heup district. The foundation has helped villagers build schools, install wells and organise a weaving co-operative. But those villagers told Mr. Thorn that what they needed most was access to the Internet. To have any hope of meeting that need, in an environment which is both physically harsh and far removed from technical support, Mr. Thorn realised that a robust computer was the first requirement.

install *v.* 安装

harsh *a.*严厉的,让人不舒服的

robust *a.* 强壮的,健康的

He therefore turned to engineers working with the Jhai Foundation, who devised a machine that has no moving, and few delicate, parts. Instead of a hard disk, the Jhai PC relies on flash-memory chips to store its data. Its screen is a liquid-crystal display, rather than an energy-guzzling glass cathode-ray tube — an exception to the rule that the components used are old-fashioned, and therefore cheap. (No Pentiums, for example, just a 486-type processor.) Mr. Thorn estimates that, built in quantity, each Jhai PC would cost around $ 400. Furthermore, because of its simplicity, a Jhai PC can be powered by a car battery charged with bicycle cranks — thus removing the need for a connection to

devise *v.* 设计,策划

energy-guzzling *a.* 高耗能的

component *n.* 组成

the grid.

Wireless Internet cards connect each Jhai PC to a solar-powered hilltop relay station which then passes the signals on to a computer in town that is connected to both the Lao phone system (for local calls) and to the Internet. Meanwhile, the Linux-based software that will run the computers is in the final stages of being "localised" into Lao by a group of expatriates in America.

One thing that the new network will allow villagers to do is decide whether it is worth going to market. Phon Hong, the local market town, is 30 km away, so it is worth knowing the price of rice before you set off to sell some there. Links farther afield may allow decisions about growing crops for foreign markets to be taken more sensibly— and help with bargaining when these are sold. And there is also the pleasure of using Internet telephony to talk to relatives who have gone to the capital, Vientiane, or even abroad.

If it works, the Jhai PC and its associated network could be a widespread success. So far, the foundation has had expressions of interest from groups working in Peru, Chile and South Africa. The prototype should be operational in Laos this December and it, or something very much like it, may soon be bridging the digital divide elsewhere as well.

expatriate *v.* 驱逐出国，移居

bargain *v.* 讨价还价

widespread *a.* 广为传播的

prototype *n.* 原型

长难句分析

1. Its screen is a liquid-crystal display, rather than an energy-guzzling glass cathode-ray tube — an exception to the rule that the components used are old-fashioned, and therefore cheap.

◆ **结构分析** 该句主干为 Its screen is a liquid-crystal display... rather than 这个连词引导了一个比较状语，意为"胜于"，在两者进行比较时，否定后者，肯定前者，可以翻译为"而不是"。此外这一句中还含有一个带有同位语从句的插入语，即 an exception to。

2. Wireless Internet cards connect each Jhai PC to a solar-powered hilltop relay station which then passes the signals on to a computer in town that is connected to both the

Lao phone system（for local calls）and to the Internet.

❖**结构分析** 该句主干为 Wireless Internet cards connect each Jhai PC to a... relay station...
本句是一个复合句，包含两个定语从句，一个由 which 引导来修饰 relay
station,另外一个由 that 引导修饰 computer。

参考译文

"个人电脑是有史以来最好的发明,"比尔·盖茨在 2000 年的一个"数字红利"会议上如此说到。他甚至想知道,有没有可能为那些尚未通电国家的穷人制造计算机。答案是肯定的,而且甚至还不止于此。在老挝的一个既不通电也没有电话的偏僻地区,村民们现在可以登录互联网了。

李·索恩是一个美国—老挝组织"Jhai 基金会"的负责人,他在班欣合(Hin Heup)地区已经工作了将近 5 年。该基金会帮助村民办学、打井、还组织了一个编织合作社。但那些村民告诉索恩先生他们最需要的是上网。在这样一个条件恶劣,远离技术支持的环境里,想要满足这种需求,索恩先生意识到一台好用的电脑是当务之急。

因此他向"Jhai 基金会"的技术人员求助,于是他们发明了一台没有活动部件,也没有多少精致组件的电脑。Jhai 电脑没有硬盘,而是依靠闪存芯片存储资料。它的屏幕是一个液晶显示器,而不是耗电的玻璃纯屏显示器——这打破了使用过时廉价组件(比如,处理器不是奔腾系列,而只是 486 类型)的原则。索恩先生估计,如果批量生产的话,每台 Jhai 电脑的成本大概是 400 美元。此外,由于设计简单,Jhai 电脑还可以用借助自行车曲柄充电的汽车电池来提供电源——这样就不必连接电网了。

无线网卡将每一台 Jhai 电脑和一个山顶太阳能中转站连接在一起,通过这个中转站,信号可以传送到镇上的一台连接老挝电话系统(用于本地电话)和互联网的电脑。与此同时,基于 Linux 系统的电脑运行软件也正处于用老挝语进行"本地化"的最后阶段,从事这一项工作的是一群移居美国的老挝人。

村民们用这个新网络可以决定要不要走向市场。孟莲洪(Phon Hong)是当地的集镇,距离村子有 30 公里,因此在去集镇卖大米之前了解一下米价还是很有用的。如果能和更远的地方进行沟通，那么人们就可以更加理智地对待国外市场的需求——而且这种沟通还有助于在销售的时候讨价还价。此外,人们还可以使用网络电话与在首都万象甚至国外的亲人进行通话。

如果这种电脑可行的话,Jhai 电脑及其相关网络将取得巨大的成功。目前,秘鲁、智利和南非的一些团体已经向基金会表示了他们的关注。今年 12 月,第一台电脑即将在老挝投入使用,其他与之类似的电脑将很快填平数字化鸿沟。

Passage 2

DOTCOMS may be moribund, but inside companies, the Internet is still finding cost-saving new uses. "B2E — business-to-employee — didn't have a crash," says Bipin Patel, in charge of developing the potential of the corporate intranet at the Ford Motor Company. "It's still growing."

Ford has gone further than most companies to get its employees online: it offered its American employees personal computers, and 90% of them accepted. Ford hopes that the free PCs will save its own and its employees' time by moving services online. General Motors, Ford's great rival, considered a similar scheme but found that most employees willing to use PCs already had them. It is helping staff to pay for high-bandwidth connections instead.

At Ford, the human-resources department has pioneered a scheme to provide up-to-the-minute information to employees about pay and benefits. In the past, employees sometimes found that it took weeks to get a copy of the pay information they needed to do their tax returns, and the department's staff spent mind-numbing hours answering the same questions from hundreds of different employees. Now employees can look at a password-protected site that displays their payslips over the previous 18 months. They can see all deductions, and the hours they worked. All this information was on the human-resources database: displaying it to employees has saved staff time.

"People want more and more of this self-service information, which they can manage themselves," observes Mr. Patel. "There is no such thing as information overload here, because it's their information." Even training seems to work better online: Ford employees can now download a range of courses, including one on "Listening and Handling

moribund	a. 垂死的
intranet	n. 专用网,企业网
pioneer	v. 开创
up-to-the-minute	最新的
mind-numbing	a. 伤脑筋的
payslip	n. 工资单
deduction	n. 扣除,推论
overload	n. 超载

Tough Situations", all designed for digestion in 10 or 15 minute gobbets. The company claims to have cut training costs by $ 2 million during the past six months, as fewer people leave their desks to learn.

digestion *n.* 消化

The company also uses its intranet to communicate with its staff around the world. Jacques Nasser, Ford's boss, sends out "Let's chat" notes once a week. In fact, Mr. Nasser does most of the chatting. He gets hundreds of e-mails in reply, but the communication is basically a one-way flow. The company also runs chatrooms, in which employees can question various inhouse experts and outside analysts live on the corporate intranet.

inhouse *a.* 内部的

In time, thinks Mr. Patel, communications technology will reshape corporate behaviour. It will encourage collaboration and team-working. Already, the Internet is causing disintermediation within companies, he argues, just as it did in e-commerce: the human-resources department does much less administration once the benefits system is more self-service, but rather more advising and consulting. One day, working in human resources might even be fun.

disintermediation *n.* 去中介化

consult *v.* 请教，商议

长难句分析

Already, the Internet is causing disintermediation within companies, he argues, just as it did in e-commerce: the human-resources department does much less administration once the benefits system is more self-service, but rather more advising and consulting.

❖结构分析 本句的主句是 The Internet is causing disintermediation within companies... he argues 是插入语，连词 as 的意思是"如同，正如"，did 指代的是 cause disintermediation；冒号后的内容是对 just as it did in e-commerce 的解释说明。

参考译文

网络公司(DOTCOMS)也许即将灭亡,但是在公司内部,因特网仍然是节省成本的新办法。"B2E(企业对职员)并没有失败。"福特汽车公司负责开发企业内部网潜力的拜平·帕特尔说,"相反,它仍然在发展。"

在说服员工上网方面福特汽车公司比多数公司走得更远:它给它的美国员工提供个人电脑,而 90% 的员工都接受了。福特汽车公司希望把一些服务性信息放到网上,能够节省公司及其员工的时间。福特汽车公司的主要竞争对手通用汽车公司已考虑实施相似的计划,但发现多数愿意使用个人电脑的员工已经有了电脑。因此,它正在帮助职员支付高速宽带连接费用。

在福特公司,人力资源部率先制定了一项计划,为员工提供有关薪水和津贴的最新信息。在过去,员工有时发现,他们要等上好几个几周才能得到一张用于纳税的薪水信息的复印件,而人力资源部的职员却不得不晕头转向地花好几个小时来回答几百个不同员工提出的同样的问题。现在,职员们可以在密码保护的网站上查看他们过去 18 个月的工资单。他们可查看所有的扣除额、工作时间等信息。所有这些信息都放在人力资源部的数据库里:把这些信息显示出来节省了员工的时间。

"人们越来越多地需要这类自助信息,而这些信息是他们自己就可以管理的。"帕特尔先生说,"这里根本没有所谓的信息超载一说,因为这是他们的信息。"甚至在线培训似乎也进行得更好一些:现在,福特公司的员工从网上下载系列课程,其中包括一个有关"倾听和处理棘手情况"的课程。所有这些课程的设计保证学员能在 10—15 分钟内消化理解。公司声称,在过去的 6 个月里,培训费减少了两百万美元,因为几乎没有人丢下他们的工作去学习。

公司还用公司的内部网与世界各地的员工进行通信联络。福特公司的老板雅克·纳赛尔每周发一个"让我们聊天"的帖子。实际上,多数情况都是纳赛尔先生在聊天。他收到回复的电子邮件有几百封,但交流基本上是单向的。福特公司还经营聊天室。员工们可在聊天室向在线做客的公司内的专家和公司外的分析人员提各种各样的问题。

帕特尔认为,通信技术最终将再造公司的行为方式。它将鼓励合作和团队精神。他论述说,正如电子商务中发生的脱媒现象一样—— 一旦津贴制度变得更加自助化,人力资源部所做的行政管理方面的工作会少得多, 他们更多的是提供建议和咨询——互联网也正在导致公司之间的非中介化现象。总有一天,在人力资源部工作甚至会充满乐趣。

Passage 3

In the cause of equal rights, feminists have had much to complain about. But one striking piece of inequality has been conveniently overlooked: lifespan. In this area, women have the upper hand. All round the world, they live longer than men. Why they should do so is not immediately obvious. But the same is true in many other species. From lions to antelope and from sea lions to deer, males, for some reason, simply can't go the distance. One theory is that males must compete for female attention. That means evolution is busy selecting for antlers, aggression and alloy wheels in males, at the expense of longevity. Females are not subject to such pressures. If this theory is correct, the effect will be especially noticeable in those species where males compete for the attention of lots of females. Conversely, it will be reduced or absent where they do not.

To test that idea, Tim Clutton-Brock of Cambridge University and Kavita Isvaran of the Indian Institute of Science in Bengalooru decided to compare monogamous and polygynous species(in the latter, a male monopolises a number of females). They wanted to find out whether polygynous males had lower survival rates and aged faster than those of monogamous species. To do so, they collected the relevant data for 35 species of long-lived birds and mammals.

As they report, the pattern was much as they expected. In 16 of the 19 polygynous species in their sample, males of all ages were much more likely to die during any given period than were females. Furthermore, the older they got, the bigger the mortality gap became. In other words, they aged faster. Males from monogamous species did not show these patterns. The point about polygyny is that if one male has exclusive access to, say, ten females, another nine males will be waiting to topple the harem master as soon as he shows the first sign of weakness. The intense competitive pressure means that individuals who succeed put all their

feminist *n.* 女性主义者

overlook *v.* 忽视

antler *n.* 鹿茸
longevity *n.* 长寿

conversely *ad.* 相反地

monogamous *a.* 一夫一妻的

polygynous *a.* 一夫多妻的

mammal *n.* 哺乳动物

mortality *n.* 死亡率

topple *v.* 推翻,倒塌

efforts into one or two breeding seasons.

breed *v.* 饲养，繁殖

That obviously takes its toll directly. But a more subtle effect may also be at work. Most students of ageing agree that an animal's maximum lifespan is set by how long it can reasonably expect to escape predation, disease, accident and damaging aggression by others of its kind. If it will be killed quickly anyway, there is not much reason for evolution to divert scarce resources into keeping the machine in tip-top condition. Those resources should, instead, be devoted to reproduction. And the more threatening the outside world is, the shorter the maximum lifespan should be.

predation *n.* 捕食，掠夺
行为

tip-top *a.* 最好的，一流的

There is no reason why that logic should not work between the sexes as well as between species. The test is to identify a species that has made its environment so safe that most of its members die of old age, and see if the difference continues to exist. Fortunately, there is such a species: man. Dr. Clutton-Brock reckons that the sex difference in both human rates of ageing and in the usual age of death is an indicator that polygyny was the rule in humanity's evolutionary past — as it still is, in some places. That may not please some feminists, but it could be the price women have paid for outliving their menfolk.

长难句分析

1. **The point about polygyny is that if one male has exclusive access to, say, ten females, another nine males will be waiting to topple the harem master as soon as he shows the first sign of weakness.**

   ❖结构分析　该句主干为 The point is that if..., another nine males will be... 这是一个复合句，that 引导的是句子的表语从句；该表语从句中，if 引导的是条件状语从句，as soon as 引导的是时间状语从句。

2. **Dr. Clutton-Brock reckons that the sex difference in both human rates of aging and in the usual age of death is an indicator that polygyny was the rule in humanity's evolutionary past — as it still is, in some places.**

   ❖结构分析　该句主干为 Dr. Clutton-Brock reckons that... 这是一个复合句。that 引导的是宾语从句；该宾语从句中，indicator 后面 that 引导的是定语从句。

参考译文

在权利平等的问题上,女性会有许多抱怨之处。但有一个明显的不平等现象一直被人们所忽略:寿命。在这一方面,妇女处于优势地位。全世界各地的女性都要比男性寿命长。虽然原因尚不清楚,但是许多物种也存在相同的情况。从狮子到羚羊,从海狮到鹿,雄性总是活得不够长。一种理论认为,雄性必须通过竞争来获得雌性的注意,这就意味着进化在男性中间选择鹿角、侵略和合金轮子,其代价就是寿命,而女性却不用面对这种压力。如果这个理论成立的话,那么在那些雄性要通过竞争来引起雌性注意的物种中,雌性比雄性长寿的现象就应该格外明显。相反,在没有此类竞争的物种中,这种区别会较少甚至没有。

为了证实这种想法,剑桥大学的蒂姆·克拉顿布罗克和印度科学研究院的卡维塔·艾斯瓦拉决定对比研究单配物种和多配物种(后者为一个雄性有多个雌性配偶)。他们的目的在于研究是否多配物种雄性的存活率比单配物种低一些,也老得快一些。为了达到这一目的,他们搜集了 35 种寿命较长的鸟类和哺乳类动物的信息。

他们称结果与他们预想的差不多。他们选择的 19 种多配物种中,有 16 种物种各个年龄段的雄性在任何时期都比雌性更容易死亡。而且,随着年龄的增长,它们的死亡率差距就越大。也就是它们老得越快。而单配物种的雄性没有这些特征。多配物种中,如果某一个雄性单独拥有 10 个雌性,那么它一旦出现衰老的迹象,另外 9 个雄性就会推倒这位占有多个雌性的主人。强大的竞争压力意味着胜利的那些雄性个体会把所有的精力放在一个或两个繁殖季节。

很明显这会直接缩短雄性的寿命。但是还存在一个更不易察觉的影响。研究老化的学生都认为动物寿命最大程度上取决于逃避捕食、疾病、意外和同类进攻等因素。如果它们很快就杀死,那么进化就不可能将有限的资源用于保证机器处于最好的状态了。相反地,这些资源应当用于繁殖。外界的环境越危险,寿命就应该越短。

同理,这种逻辑在性别或物种之间也存在。该实验旨在找到一种能将自己的环境保护得非常安全,以便其大多数成员都可以在老年死去的物种,从而检验上述差异是否持续存在。幸运的是还有这么一个物种——人类。克拉顿·布罗克博士估计人类衰老速度的性别差异和死亡的正常年龄标志着一夫多妻可能是人类进化的法则,因为现在在某些地方还存在着这种现象。一些女性主义者可能会不高兴了,但这可能就是女性比男性寿命更长所要付出的代价吧。

Passage 4

Launching people into space may make headlines but it does little useful science. So when George Bush redirected America's space agency, NASA, away from scientific research and towards a manned return to the moon in 2004, many scientists were disappointed. Now the agency has finally offered some small morsels of comfort in the form of four projects that could accompany efforts for a lunar return.

The most exciting of these is the plan for a radio telescope that could be placed on the far side of the moon. Such a device would look back at the early universe to the time when large-scale structures such as galaxies and stars formed. A lunar-based radio telescope would be able to detect long wavelengths that cannot be sensed on Earth because they are absorbed by the outermost layers of the planet's atmosphere. Moreover by pointing the telescope away from the din of shorter-wavelength radio waves that are used for communication on Earth, astrophysicists would be able to see the early universe in unprecedented detail.

Finding alien life might also be possible with such a telescope. It would be able to map the magnetic fields of stars and exoplanets (planets that circle stars outside the solar system). It is the magnetic field of the Earth that protects its inhabitants from being bombarded by high-energy particles from space that would otherwise leave the planet sterile. Detecting a magnetic field surrounding an Earth-like exoplanet would prove a promising sign for finding extraterrestrial life.

The proposal, led by Joseph Lazio, of the Naval Research Laboratory in Washington, DC, is to create an array of three arms arranged in a Y-shape, each of which would be 500 metres long and contain 16 antennae. Each arm would be made of a plastic film that could be rolled out onto the surface of the moon, either by robots or by

launch *v.* 发射,推动

morsel *n.* 少量
lunar *a.* 月球的

telescope *n.* 望远镜

galaxy *n.* 银河系

wavelength *n.* 波长
outermost *a.* 最外层的

astrophysicist *n.* 天体物理学家

alien *a.* 外国的,外星的

exoplanet *n.* 外行星

bombard *v.* 炮击,攻击

sterile *a.* 贫瘠的,无生育能力的

extraterrestrial *a.* 外星的

antennae *n.* 触角

astronauts

A second project, headed by Michael Collier, of the NASA Goddard Space Flight Center, would examine how the solar wind — a stream of charged particles ejected from the sun — interacts with the tenuous lunar atmosphere close to the moon's surface. Such bombardment produces low-energy X-rays that would be detected on the surface of the moon.

The third and fourth projects are similar both to each other and to earlier ventures dropped on the moon by the Apollo and the Soviet Luna missions in the late 1960s and 1970s. Some 35 years on, reflectors placed on the lunar surface are still used by scientists interested in geophysics and geodesy (for example, how the moon's gravitational field shifts over time). Most of the reflectors are clustered close to the lunar equator. The proposals, led by Stephen Merkowitz, also of NASA's Goddard Space Flight Centre, and Douglas Currie, of the University of Maryland, are to sprinkle some more sophisticated versions over more of the moon's surface.

Such efforts may attract little attention compared with the launch of the space shuttle Endeavour this week. Nevertheless, when NASA argues that putting people into space inspires young people to study science, it is precisely these endeavours that it wishes to encourage.

astronaut *n.* 宇航员

eject *v.* 驱逐，喷射

venture *n.* 冒险，风险

geodesy *n.* 测地学
reflector *n.* 反射器
equator *n.* 赤道

sprinkle *v.* 撒

shuttle *n.* 飞机，穿梭

长难句分析

1. **So when George Bush redirected America's space agency, NASA, away from scientific research and towards a manned return to the moon in 2004, many scientists were disappointed.**

   ◆结构分析 该句主干为 So when George Bush redirected... away from... and towards... , many scientists were... 这是一个复合句，前面 when 引导的是时间状语从句。

2. **A second project, headed by Michael Collier, of the NASA Goddard Space Flight Center, would examine how the solar wind — a stream of charged particles ejected from the sun — interacts with the tenuous lunar atmosphere close to the moon's surface.**

❖结构分析 该句主干为 A second project would examine...这是一个复合句,how 引导的是宾语从句;headed... 分词结构修饰前面的 project。

参考译文

把人送入太空也许能成为头条新闻,但是对科学研究却没有什么帮助。因此,当乔治·布什在 2004 年要求美国宇航局将重点从科学研究转移到载人回归月球时,很多科学家都倍感失望。现在,美国宇航局为回归月球计划增加了四项科研项目,总算给大家带来了些许安慰。

这些项目中最激动人心的是一种可以安装在月球背面的无线电天文望远镜。通过这种望远镜,人们可以了解到从宇宙早期至大规模天体结构如星云和恒星形成的时期。安装在月球上的无线电天文望远镜可以探测到那些无法在地球表面被检测到的长波,因为这些长波都被地球大气层的最外层吸收了。此外,天体物理学家们使该望远镜远离地球上频繁用于通信的较短波长无线电波,从而能够史无前例地细致观察早期的宇宙。

使用这台望远镜也许还可以寻找外星生物。因为它能够描绘出恒星和太阳系外行星(太阳系之外围绕恒星运动的行星)的磁场图。正是由于地球磁场的保护,地球上居住着的生物才能幸免于来自太空中高能量粒子的袭击,否则这个星球就会变成一片不毛之地。如果能够检测到某个太阳系外行星也像地球一样被磁场包围,就有希望找到地球以外的生命。

该计划由美国华盛顿特区海军研究实验室的约瑟夫·拉齐奥领导,目标是创造出一个以三臂状构成 Y 字形的天线阵,其中每只臂长 500 米,含 16 根天线,用塑料薄膜制成,以便由机器人或宇航员平铺在月球表面。

第二项计划的负责人是美国宇航局戈达德太空飞行中心的迈克尔·科利尔,该计划将研究太阳风(太阳喷发出的一束带电粒子流)如何与月球表面附近稀薄的大气相互作用。这种作用产生的低能量 X 射线可以在月球表面被探测到。

第三和第四项计划彼此相似,并与早前于 20 世纪 60 年代末和 70 年代进行的阿波罗计划和前苏联的登月计划也大同小异。现在那些放置于月球表面的反射器已差不多工作了 35 年,且仍然为那些对地球物理学和测地学(如研究月球引力场如何随时间而变化)感兴趣的科学家们服务着。大多数反射器都安装在靠近月球赤道的地方。这两项计划的主管人是美国宇航局戈达德太空飞行中心的斯蒂芬·默科维茨以及马里兰大学的道格拉斯·柯里,其目标是在月球上更大范围地布置一些尖端反射器。

与本周发射的"奋进号"航天飞机相比,这些月球计划可能不会引起多大关注,但是,当美国宇航局极力主张载人航天可以激励年轻人学习科学时,为月球计划而"奋进"的精神也正是它所要鼓舞的。

Passage 5

At the close of the *Kyoto Global-Warming Treaty* discussions held in Bonn last week, exhausted negotiators from nearly every country on earth had reason to be proud. They had done what no one expected — they reached a breakthrough agreement to limit greenhouse gases. During the concluding remarks, as each speaker praised the next, only the chief U.S. official on the scene drew an undiplomatic response. When Paula Dobriansky told the gathering that the Bush Administration "will not abdicate our responsibility" to address global warming, the hall filled with boos. That's because the U.S., the world's largest producer of greenhouse gases, sat on the sidelines in Bonn.

George W. Bush has yet to decide what, if anything, he will do to combat global warming. But he believes the Kyoto treaty is fatally flawed because it doesn't require developing countries to limit their fossil-fuel use immediately, as it does industrialized countries. So he kept the U.S. out of the discussions. In doing so, the Administration may have lost its last opportunity to help shape the international response to the problem. And Bush may be in danger of losing control over climate action domestically. After months of internal debate, the Administration is still "consulting" on the issue.

That noise you hear is Congress rushing to fill the leadership vacuum. At least six climate plans have been proposed so far. The first is sponsored by former Republican, now Independent Senator Jim Jeffords, chairman of the Senate Environment Committee, who proposes to cut greenhouse-gas emissions from power plants. Congressional action this week will center on reducing emissions by raising vehicle fuel-efficiency standards, including those for SUVs. If SUVs had to meet the same standards as cars — something Massachusetts Representative Ed Markey will propose this week — they could save

exhausted	a. 精疲力竭的
breakthrough	n. 突破
concluding	a. 结束的
gathering	n. 聚集, 与会者
abdicate	v. 让位, 放弃
combat	v. 对抗
flawed	a. 有缺陷的
shape	v. 塑造, 影响
domestically	ad. 国内地
vacuum	n. 真空
sponsor	v. 赞助
emission	n. 释放, 发射
representative	n. 代表

consumers an estimated $7 billion at the pump this year and cut gasoline demand by tens of billions of gallons over 10 years.

pump *n.* 抽水机,打气筒

The "drill Detroit, not the Arctic" campaign will find some support this week when the National Academy of Sciences releases a long-awaited study. The report, toned down after the auto industry protested that raising fuel-efficiency standards, by making cars lighter, makes vehicles less safe, is still likely to conclude that fuel efficiency can be increased at least 25% with existing technology.

drill *v.* 钻孔

long-awaited *a.* 期待已久的

If a fuel-efficiency bill reaches his desk, Bush could be in a bind — caught between auto lobbyists(his chief of staff used to be one) and his concern for energy security. With new technology putting impressive fuel efficiency within reach, it will be hard for him to oppose measures that could reduce the national appetite for foreign oil by millions of barrels a year.

lobbyist *n.* 说客,活动议案通过者

appetite *n.* 胃口

长难句分析

The report, toned down after the auto industry protested that raising fuel-efficiency standards, by making cars lighter, makes vehicles less safe, is still likely to conclude that fuel efficiency can be increased at least 25% with existing technology.

❖结构分析 该句主干为 The report... is still likely to conclude that... 这句话的主语是 the report，后面跟的过去分词 toned down 作伴随状语来修饰 the report; toned down 后面又跟了 after 引导的时间状语从句,从句中又有一个 that 引导的宾语从句，宾语从句中 raising fuel-efficiency standards 是主语，由 by making cars lighter 来修饰；这句话的谓语是 is still likely...; 谓语后又跟了一个 that 引导的宾语从句。

参考译文

上周在波恩举行的商讨《京都议定书》会议结束的时候,来自世界各国的筋疲力尽的谈判者完全有理由感到自豪。他们取得的成果是任何人都没有预料到的——就限制温室气体排放问题达成了一项突破性协议。在致闭幕词的时候,与会的每一位发言人都对此表示称

赞,唯独美国官方代表做出了毫无外交策略的回应。当保拉·多布里扬斯基向大会宣布布什政府"不会放弃自己的责任"去处理全球变暖这一问题时,全场报以唏嘘声。这是因为美国作为全球温室气体排放量最大的国家在波恩会议上完全是一种局外人的态度。

如果真有什么可做的话,乔治·W.布什必须决定应该为遏制全球气候变暖做些什么。但是他认定京都协定有致命的缺陷,因为它没有要求发展中国家同其他工业国那样,立即限制矿物燃料的使用,因此美国没有参与讨论。这样做的结果是,布什政府可能失去了最后的机会去影响国际社会对此问题做出的反应。在国内,布什可能会有对气候问题处于失控状态的危险。经过几个月的内部讨论之后,布什政府对这一问题仍然处于"磋商"阶段。

你所听到的都是一些国会成员争先抢后去填补领导层空缺的议论。至今已提出了至少六种有关气候治理的计划。第一种计划是由吉姆·杰福兹提出的。吉姆·杰福兹是前共和党派,现在的无党派参议员,并任参议院环境工程委员会主席。他提议减少电厂的温室气体排放量。本周国会议题是围绕通过提高机动车燃料效率标准来减少气体排放量这一论点展开的,其中也包括提高越野车的标准。如果越野车要达到的标准和小汽车一样的话——这是本周来自马萨诸塞州的代表爱德·马奇提出来的——那么消费者今年估计仅气泵一项就能节省 70 亿美元,十年中汽油需求量能减少好几百亿加仑。

本周国家科学研究院公布了一项令人期待已久的研究,这项研究将会使"在底特律而不要在北极进行石油勘探"这一运动从中获得一些支持。由于汽车生产企业的抗议——通过减轻车身的重量来提高燃油效率的标准会使汽车的安全性降低,这项报告处以低调,但仍可能得出这样的结论:现在的科技水平能使燃料效率至少提高 25%。

如果一份有关燃料效率的议案送到布什的案头,他会进退两难——夹在汽车企业的说客(他的参谋长就是其中一个)和自己对能源安全问题的担忧之间。应用新科技能达到令人满意的燃油效率,那么也就使他很难反对能减少国人每年对外国石油几百万桶的需求量的方案。

第三章 真经与实战

1. 本部分的内容与结构

　　真题的使用是考研备考过程中最重要的一部分内容,因为真题是最直接的材料,接触真题就好比是与对手短兵相接,双方没有任何距离。真题是最佳的复习材料,这一点毋庸置疑,也为广大考生的学习经验所证明。但是,关键的问题在于如何使用这些珍贵的复习材料,使其发挥最大的作用。本部分是近六年考研真题的阅读部分,包括 A、B 和 C 节。原文不做任何改动和标记,后面对每一篇文章都有"长难句解析"和"参考译文",对每一道试题都有明了的解析,以帮助读者全面了解考研试题的性质、内容、难度、出题方式等。

2. 考研英语阅读理解的类型与解题思路

(1) A 节的特点与解题思路

　　考研真题大都选自英语报刊杂志,再根据出题的要求进行一些修改而成的,总的来说都有一定难度。从题材上来看,科技、经济和文化方面的内容占了较大比例,而一些比较敏感的政治、宗教问题则不易出现在题中,除非只是对其做介绍。在阅读过程中,首先要注意的是文章的整体结构问题。由于大多数文章都属于说明文和议论文。记叙性质的文章,也往往包括说明或议论的成份。但英语文章在结构上有其自身的特点,如一般的议论或说明性文章在结构上都呈区的形态,也就是说两头大,中间小,重要的内容和信息都包含在文章和段落的开头和结尾,中间不过是说明或解释。并且,由于英语里面有一些明确地表达转折或递进的连接词,在阅读的时候也要注意它们的存在。

　　当然,有的作者喜欢用其他的写作方式,比如先提出某种现象,再列举别人的观点,然后才在批判他人观点的基础上提出自己的观点,最后进行总结等等,或者先提出问题,再谈论某些现象,逐一考查,最后提出自己对问题的看法等等。纸上谈兵很容易,但实际上做起来却不那么得心应手,必须要有深厚的基础才行。解决问题的关键就在于对真题的了解程度。

　　就出题的方式而言,一般以细节题为主,也就是说考查考生对文中某一个细节的理解。这种题型考查的就是对个别句子的理解能力和考生的细心程度,做这类题时只要小心仔细,在充分理解上下文的基础上是不难解决的。但是,从近两年的出题趋势来看,综合性的题目越来越多,比如,主旨大意题(对文章的主要内容进行概括,比如为文章选题目等)、态度题

(作者或文中某个人物对某事的态度,是支持还是反对等)、归纳题(对某个段落进行归纳)等等。此外,从题型上看还有推断题(就是让考生在文章所提供的信息的基础上推断出没有讲出的内容)、词义猜测题(根据上下文对某个词或词组的意思进行猜测)等等。很难说某一种题型会有特定的解题方法,只有在实践中进行磨练才能掌握做题的技巧因此,应该下功夫使真题得到充分的利用。

（2）B 节的特点与解题思路

B 节是 2005 年开始新增的题型,旨在考查考生对英语文章篇章逻辑结构的理解,以及对全文或段落结构的概括能力等。部分考生对这部分试题感到不太适应,但实际上从文章难度来看,B 节内容比 A 节更容易一些,长难句子更少。关键在于解题的思路要调整。一般来说,英语文章的逻辑结构是很清楚的,上下文之间的关系也比较紧密。因此,考生首先要注意选项中和上下文之间的一些提示性关键词,如人名、地名,某个重要出现的词语等。其次要注意表示逻辑关系的连接词,比如 however, but, furthermore, therefore 等等,理清其逻辑关联。第三,除了这些细节性的技巧之外,还要注意内容上的整体关联。比如 2009 年的第 43 题就是如此,并列提出两种关于文化的观点,后文分别对它们进行说明。

（3）C 节的特点与解题思路

英译汉部分是从 2003 年开始加入阅读理解的,作为 Part B,从 2005 年开始新增"选择搭配"题型以后,成为阅读理解的 Part C。C 节令众多考生都感到头疼,一方面有词汇方面的困难,另一方面则有句子结构的问题,很多人不知如何下手。还有考生反映,明明英语看懂了,就是用汉语写不出来。这一系列问题都表明一般考生对翻译的方法和技巧不甚明了。从历年考题来看,需要翻译的句子大都是复合句,除了偶尔难度较大外,结构算不上太复杂。本书从第一章就有"长难句分析"这一环节,针对的也是这一题型。

在翻译时,首要工作是要明白句子的主干是什么。英语句子的特点就在于,无论它有多么长,多么复杂,必定有一个主谓结构在那里,也就是说,首先要明白哪个是句子的主语,哪个是谓语;第二步是把其他相关的部分再翻译出来。由于已经明白句子的主干是什么,这些部分的内容就可以很轻松地加到主干上去。第三步是根据汉语的语言习惯重新组织句子,要尽量做到逻辑清晰,最好和英文原文能对应起来。翻译能力的提高是一个循序渐进的过程,不能一蹴而就,但相信考生如果能遵循翻译的规律,掌握方法,在短时间内会有很大提高。因此,一定要先自己尝试翻译,然后参考书中的译文,找到自己的不足之处。

3. 学习步骤与使用方法

（1）不要畏难,直接进入真题

对于有些英语基础比较薄弱的同学来说,做考研题时总会感觉到力不从心,因此有畏难心理。我们的要求是,直奔主题! 也不要怕做不好,关键的问题在于进入真实的场景中去感受考研试题。感性理解考研题是解决问题的第一步。

(2) 借助工具书对课文进行仔细阅读

字典是这个阶段不可或缺的工具,要求把每一个感觉到生疏的词都查出来,记在单词本上。这个过程可能会很枯燥,但却是必须的。记忆单词要求结合记忆规律,不断重复。同时,反复阅读已经细读过的内容,使这些单词不断复现,加深印象。无论如何,解决单词问题既要靠"记",也要靠"读",二者兼顾才能达到良好的效果。

(3) 借助本书中提供的"长难句分析"和"参考译文",对文章进行仔细对比阅读

记住,要研究每一句话,包括词汇、结构、意义。所谓熟能生巧,只有把这些文章都了如指掌,才能悟到考研试题文章的解题精要。当然每年的考试中不会出现重复的文章,但同一类型的文章和题型却是一再重复的。通过精主导,"长难句分析"和"参考译文"准确把握出题规律。

(4) 借助"试题分析",认真理解每一道题

本部分的"试题分析"从实践出发,既帮助考生理解试题的含义,又在方法上进行指导。每个人面对同一道试题的反应固然不同,但总的解题思路还是有规律的,方法也很重要。所以,"试题分析"这部分一方面加深对试题和相关文章的理解,另一方面则在方法上进行点拨,启发读者针对不同题型使用相应的解题策略。

(5) 复习与重复

仅仅理解是不够的。我们的要求要远远高过这一点:希望读者把每篇文章、每道考题都熟记在心,不仅是文章内容也包括句子和词汇。只有读熟了、读精了、读透了,才能真正掌握到考研试题的规律所在。

2005年 考研英语全真试题
（阅读理解部分）

Part A

Directions:

*Read the following four texts. Answer the questions below each text by choosing A, B, C or D. Mark your answers on **ANSWER SHEET 1**.*

Text 1

Everybody loves a fat pay rise. Yet pleasure at your own can vanish if you learn that a colleague has been given a bigger one. Indeed, if he has a reputation for slacking, you might even be outraged. Such behavior is regarded as "all too human" with the underlying assumption that other animals would not be capable of this finely developed sense of grievance. But a study by Sarah Brosnan and Frans de Waal of Emory University in Atlanta, Georgia, which has just been published in *Nature*, suggests that it is all too monkey, as well.

The researchers studied the behaviour of female brown capuchin monkeys. They look cute. They are good-natured, co-operative creatures, and they share their food readily. Above all, like their female human counterparts, they tend to pay much closer attention to the value of "goods and services" than males.

Such characteristics make them perfect candidates for Dr. Brosnan's and Dr. de Waal's study. The researchers spent two years teaching their monkeys to exchange tokens for food. Normally, the monkeys were happy enough to exchange pieces of rock for slices of cucumber. However, when two monkeys were placed in separate but adjoining chambers, so that each could observe what the other was getting in return for its rock, their behaviour became markedly different.

In the world of capuchins, grapes are luxury goods (and much preferable to cucumbers). So when one monkey was handed a grape in exchange for her token, the second was reluctant to hand hers over for a mere piece of cucumber. And if one received a grape without having to provide her token in exchange at all, the other either tossed her own token at the researcher or out of the chamber, or refused to accept the slice of cucumber. Indeed, the mere presence of a grape in the other chamber(without an actual monkey to eat it) was enough to induce resentment in a female capuchin.

The researchers suggest that capuchin monkeys, like humans, are guided by social emotions. In the wild, they are a co-operative, group-living species. Such co-operation is likely to be stable only when each animal feels it is not being cheated. Feelings of righteous indignation, it seems, are not the preserve of people alone. Refusing a lesser reward completely makes these feelings abundantly clear to other members of the group. However, whether such a sense of fairness evolved independently in capuchins and humans, or whether it stems from the common ancestor that the species had 35 million years ago, is, as yet, an unanswered question.

21. In the opening paragraph, the author introduces his topic by _____.

    A. posing a contrast   B. justifying an assumption

    C. making a comparison   D. explaining a phenomenon

22. The statement "it is all too monkey" (Last line, Paragraph 1) implies that _____.

    A. monkeys are also outraged by slack rivals

    B. resenting unfairness is also monkeys' nature

    C. monkeys, like humans, tend to be jealous of each other

    D. no animals other than monkeys can develop such emotions

23. Female capuchin monkeys were chosen for the research most probably because they are _____.

    A. more inclined to weigh what they get

    B. attentive to researchers' instructions

    C. nice in both appearance and temperament

    D. more generous than their male companions

24. Dr. Brosnan and Dr. de Waal have eventually found in their study that the monkeys _____.

    A. prefer grapes to cucumbers

    B. can be taught to exchange things

    C. will not be co-operative if feeling cheated

    D. are unhappy when separated from others

25. What can we infer from the last paragraph?

    A. Monkeys can be trained to develop social emotions.

    B. Human indignation evolved from an uncertain source.

    C. Animals usually show their feelings openly as humans do.

    D. Cooperation among monkeys remains stable only in the wild.

Text 2

Do you remember all those years when scientists argued that smoking would kill us but the doubters insisted that we didn't know for sure? That the evidence was inconclusive, the science uncertain? That the antismoking lobby was out to destroy our way of life and the government should stay out of the way? Lots of Americans bought that nonsense, and over three decades, some 10 million smokers went to early graves.

There are upsetting parallels today, as scientists in one wave after another try to awaken us to the growing threat of global warming. The latest was a panel from the National Academy of Sciences, enlisted by the White House, to tell us that the Earth's atmosphere is definitely warming and that the problem is largely man-made. The clear message is that we should get moving to protect ourselves. The president of the National Academy, Bruce Alberts, added this key point in the preface to the panel's report: "Science never has all the answers. But science does provide us with the best available guide to the future, and it is critical that our nation and the world base important policies on the best judgments that science can provide concerning the future consequences of present actions."

Just as on smoking, voices now come from many quarters insisting that the science about global warming is incomplete, that it's OK to keep pouring fumes into the air until we know for sure. This is a dangerous game: by the time 100 percent of the evidence is in, it may be too late. With the risks obvious and growing, a prudent people would take out an insurance policy now.

Fortunately, the White House is starting to pay attention. But it's obvious that a majority of the president's advisers still don't take global warming seriously. Instead of a plan of action, they continue to press for more research — a classic case of "paralysis by analysis".

To serve as responsible stewards of the planet, we must press forward on deeper atmospheric and oceanic research. But research alone is inadequate. If the Administration won't take the legislative initiative, Congress should help to begin fashioning conservation measures. A bill by Democratic Senator Robert Byrd of West Virginia, which would offer financial incentives for private industry, is a promising start. Many see that the country is getting ready to build lots of new power plants to meet our energy needs. If we are ever going to protect the atmosphere, it is crucial that those new plants be environmentally sound.

26. An argument made by supporters of smoking was that _____.

    A. there was no scientific evidence of the correlation between smoking and death

    B. the number of early deaths of smokers in the past decades was insignificant

    C. people had the freedom to choose their own way of life

    D. antismoking people were usually talking nonsense

27. According to Bruce Alberts, science can serve as _____.

    A. a protector   B. a judge   C. a critic   D. a guide

28. What does the author mean by "paralysis by analysis" (Last line, Paragraph 4)?

    A. Endless studies kill action.

    B. Careful investigation reveals truth.

    C. Prudent planning hinders progress.

    D. Extensive research helps decision-making.

29. According to the author, what should the Administration do about global warming?

    A. Offer aid to build cleaner power plants.

    B. Raise public awareness of conservation.

    C. Press for further scientific research.

    D. Take some legislative measures.

30. The author associates the issue of global warming with that of smoking because _____.

    A. they both suffered from the government's negligence

    B. a lesson from the latter is applicable to the former

    C. the outcome of the latter aggravates the former

    D. both of them have turned from bad to worse

Text 3

    Of all the components of a good night's sleep, dreams seem to be least within our control. In dreams, a window opens into a world where logic is suspended and dead people speak. A century ago, Freud formulated his revolutionary theory that dreams were the disguised shadows of our unconscious desires and fears; by the late 1970s, neurologists had switched to thinking of them as just "mental noise" — the random byproducts of the neural-repair work that goes on during sleep. Now researchers suspect that dreams are part of the mind's emotional thermostat, regulating moods while the brain is "off-line." And one leading authority says that these intensely powerful mental events can be not only harnessed but actually brought under conscious control, to help us sleep and feel better, "It's your dream," says Rosalind Cartwright, chair of psychology at Chicago's Medical Center. "If you don't like it, change it."

    Evidence from brain imaging supports this view. The brain is as active during REM (rapid eye movement) sleep — when most vivid dreams occur — as it is when fully awake, says Dr. Eric Nofzinger at the University of Pittsburgh. But not all parts of the brain are equally involved; the limbic system (the "emotional brain") is especially active, while the prefrontal cortex (the center of intellect and reasoning) is relatively quiet. "We wake up from dreams happy or depressed, and those feelings can stay with us all day." says Stanford sleep researcher Dr. William Dement.

    The link between dreams and emotions shows up among the patients in Cartwright's clinic. Most people seem to have more bad dreams early in the night, progressing toward happier ones before awakening, suggesting that they are working through negative feelings generated during the day. Because our conscious mind is occupied with daily life we don't always think about the emotional significance of the day's events — until, it appears, we begin to dream.

    And this process need not be left to the unconscious. Cartwright believes one can exercise conscious control over recurring bad dreams. As soon as you awaken, identify what is upsetting about the dream. Visualize how you would like it to end instead; the next time it occurs, try to wake up just enough to control its course. With much practice people can learn to, literally, do it in their sleep.

At the end of the day, there's probably little reason to pay attention to our dreams at all unless they keep us from sleeping or "we wake up in a panic," Cartwright says. Terrorism, economic uncertainties and general feelings of insecurity have increased people's anxiety. Those suffering from persistent nightmares should seek help from a therapist. For the rest of us, the brain has its ways of working through bad feelings. Sleep — or rather dream — on it and you'll feel better in the morning.

31. Researchers have come to believe that dreams _____.

    A. can be modified in their courses

    B. are susceptible to emotional changes

    C. reflect our innermost desires and fears

    D. are a random outcome of neural repairs

32. By referring to the limbic system, the author intends to show _____.

    A. its function in our dreams

    B. the mechanism of REM sleep

    C. the relation of dreams to emotions

    D. its difference from the prefrontal cortex

33. The negative feelings generated during the day tend to _____.

    A. aggravate in our unconscious mind

    B. develop into happy dreams

    C. persist till the time we fall asleep

    D. show up in dreams early at night

34. Cartwright seems to suggest that _____.

    A. waking up in time is essential to the ridding of bad dreams

    B. visualizing bad dreams helps bring them under control

    C. dreams should be left to their natural progression

    D. dreaming may not entirely belong to the unconscious

35. What advice might Cartwright give to those who sometimes have bad dreams?

    A. Lead your life as usual.   B. Seek professional help.

    C. Exercise conscious control.   D. Avoid anxiety in the daytime.

Text 4

Americans no longer expect public figures, whether in speech or in writing, to command the English language with skill and gift. Nor do they aspire to such command themselves. In his latest book, *Doing Our Own Thing: The Degradation of Language and Music and Why We Should, Like, Care*, John McWhorter, a linguist and controversialist of mixed liberal and conservative views, sees the triumph of 1960s counter-culture as responsible for the decline of formal English.

Blaming the permissive 1960s is nothing new, but this is not yet another criticism against the decline in education. Mr. McWhorter's academic speciality is language history and change, and he sees the gradual disappearance of "whom," for example, to be natural and no more regrettable than the loss of the case-endings of Old English.

But the cult of the authentic and the personal, "doing our own thing," has spelt the death of formal speech, writing, poetry and music. While even the modestly educated sought an elevated tone when they put pen to paper before the 1960s, even the most well regarded writing since then has sought to capture spoken English on the page. Equally, in poetry, the highly personal, performative genre is the only form that could claim real liveliness. In both oral and written English, talking is triumphing over speaking, spontaneity over craft.

Illustrated with an entertaining array of examples from both high and low culture, the trend that Mr. McWhorter documents is unmistakable. But it is less clear, to take the question of his subtitle, why we should, like, care. As a linguist, he acknowledges that all varieties of human language, including non-standard ones like Black English, can be powerfully expressive — there exists no language or dialect in the world that cannot convey complex ideas. He is not arguing, as many do, that we can no longer think straight because we do not talk proper.

Russians have a deep love for their own language and carry large chunks of memorized poetry in their heads, while Italian politicians tend to elaborate speech that would seem old-fashioned to most English-speakers. Mr. McWhorter acknowledges that formal language is not strictly necessary, and proposes no radical education reforms — he is really grieving over the loss of something beautiful more than useful. We now take our English "on paper plates instead of china." A shame, perhaps, but probably an inevitable one.

36. According to McWhorter, the decline of formal English _____.

    A. is inevitable in radical education reforms

    B. is but all too natural in language development

    C. has caused the controversy over the counter-culture

    D. brought about changes in public attitudes in the 1960s

37. The word "talking" (Line 6, Paragraph 3) denotes _____.

    A. modesty   B. personality

    C. liveliness   D. informality

38. To which of the following statements would McWhorter most likely agree?

    A. Logical thinking is not necessarily related to the way we talk.

    B. Black English can be more expressive than standard English.

    C. Non-standard varieties of human language are just as entertaining.

    D. Of all the varieties, standard English can best convey complex ideas.

39. The description of Russians' love of memorizing poetry shows the author's _____.

    A. interest in their language

    B. appreciation of their efforts

    C. admiration for their memory

    D. contempt for their old-fashionedness

40. According to the last paragraph, "paper plates" is to "china" as _____.

    A. "temporary" is to "permanent"

    B. "radical" is to "conservative"

    C. "functional" is to "artistic"

    D. "humble" is to "noble"

Part B

Directions:

*In the following text, some sentences have been removed. For Questions 41—45, choose the most suitable one from the list A—G to fit into each of the numbered blanks. There are two extra choices, which do not fit in any of the gaps. Mark your answers on **ANSWER SHEET 1**.*

Canada's premiers (the leaders of provincial governments), if they have any breath left after complaining about Ottawa at their late July annual meeting, might spare a moment to do something, together, to reduce health-care costs.

They're all groaning about soaring health budgets, the fastest-growing component of which are pharmaceutical costs.

41. _____

What to do? Both the Romanow commission and the Kirby committee on health care — to say nothing of reports from other experts — recommended the creation of a national drug agency. Instead of each province having its own list of approved drugs, bureaucracy, procedures and limited bargaining power, all would pool resources, work with Ottawa, and create a national institution.

42. _____

But "national" doesn't have to mean that. "National" could mean interprovincial — provinces combining efforts to create one body.

Either way, one benefit of a "national" organization would be to negotiate better prices, if possible, with drug manufacturers. Instead of having one province — or a series of hospitals within a province — negotiate a price for a given drug on the provincial list, the national agency would negotiate on behalf of all provinces.

Rather than, say, Quebec, negotiating on behalf of seven million people, the national agency would negotiate on behalf of 31 million people. Basic economics suggests the greater the potential consumers, the higher the likelihood of a better price.

43. _____

A small step has been taken in the direction of a national agency with the creation of the Canadian Co-ordinating Office for Health Technology Assessment, funded by Ottawa and the provinces. Under it, a Common Drug Review recommends to provincial lists which new drugs should be included. Predictably, and regrettably, Quebec refused to join.

A few premiers are suspicious of any federal-provincial deal-making. They (particularly Quebec and Alberta) just want Ottawa to fork over additional billions with few, if any, strings attached. That's one reason why the idea of a national list hasn't gone anywhere, while drug costs keep rising fast.

44. _____

Premiers love to quote Mr. Romanow's report selectively, especially the parts about more federal money. Perhaps they should read what he had to say about drugs: "A national drug agency would provide governments more influence on pharmaceutical companies in order to constrain the ever-increasing cost of drugs."

45. _____

So when the premiers gather in Niagara Falls to assemble their usual complaint list, they should also get cracking about something in their jurisdiction that would help their budgets and patients.

[A] Quebec's resistance to a national agency is provincialist ideology. One of the first advocates for a national list was a researcher at Laval University. Quebec's Drug Insurance Fund has seen its costs skyrocket with annual increases from 14.3 percent to 26.8 percent!

[B] Or they could read Mr. Kirby's report: "the substantial buying power of such an agency would strengthen the public prescription-drug insurance plans to negotiate the lowest possible purchase prices from drug companies."

[C] What does "national" mean? Roy Romanow and Senator Michael Kirby recommended a federal-provincial body much like the recently created National Health Council.

[D] The problem is simple and stark: health-care costs have been, are, and will continue to increase faster than government revenues.

[E] According to the Canadian Institute for Health Information, prescription drug costs have risen since 1997 at twice the rate of overall health-care spending. Part of the increase comes from drugs being used to replace other kinds of treatments. Part of it arises from new drugs costing more than older kinds. Part of it is higher prices.

[F] So, if the provinces want to run the health-care show, they should prove they can run it, starting with an interprovincial health list that would end duplication, save administrative costs, prevent one province from being played off against another, and bargain for better drug prices.

[G] Of course, the pharmaceutical companies will scream. They like divided buyers; they can lobby better that way. They can use the threat of removing jobs from one province to another. They can hope that, if one province includes a drug on its list, the pressure will cause others to include it on theirs. They wouldn't like a national agency, but self-interest would lead them to deal with it.

Part C

Directions:

Read the following text carefully and then translate the underlined segments into Chinese. Your translation should be written clearly on ANSWER SHEET 2.

It is not easy to talk about the role of the mass media in this overwhelmingly significant phase in European history. History and news become confused, and one's impressions tend to be a mixture of skepticism and optimism. (46) Television is one of the means by which these feelings are created and conveyed — and perhaps never before has it served so much to connect different peoples and nations as in the recent events in Europe. The Europe that is now forming cannot be anything other than its peoples, their cultures and national identities. With this in mind we can begin to analyze the European television scene. (47) In Europe, as elsewhere, multi-media groups have been increasingly successful: groups which bring together television, radio, newspapers, magazines and publishing houses that work in relation to one another. One Italian example would be the Berlusconi group, while abroad Maxwell and Murdoch come to mind.

Clearly, only the biggest and most flexible television companies are going to be able to compete in such a rich and hotly-contested market. (48) This alone demonstrates that the television business is not an easy world to survive in, a fact underlined by statistics that show that out of eighty European television networks, no less than 50% took a loss in 1989.

Moreover, the integration of the European community will oblige television companies to cooperate more closely in terms of both production and distribution.

(49) Creating a "European identity" that respects the different cultures and traditions which go to make up the connecting fabric of the Old Continent is no easy task and demands a strategic choice — that of producing programs in Europe for Europe. This entails reducing our dependence on the North American market, whose programs relate to experiences and cultural traditions which are different from our own.

In order to achieve these objectives, we must concentrate more on co-productions, the exchange of news, documentary services and training. This also involves the agreements between European countries for the creation of a European bank for Television Production which, on the model of the European Investments Bank, will handle the finances necessary for production costs. (50) In dealing with a challenge on such a scale, it is no exaggeration to say "United we stand, divided we fall" — and if I had to choose a slogan it would be "Unity in our diversity". A unity of objectives that nonetheless respect the varied peculiarities of each country.

2005年考研英语全真试题
（阅读理解部分）解析

Part A

Text 1

长难句分析

1. However, when two monkeys were placed in separate but adjoining chambers, so that each could observe what the other was getting in return for its rock, their behaviour became markedly different.

❖ **结构分析** when 引导的时间状语从句中的主干是 Two monkeys were placed in separate but adjoining chambers.后面是 so that 引导的一个目的状语从句：so that each could observe,接着是 what 引导的一个宾语从句：what the other was getting in return for its rock。

2. However, whether such a sense of fairness evolved independently in capuchins and humans, or whether it stems from the common ancestor that the species had 35 million years ago, is, as yet, an unanswered question.

❖ **结构分析** 句子主干为 Whether... or whether... is an unanswered question. such a sense of fairness evolved independently in capuchins and humans 中 evolve 是谓语,意为"进化"。... it stems from the common ancestor that 中 it 指的是 a sense of fairness。the species 指的是 capuchins and humans。

试 题 分 析

21. [C] 结构题。文章主要内容是讲僧帽猴也有情绪问题,第一段开始却先从人类说起,然后又过渡到文章主旨,是拿人的行为和猴子的行为做比较,答案是C"进行比较"。在解题时,要逐一进行对比和排除。B"验证假设"和D"解释现象"显然和作者的举例方法不符,可排除。A 和 C 关键是要理解 contrast 和 comparison 这两个词的区别,汉语中都可被译成"对比",但意思却不同。contrast 含有强调所对比之物之间的差异,即是说用这个词来表示两件事情的不同。而 comparison 则有"比喻,对比"的含义。

22. [B] 词义题。all too monkey 是对应于 all too human 而言的。人对不公的愤怒是普遍现象,all too human 指的就是"人之常情"。而研究发现,猴子也有类似的情感,对不公平现象的憎恶是"猴之常情"。因此,答案应该是 B"憎恶不公也是猴子的天性";A"猴子也会被懒散的对手激怒"只是不公平的一个例子;C"像人类一样,猴子也往往会相互嫉妒"和文章讨论的主旨无关,文章谈论的不是嫉妒;D"除了猴子,其他动物都不能进化出这样的情感"文章没有提到。

23. [A] 细节题。第二段说雌性棕僧帽猴看起来很聪明,它们性情温顺,善于合作,并且乐于与同伴分享食物,更重要的是它们比雄性更关心"商品和服务"的价值。可见 A"更倾向于权衡它们所得到的东西"为最佳答案,我们要注意题中的"above all"的意思是"最重要的,首要的"。

24. [C] 细节题。布罗斯南和德瓦尔博士最终在他们的研究中发现,猴子会怎么样。A"更喜欢葡萄而不是黄瓜"可排除,第四段第一句话说明它不是布罗斯南进行实验的结果;B"能被教会交换东西"也可排除,因为这不是实验的目的;D 没有被提到。答案是 C"如果感觉被欺骗就会拒绝合作",最后一段明确说,在动物没有感觉上当受骗时,它们之间的协作关系才可能稳定。

25. [B] 推断题。最后一段说,僧帽猴同人类一样,受社会情感的引导。人和猴子都有公平感,目前还不清楚, 这种公平感是人类和僧帽猴各自独立进化而来的, 还是来自二者 3,500 万年前共同的祖先。因此,答案是 B"人类表示愤慨的感情来源不确定"。

参考译文

每个人都喜欢薪水大幅增长。然而在得知一位同事的的薪水比你加得更多时,你的喜悦感就会消失。确实,如果他有工作松弛的坏名声,你甚至会感到愤怒。这样的行为被当做是"人之常情",其潜台词就是其他动物没有这种发展完善的感情能力。但是佐治亚州亚特兰大埃默里大学的萨拉·布罗斯南和弗兰斯·德瓦尔的研究表明,猴子也有类似的情感表达!他们的研究刚刚在《自然》杂志上发表。

他们对雌性棕僧帽猴的行为进行了研究。这些猴子看起来很聪明,它们性情温顺,善于合作,并且乐于与同伴分享食物。更重要的是,就像是人类女性一样,它们比雄性更关心"商品和服务"的价值。

这些特性使它们成为布罗斯南和德瓦尔博士最完美的研究对象。他们用了两年的时间教这些猴子用代币交换食物。通常情况下,这些猴子很乐意用石块换黄瓜片。但是,当两只猴子被放置进分离但相邻的房间时,因为它们能看到对方用石块换到的是什么,它们的行为会变得不同往常。

在僧帽猴的世界中,葡萄是奢侈品(比黄瓜受欢迎得多)。因此当一只猴子用代币换来葡萄时,另外一只猴子就不乐意用代币换来黄瓜。如果一只猴子没有用代币就得到一颗葡萄的话,另外一只要么就代币扔向研究者或扔出房间,或者拒绝接受黄瓜片。事实上,只要另一个房间里出现了葡萄(实际上没有猴子去吃它),就足以引起雌性僧帽猴的不满。

两位研究者指出,僧帽猴同人类一样,受社会情感的引导。在野生世界,它们是相互协作、群居的物种。当所有动物都没有感觉上当受骗时，它们之间的协作关系才可能稳定。因正当理由而愤怒似乎并不是人类所独有的情感。拒绝较少的回报使这些情感能明白无误地传达给同伴。<u>然而，这种公平感是人类和僧帽猴各自独立进化而来的，还是来自二者3,500万前共同的祖先，还是一个尚未解决的问题。</u>

Text 2

长难句分析

1. **The latest was a panel from the National Academy of Sciences, enlisted by the White House, to tell us that the Earth's atmosphere is definitely warming and that the problem is largely man-made.**

   ❖ 结构分析 主句中panel指的是由科学家组成的专门小组，或称专家团，后面的enlisted是过去分词作定语，意为"由白宫召集的专家团"。to tell us that 是目的状语，后面是由that... and that 引导的两个宾语从句。

2. **But science does provide us with the best available guide to the future, and it is critical that our nation and the world base important policies on the best judgments that science can provide concerning the future consequences of present actions.**

   ❖ 结构分析 本句包括由and连接的两个并列句，第一个句子science does provide us with the best available guide to the future 中does表示强调，意为"确实"，and it is critical that 后面是表语从句，从句主干为 the world base important policies on the best judgments，其中base... on 意为"把…建立在…基础上"。后面的that can science can provide 和 concerning the future consequences of present actions 都修饰 the best judgments，即"科学所能提供的最佳判断"与"现在行为会对将来产生什么后果的最佳判断"。

试题分析

26. **[C]** 细节题。第一段用了几个反问句来表达作者的观点，科学家们说吸烟会导致死亡时，他们认为证据不够确凿。反对吸烟的游说团是在破坏我们的生活方式，很多美国人都接受了这一无稽之谈。因此答案应该为C"人们有权选择自己的生活方式"；A"没有科学证据表明吸烟与死亡之间的联系"之所以不对是因为原文用的是 the evidence was inconclusive，证据不足而不是没有证据；D"反对吸烟的人是在胡说八道"错误理解了nonsense的语境，是作者认为那些支持者的争论是胡说八道；B"过去几十年因吸烟而导致的早亡并不显著"和一千万人死于吸烟显然不符。

27. **[D]** 细节题。第二段中提到 science does provide us with the best available guide to the future，参考长难句分析2。答案为D"引导者"。

28. **[A]** 词义猜测题。第四段提到白宫已开始关注环境问题，但是大多数的总统顾问们仍然还没把全球变暖当回事儿。他们没有提出行动计划，而是要求继续研究——这是"分析导致瘫痪"的典型案例。关键词就是 research 和 action,所以 paralysis by analysis 的意思应该是 A"没完没了的研究会毁掉行动"。

29. [D] 细节题。作者坦白地说,仅有研究是不够的。所以 A"给建设更清洁的电厂提供援助"不正确,因为作者说很多国家正在准备建造新的发电厂以满足我们的能源需要,但关键的一点就是这些发电厂对环境无害,这仅是其中一个例子;B"唤起公众的保护意识"没有被提到;C"要求更进一步进行科学研究"不对;作者说,如果行政部门没有首先提出法案,议会应当实施环境保护措施。因此,答案应该为 D"采取立法措施"。

30. [B] 结构题。作者在一开始提出吸烟问题,是以此为例,引出下面要谈的全球变暖问题,因此二者之间的联系仅在于吸烟问题与环境问题二者所遭受到的共同境遇,至于这两者之间是否存在什么因果联系,作者并没有说。因此 C"后者产生的后果加重了前者"可排除;A 和 D 也不正确,因为其内容和文章基本上没有关系;从文章结构上来看,作者把全球变暖问题和吸烟联系起来,是让人从对待吸烟这个事情上得到的教训引出我们现在就该重视环境问题的话题。故答案为 B"从后者得到的教训也适用于前者"。

参考译文

你是否还记得,当科学家们说吸烟会导致死亡时,怀疑者坚持认为我们并不能确信这种观点?难道证据不够确凿,科学也靠不住?反对吸烟的游说团是在破坏我们的生活方式,政府应该站在一边不应干涉?很多美国人都接受了这一无稽之谈。在过去的 30 年中,大概有一千万烟民早逝。

现在也有让人不安的类似事件发生。科学家们一次又一次地努力使我们明白全球变暖所带来的威胁日益增加。最近,白宫召集了一批来自国家科学院的专家团,他们认为地球的大气层毫无疑问地在变暖,人为因素是其主要原因。很明确的信息是,我们是时候行动起来保护自己了。国家科学院院长布鲁斯·艾伯茨在报告的前言中表达了一个重要观点,他说:"科学无法回答所有问题。但是科学确实给我们提供了面对未来时最好的指导,并且我们的国家和全世界应该把重要政策的制订建立在科学所能提供的最佳判断之上,即我们目前的行为对将来会产生什么后果。这一点至关重要。"

就像对待吸烟的问题一样,现在有来自各方面的声音,他们坚持认为关于全球变暖的科学是不完善的,在这个问题确定之前,我们可以继续把废气排到大气中。这真是个危险的游戏:等到有了百分之百的证据时就已经太晚了。风险很明显并且越来越大,一个谨慎的人现在就应该为此而购买保险了。

幸运的是,白宫已开始关注这一问题。但显然,大多数的总统顾问们仍然还没把全球变暖当回事儿。他们没有提出行动计划,而是要求继续研究——这是"分析导致瘫痪"的典型案例。

作为地球上的管理员,我们应该奋力向前,对大气和海洋进行更深入的研究。但是仅有研究是不够的。如果行政部门没有首先提出法案,议会应当实施环境保护措施。来自弗吉尼亚的民主党参议员罗伯特·伯德提出议案,要求在财政上鼓励私人企业保护环境,这是一个良好的开端。很多人看到,我们的国家正在准备建造新的发电厂以满足我们的能源需要。如果我们要保护大气层,关键的一点就是这些发电厂对环境无害。

Text 3

长难句分析

1. And one leading authority says that these intensely powerful mental events can be not only harnessed but actually brought under conscious control, to help us sleep and feel better, "It's your dream," says Rosalind Cartwright, chair of psychology at Chicago's Medical Center. "If you don't like it, change it."

❖ **结构分析** one leading authority says that 后的宾语从句中用了 not only... but (also)句式,意为"既能被控制,实际上也能被意识支配。"to help 是不定式表示目的。我们在实际阅读中,人名及其头衔可以先略过。所以句子看起来很长,把用处不大的信息去掉,就简单多了。

2. Most people seem to have more bad dreams early in the night, progressing toward happier ones before awakening, suggesting that they are working through negative feelings generated during the day.

❖ **结构分析** progressing toward 是非谓语动词作伴随状语,其逻辑主语为 most people, suggesting 也是状语,意为"上面的情况说明…"。其后是一个 that 引导的宾语从句。generated during the day 也是一个非谓语动词短语,修饰 feelings。

试题分析

31. [A] 细节题。 第一段说一个世纪以前,弗洛伊德发表了他革命性的理论,即梦是潜意识中欲望和恐惧的伪装表现。可见 C"反映了我们内心的愿望和恐惧"是弗洛伊德的观点,而不是现在的看法;作者接着说,到 20 世纪 70 年代后期神经学家则认为,梦是"精神噪音",是在我们睡眠时进行的神经修复工作随机产生的副产品。D"是神经修复的随机产物"也可排除,因为这也不是现在的看法;文中提到"现在研究者怀疑,梦是我们大脑的情绪自动调节器的一部分,当大脑'下线'时帮助我们调节情绪。"可见 B"对感情变化很敏感"也不正确,梦是调节情绪而不是被情绪所控制;根据"这些强烈的大脑运动不仅能被控制,实际上还能被意识所支配。"可知答案为 A"在其过程中能被改变"。

32. [C] 结构题。"脑边缘系统"一词出现在第二段,是在解释睡眠的 REM(眼球快速转动)阶段。作者说,并不是大脑的所有部分都处于同样状态;脑边缘系统(大脑控制感情的部分)尤其活跃,而前额皮层(大脑中思维和推理的中心)则相对平静。因此答案应为 C "梦与情感的关系"。作者没有对它和前额皮层进行对比的意思,而旨在说明在 REM 阶段大脑各部分活动的情况不同。

33. [D] 细节题。第三段说在卡特赖特诊所就医的病人身上可以看到梦与情感之间的联系。多数人似乎在晚上早些时候会有更多噩梦,在睡醒之前会逐渐转向美梦,这表明他们在消除白天某些负面情绪。所以在白天所产生的负面情绪经常在晚上早些时候出现在梦里,答案应为 D。

34. [D] 推断题。卡特赖特认为人可以用意识对反复出现的噩梦进行控制。想象如何做才会使这种不安终止;如果再次出现时,努力醒来就能控制梦的进程。通过练习人们可以学会直接在睡眠中控制梦。因此,答案应为 D"梦也许不完全属于无意识";A"及时醒来对消除噩梦是必要的"不对,因为文章只说醒来可控制梦的进程而没有说它对消除噩梦的作用;B"想象噩梦有助于控制它们"曲解了文章的意思,不是让人想象噩梦,而是想那些使我们不安的东西;C"应该让梦自然进展"和文章意思相反。

35. [A] 推断题。最后一段说,那些深受噩梦折磨的人应该向医生求助。对其他人来说,大脑有其自己对付不良情绪的方法。可见答案应该为 A"像平时一样生活",而不是 B"向专业人士求助",这里最重要的就是要分清题干中所用的词 sometimes 与文章中使用的 persistent(持久,稳固的)之间在程度上的重大区别,不然会误选 B。

参考译文

在良好睡眠的所有要素中,梦好像是最不能人为控制的。梦为我们打开了一扇通往另一个世界的窗口,在那里没有逻辑,死者也开口说话。一个世纪以前,弗洛伊德发表了他具有革命性的理论,即梦是潜意识中欲望和恐惧的伪装表现。到 20 世纪 70 年代后期,神经学家则认为,梦只是"精神噪音"——是在我们睡眠时进行的神经修复工作随机产生的副产品。现在研究者怀疑,梦是我们大脑的情绪自动调节器的一部分,当大脑"下线"时帮助我们调节情绪。有一位权威人士说,这些强烈的大脑运动不仅能被控制,实际上还能被意识所支配,帮助我们睡得更好,感觉更棒。芝加哥医疗中心心理学部主任罗莎琳德·卡特赖特说:"这就是你的梦。如果你不喜欢,就改变它。"

来自大脑图像的证据支持这种观点。匹兹堡大学的埃里克·诺夫辛格博士说,在 REM(眼球快速转动)阶段——最生动的梦发生时——大脑活动和我们完全清醒时一样。但并不是大脑的所有部分都处于同样状态;脑边缘系统(大脑控制感情的部分)尤其活跃,而前额皮层(大脑中思维和推理的中心)则相对平静。斯坦福大学睡眠研究人员威廉·德门特博士说,"我们从梦中醒来,感到高兴或沮丧,这些感觉会伴随我们一整天。"

在卡特赖特诊所就医的病人身上可以看到梦与情感之间的联系。多数人似乎在晚上早些时候会有更多噩梦,在睡醒之前会逐渐转向美梦,这表明他们在消除白天某些负面情绪。因为我们有意识的思绪被白天的生活所占据,所以我们不会老是想着白天所发生的事件对情绪的影响,直到我们开始做梦,看起来事情就是这样的。

这一过程不会留给无意识去完成。卡特赖特认为,人可以用意识对反复出现的噩梦进行控制。你一醒来就要辨别是什么使你在梦里感到不安。想象你如何做才会使这种不安终止;如果再次出现时,努力醒来就能控制梦的进程。通过练习人们会学会直接在睡眠中控制梦。

一天结束的时候,也许没有多少理由让我们关注梦,除非它们使我们睡不着或"在苦痛中醒来"卡特赖特如是说。恐怖主义、经济不稳定和没有安全感增加了人们的焦虑。那些深受噩梦折磨的人应该向医生求助。对其他人来说,大脑有其自己对付不良情绪的方法。带着这样的想法睡吧——甚至梦吧——你会在早晨醒来时感觉好多了。

Text 4

长难句分析

1. In his latest book, *Doing Our Own Thing: The Degradation of Language and Music and Why We Should, Like, Care,* John McWhorter, a linguist and controversialist of mixed liberal and conservative views, sees the triumph of 1960s counter-culture as responsible for the decline of formal English.

❖**结构分析** 句子主干为 John McWhorter sees the triumph of 1960s counterculture as responsible for the decline of formal English. 其他成分大多是在对约翰·麦克沃特进行介绍,在实际阅读中可以先忽略。

2. As a linguist, he acknowledges that all varieties of human language, including non-standard ones like Black English, can be powerfully expressive — there exists no language or dialect in the world that cannot convey complex ideas.

❖**结构分析** 句子主干为 He acknowledges that all varieties of human language can be powerfully expressive. 破折号后的部分 there exists no language or dialect in the world 是主句,后面是一个修饰 language or dialect 的定语从句。

试 题 分 析

36. [B] 细节题。我们可以根据文章内容逐一进行对比和排除。第一段最后一句话说,他认为反文化的胜利应该对正式英语的衰落负责而没有说反文化因此而引起争议,故 C "引起了对反文化的争议"是不正确的;麦克沃特认为像 whom 这样词的逐步消失是自然的,并不比古英语中尾格的消失更让人感到遗憾。因此答案 B"在语言进化过程中是很自然的"是正确的;文章没有谈到教育改革和正式英语衰落的关系,因此不选 A"在激进的教育改革中是不可避免的";D"在 20 世纪 60 年代带来了公众态度的变化"也是倒因为果,不是因为正式英语的衰落带来了公众态度的变化,而是"对真实和个人感情的崇拜,'做你自己的事',导致了正式演讲、写作、诗歌和音乐的死亡。"

37. [D] 词义猜测题。作者说,在 20 世纪 60 年代以前,那些受过不多教育的人也尽力使用优雅的修辞,但从那以后,即使是被认为是最好的文章也力图在写作中运用口语。接下来说,in both oral and written English, talking is triumphing over speaking, spontaneity over craft。可见,talk 和 speak 分别代表口语和优雅的词汇。答案为 D"不正式的"。

38. [A] 推断题。文章最后说,包括像黑人英语这样不标准的语言在内的各种人类语言都是强有力的表达工具——世界上没有哪种语言或方言不能表达出复杂的观点。麦克沃特并不像其他人那样认为,因为我们不能恰当地说话,所以我们不能有条理地思考。由此可知,A"逻辑思维与我们谈话的方式没有必然联系"是正确的;B"黑人英语比正规英语表达力更强"与 D"标准英语是所有语言中最能表达复杂思想"和上面的说法相矛盾;C 没有被提到。

39. [B] 推断题。作者说,俄罗斯人深爱着他们自己的语言,并且能记住大段的诗句,而意大利的政治家们则喜欢在演讲时使用对多数英语使用者来说过时的语言。麦克沃特承认正式语言并非一定必要,他是为某种美丽的而不是有用的东西的消失感到难过。由此可推论,作者是在为自己语言的遭遇感到遗憾,从而欣赏他们的努力,B 与此相符;因此他不可能是轻视俄国人的守旧,D 排除;A"对俄语感兴趣"也不可能,因为作者举俄罗斯和意大利为例与对他们的语言感兴趣与否无关;C 提到的记忆力和文章无关。

40. [C] 词义猜测题。可参考对 37 题的解析。答案为 C"功能的与艺术的",这里仍然是正式语言与非正式语言的对比。正式语言就像是写在瓷器上的,有艺术功能,而日常语言则只具有实用功能,像纸盘子一样。这里 D"低俗的与高雅的"选项有一定的迷惑性,但作者没有认为日常语言是"低俗的",只是从语言发展的角度来谈论正式英语的衰落。

参考译文

美国人不再期望公众人物在讲演或文章中能熟练而有天赋地使用英语。他们自己也不再热望能这样掌握英语。语言学家约翰·麦克沃特是一个兼有自由和保守观点的辩论家。在他最近出版的《做我们自己的事:语言和音乐能力的退化及其被关注的原因》一书中,他认为二十世纪 60 年代反文化运动的胜利应该对正式英语的衰落负责。

谴责过于宽容的 20 世纪 60 年代不是什么新鲜事儿,但这不是对教育水平下滑的另一种批评。麦克沃特先生的专业是语言史和语言演变,他认为像"whom"这样词的逐步消失是自然的,并不比古英语中尾格的消失更让人感到遗憾。

但是对真实和个人感情的崇拜,"做你自己的事",导致了正式演讲、写作、诗歌和音乐的死亡。在 20 世纪 60 年代以前,甚至那些受过不多教育的人也在他们书写时追求尽力使用优雅的修辞,但从那以后,即使是被认为是最好的文章也力图在写作中运用口语。同样地,在诗歌中只有那种高度个人化、具有述行性的流派才是唯一有活力的形式。无论是在口头还是书面英语中,说话胜过演讲,自发性胜过艺术性。

从高雅文化和低俗文化中得来的一系列有趣的例子可以说明麦克沃特所证明的趋势并没有错。但是并不太清楚的是,以他的副标题为例,我们为什么要关注这件事。作为一位语言学家,他承认包括像黑人英语这样不标准的语言在内的各种人类语言都是强有力的表达工具——世界上没有哪种语言或方言不能表达出复杂的观点。他并不像其他人那样认为,因为我们不能恰当地说话,所以我们不能有条理地思考。

俄罗斯人深爱他们自己的语言，并且能记住大段的诗句，而意大利的政治家们则喜欢在演讲时使用对多数英语使用者来说过时的语言。麦克沃特承认正式语言并非一定必要，也没有提出激进的教育改革方案——他是为某种美丽的而不是有用的东西的消失感到难过。现在我们把英语看成是写在"纸上的而不是瓷器上的"。这也许是一种遗憾，但却更可能无法避免。

Part B

试题分析

41. [E] 解题的关键在于对文章的结构进行逻辑分析，主要考查对语篇的把握能力。41 题出现在前两段之后，从文章结构来看，第一段无非是引子，重点不在于加拿大的那些官员们而在于医疗费用。第二段特别提到了医药费用的增长，而第四段仍然是讲药物的问题，可以判断，41 题所选内容应该和"药费"有关，因此答案应该为 E，与第二、四段都有逻辑关系。

42. [C] 这道题比较容易选择，从结构上来看是承接上文的"national"一词而来的。但是，应该注意的是这样明显的答案也许会是一个陷阱，因此仍要注意下文中的内容是否与此有衔接，第六段又提到"national"一词，并对此做了进一步的解释，因此可以确定 C 无误。注意，选项与上下文之间的逻辑关系是解题的关键。

43. [G] 此题难度较大，原因就在于很难一眼就看出选项与上下文之间的逻辑关系。在这一题之前，文章所谈论的是药费问题及解决问题的设想。成立国家级的委员会，作者说，这样可为消费者争取更合理的价格。根据上下文，可能的答案是 A 和 G。A 之所以可能是因为提到了魁北克，仿佛是承接上文，但仔细阅读会发现如果 A 的话，应该放在下一段之后，因为下一段作者说"遗憾的是魁北克可能会拒绝加入"，A 再解释为什么会这样。G 实际上是一个转折，说的是药品商的态度，同时也在解释为什么全国性机构更能为患者带来好处。

44. [F] 文章第十、十一段说，尽管由渥太华和各省出资建立的加拿大医疗技术评估联合协作办事处使人们向建立国家级代理机构的方向迈出一小步，但是有些省长对联邦与各省之间的协作感到怀疑。魁北克等省只是想让加拿大政府额外支付金钱，这是没办法建立国家级机构而同时又使药物价格飞涨的原因。F 就是对这一现象的说明。

45. [B] 这里其实是一个转折。作者在第十三段说，省长们喜欢引用罗曼诺的报告，尤其是有关联邦应该提供更多资金支持的那一部分。作者建议他们读关于国家代理机构的部分，或者科尔比的报告。他引用的这两部分都是为了支持自己的论点：国家级代理机构有利于降低药价，这也是作者最终所要表达的意思。

参考译文

如果加拿大的省长们在 7 月底的年会上抱怨过政府之后还有什么精力的话，他们也许会花点时间去做点事情,一起行动,降低一下医疗费用。

他们都对医疗预算的大幅增长怒气冲天,其中增长最快的是药物的费用。

41. 根据加拿大医疗信息研究所的数据,自从1997年以来的增长处方药的费用是整个医疗费用涨幅的两倍。增长的费用部分源于那些被用来代替其他治疗方法的药物,部分是因为新药物的花费比其他原来使用的药物要高,也有一部分源自价格的提高。

该怎么办呢?罗曼诺和科尔比这两个医疗委员会都推荐建立一个国家级的药物管理机构。不让各省有独立的批准药物清单、官僚机构、管理程序和有限的讨价还价能力,各省都要集中资源同政府合作,从而建立一个国家级的机构。

42. "国家级"的意味着什么呢?罗伊·罗曼诺和迈克尔·科尔比议员都建议成立一个像最近成立的国家卫生委员会那样的联邦和地方政府的协作机构。

但是"国家级"并不是那种意思。"国家级"可能指的是省际间的——各省共同努力创建一个机构。

无论是哪种方法,一个"国家级"的机构所带来的好处将会是跟药品制造商进行协商,如果可能的话可以降低药价。不是要一个省,或者一个省内的各家医院,为了省里清单上的特定药品而和制造商进行价格谈判,而是用国家级代理机构代表所有省份去和他们谈判。

比如,不是让魁北克为了其七百万人而去谈判,国家级的代理机构将会代表三千一百万人的利益。基础经济学表明,潜在消费者的数量越多,获得更合理价格的可能性就会越大。

43. 当然,医药公司也会对此大声尖叫。他们喜欢被分割开的顾客,这样他们就可以方便地游说。他们可能威胁把工作从一个省转移到另一个省。他们希望如此,如果一个省把某种药物列入自己的清单,会迫使其他省也把它列进去。他们不喜欢国家级的管理机构,但是为了私利他们将与这些机构打交道。

由渥太华和各省出资建立的加拿大医疗技术评估联合协作办事处使人们向建立国家级代理机构的方向迈出一小步。在其下,一个公共药品评估委员会建议各省所列的清单里应该包括一些新药。可以预测,但很让人遗憾,魁北克省会拒绝加入。

一些省长对任何联邦与地方政府之间的协作而进行的交易表示怀疑。他们(尤其是魁北克和阿尔伯达两个省的省长) 只是想让加拿大政府额外支付几十亿美元而没有多少附带条件。这也是为什么确定全国性清单的想法至今无法得到普遍认可,而同时药物价格又飞涨的原因。

44. 因此,如果各省想要对整个医疗事务负责,它们应该证明自己有能力做到这一点,开始制订省际间的药品清单,既可以杜绝重复,又可以节约管理成本,预防省与省之间的勾心斗角,并能够为得到更合理的药价而进行讨价还价。

省长们喜欢有选择地引用罗曼诺的报告,尤其是有关联邦应该提供更多资金支持的那一部分。也许他们应该读一读他关于药品所说的话:"国家级代理机构将会使政府能会药品公司产生更大的影响,目的是限制药品花费的不断增长。"

45. 或者他们应该读一下科尔比的报告:"这样一个代理机构的实际购买能力会加强公众处方药保险计划,以便在同医药公司的谈判中获得最低价格的药品。"

因此,当省长们聚集在尼亚加拉大瀑布开会并像通常那样对清单进行抱怨时,他们应该也开始利用自己的权限做点对预算和病人有利的事情。

Part C

试题分析

46. **全句译文**：电视是激发与传递感情的手段之一。也许在最近欧洲发生的事件中,就加强不同的民族和国家之间的联系而言,电视还从来没有起到如此巨大的作用。

翻译提示：这是由 and 连接的两个并列句。第一个句子中的 means 意为"工具或者手段",后面的 by which 是定语从句,which 代表 means,从句意为"通过这种手段/方式情感被创造和传递"。and 后的句子由 never before 在句首,句子要倒装,正常语序为 it has never served so much...

47. **全句译文**：在欧洲,就像在任何地方,多媒体集团变得越来越成功。这些集团把密切相关的电视台、电台、报纸、杂志、出版社整合到了一起。

翻译提示：句子主干为 Multi-media groups have been increasingly successful.后面的句子成分是对这种情况的说明。increasingly 作副词,意为"逐渐地,越来越…"。in relation to 意为"与…相关"。

48. **全句译文**：仅这一点就足以表明电视行业并不是一个容易生存的领域。这个事实通过统计数字可以一目了然,统计表明 80 家欧洲电视网中在 1989 年出现亏损的不低于 50%。

翻译提示：第一个 that 后面接的是宾语从句 the television business is not...。a fact 是前面句子的同位语,underlined 是过去分词作定语,修饰 fact。

49. **全句译文**：创造一个尊重不同文化和传统的"欧洲身份"绝非易事,需要战略性选择,这些文化与传统组成了连接老欧洲的纽带。

翻译提示：Creating an European identity 作主语,that 引导定语从句修饰它。which 引导的从句修饰 cultures and traditions,于是主句就是 Creating a "European identity" is no easy task and demands a strategic choice.

50. **全句译文**：在应付一个如此规模的挑战的过程中,我们可以毫不夸张地说,"合即立,分即垮",如果我们一定要选择一个标语的话,那就是"分中有合"。

翻译提示：In dealing with a challenge... 部分作状语。it is no exaggeration to say 是一个固定用法,意为"我们可以毫不夸张地说"。United we stand, divided we fall.是句名言。

参考译文

　　在欧洲历史的这段关键时期去谈论大众媒体的角色,并非易事。历史与新闻相互混合,我们对此的反应则是怀疑与乐观的混合。(46)电视是激发与传递感情的手段之一。也许在最近欧洲发生的事件中,就加强不同的民族和国家之间的联系而言,电视还从来没有起到如此巨大的作用。正在成形中的欧洲就是其各个民族,各个文化以及民族身份的总和。记住这一点,我们就可以开始分析欧洲的电视场景。(47)在欧洲,就像在任何地方,多媒体集团变得越来越成功。这些集团把密切相关的电视台、电台、报纸、杂志、出版社整合到了一起。我们意大利的例子就是贝卢斯科尼团队,国外的例子就是麦克斯韦尔和默多克了。

很显然,只有最大的、最灵活的电视公司才有能力在这样一个繁荣且充满竞争力的市场中进行竞争。(48)仅这一点就足以表明电视行业并不是一个容易生存的领域。这个事实通过统计数字可以一目了然,统计表明 80 家欧洲电视网中在 1989 年出现亏损的不低于 50%。

另外,欧洲的整合将促使电视公司彼此之间加强合作,无论是在生产还是分配领域。

(49)创造一个尊重不同文化和传统的"欧洲身份"绝非易事,需要战略性选择,这些文化与传统组成了连接老欧洲的纽带——欧洲节目为欧洲。这将减轻我们对北美市场的依赖程度,他们的节目因为经验与文化传统而与我们有所不同。

为了取得这些目标,我们必须将精力集中于合作生产、新闻的交流、文献合作与培训等方面。这同时也涉及到了欧洲国家之间的协议,以欧洲投资银行为蓝本,为电视生产创建一家欧洲银行,这样便可以应对生产成本所面对的财政问题。(50)在应付一个如此规模的挑战的过程中,我们可以毫不夸张地说,"合即立,分即垮"——如果我们一定要选择一个标语的话,那就是"分中有合。"目标的统一意味着对每个国家的特殊利益都予以应有的关注。

2006年 考研英语全真试题
(阅读理解部分)

Part A

Directions:

*Read the following four texts. Answer the questions below each text by choosing A, B, C or D. Mark your answers on **ANSWER SHEET 1**.*

Text 1

In spite of "endless talk of difference", American society is an amazing machine for homogenizing people. There is "the democratizing uniformity of dress and discourse, and the casualness and absence of deference" characteristic of popular culture. People are absorbed into "a culture of consumption" launched by the 19th-century department stores that offered "vast arrays of goods in an elegant atmosphere. Instead of intimate shops catering to a knowledgeable elite," these were stores "anyone could enter, regardless of class or background. This turned shopping into a public and democratic act." The mass media, advertising and sports are other forces for homogenization.

Immigrants are quickly fitting into this common culture, which may not be altogether elevating but is hardly poisonous. Writing for the National Immigration Forum, Gregory Rodriguez reports that today's immigration is neither at unprecedented levels nor resistant to assimilation. In 1998 immigrants were 9.8 percent of population; in 1900, 13.6 percent. In the 10 years prior to 1990, 3.1 immigrants arrived for every 1,000 residents; in the 10 years prior to 1890, 9.2 for every 1,000. Now, consider three indices of assimilation — language, home ownership and intermarriage.

The 1990 Census revealed that "a majority of immigrants from each of the fifteen most common countries of origin spoke English 'well' or 'very well' after ten years of residence." The children of immigrants tend to be bilingual and proficient in English. "By the third generation, the original language is lost in the majority of immigrant families." Hence the description of America as a "graveyard" for languages. By 1996 foreign-born immigrants who had arrived before 1970 had a home ownership rate of 75.6 percent, higher than the 69.8 percent rate among native-born Americans.

Foreign-born Asians and Hispanics "have higher rates of intermarriage than do U.S.-born whites and blacks." By the third generation, one third of Hispanic women are married to non-

Hispanics, and 41 percent of Asian-American women are married to non-Asians.

Rodriguez notes that children in remote villages around the world are fans of superstars like Arnold Schwarzenegger and Garth Brooks, yet "some Americans fear that immigrants living within the United States remain somehow immune to the nation's assimilative power."

Are there divisive issues and pockets of seething anger in America? Indeed. It is big enough to have a bit of everything. But particularly when viewed against America's turbulent past, today's social indices hardly suggest a dark and deteriorating social environment.

21. The word "homogenizing" (Line 2, Paragraph 1) most probably means _____.

    A. identifying   B. associating

    C. assimilating   D. monopolizing

22. According to the author, the department stores of the 19th century _____.

    A. played a role in the spread of popular culture

    B. became intimate shops for common consumers

    C. satisfied the needs of a knowledgeable elite

    D. owed its emergence to the culture of consumption

23. The text suggests that immigrants now in the U. S. _____.

    A. are resistant to homogenization

    B. exert a great influence on American culture

    C. are hardly a threat to the common culture

    D. constitute the majority of the population

24. Why are Arnold Schwarzenegger and Garth Brooks mentioned in Paragraph 5?

    A. To prove their popularity around the world.

    B. To reveal the public's fear of immigrants.

    C. To give examples of successful immigrants.

    D. To show the powerful influence of American culture.

25. In the author's opinion, the absorption of immigrants into American society is _____.

    A. rewarding   B. successful   C. fruitless   D. harmful

Text 2

Stratford-on-Avon, as we all know, has only one industry — William Shakespeare — but there are two distinctly separate and increasingly hostile branches. There is the Royal Shakespeare Company(RSC), which presents superb productions of the plays at the Shakespeare Memorial Theatre on the Avon. And there are the townsfolk who largely live off the tourists who come, not to see the plays, but to look at Anne Hathaway's Cottage, Shakespeare's birthplace and the other sights.

The worthy residents of Stratford doubt that the theatre adds a penny to their revenue. They frankly dislike the RSC's actors, them with their long hair and beards and sandals and noisiness.

It's all deliciously ironic when you consider that Shakespeare, who earns their living, was himself an actor (with a beard) and did his share of noise-making.

The tourist streams are not entirely separate. The sightseers who come by bus — and often take in Warwick Castle and Blenheim Palace on the side — don't usually see the plays, and some of them are even surprised to find a theatre in Stratford. However, the playgoers do manage a little sight-seeing along with their playgoing. It is the playgoers, the RSC contends, who bring in much of the town's revenue because they spend the night (some of them four or five nights) pouring cash into the hotels and restaurants. The sightseers can take in everything and get out of town by nightfall.

The townsfolk don't see it this way and local council does not contribute directly to the subsidy of the Royal Shakespeare Company. Stratford cries poor traditionally. Nevertheless every hotel in town seems to be adding a new wing or cocktail lounge. Hilton is building its own hotel there, which you may be sure will be decorated with Hamlet Hamburger Bars, the Lear Lounge, the Banquo Banqueting Room, and so forth, and will be very expensive.

Anyway, the townsfolk can't understand why the Royal Shakespeare Company needs a subsidy. (The theatre has broken attendance records for three years in a row. Last year its 1,431 seats were 94 percent occupied all year long and this year they'll do better.) The reason, of course, is that costs have rocketed and ticket prices have stayed low.

It would be a shame to raise prices too much because it would drive away the young people who are Stratford's most attractive clientele. They come entirely for the plays, not the sights. They all seem to look alike (though they come from all over) — lean, pointed, dedicated faces, wearing jeans and sandals, eating their buns and bedding down for the night on the flagstones outside the theatre to buy the 20 seats and 80 standing-room tickets held for the sleepers and sold to them when the box office opens at 10:30 a.m..

26. From the first two paragraphs, we learn that _____.

    A. the townsfolk deny the RSC's contribution to the town's revenue

    B. the actors of the RSC imitate Shakespeare on and off stage

    C. the two branches of the RSC are not on good terms

    D. the townsfolk earn little from tourism

27. It can be inferred from Paragraph 3 that _____.

    A. the sightseers cannot visit the Castle and the Palace separately

    B. the playgoers spend more money than the sightseers

    C. the sightseers do more shopping than the playgoers

    D. the playgoers go to no other places in town than the theater

28. By saying "Stratford cries poor traditionally" (Line 2, Paragraph 4), the author implies that _____.

    A. Stratford cannot afford the expansion projects

    B. Stratford has long been in financial difficulties

C. the town is not really short of money

D. the townsfolk used to be poorly paid

29. According to the townsfolk, the RSC deserves no subsidy because _____.

    A. ticket prices can be raised to cover the spending

    B. the company is financially ill-managed

    C. the behavior of the actors is not socially acceptable

    D. the theatre attendance is on the rise

30. From the text we can conclude that the author _____.

    A. is supportive of both sides

    B. favors the townsfolk's view

    C. takes a detached attitude

    D. is sympathetic to the RSC

Text 3

When prehistoric man arrived in new parts of the world, something strange happened to the large animals. They suddenly became extinct. Smaller species survived. The large, slow-growing animals were easy game, and were quickly hunted to extinction. Now something similar could be happening in the oceans.

That the seas are being overfished has been known for years. What researchers such as Ransom Myers and Boris Worm have shown is just how fast things are changing. They have looked at half a century of data from fisheries around the world. Their methods do not attempt to estimate the actual biomass(the amount of living biological matter) of fish species in particular parts of the ocean, but rather changes in that biomass over time. According to their latest paper published in *Nature*, the biomass of large predators(animals that kill and eat other animals) in a new fishery is reduced on average by 80% within 15 years of the start of exploitation. In some long-fished areas, it has halved again since then.

Dr. Worm acknowledges that these figures are conservative. One reason for this is that fishing technology has improved. Today's vessels can find their prey using satellites and sonar, which were not available 50 years ago. That means a higher proportion of what is in the sea is being caught, so the real difference between present and past is likely to be worse than the one recorded by changes in catch sizes. In the early days, too, longlines would have been more saturated with fish. Some individuals would therefore not have been caught, since no baited hooks would have been available to trap them, leading to an underestimate of fish stocks in the past. Furthermore, in the early days of longline fishing, a lot of fish were lost to sharks after they had been hooked. That is no longer a problem, because there are fewer sharks around now.

Dr. Myers and Dr. Worm argue that their work gives a correct baseline, which future management efforts must take into account. They believe the data support an idea current among marine biologists, that of the "shifting baseline." The notion is that people have failed to detect the massive changes which have happened in the ocean because they have been looking back only a relatively short time into the past. That matters because theory suggests that the maximum sustainable yield that can be cropped from a fishery comes when the biomass of a target species is about 50% of its original levels. Most fisheries are well below that, which is a bad way to do business.

31. The extinction of large prehistoric animals is noted to suggest that _____.

   A. large animal were vulnerable to the changing environment

   B. small species survived as large animals disappeared

   C. large sea animals may face the same threat today

   D. slow-growing fish outlive fast-growing ones

32. We can infer from Dr. Myers and Dr. Worm's paper that _____.

   A. the stock of large predators in some old fisheries has reduced by 90%

   B. there are only half as many fisheries as there were 15 years ago

   C. the catch sizes in new fisheries are only 20% of the original amount

   D. the number of larger predators dropped faster in new fisheries than in the old

33. By saying "these figures are conservative" (Line 1, Paragraph 3), Dr. Worm means that _____.

   A. fishing technology has improved rapidly

   B. the catch-sizes are actually smaller than recorded

   C. the marine biomass has suffered a greater loss

   D. the data collected so far are out of date

34. Dr. Myers and other researchers hold that _____.

   A. people should look for a baseline that can work for a longer time

   B. fisheries should keep their yields below 50% of the biomass

   C. the ocean biomass should be restored to its original level

   D. people should adjust the fishing baseline to the changing situation

35. The author seems to be mainly concerned with most fisheries' _____.

   A. management efficiency

   B. biomass level

   C. catch-size limits

   D. technological application

Text 4

Many things make people think artists are weird. But the weirdest may be this: artists' only job is to explore emotions, and yet they choose to focus on the ones that feel bad.

This wasn't always so. The earliest forms of art, like painting and music, are those best suited for expressing joy. But somewhere from the 19th century onward, more artists began seeing happiness as meaningless, phony or, worst of all, boring, as we went from Wordsworth's daffodils to Baudelaire's flowers of evil.

You could argue that art became more skeptical of happiness because modern times have seen so much misery. But it's not as if earlier times didn't know perpetual war, disaster and the massacre of innocents. The reason, in fact, may be just the opposite: there is too much damn happiness in the world today.

After all, what is the one modern form of expression almost completely dedicated to depicting happiness? Advertising. The rise of anti-happy art almost exactly tracks the emergence of mass media, and with it, a commercial culture in which happiness is not just an ideal but an ideology.

People in earlier eras were surrounded by reminders of misery. They worked until exhausted, lived with few protections and died young. In the West, before mass communication and literacy, the most powerful mass medium was the church, which reminded worshippers that their souls were in danger and that they would someday be meat for worms. Given all this, they did not exactly need their art to be a bummer too.

Today the messages the average Westerner is surrounded with are not religious but commercial, and forever happy. Fast-food eaters, news anchors, text messengers, all smiling, smiling, smiling. Our magazines feature beaming celebrities and happy families in perfect homes. And since these messages have an agenda — to lure us to open our wallets — they make the very idea of happiness seem unreliable. "Celebrate!" commanded the ads for the arthritis drug Celebrex, before we found out it could increase the risk of heart attacks.

But what we forget — what our economy depends on us forgetting — is that happiness is more than pleasure without pain. The things that bring the greatest joy carry the greatest potential for loss and disappointment. Today, surrounded by promises of easy happiness, we need art to tell us, as religion once did, Memento mori: remember that you will die, that everything ends, and that happiness comes not in denying this but in living with it. It's a message even more bitter than a clove cigarette, yet, somehow, a breath of fresh air.

36. By citing the examples of poets Wordsworth and Baudelaire, the author intends to show that _____.

    A. poetry is not as expressive of joy as painting or music

    B. art grows out of both positive and negative feelings

    C. poets today are less skeptical of happiness

    D. artists have changed their focus of interest

37. The word "bummer" (Line 5, Paragraph 5) most probably means something _____.

    A. religious   B. unpleasant

    C. entertaining   D. commercial

38. In the author's opinion, advertising _____.

    A. emerges in the wake of the anti-happy art

    B. is a cause of disappointment for the general public

    C. replaces the church as a major source of information

    D. creates an illusion of happiness rather than happiness itself

39. We can learn from the last paragraph that the author believes _____.

    A. happiness more often than not ends in sadness

    B. the anti-happy art is distasteful but refreshing

    C. misery should be enjoyed rather than denied

    D. the anti-happy art flourishes when economy booms

40. Which of the following is true of the text?

    A. Religion once functioned as a reminder of misery.

    B. Art provides a balance between expectation and reality.

    C. People feel disappointed at the realities of modern society.

    D. Mass media are inclined to cover disasters and deaths.

Part B

Directions:

In the following article, some sentences have been removed. For Questions 41—45, choose the most suitable one from the list A—G to fit into each of the numbered gaps. There are two extra choices, which you do not need to use in any of the blanks. Mark your answers on ***ANSWER SHEET 1****.*

On the north bank of the Ohio river sits Evansville, Ind., home of David Williams, 52. and of a riverboat casino(a place where gambling games are played). During several years of gambling in that casino, Williams, a state auditor earning $35,000 a year, lost approximately $175,000. He had never gambled before the casino sent him a coupon for $20 worth of gambling.

He visited the casino, lost the $20 and left. On his second visit he lost $800. The casino issued to him, as a good customer, a "Fun Card", which when used in the casino earns points for meals and drinks, and enables the casino to track the user's gambling activities. For Williams, those activities become what he calls "electronic heroin".

(41) _____ In 1997 he lost $21,000 to one slot machine in two days. In March 1997 he lost $72,186. He sometimes played two slot machines at a time, all night, until the boat docked at 5 a.m., then went back aboard when the casino opened at 9 a.m. Now he is suing the casino, charging that it should have refused his patronage because it knew he was addicted. It did know he had a problem.

In March 1998 a friend of Williams's got him involuntarily confined to a treatment center for addictions, and wrote to inform the casino of Williams's gambling problem. The casino included a photo of Williams among those of banned gamblers, and wrote to him a "cease admissions" letter. Noting the medical/psychological nature of problem gambling behavior, the letter said that before being readmitted to the casino he would have to present medical/psychological information demonstrating that patronizing the casino would pose no threat to his safety or well-being.

(42) _____

The Wall Street Journal reports that the casino has 24 signs warning: "Enjoy the fun... and always bet with your head, not over it." Every entrance ticket lists a toll-free number for counseling from the Indiana Department of Mental Health. Nevertheless, Williams's suit charges that the casino, knowing he was "helplessly addicted to gambling," intentionally worked to "lure" him to "engage in conduct against his will." Well.

(43) _____

The fourth edition of the *Diagnostic and Statistical Manual of Mental Disorders* says "pathological gambling" involves persistent, recurring and uncontrollable pursuit less of money than of thrill of taking risks in quest of a windfall.

(44) _____ Pushed by science, or what claims to be science, society is reclassifying what once were considered character flaws or moral failings as personality disorders akin to physical disabilities.

(45) _____

Forty-four states have lotteries, 29 have casinos, and most of these states are to varying degrees dependent on — you might say addicted to — revenues from wagering. And since the first Internet gambling site was created in 1995. competition for gamblers' dollars has become intense. The Oct. 28 issue of *Newsweek* reported that 2 million gamblers patronize 1,800 virtual casinos every week. With $3.5 billion being lost on Internet wagers this year, gambling has passed pornography as the Web's most profitable business.

[A] Although no such evidence was presented, the casino's marketing department continued to pepper him with mailings. And he entered the casino and used his Fun Card without being detected.

[B] It is unclear what luring was required, given his compulsive behavior. And in what sense was his will operative?

[C] By the time he had lost $5,000 he said to himself that if he could get back to even, he would quit. One night he won $5,500. but he did not quit.

[D] Gambling has been a common feature of American life forever, but for a long time it was broadly considered a sin, or a social disease. Now it is a social policy: the most important and aggressive promoter of gambling in America is the government.

[E] David Williams's suit should trouble this gambling nation. But don't bet on it.

[F] It is worrisome that society is medicalizing more and more behavioral problems, often defining as addictions what earlier, sterner generations explained as weakness of will.

[G] The anonymous, lonely, undistracted nature of online gambling is especially conducive to compulsive behavior. But even if the government knew how to move against Internet gambling, what would be its grounds for doing so?

Part C

Directions:

*Read the following text carefully and then translate the underlined segments into Chinese. Your translation should be written clearly on **ANSWER SHEET 2.***

Is it true that the American intellectual is rejected and considered of no account in his society? I am going to suggest that it is not true. Father Bruckberger told part of the story when he observed that it is the intellectuals who have rejected America. But they have done more than that. They have grown dissatisfied with the role of intellectual. It is they, not America, who have become anti-intellectual.

First, the object of our study pleads for definition. What is an intellectual? (46) I shall define him as an individual who has elected as his primary duty and pleasure in life the activity of thinking in a Socratic (苏格拉底的) way about moral problems. He explores such problems consciously, articulately, and frankly, first by asking factual questions, then by asking moral questions, finally by suggesting action which seems appropriate in the light of the factual and moral information which he has obtained. (47) His function is analogous to that of a judge, who must accept the obligation of revealing in as obvious a manner as possible the course of reasoning which led him to his decision.

This definition excludes many individuals usually referred to as intellectuals — the average scientist, for one. (48) I have excluded him because, while his accomplishments may contribute to the solution of moral problems, he has not been charged with the task of approaching any but the factual aspects of those problems. Like other human beings, he encounters moral issues even in the everyday performance of his routine duties — he is not supposed to cook his experiments, manufacture evidence, or doctor his reports. (49) But his primary task is not to think about the moral code which governs his activity, any more than a businessman is expected to dedicate his energies to an exploration of rules of conduct in business. During most of his waking life he will take his code for granted, as the businessman takes his ethics.

The definition also excludes the majority of teachers, despite the fact that teaching has traditionally been the method whereby many intellectuals earn their living. (50) They may teach very well and more than earn their salaries, but most of them make little or no independent reflections on human problems which involve moral judgment. This description even fits the majority of eminent scholars. Being learned in some branch of human knowledge is one thing, living in "public and illustrious thoughts," as Emerson would say, is something else.

2006年 考研英语全真试题

（阅读理解部分）解析

Part A

Text 1

长难句分析

Rodriguez notes that children in remote villages around the world are fans of superstars like Arnold Schwarzenegger and Garth Brooks, yet "some Americans fear that immigrants living within the United States remain somehow immune to the nation's assimilative power."

❖**结构分析** that 引导的宾语从句的主干是 Children in remote villages are fans of superstars. yet 是表转折的并列连词，some Americans fear that 后又是一个宾语从句，其主干是 Immigrants remain immune to the nation's assimilative power.

试题分析

21. [C] 词义猜测题。根据上下文进行判断。开头用 in spite of 说明是转折，句子前后意思相反。因此，后面的词应是 difference 的反义词，答案是 C "同化"。文章后面的部分也可印证这个判断，无论是移民对语言的使用还是对大众文化的认同，都说明美国实际上是个同化机器。

22. [A] 细节题。第一段说，19 世纪百货商店开创了"消费文化"，任何人都能进来，无论你是什么阶级、有什么背景。这使购物成为一个公共的、民主的行为。大众媒体、广告和体育运动都是同化力量的来源。因此，先排除意思相反的 C "满足了知识渊博的社会精英的需要"；答案 B "成了普通消费者的私有商店"很有迷惑性，关键在于 intimate 一词的意思。原文中 intimate 一词意为"私有的"，这句话是说百货商店和那些迎合精英阶层的私有商店不同，既然任何人都能进，何来私有一说呢？因此 B 也不正确；D "百货商店的发展要归功于消费文化"本末倒置，是百货商店开创了大众文化，而不是相反；因此答案为 A "对大众文化的传播起到了关键作用"。

23. [C] 推断题。根据第二段的内容，移民既不拒绝大众文化，也不拒绝同化。因此 A "抵制同化"可排除；D "占人口的大多数"明显错误，因为在 1988 年移民只占人口的 9.8%；那问题就在于移民对美国文化的影响有多大。第二段说，移民很快就能适应大众文化，第三段又以语言为例,第四段以婚姻为例,都是说明是移民适应美国文化,而不是改变它。因此,答案应为C"对大众文化几乎没有影响",而不是 B"对美国文化造成重大影响"。

24. [D] 结构题。文章在前面的部分讲美国大众文化的同化力量,第五段先用施瓦辛格等例子来说明这一点,后面又有一个转折,说有些美国人还担心移民没有受到同化力量的影响。D"为了表现美国文化的巨大影响"为正确答案;可先排除掉 A"为了证明他们在全世界受欢迎",这和文章主旨没关系;B"为了揭示大众对移民的恐惧"和举的两个例子明显不符;C"为了列举成功移民的例子"也明显不对,因为即使不认识这两个人的名字,但他们是"superstars",而不是外来移民的代表。

25. [B] 态度题。从文章来看,作者认为美国文化对移民的作用是非常大的,同化力量也很强。第一段点出美国实际上具有很强的同化力量,后面三段以大众文化、语言、婚姻等为例说明美国的同化很成功。因此,答案是 B。

参考译文

　　尽管"对差异的讨论无休无止",但美国社会是一个神奇的能够同化人民的社会。这里存在"服饰和话语上民主化的一致,漫不经心、尊重的缺失",这些是大众文化的特色。人们被 19 世纪百货商店所开创的"消费文化"深深吸引,这些商店"在优雅的环境中提供各类商品,不同于迎合知识精英的私有商店,而是任何人都能进来,无论你是什么阶级、有什么背景。这使购物成为一个公共的、民主的行为"。大众媒体、广告和体育运动也都是同化力量的来源。

　　移民正在很快适应这种大众文化,它总的来说并不能提升人的境界,但却也没有什么害处。格雷戈里·罗德里格斯是国家移民论坛的撰稿人,他的报告说现在的移民既没有达到空前的水平,也不拒绝被同化。1988 年的移民数量占人口的 9.8%,1900 年的比例则是 13.6%。在 1990 年之前的十年,每 1,000 个居民中有 3.1 个移民;而在 1890 年之前的十年,每 1,000 个居民中有 9.2 个移民。现在有三个同化指标:语言、房屋所有权和异族联姻。

　　1990 年统计数字表明,"在美国居住十年之后,来自最常移民的 15 个国家的居民英语说得'好'或'很好'"。移民者的子女常常能使用双语,精通英语。"到了第三代移民,在大多数家庭中,他们的本国语言将不再被使用。"因此,美国被描述为语言的"坟墓"。到 1996 年,出生于国外,在 1970 年前到达美国的移民的房产拥有率高达 75.6%,这高于土生土长的美国人的 69.8%的比率。

　　出生于国外的亚洲人和西班牙人 "异族通婚率高于在美国出生的黑人和白人之间的通婚率"。到了第三代,三分之一的西班牙妇女会与异族通婚,41%的亚裔妇女会嫁给非亚裔人士。

　　罗德里格斯提到, 世界各地边远地区乡村的孩子是阿诺德·施瓦辛格和加斯·布鲁克斯等超级巨星的影迷。然而"一些美国人担心生活在美国的移民没有受到国家同化力量的影响。"

　　美国是否存在分裂和骚动问题？是这样的。美国很大，任何东西都会有那么一点点。尤其是与美国过去的动乱年代相比较，今天的社会指数并不能表明社会环境正在日益黑暗和恶化。

Text 2

长难句分析

1. It is the playgoers, the RSC contends, who bring in much of the town's revenue because they spend the night〔some of them four or five nights〕pouring cash into the hotels and restaurants.

❖ 结构分析　句子主干是个强调句型 It is the playgoers who bring in much of the town's revenue。the RSC contends 是插入语，补充说明是 RSC 公司这样认为的。because 引导的从句中，pouring cash into the hotels and restaurants 是非谓语动词，作 spend 的伴随状语，即他们在小镇过夜的同时，大把地花钱。

2. Hilton is building its own hotel there, which you may be sure will be decorated with Hamlet Hamburger Bars, the Lear Lounge, the Banquo Banqueting Room, and so forth, and will be very expensive.

❖ 结构分析　which 引导非限制性定语从句，修饰 hotel。you may be sure 是插入语，which will be... and will be 才是句子的主干，是由 and 连接的两个并列成分。

3. They all seem to look alike〔though they come from all over〕— lean, pointed, dedicated faces, wearing jeans and sandals, eating their buns and bedding down for the night on the flagstones outside the theatre to buy the 20 seats and 80 standing-room tickets held for the sleepers and sold to them when the box office opens at 10:30 a.m.

❖ 结构分析　破折号之后的修饰部分很长，lean, pointed, dedicated faces 是三个形容词修饰看戏者的面部，后面的 wearing，eating 和 bedding 是三个伴随状语，说明这些人穿什么、吃什么、睡什么。bedding down for the night on... to buy the 20 seats... held for the sleepers and sold to them when... 中，to buy 是目的状语，意为"为了买…"。held 是过去分词作定语，修饰 tickets，即为过夜人准备的票，sold to them 充当相同成分也修饰 tickets，这些票被买给他们。这部分的意思就是"为了买 20 张座位票和 80 张为过夜人准备的站票。"

试题分析

26. 〔A〕细节题。文章开头就说莎士比亚是艾芬河畔斯特拉德福德的唯一产业，但是却有个敌对的分支。因此 C 可被排除，皇家莎士比亚公司就是两个分支中的一个；又说镇上的居民主要靠旅游业为生，可知 D 也错误；斯特拉德福德的可敬的居民们怀疑剧院是否能给他们的收入带来丝毫好处,可知 A "当地居民认为皇家莎士比亚公司对城镇收入没有贡献"是正确答案;B "皇家莎士比亚公司的演员无论在台上还是台下都模仿莎士比亚"没有根据。

27. [B] 推断题。第三段说观光者通常不看戏剧演出,其中有些人甚至对这里竟然有剧院感到奇怪。然而,看戏剧的人通常会设法参观某些地方。皇家莎士比亚公司认为,这些前来看戏的人在这里过夜,把钱花到旅馆和餐厅。而观光者则在夜幕降临之前就参观完景点,离开这个小城。可见 B "看戏者比观光者花的钱更多"为正确答案;A 和 C 文中没有提及可排除;D "看戏者除了剧院哪里都不去"和文章说的相反。

28. [C] 推断题。作者说 "Stratford cries poor traditionally"(第四段第二行)这句话后,马上说镇上的每一家旅馆都似乎在扩大规模,而希尔顿正在那里建造昂贵的酒店,可见作者并不认为那里真的没钱,答案为 C "斯特拉德福德并非真的没钱"。

29. [D] 细节题。第五段说当地居民不能理解为什么皇家莎士比亚公司需要政府补助,剧院已经连续三年都打破原来的上座率,答案为 D "戏院的上座率在上升";作者认为原因就是费用在飞快上涨而票价却仍然很低。所以,A "可提高票价满足开支"不是当地居民的意见;B 没有提到;C 不是居民反对给公司补贴的原因。

30. [D] 综合归纳题。第二段讲到,小镇居民看不惯演员们的行为,作者说莎士比亚本人就曾经是这样的,态度明确同情演员。第三段作者更是认为,观光者不看演出,看戏者却观光,使他们给城镇带来大部分收入。第四段就财政补贴的事,作者最后说虽然上座率高,但居民们没有注意到费用也在上涨,是替莎士比亚公司辩护。总之,作者是同情该公司的。答案为 D "同情皇家莎士比亚公司"。

参考译文

众所周知,莎士比亚是艾芬河畔斯特拉德福德的唯一产业,但是却有两种截然不同、日益敌对的分支。皇家莎士比亚公司(RSC)在艾芬河畔的莎士比亚纪念剧院上演莎士比亚最好的戏剧作品。镇上的居民主要靠旅游业为生,但游客来这里不是看戏剧演出的,而是要看安妮·海瑟威的故居,莎士比亚的出生地和其他景点的。

斯特拉德福德的可敬的居民们怀疑剧院是否能给他们的收入带来丝毫好处。他们坦言不喜欢皇家莎士比亚公司的演员,他们留着长长的头发和胡须,穿着便鞋,闹哄哄的。颇具讽刺意味的是,莎士比亚本人就是个演员(蓄着胡须)并以此谋生的,也曾经制造过类似的喧闹。

游客们并没有完全被分流。坐汽车来的观光者通常会参观附近的沃里克城堡和布莱尼姆宫,他们通常不看戏剧演出,其中有些人甚至对这里竟然有剧院感到奇怪。然而,看戏剧的人通常会设法参观某些地方。皇家莎士比亚公司认为,正是这些前来看戏的人带来了城镇的大部分收入,因为他们在这里过夜(有人会呆四五个晚上),把钱花到旅馆和餐厅。而观光者则在夜幕降临之前就参观完景点,离开这个小镇。

但是小镇居民们并不这样想,地方议政厅也不直接给皇家莎士比亚公司提供财政补贴。斯特拉特福德一直在哭穷。然而镇上的每一家旅馆都似乎在增加侧厅或鸡尾酒厅。希尔顿正在那里建造酒店,那里肯定会有哈姆雷特汉堡酒吧、李尔厅、班柯宴会厅等,并且价格将会十分昂贵。

无论如何,当地居民不能理解为什么皇家莎士比亚公司需要政府补助。(剧院已经连续三年打破上座率纪录。去年 1431 个座位的上座率为 94%,今年情况将会更好。)当然,原因是费用在飞快上涨而票价却仍然很低。

大幅提高票价将会是遗憾之事,因为这将会把那些年轻人赶走,他们对斯特拉特福德来说是最具吸引力的客户。他们来到这里完全是为了看戏而不是观光。他们好像很相似(虽然他们来自四面八方)——他们都有瘦瘦尖尖、充满热情的脸庞,穿着牛仔服和便鞋,吃着圆面包,晚上就睡在外面的石板上,上午 10:30 开始售票时他们就买 20 张座位票和 80 张为过夜人准备的站票。

Text 3

长难句分析

1. **That means a higher proportion of what is in the sea is being caught, so the real difference between present and past is likely to be worse than the one recorded by changes in catch sizes.**

   ❖结构分析 a higher proportion of what is in the sea is being caught 中 what is in the sea 指海洋生物。is being caught 是被动语态的现在进行时,这部分的意思是"海洋生物中有更大一部分正在被捕捞。"so 引导结果状语从句,从句主干是 the difference is likely to be worse,即差别可能更大,than the one recorded by changes in catch sizes 中 the one 指的是 the difference, recorded 是定语,相当于 that is recorded by changes in catch sizes。

2. **That matters because theory suggests that the maximum sustainable yield that can be cropped from a fishery comes when the biomass of a target species is about 50% of its original levels.**

   ❖结构分析 That matters... 是主句,意思是"那很重要",matter 是不及物动词,意为"要紧,有关系"。 because 从句的主干是 The maximum sustainable yield comes. that can be cropped from a fishery 是定语从句,修饰 yield。when 引导状语从句。

试题分析

31. [C] 结构题。首先要理解作者的意图。第一段提到史前大型动物的灭绝是为了引出下文,即现在大型海洋生物也受到同样的威胁:过度捕杀。所以,A"大型动物更易受到环境变化的影响"可排除,因为作者所谈论的是人为因素而非环境因素;D"生长比较慢的动物比生长更快动物要长寿"没有提及也可排除;B"大型动物灭绝时,小型动物存活下来"可能是事实,但和文章没有关系;答案为 C"现在大型海洋动物将面临同样的威胁",这是作者提到这件事的意图所在。

32. [A] 细节推断题。第二段提到迈尔斯和沃尔姆的研究是计算不同时期鱼的数量的变化。根据他们的论文,在特定渔场内,大型食肉性鱼类的总体数量 15 年内平均降低了 80%。在一些捕鱼历史悠久的地区,从那以后,大型食肉型鱼类的数量又下降了 50%。可见,15 年内大型肉食性鱼类只剩下了原来的 20%,又在此基础上下降了一半,只有 10%,减少了 90%,A 为正确答案。

33. [C] 推断题。沃尔姆说这是保守数字,原因之一是捕鱼技术提高了。因此 A 可排除,技术发展只是数字变化的原因。他接着说,现在和过去的真正差别可能会比记录下来的捕捞数量的变化更大,在早期所使用的方法可能导致过去对鱼类资源的估计不足。所以 C"海洋生物总量遭受了更大的损失"为正确答案;B"实际的捕捞数量比记录的要少"和原文意思相反,而 D 并没有提到。

34. [D] 细节题。最后一段,迈尔斯等人认为由于人类只在一个相对较短的时间内回顾过去,所以没能察觉海洋所发生的巨大变化,所以要把这个因素考虑进去对底线进行调整。可见答案应该为 D"人们应该根据情况的变化而调整捕捞底线";A"人们应该寻找一条发挥作用时间更长的底线"与这个意思不符;文章说当目标鱼量降至原来的 50% 时,人们才能从渔场获得最大可持续产出量,但是这并不能推断出 B"渔场应该把产出量保持在总量的50%"这个结论,所以 B 也不合适;C"海洋生物数量应该恢复到原有水平"文章也没有提到。

35. [B] 主旨大意题。A 和 D 可以快速排除,因为作者所关注的问题是海洋生物的数量问题而不是渔场的管理和技术;答案 B 和 C 的区别在于,B 强调生物数量水平,C 强调渔场的捕获量。作者从第一段就说,海洋大型动物可能会灭绝,第二段开始引用了迈尔斯等人的研究,所关注的是"大型食肉型动物的总体数量"。作者之所以谈到"捕获量"问题和"底线",还是出于对海洋动物总体数量的关注。所以 B"生物数量水平"是最佳答案。作者关注的似乎主要是大多数渔场的生物数量水平。

参考译文

当史前人类到达地球上新的地方时,奇怪的事情发生了:大型动物突然灭绝了,而体形较小的物种则存活了下来。体形较大、成长缓慢的动物很容易成为被猎杀的对象,所以很快灭绝。现在类似的事情可能正在海洋发生。

很多年以来,人们都知道海洋正在被过度捕捞。如兰塞姆·迈尔斯和鲍里斯·沃尔姆这样的研究者提示出事情变化得究竟有多快。他们调查了半个世纪以来世界各地的渔业数据。他们的方法不是试图估算在特定区域内实际的鱼数量,而是计算不同时期鱼的数量的变化。根据他们最近在《自然》杂志上发表的论文,在特定渔场内,大型食肉性鱼类的总体数量在开始进行海洋开发的 15 年内平均降低了 80%。此后,在一些捕鱼历史悠久的地区,大型食肉鱼类的数量又下降了 50%。

沃尔姆博士承认这些是保守数字。其中原因之一在于,捕鱼技术提高了。现在的渔船能够用卫星或声纳定位仪找到猎物,而这些技术在 50 年之前是没有的。这就意味着有更多的海洋生物被捕捞,因此现在和过去的真正差别可能会比记录下来的捕捞数量的变化更大。在早期,多钩长线会挂满了鱼,一些鱼可能因此而没有上钩,只是因为没有更多的挂着鱼饵的鱼钩在引诱它们,这导致过去对鱼类资源的估计不足。此外,在早期使用多钩长线时,许多鱼在上钩之后又被鲨鱼吃掉了。由于鲨鱼数量的下降,现在这已经不再是个问题。

迈尔斯和沃尔姆博士认为他们的工作设立了一条合理的底线,未来进行管理时要把它考虑在内。他们相信数据支持一种目前海洋生物学家所持的观点,即改变底线。这一观点认为,人类没能察觉海洋所发生的巨大变化,因为他们只在一个相对较短的时间内回顾过去。这很重要,因为有理论表明,当目标鱼量降至原来的 50% 时,人们才能从渔场获得最大可持续产出量。大部分渔场中鱼的存活量远远低于这个数值,这样的生意可不好做。

Text 4

长难句分析

1. **But somewhere from the 19th century onward, more artists began seeing happiness as meaningless, phony or, worst of all, boring, as we went from Wordsworth's daffodils to Baudelaire's flowers of evil.**

   ❖结构分析　主句中 began seeing happiness as... 意为"开始把快乐看做是…",后面三个形容词作表语。somewhere 在这里的意思是"大约,差不多"。as we went from... to 意为"就像我们从…转向…一样"。

2. **In the West, before mass communication and literacy, the most powerful mass medium was the church, which reminded worshippers that their souls were in danger and that they would someday be meat for worms.**

   ❖结构分析　主句为 The most powerful mass medium was the church. which reminded worshippers that... and... 是非限制性定语从句,which 指代 church, remind sb. that 意为"提醒某人某事",that 后面是由 and 连接的两个宾语从句。

3. **Today, surrounded by promises of easy happiness, we need art to tell us, as religion once did, Memento mori: remember that you will die, that everything ends, and that happiness comes not in denying this but in living with it.**

   ❖结构分析　surrounded by 的逻辑主语是句子主语 we, 意为"我们被…包围"。主句是 We need art to tell us Memento mori. remember that 是对 Memento mori 的解释,后面用了三个 that, 说明是三个并列的成分。 happiness comes not in... but in 意为"幸福不是在于…而是在于…",this 指的是死亡。

试 题 分 析

36.［D］结构题。作者认为艺术原来是善于表达快乐的,但后来又认为快乐没有意思。华兹华斯和波德莱尔是这种变化过程的代表。因此答案是 D。A 和 B 都没有提到;C"现在的诗人对幸福怀疑更少"和文章的意思相反。

37.［B］词义猜测题。第三段作者说,在现今社会有太多可恶的快乐,所以艺术才表达痛苦。在第四段中,作者说表达痛苦的艺术几乎是和大众媒介的出现同步的,第五段接着说,生活在早期社会的人们更加痛苦,当时最有力的大众媒介是教堂,它能提醒礼拜者他们的灵魂正在遭受危险,他们总有一天会成为虫子的食物等。所以,在大众媒介出现之前,艺术是不怎么表达痛苦的。因此,答案应为 B"娱乐的"。

38.［D］推断题。第四段说广告最能表达快乐,所以 B"是造成公众失望的原因"不对;表达痛苦的艺术几乎是和大众媒介的出现同步的,随之而来的是商业文化。广告是商业文化的代表,因此答案 A"出现于反快乐的艺术之初"是错误的;C 项没有提及;D"制造了幸福的幻觉而不是幸福本身"正确,因为文章明确说:"快乐在这种文化中不仅是一种理想还是一种意识形态。"理想和意识形态就是说明广告所制造出来的是一种幻觉。

39.［B］归纳题。最后一段说,幸福不仅仅是没有痛苦的快乐。那些能给我们带来极大快乐的东西也最有可能失去和让人失望。所以答案 A"快乐经常以悲伤结束"不正确,因为快乐和悲伤交织,但并不是说以悲伤结束;作者接着说,现在,我们需要艺术(就像宗教曾经所做的那样)来告诉我们死亡的象征:幸福不是来自对死亡的拒绝而是来自对死亡的接受。这是比丁香烟叶还苦的信息,但是,却会使我们呼吸到新鲜的空气。所以,B"反快乐的艺术令人不快,却让人感到清新"是正确答案;C"应该享受痛苦而不是拒绝它"不正确,原文讲的是对死亡的接受而不是对痛苦的享受;D 在最后一段没有被提到。

40.［A］细节题。第五段谈到教堂,说它能提醒礼拜者他们的灵魂正在遭受危险,他们总有一天会成为虫子的食物。因此 A"宗教曾被作为痛苦的提醒物而存在"正确;B 和 C 都没有提到;D"大众传媒倾向于报道灾难和死亡事件"与文章意思相反,因为大众传媒给公众带来快乐而不是痛苦。

参考译文

　　许多事情使人认为艺术家们都很怪异,但最怪的事情可能是:艺术家唯一的工作就是探索情感,可是他们却把注意力集中在那些负面情感上。

　　情况并非一直是这样的。最早的艺术形式,比如绘画和音乐,都最适合表达快乐的情感。但是大概从 19 世纪以来,更多的艺术家开始认为快乐是无意义的、虚假的,最糟糕的是,他们认为快乐是让人厌倦的,就像我们从华兹华斯的"水仙花"转向波德莱尔的"恶之花"这个过程一样。

也许你会说,由于现代社会有太多的不幸,艺术才对快乐持怀疑态度。但是,早些时候也有无休止的战争、灾难和对无辜者的屠杀。事实上,原因可能与此相反:在现今社会有太多可恶的快乐!

究竟什么样的现代表达方式能几乎完全表达快乐呢?广告。表达痛苦的艺术几乎是和大众媒介的出现同步的,随之而来的是商业文化,快乐在这种文化中不仅是一种理想还是一种意识形态。

生活在早期社会的人们被痛苦的记忆所包围。他们要工作到疲惫不堪,生活没多少保障并且容易早亡。在西方,在大众传播出现、人们开始读书识字之前,最有力的大众媒介是教堂,它能提醒礼拜者他们的灵魂正在遭受危险,他们总有一天会成为虫子的食物。考虑到所有这些,他们不需要让艺术当成是让人不快的东西。

现在普通的西方人不是被宗教而是被商业所包围,永远都让人快快乐乐。那些吃快餐的人,新闻主持人和邮递员都不停地微笑,微笑再微笑。我们的杂志以容光焕发的名人和住在漂亮房子里的幸福家庭为对象。并且既然这些信息有意要引诱我们打开钱包,他们就会让幸福这一感觉变得不可靠。西乐葆可以治疗关节炎的广告让我们欢欣鼓舞,但不久我们就发现它只能增加我们患上心脏病的机率。

但是我们所忘记的东西是——我们的经济所依赖的就是我们的忘记——幸福不仅仅是没有痛苦的快乐。那些能给我们带来极大快乐的东西也最有可能失去和让人失望。现在,我们四周到处都是可以很容易得到幸福的承诺,我们需要艺术(就像宗教曾经所做的那样)来告诉我们死亡的象征:记住你会死去,所有事情都会终结,幸福不是来自对死亡的拒绝而是来自对死亡的接受。这是比丁香烟叶还苦的信息,但是,却会使我们呼吸到新鲜的空气。

Part B

试 题 分 析

41. [C] 从文章的结构来看,威廉斯只是作者引出自己话题的一个引子,首先介绍他如何一步步成为一个赌徒,后再论述自己对赌博业的看法。从该题的位置来看,答案应该在C和E之间,因为这两个选项是关于威廉斯个案的。但E是总结性的说法,与上下文不符,而C正是描述他沦为赌徒过程中的一个环节,因此C为最佳答案。

42. [A] 第三段讲的是威廉斯被送入治疗中心戒赌并通知赌场,而赌场也给他发了书面通知,要求他必须出示医学证明才能重新进入赌场。第五段说,威廉斯在起诉书中说,该赌场明知他"不能自拔地赌博上瘾",仍有意地"引诱"他"参与违背自己意愿的活动。"这样看来,赌场并没有尽到自己的责任。而备选答案中只有A能起到上下文的连接作用,即是说,赌场实际上没有尽到责任,赌场仍然在给他发送信件,而当威廉斯去赌场使用开心卡的时候,也没有人注意到他。

43. [B] 此题较易解答。上一段说赌场里有警示标志,入场券里也印有心理咨询的电话号码,但威廉斯称自己受到引诱。所以 lure 是其中最明显的一个线索,B的意思就是由于有强迫症,威廉斯根本就不用什么引诱了,他已经毫无意志力。

44. [F] 此题的上一段提到,《精神紊乱的诊断与统计手册》第四版中说,"病理性赌博"是一种顽固的、容易复发的、无法控制的对失去钱财的追逐,而不是追求在发横财的冒险过程中寻求刺激。而在本段的后半部分中,作者说在科学的推动下,社会把性格缺陷或道德缺失的问题当做是类似身体残疾的人性紊乱。因此,选项中的 medicalizing, behavioral problems,和 weakness of will 等都是解题的关键词。此外,选项中的部分和这一段的后半部分都谈到了人们现在和过去对同一问题的看法。其他几个备选答案可以逐一排除。

45. [D] 从上下文来看,在此之前的部分讲的是威廉斯的个案,接下来可能继续说威廉斯的问题,也可能转到作者对全文的总结方面。备选答案中 E 和 D 都和上文具有一定的承接关系。但最后一段列举了美国赌业的一结数据和赌博业的繁荣,因此 D 项最后说美国政府成了赌博业的坚定支持者,正好可以与下文衔接。

参考译文

在俄亥俄河北岸坐落着埃文斯维尔城,它是大卫·威廉斯的家乡,也是一个经营海上赌博游戏的娱乐场所。威廉斯 52 岁,是俄亥俄的一名审计员,年收入为 3 万 5 千美元,在这里赌博的几年间,他输掉了大约 17 万 5 千美元。该赌场曾送给他 20 美元的赌资,在此之前他从未赌过。

他去了赌场,输掉了那 20 美元然后离开了。他第二次光顾这里输了 800 美元。因为他是一个好顾客,赌场就发给他一张"开心卡",这张卡的作用是可以在赌场使用,赢得餐饮点数,也可以使赌场跟踪使用者的赌博活动。对于威廉斯,用他自己的话来说,这些行为是"电子海洛因"。

(41)当他输掉 5,000 美元时,他对自己说如果他能捞回本来,他就不再去赌了。有一天晚上,他赢了 5,000 美元,但他没有停止赌博。在 1997 年他在同一台老虎机上两天输掉了 21,000 美元。同年 3 月,他输掉了 72,186 美元。他有时同时打两台老虎机,整夜不休息直到凌晨 5:00,然后在晚上 9:00 赌场开始营业时再回来。目前他正在起诉这个赌场,声称当它知道自己已经上瘾时,该赌场应该拒绝他继续赌博。赌场确实知道他出了一些问题。

在 1998 年 3 月,威廉斯的一个朋友在他不情愿的情况下把他送进了戒瘾治疗中心,并书面通知了那家赌场。赌场把威廉斯的照片放到被禁止的名单当中,并给他发了"终止入场"的函件。该函件称,由于注意到了赌博行为问题的医学和心理学性质,在重新允许他进入赌场之前,他必须要出示"医学/心理学"的数据,证明参与赌博不会对他的安全和身体健康造成威胁。

(42)虽然没有提交这样的证据,赌场的营销部门还是继续给他发送信件。他去赌场并使用开心卡的时候也没被人发觉。

《华尔街日报》报道,这家赌场有 24 个警示标语,上面写着"玩得开心…保持清醒,切勿过头"。每张入场券上都印有一个印第安纳州精神健康处免费心理咨询的号码。然而,威廉斯在起诉书中称,该赌场明知他"不能自拔地赌博上瘾",仍有意地"引诱"他"参与违背自己意愿的活动。"

(43)由于他患有强迫症,真不清楚他还需要什么引诱,也不清楚他的意志在哪种意义上还在起作用。

《精神紊乱的诊断与统计手册》第四版中说,"病理性赌博"是一种顽固的、容易复发的、无法控制的对失去钱财的追逐,而不是追求在发横财的冒险过程中寻求刺激。

(44)令人担忧的是,社会把越来越多的行为问题纳入到医学问题之中,常常把原来那些更严格的前辈们所说的"意志薄弱"定义为上瘾。在科学或所谓的科学的推动下,社会对过去人们曾经认为的性格缺陷或道德缺失的问题进行重新归类, 把他们当做是类似身体残疾的人性紊乱。

(45)赌博将永远是美国生活的一个特征,然而很长时期以来人们普遍认为这是一种罪过,或是社会病态。现在,赌博却变成了一项社会政策:美国政府是赌博业最重要、最坚决的支持者。

有 44 个州在经营博彩业,29 个州拥有赌场,大多数州都在不同程度上依赖赌博——也许你会说它们也上瘾了——将其当做财政收入的一部分。自从 1995 年首家互联网才干网站开通,对参与者钱财的竞争也变得激烈起来。10 月 28 日的《新闻周刊》报道,每周有两百万赌徒光顾 1,800 家赌场。有 35 亿美元金钱在互联网上被输掉,这使赌博业超越了色情业,成为网上最赚钱的行业。

Part C

试题分析

46. 全句译文:我将他定义为这样的人,他以苏格拉底的方式去思考道德问题,并把这种行为视为自己生命中的首要责任与乐趣。

翻译提示:who 引导一个定语从句,从句的正常语序应该是 who has elected the activity of thinking about moral problems in a Socratic(苏格拉底) way as his primary duty and pleasure in life,于是这句话的意思就是,他以苏格拉底的方式去思考道德问题,他把这种行为方式视为自己生命中的首要责任与乐趣。其中 define sb./sth. as 意为"把某人/某事定义为"。

47. 全句译文:他的作用与法官类似,必须承担这样的责任,即用尽可能明了的方式来展示自己做出决定的推理过程。

翻译提示:这个句子中包含两个定语从句,分别为 who 和 which 所引导,但并不复杂,翻译时先单独译出。其中 analogous 意为"类似的,可类比的"。

48. 全句译文:我之所以把他(普通科学家)排除在外,是因为尽管他的成就可能会有助于道德问题的解决,但他所承担的任务只不过是这些问题的事实层面。

翻译提示:because 引导的原因状语从句插入了 while 引导的状语从句, 翻译的时候可以

先把它省过去,单独译出来。其中 be charged with 意为"承担"。 any but 意为
"只是"。

49. 全句译文:但是,他的首要任务并不是思考支配自己行为的道德律令,就如同我们不能指
望商人专注于探索自己的行业规范一样。

翻译提示:which 引导的定语从句修饰 activity,这里 code 意为"法典,律条",是个法学术
语。not any more than 的意思是"两者可以等量齐观,不相上下",表程度。
dedicate sth. to sth. 意为"致力于,专注于"。

50. 全句译文:他们可能教得很好,不仅仅是挣点薪水。但他们大多数人却很少或根本就没有
对牵涉到道德判断的人类问题进行独立思考。

翻译提示:which 引导定语从句修饰 human problems。其中 more than 的意思是"不仅仅,
在程度上超过"。这半句的意思是"他们可能教得很好,不仅仅是挣薪水。"
make reflections on 意为"对…反思"。 involve 意为"涉及,牵涉"。

参考译文

　　据说美国知识分子被人拒绝以致在社会上毫无地位,这确有其事吗?我将证明事实并非
如此。当布鲁克贝格尔神父认识到其实是知识分子拒绝了美国,他说出了部分真相。但他们
所做的不止于此。他们对知识分子这一角色日渐不满。是他们自己,而非美国,成为反知识分
子势力。

　　首先,我们的研究目标是寻求定义。何谓知识分子?(46)我将知识分子定义为这样的人,
他以苏格拉底的方式去思考道德问题,并把这种行为方式视为自己生命中的首要责任与乐
趣。他认真、严肃、真诚地去探索这些问题,先是询问事实问题,继而追问道德问题,最后在事
实与道德信息的烛照下,给出自己富有启发性的行为指导。(47)他的作用与法官类似,必须
承担这样的责任,即用尽可能明了的方式来展示自己做出决定的推理过程。

　　这一定义就将很多所谓的知识分子排除在外,如普通的科学家。(48)我之所以把他排除
在外,是因为尽管他的成就可能会有助于道德问题的解决,但他所承担的任务只不过是这些
问题的事实层面。就像任何人类一样,他也会在行使自己的日常职责时遭遇道德问题,他不
能操控自己的实验,不能伪造证据,或是对结果做手脚。(49)但是,他的首要任务并不是思考
支配自己行为的道德律令,就如同我们不能指望商人专注于探索自己的行业规范一样。在他
大部分生活中,他都将法律当做是自然而然的,就像商人对待商业规则一样。

　　这一定义同时也排出了大部分的教师,尽管这一职业一般视为知识分子的传统谋生手
段。(50)他们可能教得很好,不仅仅是挣一份薪水,但他们大多数人却很少或根本就没有对
牵涉到道德判断的人类问题进行独立思考。这种描述甚至也适用于很多优秀学者。对人类知
识的某一领域有所研究是一回事儿,但正如艾默生所说,生活在"公共与伟大的思想中",那
就是另一回事儿了。

2007年 考研英语全真试题
（阅读理解部分）

Part A

Directions:

*Read the following four texts. Answer the questions below each text by choosing A, B, C or D. Mark your answers on **ANSWER SHEET 1**.*

Text 1

If you were to examine the birth certificates of every soccer player in 2006's World Cup tournament, you would most likely find a noteworthy quirk: elite soccer players are more likely to have been born in the earlier months of the year than in the later months. If you then examined the European national youth teams that feed the World Cup and professional ranks, you would find this strange phenomenon to be even more pronounced.

What might account for this strange phenomenon? Here are a few guesses: a) certain astrological signs confer superior soccer skills; b) winter-born babies tend to have higher oxygen capacity, which increases soccer stamina; c) soccer-mad parents are more likely to conceive children in springtime, at the annual peak of soccer mania; d) none of the above.

Anders Ericsson, a 58-year-old psychology professor at Florida State University, says he believes strongly in "none of the above". Ericsson grew up in Sweden, and studied nuclear engineering until he realized he would have more opportunity to conduct his own research if he switched to psychology. His first experiment, nearly 30 years ago, involved memory: training a person to hear and then repeat a random series of numbers. "With the first subject, after about 20 hours of training, his digit span had risen from 7 to 20," Ericsson recalls. "He kept improving, and after about 200 hours of training he had risen to over 80 numbers."

This success, coupled with later research showing that memory itself is not genetically determined, led Ericsson to conclude that the act of memorizing is more of a cognitive exercise than an intuitive one. In other words, whatever inborn differences two people may exhibit in their abilities to memorize, those differences are swamped by how well each person "encodes" the information. And the best way to learn how to encode information meaningfully, Ericsson determined, was a process known as deliberate practice. Deliberate practice entails more than simply repeating a task. Rather, it involves setting specific goals, obtaining immediate feedback and concentrating as much on technique as on outcome.

Ericsson and his colleagues have thus taken to studying expert performers in a wide range of pursuits, including soccer. They gather all the data they can, not just performance statistics and biographical details but also the results of their own laboratory experiments with high achievers. Their work makes a rather startling assertion: the trait we commonly call talent is highly overrated. Or, put another way, expert performers — whether in memory or surgery, ballet or computer programming — are nearly always made, not born.

21. The birthday phenomenon found among soccer players is mentioned to _____.

    A. stress the importance of professional training

    B. spotlight the soccer superstars in the World Cup

    C. introduce the topic of what makes expert performance

    D. explain why some soccer teams play better than others

22. The word "mania" (Line 4, Paragraph 2) most probably means _____.

    A. fun   B. craze   C. hysteria   D. excitement

23. According to Ericsson, good memory _____.

    A. depends on meaningful processing of information

    B. results from intuitive rather than cognitive exercises

    C. is determined by genetic rather than psychological factors

    D. requires immediate feedback and a high degree of concentration

24. Ericsson and his colleagues believe that _____.

    A. talent is a dominating factor for professional success

    B. biographical data provide the key to excellent performance

    C. the role of talent tends to be overlooked

    D. high achievers owe their success mostly to nurture

25. Which of the following proverbs is closest to the message the text tries to convey?

    A. Faith will move mountains.   B. One reaps what one sows.

    C. Practice makes perfect.   D. Like father, like son.

Text 2

For the past several years, the *Sunday* newspaper supplement *Parade* has featured a column called "Ask Marilyn". People are invited to query Marilyn vos Savant, who at age 10 had tested at a mental level of someone about 23 years old; that gave her an IQ of 228 — the highest score ever recorded. IQ tests ask you to complete verbal and visual analogies, to envision paper after it has been folded and cut, and to deduce numerical sequences, among other similar tasks. So it is a bit confusing when vos Savant fields such queries from the average Joe (whose IQ is 100) as, What's the difference between love and fondness? Or what is the nature of luck and coincidence? It's not obvious how the capacity to visualize objects and to figure out numerical patterns suits one to answer questions that have eluded some of the best poets and philosophers.

Clearly, intelligence encompasses more than a score on a test. Just what does it mean to be smart? How much of intelligence can be specified, and how much can we learn about it from neurology, genetics, computer science and other fields?

The defining term of intelligence in humans still seems to be the IQ score, even though IQ tests are not given as often as they used to be. The test comes primarily in two forms: the Stanford-Binet Intelligence Scale and the Wechsler Intelligence Scales(both come in adult and children's version). Generally costing several hundred dollars, they are usually given only by psychologists, although variations of them populate bookstores and the World Wide Web. Superhigh scores like vos Savant's are no longer possible, because scoring is now based on a statistical population distribution among age peers, rather than simply dividing the mental age by the chronological age and multiplying by 100. Other standardized tests, such as the Scholastic Assessment Test (SAT) and the Graduate Record Exam (GRE), capture the main aspects of IQ tests.

Such standardized tests may not assess all the important elements necessary to succeed in school and in life, argues Robert J. Sternberg. In his article "How Intelligent Is Intelligence Testing? ", Sternberg notes that traditional test best assess analytical and verbal skills but fail to measure creativity and practical knowledge, components also critical to problem solving and life success. Moreover, IQ tests do not necessarily predict so well once populations or situations change. Research has found that IQ predicted leadership skills when the tests were given under low-stress conditions, but under high-stress conditions, IQ was negatively correlated with leadership — that is, it predicted the opposite. Anyone who has toiled through SAT will testify that test-taking skill also matters, whether it's knowing when to guess or what questions to skip.

26. Which of the following may be required in an intelligence test?

    A. Answering philosophical questions.

    B. Folding or cutting paper into different shapes.

    C. Telling the differences between certain concepts.

    D. Choosing words or graphs similar to the given ones.

27. What can be inferred about intelligence testing from Paragraph 3?

    A. People no longer use IQ scores as an indicator of intelligence.

    B. More versions of IQ tests are now available on the Internet.

    C. The test contents and formats for adults and children may be different.

    D. Scientists have defined the important elements of human intelligence.

28. People nowadays can no longer achieve IQ scores as high as vos Savant's because _____.

    A. the scores are obtained through different computational procedures

    B. creativity rather than analytical skills is emphasized now

C. vos Savant's case is an extreme one that will not repeat

D. the defining characteristic of IQ tests has changed

29. We can conclude from the last paragraph that _____.

    A. test scores may not be reliable indicators of one's ability

    B. IQ scores and SAT results are highly correlated

    C. testing involves a lot of guesswork

    D. traditional test are out of date

30. What is the author's attitude towards IQ tests?

    A. Supportive.   B. Skeptical.   C. Impartial.   D. Biased.

Text 3

During the past generation, the American middle-class family that once could count on hard work and fair play to keep itself financially secure had been transformed by economic risk and new realities. Now a pink slip, a bad diagnosis, or a disappearing spouse can reduce a family from solidly middle class to newly poor in a few months.

In just one generation, millions of mothers have gone to work, transforming basic family economics. Scholars, policymakers, and critics of all stripes have debated the social implications of these changes, but few have looked at the side effect: family risk has risen as well. Today's families have budgeted to the limits of their new two-paycheck status. As a result, they have lost the parachute they once had in times of financial setback — a back-up earner(usually Mom) who could go into the workforce if the primary earner got laid off or fell sick. This "added-worker effect" could support the safety net offered by unemployment insurance or disability insurance to help families weather bad times. But today, a disruption to family fortunes can no longer be made up with extra income from an otherwise-stay-at-home partner.

During the same period, families have been asked to absorb much more risk in their retirement income. Steelworkers, airline employees, and now those in the auto industry are joining millions of families who must worry about interest rates, stock market fluctuation, and the harsh reality that they may outlive their retirement money. For much of the past year, President Bush campaigned to move Social Security to a saving-account model, with retirees trading much or all of their guaranteed payments for payments depending on investment returns. For younger families, the picture is not any better. Both the absolute cost of healthcare and the share of it borne by families have risen-and newly fashionable health-savings plans are spreading from legislative halls to Wal-Mart workers, with much higher deductibles and a large new dose of investment risk for families' future healthcare. Even demographics are working against the middle class family, as the odds of having a weak elderly parent — and all the attendant need for physical and financial assistance — have jumped eightfold in just one generation.

From the middle-class family perspective, much of this, understandably, looks far less like an opportunity to exercise more financial responsibility, and a good deal more like a frightening acceleration of the wholesale shift of financial risk onto their already overburdened shoulders. The financial fallout has begun, and the political fallout may not be far behind.

31. Today's double-income families are at greater financial risk in that _____.

　　A. the safety net they used to enjoy has disappeared

　　B. their chances of being laid off have greatly increased

　　C. they are more vulnerable to changes in family economics

　　D. they are deprived of unemployment or disability insurance

32. As a result of President Bush's reform, retired people may have _____.

　　A. a higher sense of security　　　　B. less secured payments

　　C. less chance to invest　　　　　　D. a guaranteed future

33. According to the author, health-savings plans will _____.

　　A. help reduce the cost of healthcare

　　B. popularize among the middle class

　　C. compensate for the reduced pensions

　　D. increase the families' investment risk

34. It can be inferred from the last paragraph that _____.

　　A. financial risks tend to outweigh political risks

　　B. the middle class may face greater political challenges

　　C. financial problems may bring about political problems

　　D. financial responsibility is an indicator of political status

35. Which of the following is the best title for this text?

　　A. The Middle Class on the Alert.

　　B. The Middle Class on the Cliff.

　　C. The Middle Class in Conflict.

　　D. The Middle Class in Ruins.

Text 4

It never rains but it pours. Just as bosses and boards have finally sorted out their worst accounting and compliance troubles, and improved their feeble corporation governance, a new problem threatens to earn them — especially in America — the sort of nasty headlines that inevitably lead to heads rolling in the executive suite: data insecurity. Left, until now, to odd, low-level IT staff to put right, and seen as a concern only of data-rich industries such as banking, telecoms and air travel, information protection is now high on the boss's agenda in businesses of every variety.

Several massive leakages of customer and employee data this year — from organizations as diverse as Time Warner, the American defense contractor Science Applications International Corp and even the University of California, Berkeley — have left managers hurriedly peering into their intricate IT systems and business processes in search of potential vulnerabilities.

"Data is becoming an asset which needs to be guarded as much as any other asset," says Haim Mendelson of Stanford University's business school. "The ability to guard customer data is the key to market value, which the board is responsible for on behalf of shareholders." Indeed, just as there is the concept of Generally Accepted Accounting Principles(GAAP), perhaps it is time for GASP, Generally Accepted Security Practices, suggested Eli Noam of New York's Columbia Business School. "Setting the proper investment level for security, redundancy, and recovery is a management issue, not a technical one," he says.

The mystery is that this should come as a surprise to any boss. Surely it should be obvious to the dimmest executive that trust, that most valuable of economic assets, is easily destroyed and hugely expensive to restore — and that few things are more likely to destroy trust than a company letting sensitive personal data get into the wrong hands.

The current state of affairs may have been encouraged — though not justified — by the lack of legal penalty (in America, but not Europe) for data leakage. Until California recently passed a law, American firms did not have to tell anyone, even the victim, when data went astray. That may change fast: lots of proposed data-security legislation is now doing the rounds in Washington, D.C. Meanwhile, the theft of information about some 40 million credit-card accounts in America, disclosed on June 17th, overshadowed a hugely important decision a day earlier by America's Federal Trade Commission(FTC) that puts corporate America on notice that regulators will act if firms fail to provide adequate data security.

36. The statement "It never rains but it pours" is used to introduce _____.

    A. the fierce business competition

    B. the feeble boss-board relations

    C. the threat from news reports

    D. the severity of data leakage

37. According to Paragraph 2, some organizations check their systems to find out _____.

    A. whether there is any weak point

    B. what sort of data has been stolen

    C. who is responsible for the leakage

    D. how the potential spies can be located

38. In bringing up the concept of GASP the author is making the point that _____.

    A. shareholders' interests should be properly attended to

    B. information protection should be given due attention

    C. businesses should enhance their level of accounting security

    D. the market value of customer data should be emphasized

39. According to Paragraph 4, what puzzles the author is that some bosses fail to _____.

A. see the link between trust and data protection

B. perceive the sensitivity of personal data

C. realize the high cost of data restoration

D. appreciate the economic value of trust

40. It can be inferred from Paragraph 5 that _____.

A. data leakage is more severe in Europe

B. FTC's decision is essential to data security

C. California takes the lead in security legislation

D. legal penalty is a major solution to data leakage

Part B

Directions:

You are going to read a list of headings and a text about what parents are supposed to do to guide their children into adulthood. Choose a heading from the list A—G that best fits the meaning of each numbered part of the text(41—45). The first and last paragraphs of the text are not numbered. There are two extra headings that you do not need to use. Mark your answers on ANSWER SHEET 1.

A. Set a Good Example for Your Kids

B. Build Your Kids' Work Skills

C. Place Time Limits on Leisure Activities

D. Talk about the Future on a Regular Basis

E. Help Kids Develop Coping Strategies

F. Help Your Kids Figure Out Who They Are

G. Build Your Kids' Sense of Responsibility

How Can a Parent Help?

Mothers and fathers can do a lot to ensure a safe landing in early adulthood for their kids. Even if a job's starting salary seems too small to satisfy an emerging adult's need for rapid content, the transition from school to work can be less of a setback if the start-up adult is ready for the move. Here are a few measures, drawn from my book *Ready or Not, Here Life Comes*, that parents can take to prevent what I call "work-life unreadiness":

41	

You can start this process when they are 11 or 12. Periodically review their emerging strengths and weaknesses with them and work together on any shortcomings, like difficulty in communicating well or collaborating. Also, identify the kinds of interests they keep coming back to, as these offer clues to the careers that will fit them best.

42	

Kids need a range of authentic role models — as opposed to members of their clique, pop stars and vaunted athletes. Have regular dinner-table discussions about people the family knows and how they got where they are. Discuss the joys and downsides of your own career and encourage your kids to form some ideas about their own future. When asked what they want to do, they should be discouraged from saying "I have no idea." They can change their minds 200 times, but having only a foggy view of the future is of little good.

43	

Teachers are responsible for teaching kids how to learn; parents should be responsible for teaching them how to work. Assign responsibilities around the house and make sure homework deadlines are met. Encourage teenagers to take a part-time job. Kids need plenty of practice delaying gratification and deploying effective organizational skills, such as managing time and setting priorities.

44	

Playing video games encourages immediate content. And hours of watching TV shows with canned laughter only teaches kids to process information in a passive way. At the same time, listening through earphones to the same monotonous beats for long stretches encourages kids to stay inside their bubble instead of pursuing other endeavors. All these activities can prevent the growth of important communication and thinking skills and make it difficult for kids to develop the kind of sustained concentration they will need for most jobs.

45	

They should know how to deal with setbacks, stresses and feelings of inadequacy. They should also learn how to solve problems and resolve conflicts, ways to brainstorm and think critically. Discussions at home can help kids practice doing these things and help them apply these skills to everyday life situations.

What about the son or daughter who is grown but seems to be struggling and wandering aimlessly through early adulthood? Parents still have a major role to play, but now it is more delicate. They have to be careful not to come across as disappointed in their child. They should exhibit strong interest and respect for whatever currently interests their fledging adult (as naive or ill conceived as it may seem) while becoming a partner in exploring options for the future. Most of all, these new adults must feel that they are respected and supported by a family that appreciates them.

Part C

Directions:
*Read the following text carefully and then translate the underlined segments into Chinese. Your translation should be written clearly on **ANSWER SHEET 2**.*

The study of law has been recognized for centuries as a basic intellectual discipline in European universities. However, only in recent years has it become a feature of undergraduate programs in Canadian universities. (46) Traditionally, legal learning has been viewed in such institutions as the special preserve of lawyers, rather than a necessary part of the intellectual equipment of an educated person. Happily, the older and more continental view of legal education is establishing itself in a number of Canadian universities and some have even begun to offer undergraduate degrees in law.

If the study of law is beginning to establish itself as part and parcel of a general education, its aims and methods should appeal directly to journalism educators. Law is a discipline which encourages responsible judgment. On the one hand, it provides opportunities to analyze such ideas as justice, democracy and freedom. (47) On the other, it links these concepts to everyday realities in a manner which is parallel to the links journalists forge on a daily basis as they cover and comment on the news. For example, notions of evidence and fact, of basic rights and public interest are at work in the process of journalistic judgment and production just as in courts of law. Sharpening judgment by absorbing and reflecting on law is a desirable component of a journalist's intellectual preparation for his or her career.

(48) But the idea that the journalist must understand the law more profoundly than an ordinary citizen rests on an understanding of the established conventions and special responsibilities of the news media. Politics or, more broadly, the functioning of the state, is a major subject for journalists. The better informed they are about the way the state works, the better their reporting will be. (49) In fact, it is difficult to see how journalists who do not have a clear grasp of the basic features of the Canadian Constitution can do a competent job on political stories.

Furthermore, the legal system and the events which occur within it are primary subjects for journalists. While the quality of legal journalism varies greatly, there is an undue reliance amongst many journalists on interpretations supplied to them by lawyers. (50) While comment and reaction from lawyers may enhance stories, it is preferable for journalists to rely on their own notions of significance and make their own judgments. These can only come from a well-grounded understanding of the legal system.

2007 年 考研英语全真试题
(阅读理解部分)解析

Part A

Text 1

○长难句分析○

1. This success, coupled with later research showing that memory itself is not genetically determined, led Ericsson to conclude that the act of memorizing is more of a cognitive exercise than an intuitive one.

❖**结构分析** 句子主干为 This success led Ericsson to conclude that.中间 coupled with later research showing that... ,这一部分,coupled with 是过去分词作状语,表示"和其他一些研究",showing 是 research 的定语,"表明…的实验"。后面 conclude that 中 that 引导宾语从句,是结论的内容,more... than 意为"与其说…还不如说"。

2. In other words, whatever inborn differences two people may exhibit in their abilities to memorize, those differences are swamped by how well each person"encodes" the information.

❖**结构分析** 主句为 Those differences are swamped by how well each person "encodes" the in-formation. whatever inborn differences two people may exhibit in their abilities to memorize 是 whatever 引导的让步状语从句,其中 two people may exhibit... 是省略连词的定语从句,修饰 differences,意为"两个人在记忆力方面所表现出来的差异"。

试 题 分 析

21. [C] 结构题。第一段和后文在内容上没有多大联系,只是一个例子引出后面作者要谈的问题。文章提到在足球运动员中发现的生日现象是为了"导入出色表现是如何形成的这一话题"。因此答案为 C。

22. [B] 词义猜测题。要根据上下文仔细判断,也可以把选项中的词代入到句中逐一试验。这个句子是 soccer-mad parents are more likely to conceive children in springtime, at the annual peak of soccer mania; 前文是 soccer-mad parents, 意为"对足球疯狂的父母",和后面的这个词对应,因此答案为 B "疯狂",意为 "每年对足球疯狂的最高峰"。

23. [A] 细节题。第四段开头说这次成功的实验和后来的研究表明,记忆本身不是由基因决定的。这使安德斯·埃里克森得出结论认为,记忆行为更是一种认知性的训练而不是天生的。因此可以排除 B"来自直觉而不是认知练习"和 C"由基因而不是由心理因素决定";D"需要即时反馈和高度集中的注意力"是说明"有意识试验需要即时反馈",而不是记忆力本身;答案为 A"依靠对信息有意义的处理过程",与"认知性训练"相关,也和对信息的"解码"能力相关——二者都是说记忆取决于对信息进行有意义的处理。

24. [D] 细节题。文章最后说,埃里克森和他的同事结论是"天赋"被高估了。换句话说,那些佼佼者们都是后天造就的,而不是天生的。因此答案是 D"佼佼者们通常把成功归于培养"。

25. [C] 主旨大意题。本文主要是讲成功来自后天的能力。先排除 B"种瓜得瓜,种豆得豆"和 D"有其父必有其子";B 讲因果关系和文章没关系;D 和原意相反。A"信念能移山"侧重于信念,和后天努力也不相符。答案为 C"练习造就完美,熟能生巧",强调后天的练习。

参考译文

　　如果查看 2006 年世界杯所有参赛队员的出生证明的话,你就会发现一个让人瞠目结舌的怪现象:优秀的足球运动员大都出生在一年的上半年,而不是下半年。如果再查看一下为世界杯和职业球队输送球员的欧洲各国家青年队,你会发现这种奇怪的现象更加突出。

　　造成这一怪现象的原因是什么呢?这里有几种猜测:a)某些星相特征赋予球员高超的球技。b)在冬季出生的婴儿可能会有更高的氧容量,这增加了球员的持久力。c)球迷父母更可能在春季怀孕,因为这是每年的足球热的高峰期。d)以上都不成立。

　　佛罗里达州立大学 58 岁的心理学教授安德斯·埃里克森说他极其赞同第四种答案"以上都不成立"。他在瑞典长大,在他意识到如果转行到心理学领域才有更多机会进行自己的研究之前,他学习的是核工程学。他在大约 30 年前进行了第一个试验,这试验与记忆有关:训练一个人听一组随机数字然后把重复。"在进行了大约 20 小时的训练之后,第一个受试者的数字记忆范围就从 7 个增加到了 20 个,"安德斯·埃里克森回忆道,"他一直在进步,200 小时的训练后,他能记忆的数字增加到了 80 个。"

　　这次成功的实验和后来的研究表明,记忆本身不是由基因决定的。这使安德斯·埃里克森得出结论认为,记忆行为更是一种认知性的训练而不是天生的。换句话说,无论两个人之间在记忆方面与生俱来的差异有多大,这些差异都能被一个人对信息的"解码"能力所抵消。了解如何对信息进行有意义的编码的最佳方式,埃里克森认为,是一种被称作"有意识训练"的过程。这种训练不仅仅需要简单地重复某个任务,而是要确立具体的目标,获得及时的反馈,既注重方法也注重结果。

　　他和他的同事开始研究包括足球在内的许多领域的佼佼者。他们尽可能地收集各种数据而不仅仅是这些人所取得成就的统计数字和传记细节,还包括他们自己对这些佼佼者所做的试验结果。他们的研究得出了让人惊讶的结论:我们高估了通常被称为"天赋"的东西。

换句话说,那些佼佼者——无论是记忆能力超强者还是外科医生,无论是芭蕾演员还是电脑程序设计师——都是后天造就的,而不是天生的。

Text 2

长难句分析

1. It's not obvious how the capacity to visualize objects and to figure out numerical patterns suits one to answer questions that have eluded some of the best poets and philosophers.

❖ **结构分析** 这个从句由 how 引导,主语是 capacity, to visualize objects and to figure out numerical patterns 是并列的不定式作定语修饰 capacity,谓语是 suits。后面是 that 引导的是定语从句,谓语 elude 的意思是"躲避,理解不了",elude sb. that 就是"使某人理解不了"。

2. Superhigh scores like vos Savant's are no longer possible, because scoring is now based on a statistical population distribution among age peers, rather than simply dividing the mental age by the chronological age and multiplying by 100.

❖ **结构分析** 主句很明了,Superhigh scores... are no longer possible.从句中的主语是非谓语动词 scoring,后面 rather than 是肯定前面的说法,否定后面的,可译为"而不是",dividing 和 multiplying 并列,表示"除以…再乘以"。

3. Research has found that IQ predicted leadership skills when the tests were given under low-stress conditions, but under high-stress conditions, IQ was negatively correlated with leadership — that is, it predicted the opposite.

❖ **结构分析** 本句结构很清楚,要注意里面的连词,that/when/but,可以先抛弃主句 research has found that 分析后面的句子。negatively correlated with leadership 意为"与领导能力负相关"。

试题分析

26. [D] 细节题。根据第一段,可先排除 A 和 C,它们都没被提到;B"把纸折成或剪成不同的形状"和 D"选出与给出词语或图案相似的选项"之间选哪个,要仔细读文章;原文 to envision paper after it has been folded and cut 的意思是对纸张被折叠或剪裁之后的形状进行想象,而不是要测试者自己去动手,所以 B 是错误的;D 符合原文 to complete verbal and visual analogies, 即对语言或形状进行类推。

27. [C] 推论题。第三段主要介绍智力测试的现状。根据第一句 the defining term of intelligence in humans still seems to be the IQ score,可知答案 A"人们不再用智商分数当做智力评判的标准"不正确;根据 although variations of them populate bookstores and the World Wide Web 似乎 B"在互联网上有更多的智力测试版本"是正确的,但实际上 them 指的是前面提到的两种主要版本,variations 是指它们的变体,而不是更多的智力测试版本;D"科学家已经定义了人类智力的重要因素"在第三段没有被提及,故可排除; 可从 the Stanford-Binet Intelligence Scale and the Wechsler Intelligence Scales (both come in adult and children's version)处确定答案为 C"成人和儿童的测试内容不一样"。

28. [A] 细节题。参考长难句分析 2,答案应为 A。现在人们无法再得到像沃斯·莎凡特那样的高分,是因为现在通过不同的计算形式得出分数。

29. [A] 细节题。最后一段多次对智商测试的结果表示怀疑,比如说测不出创造能力和实践能力,对领导能力的测试也要根据压力水平的大小来定。并且还讲到,如果测试条件和受众发生变化,其预测能力也会发生变化。因此答案应该为 A"测试结果可能无法正确反映一个人的能力";B"SAT 和 IQ 分数的关系"没有被提到;C"测试中猜测因素很多"和原文意思不符,文章只是说测试者在测试过程中可以有些猜测技巧;D"传统测试已经过时了"没有被提到。

30. [B] 归纳推论题。作者的态度比较明确地反映在最后一段,前面只是介绍并没有表态。作者认为智商测试的结果是不可靠的,也不能全面反映出测试者的全部能力。因此答案是 B"怀疑"。

参考译文

　　这些年《周日报》增刊《行列》开设了一个特色专栏"请问玛丽莲",邀请人们对玛丽莲·沃斯·莎凡特提问。她在 10 岁的时候被测定其智力水平达到了 23 岁,智商高达 223——这是有史以来的最高值。智商测试要求你完成语言和视觉类比,想象纸被折叠和剪开之后的形状,对数字顺序进行推理和其他一些类似任务。因此当沃斯·莎凡特对普通人 (其智商是 100)提出的问题(比如"爱与喜欢有什么区别","幸运与巧合的特征是什么")作出即席回答时,确实让人感到有一点点困惑。现在还不清楚,想象物体与数字推理的能力如何使人能够回答那些足以使最优秀的诗人和哲学家都感到困惑的问题。

　　显然,智力不仅仅包含一次测验的分数。聪明的含义是什么?智力在多大程度上可以被细化?我们从神经学、基因学、计算机科学和其他领域中能对智力了解多少呢?

　　虽然人们不像以前那样频繁地进行智商测验了,但是确定一个人智力的标准似乎仍然是智商分数。智商测试主要包括两种形式:斯坦福·比内智力量表和韦克斯勒智力量表(二者都分为成人和儿童两种版本)。尽管这两种智力测试的很多变体已经充斥了书店和互联网,但做这些测试一般要花费几百美元,只有心理学家才能提供。像沃斯·莎凡特那样的超级高分已经不可能再出现了,因为现在以同一年龄的人口分布统计数字为基础,而不再是简单地用实足年龄除以心理年龄再乘以 100。其他一些标准化测试,比如学术能力测试(SAT)和研究生入学考试(GRE)都具有智力测试的主要方面。

　　罗伯特·施特恩贝格认为,这些智力测试可能无法评估在学校和生活中取得成功所必须的全部重要因素。在他的文章《智力测试到底多有智慧》中,他注意到传统的测试可以评估分析和语言能力,却不能测量创造力和实践知识,这些因素也是解决问题和取得生活成功的因素。还有,当对象人群或者测试情况发生变化时,智商测试也不一定能准确预测。研究表明,当压力小时,智商测试能预测领导能力,但压力很大时,智商与领导能力却有负面关联,也就是说,事实与它的预测相反。任何费力做过 SAT 的人都可以证明,应试技巧也很重要,比如应该知道哪些题需要猜测,哪些题则要跳过等。

Text 3

长难句分析

1. **During the past generation, the American middle-class family that once could count on hard work and fair play to keep itself financially secure had been transformed by economic risk and new realities.**

   ❖ 结构分析 句子主干为 The American middle-class family had been transformed by economic risk and new realities. that once could count on hard work and fair play to keep itself financially secure 是定语从句。count on 意为"依靠,指望",to keep itself financially secure 是目的状语,"为了保持财政安全"即指收入稳定。

2. **This "added-worker effect" could support the safety net offered by unemployment insurance or disability insurance to help families weather bad times.**

   ❖ 结构分析 offered by 是表示被动的过去分词修饰 safety net,即"由失业保险和伤残保险所提供的安全网络"。weather 在这里是及物动词,意为"经得住,平安度过"。

3. **Both the absolute cost of healthcare and the share of it borne by families have risen — and newly fashionable health-savings plans are spreading from legislative halls to Wal-Mart workers, with much higher deductibles and a large new dose of investment risk for families' future healthcare.**

   ❖ 结构分析 这一长句包括 Both the absolute cost of healthcare and the share of it have risen 和 newly fashionable health-savings plans are spreading from legislative halls to Wal-Mart workers 这两个句子。with much higher deductibles and a large new dose of investment... 是伴随而来的情况,即"工资中可扣除的部分更高,未来的家庭医疗具有更大的投资风险。"

4. **From the middle-class family perspective, much of this, understandably, looks far less like an opportunity to exercise more financial responsibility, and a good deal more like a frightening acceleration of the wholesale shift of financial risk onto their already overburdened shoulders.**

   ❖ 结构分析 注意句子里的一个平行结构:far less like an opportunity to... a good deal more like...意为"不像是…而像是…,与其说是…还不如说是…"。

试题分析

31. [C] 细节归纳题。文章第二段说,现在的家庭依据新的双收入的最高值制订自己的财政预算,结果,他们失去了在金融衰退时曾经拥有过的保护伞——一个备用的挣钱者可以在主劳力失业或生病时进入劳动力市场。因此,答案应该为C"他们更易受家庭经济变化的影响";A"他们过去所享受的安全网络消失了"和D"他们被剥夺了失业或伤残保险"不正确,因为失业或伤残保险所提供的安全网不是消失了,而是说现在对双收入家庭来说作用不大了;B"他们失业的可能性增加了"没有被提到。

32. [B] 细节题。第三段说,布什总统努力将社会保障体系转变为储蓄账户模式,让退休人员把他们可靠收入的大部分或全部都进行交易,转变为由投资收益所决定的收入。可见答案B"更不稳定的收入"是正确的。

33. [D] 细节题。第三段说健康储蓄计划会带来的后果:工资中可扣除的部分更高,未来的家庭医疗具有更大的投资风险。因此答案应为D"增加家庭的投资风险"。

34. [C] 推理判断题。最后一段说,对中产家庭来说,不是让他们承担更多金融责任的机会,而是把金融风险转嫁到他们肩上。金融问题所带来的不良后果已经开始出现,而随之而来的可能是政治方面问题所带来的副作用。因此很明显答案应为C"经济问题可能会带来政治问题";A"经济风险往往大于政治风险",B"中产阶级将面临更大的政治挑战"和D"支付能力是政治地位的象征"都与这一段的意思不符。

35. [B] 主旨大意题。文章讲到中产阶级家庭目前所面临的经济压力及可能带来的政治后果,无论是对退休人员还是对年轻一些的中产家庭而言,他们所要面临的困难和风险都要超过以往。因此,答案B"悬崖边的中产阶级"才符合题意,意为"中产阶级正处于比较艰难、危险的境地"。

参考译文

过去要通过努力工作和公平竞争,一个美国的中产阶级家庭才能取得可靠的收入,而对上一代人来说,这种情况被经济风险和新的社会现实改变了。现在解雇通知书、疾病诊断证明或者配偶的去世等等,都会在几个月内在把一个稳定的中产家庭变成新的穷困家庭。

仅仅用了一代人的时间,数百万做妈妈的妇女开始去工作,这改变了基本的家庭经济结构。许多学者、政策制订者和各式的批评家们对这些变化的社会意义进行了辩论,但几乎没有人能看到它的副作用:家庭风险增高了。现在的家庭依据新的双收入的最高值制订自己的财政预算,结果,他们失去了在金融衰退时曾经拥有过的保护伞——一个备用的挣钱者(通常是母亲)可以在主劳力失业或生病时进入劳动力市场。这种"后备劳力效应"可以支持由失业保险或伤残保险提供的安全网,帮助家庭度过困难时刻。但现在,家庭经济收入的中断无法再由来自某个原来呆在家里的伴侣出去工作挣钱而得到补偿了。

同时一个家庭的退休收入也比以前更有风险。钢铁工人、航空职员和现在汽车行业的工作人员都和其他数百万的家庭一样,要为利率高低、股市震荡和得不到足以颐养天年的退休金等等现实而忧心忡忡。在去年很多时候,布什总统努力将社会保障体系转变为储蓄账户模式,让退休人员把他们可靠收入的大部分或全部都进行交易,转变为由投资收益所决定的收入。对于年轻一些的家庭而言,情况也同样糟糕。医疗方面的总支出和家庭必须分担的份额都增加了,并且新近流行的健康储蓄计划正从立法大厅推广到沃尔玛的员工,工资中可扣除的部分更高,未来的家庭医疗具有更大的投资风险。甚至人口统计也不利于中产家庭,父母因年老体弱所需要的各种费用及照顾老人时体力和经济上的支出在一代之间就增长了 8 倍。

可以理解,对中产家庭来说这些情况中的很大一部分不是让他们承担更多金融责任的机会,倒更像是把金融风险以令人恐惧的速度越来越快地转嫁到他们原就已经超负荷承受的肩上。金融问题所带来的不良后果已经开始出现,而随之而来的可能是政治方面问题所带来的副作用。

Text 4

长难句分析

1. **Just as bosses and boards have finally sorted out their worst accounting and compliance troubles, and improved their feeble corporation governance, a new problem threatens to earn them — especially in America — the sort of nasty headlines that inevitably lead to heads rolling in the executive suite: data insecurity.**

   ❖结构分析 just as 引导时间状语从句,其谓语是 have sorted out... and improved。accounting 指 "公司账目",compliance troubles. 是 "违纪问题"。 A new problem threatens to earn them a sort of nasty headlines 是主句的主干,earn sb. sth. 意为 "给某人赢得什么东西",这里的意思是 "使他们成为丑闻的标题"。that inevitably lead to... 是定语从句修饰 headlines,即 "必然导致管理层头疼不已"。

2. **Left, until now, to odd, low-level IT staff to put right, and seen as a concern only of data-rich industries such as banking, telecoms and air travel, information protection is now high on the boss's agenda in businesses of every variety.**

   ❖结构分析 句子的主语为 information protection,因此 left,seen 都和 information protection 有被动关系。left to odd, low-level IT staff to put right,即 "把信息保护交给那些业余的、低水平的临时员工";seen as a concern only of data-rich industries 意为 "把信息保护看成是只有那些数据丰富的行业才关注的事情"。

3. **Several massive leakages of customer and employee data this year — from organizations as diverse as Time Warner, the American defense contractor Science Applications International Corp and even the University of California, Berkeley — have left managers hurriedly peering into their intricate IT systems and business processes in search of potential vulnerabilities.**

❖结构分析 本句主干为 Several massive leakages of customer and employee data this year have left managers hurriedly peering into their intricate IT systems and business processes. leave sb. doing sth. 即"使某人做某事"。中间的插入成分都是公司的名字。in search of potential vulnerabilities 即"目的是寻找可能存在的安全隐患"。

4. **Surely it should be obvious to the dimmest executive that trust, that most valuable of economic assets, is easily destroyed and hugely expensive to restore — and that few things are more likely to destroy trust than a company letting sensitive personal data get into the wrong hands.**

❖结构分析 主句为 It should be obvious to the dimmest executive. 第一个 that 所引导的从句的主干是 trust is easily destroyed and hugely expensive to restore。and that... 是和前面并列的从句，里面的 few things are more likely to destroy trust than... 的意思是"最能破坏信用的事情是…",a company letting sensitive personal... 是 than 的介词宾语,letting 引出的这个短语作定语修饰 company, 即"让信息泄露出去的公司"。

试 题 分 析

36. [D] 结构题。It never rains but it pours. 这句话被用来引入文章的主旨,即信息安全的问题。因此答案应该为 D"信息泄露的严重性"。

37. [A] 细节题。参见长难句解析 3。答案为 A"是否存在弱点"。

38. [B] 细节题。第三段说数据日益成为一种资产,需要和其他资产一样好好保护。保护顾客数据资料的能力是市场价值的关键因素,建立公认安全准则(GASP)是"为数据的安全、备份和恢复设定恰当的投资标准是一个管理问题而不是技术问题。"因此答案应该为 B"应该给信息保护以更多关注"; A"应该适当关注股东的利益"不对,因为关注股东的利益不是建立 GASP 的直接目的;C 和 D 都没有被提到。

39. [A] 细节题。可参考长难句分析 4。 答案为 A"看到信用和数据保护之间的联系"。

40. [D] 推论题。第五段说,缺少法律制裁信息泄露的情况在美国更严重而不是欧洲,因此先排除掉 A"信息泄露在欧洲更为严重";美国联邦贸易委员的决议是执法者将对无法提供适当数据安全保障的公司依法进行制裁,但它的重要性不得而知,并且作者也说,这个消息并没有受到太多关注。加利福尼亚通过一项法律,但没有说什么领先地位,故 C"加利福尼亚在安全立法方面处于领先地位"也不对;依据第一句话,作者认为:"可能是缺少法律制裁才怂恿了信息泄露事件的发生(在美国而不是欧洲),虽然这一点未被证实。"然后又谈到了加利福尼亚的法律、美国联邦贸易委员的决定等,可见作者认为法律是解决问题的重要方式,答案是 D"法律惩罚是解决信息泄露的重要方式";B"联邦贸易委员会的决定对信息安全问题至关重要"也不对。

参考译文

祸不单行。就在老板和董事会最终解决了他们最糟糕的账目和纪律问题并加强了原本薄弱的公司管理之后，一个新的问题却又在迫近，使他们——尤其是在美国——成为丑闻的标题，这必将使高层们头疼不已：这就是数据的安全问题。直到现在，信息保护仍然被交给低水平的 IT 临时职员完成，人们认为只有那些需要庞大数据的行业如银行、电信和航空业才需要，而目前信息保护最终被各行各业的老板当作重要的内容而提上了议事日程。

今年某些顾客和雇员的信息数据发生几起重大泄露事件，包括时代华纳公司、美国国防承包商国际科学应用公司甚至加利福尼亚大学伯克利分校等在内的各种机构，都使这管理人员匆忙对其复杂的 IT 系统和商业流程进行检查，寻找可能存在的安全隐患。

斯坦福大学商学院的海姆·门德尔顿说，"数据日益成为一种资产，需要和其他资产一样好好保护。保护顾客数据资料的能力是市场价值的关键因素，董事会应为了股东的利益而为此负责。"纽约哥伦比亚商学院的埃利·诺姆建议，事实上，就像存在着公认会计准则（GAAP）一样，也许现在是时候建立公认安全准则（GASP）了。他说，"为数据的安全、备份和恢复设定恰当的投资标准是一个管理问题而不是技术问题。"

让人困惑的是，所有老板都会对此大吃一惊。当然即使最迟钝的行政人员也能意识到，信用是最有价值的经济财产，但它也很容易丢失，重获信用必须要付出昂贵的代价，而最能毁掉信用的事莫过于一家公司让敏感的个人数据落入他人之手。

缺少法律制裁可能怂恿了信息泄露事件的发生（在美国而不是欧洲），虽然这一点未被证实。最近在加利福尼亚通过一项法律之前，美国的公司不必将数据泄露事件告知任何人，甚至是受害者本人。这种情况也会很快得以改变：人们提出许多数据安全法案并且在华盛顿特区得到一轮又一轮的讨论。与此同时，6 月 17 日曝光美国约四千万信用卡用户信息被盗，这一事件引起的关注超过了美国联邦贸易委员会前一天所做出的重大决定，该决定提醒所有美国公司注意，执法者将对无法提供适当数据安全保障的公司依法进行制裁。

Part B

试 题 分 析

[说明] 2007 年这一部分的试题与前两年有所不同，由选择文章段落内容改为选择小标题，考查的是对每一段的内容进行综合归纳的能力和逻辑推理的能力。因此，本年的这种出题方式难度比往年稍低。

41. [F] 本文的标题是"父母如何帮助孩子"，第一段是一个总体性的介绍，本题是给第一段选一个标题，从内容看"定期探讨他们的优缺点""识别他们的兴趣类型"等都是重要的提示。因此答案应为 F"帮助孩子了解自己"。其他几个选项可以快速排除。

42. [D] 本段重复出现的词是 future，答案就为 D。A 为干扰项，虽然本段一开始就说"孩子需要真实的角色榜样"，但并非指的是父母本身要树立这样的榜样，而是用身边那些

"真实的人"作为鼓励,故 A 可排除;D"定期讨论孩子的未来"符合本段的大意。

43. [B] 老师和家长的责任并不相同,家长要教给孩子如何工作,发展劳动技能等。答案应该为 B"培养孩子的劳动技能"。

44. [C] 本段说,打电子游戏、看电视、听流行音乐等都会限制孩子的发展。从中推断,作为家长要对这些活动的时间进行限制,答案应该为 C"限制孩子的业余活动时间"。

45. [E] 这一段说,孩子应该知道如何应对挫折、压力和失败感,也应学习如果解决问题和冲突,如何集思广益及进行批判性思考,家庭讨论可以帮助孩子练习如何应对这些事情,把这些技巧应用到日常生活环境中去。答案为 E"帮助孩子发展处理问题的办法"。

参考译文

父母如何帮助孩子?

父母能为孩子做很多事情,保证他们安全过渡到早期的成年阶段。即使一份工作初期的薪水不能满足一个刚成年者对快速获得满足感的需要,但如果这个刚成年的人做好了转变的准备,那么从学校到工作岗位的转变并不会有多少挫折。这里有一些措施来自我的这本书《准备好了吗:生活已经开始了》,可以提供给父母们,让他们能够避免我所说的"没有为工作生活做好准备"。

(41) 帮助孩子了解自我

你可以在孩子 11 岁或 12 岁的时候开始这个过程。定期同他们探讨他们的优缺点,并同他们一起克服缺点,比如与别人交流或合作感到困难等。还有,识别他们拥有的兴趣类型,因为这些可以为将来适合他们的工作提供线索。

(42) 定期讨论他们的未来

孩子们需要真实的角色榜样,这与他们的小圈子、流行明星以及自负的运动员等相反。定期在餐桌上讨论家人所认识的人,他们如何达到目前地位的。讨论你自己事业的酸甜苦辣,鼓励你的孩子形成自己关于未来的某些观念。如果你问他们将来希望干什么时,应该阻止他们说"我不知道"。他们可以改变自己的想法两百回,但是对未来只有一种模糊的看法没有什么好处。

(43) 培养孩子的劳动技能

老师的责任是教给孩子怎么学习;家长则应该教给孩子如何去工作。在家中分配给孩子一些任务,并且确保他们按时完成家庭作业。鼓励孩子们从事兼职工作。他们需要大量的实践,以延缓满足感并发展有效的组织技能,比如管理时间并设定哪些问题需要优先考虑。

(44) 限制业余活动时间

打电子游戏可能带来即时的满足感。几个小时观看带有"罐头笑声"的电视节目只能都会孩子们用消极的方式处理信息。同时,用耳机长时间听相同而单调的节奏会使孩子沉浸于自己的幻想之中,而不是进行其他努力。这些活动可能会阻碍孩子的交流和思考技能的发展,使他们很难培养出从事大多数工作所需要的注意力。

(45)帮助孩子发展处理问题的办法

他们应该知道如何应对挫折、压力和失败感。他们也应学习如果解决问题和冲突,如何集思广益及进行批判性思考。家庭内部的讨论能帮助孩子练习如何应对这些事情,并帮助他们把这些技巧应用到日常生活环境中去。

对那些已经长大却似乎在整个成年早期还在无目的地挣扎和游荡的儿女们,应该怎么办?父母仍然能扮演重要的角色,但却更加微妙些。这时一定要小心翼翼,不能给孩子留下对他们失望的印象。他们应该对羽翼未丰的成年子女(天真或者像他们所表面出来的那样经常考虑不周)所表现出的无论是什么兴趣都表示浓厚的兴趣和尊重,同时成为孩子们对寻求未来选择方面的伙伴。更重要的是,这些刚刚成年的人应当觉得他们受到一个赏识他们的家庭的尊重与支持。

Part C

试 题 分 析

46. **全句译文**:长久以来,人们认为在这些机构里,法律学习是律师的特殊领域,而不是一位受教育者知识素养中必要的组成部分。

   翻译提示:句子主干为 Legal learning has been viewed as... rather than... be viewed as... 意为"被视为…"。

47. **全句译文**:另一方面,它把这些概念与日常生活联系在一起,其方式与记者在进行日常的新闻报道和评论时的做法是一致的。

   翻译提示:句子主干为 It links these concepts to everyday realities. in a manner 表示"以…方式", 后面是定语从句 which is parallel to... forge on a daily basis... 其中 be parallel to sth.意为"与…类似",forge 意为"锻造、建立、伪造",此处指记者的报道行为,可译为"做法", on a daily basis 意为"日常的"。

48. **全句译文**:但是,新闻记者必须比普通公民更深刻地了解法律,这种观点是基于对新闻媒体既定习俗和特殊责任的认识之上的。

   翻译提示:句子的主干是 the idea rests on an understanding of... the idea that 后面是 idea的同位语,对 idea 进行解释说明。翻译时可用"…这一观念"这样的句式。

49. **全句译文**:事实上,很难看到那些对加拿大宪法的基本特色缺乏清楚了解的新闻记者能够胜任政治报道。

   翻译提示:see 后面是宾语从句,how 是连词,后面句子的主干是 Journalists can do a competent job on political stories. 中间 who 引导定语从句,是说明什么样的记者"那些对加拿大宪法的基本特色都缺乏清楚了解的记者"。

50. **全句译文**:律师的评论或反馈虽然可能会为报道增色,但新闻记者凭自己对事件重要性的认识做出自己的判断是更难能可贵的。

翻译提示：主句结构主干为 it is preferable for sb. to do sth. and do sth. 意为"某人做某事和某事更为可取"，rely on sth. 意为"基于…，以…为基础"。while 引导让步状语从句，comment and reaction from lawyers 是主语，may enhance stories 是其谓语和宾语，意为"来自律师的评论和反馈可能会为报道增色"。

参考译文

对法律的研究几个世纪以来都是欧洲大学的基础知识学科。然而，只是在最近几年，法律才成为加拿大大学教育的一门学科。(46)长久以来，人们认为在这些机构里，法律学习是律师的特殊领域，而不是一位受教育者知识素养中必要的组成部分。让人高兴的是，加拿大许多大学正在树立更古老、更具欧洲大陆特色的法律教育理念，有些大学甚至开始授予法律学士学位。

如果法律学习开始成为普通教育的必要部分，其目的和方法就应该会直接吸引新闻教育者们。法律是一门鼓励人们进行有责任判断的学科。一方面，法律为分析诸如正义、民主或自由等理念提供有利时机。(47)另一方面，它把这些概念与日常生活联系在一起，其方式与记者在进行日常新闻报道和评论时的做法是一致的。比如，证据、事实、基本权利、公共利益等概念在新闻判断和生产的过程中所起的作用与在法庭上是一样的。通过对法律的学习和反省使判断更加敏锐，这是记者在为其职业生涯做准备时有利的知识组成部分。

(48)但是，新闻记者必须比普通公民更深刻地了解法律，这种观点是基于对新闻媒体既定习俗和特殊责任的认识基础之上的。政治，或在更广泛的意义上讲，国家的功能是新闻的主要对象。他们对国家运行的方式了解越多，就越能写出好的新闻报道。(49)事实上，很难看到那些对加拿大宪法的基本特色缺乏清楚了解的新闻记者能够胜任政治报道。

法律系统及发生在其中的事件是新闻记者报道的主题。虽然法律新闻报道的质量千差万别，但是许多记者过分依赖律师给他们提供的解释。(50)律师的评论或反馈虽然可能会为报道增色，但新闻记者凭自己对事件重要性的认识做出自己的判断是更难能可贵的。只有对法律系统有充分了解才能做到这些。

2008 年 考研英语全真试题
(阅读理解部分)

Part A

Directions:

Read the following four texts. Answer the questions below each text by choosing A, B, C or D Mark your answers on **ANSWER SHEET 1.**

Text 1

While still catching-up to men in some spheres of modern life, women appear to be way ahead in at least one undesirable category. "Women are particularly susceptible to developing depression and anxiety disorders in response to stress compared to men," according to Dr. Yehuda, chief psychiatrist at New York's Veteran's Administration Hospital.

Studies of both animals and humans have shown that sex hormones somehow affect the stress response, causing females under stress to produce more of the trigger chemicals than do males under the same conditions. In several of the studies, when stressed-out female rats had their ovaries(the female reproductive organs) removed, their chemical responses became equal to those of the males.

Adding to a woman's increased dose of stress chemicals, are her increased "opportunities" for stress. "It's not necessarily that women don't cope as well. It's just that they have so much more to cope with," says Dr. Yehuda. "Their capacity for tolerating stress may even be greater than men's," she observes, "it's just that they're dealing with so many more things that they become worn out from it more visibly and sooner."

Dr. Yehuda notes another difference between the sexes. "I think that the kinds of things that women are exposed to tend to be in more of a chronic or repeated nature. Men go to war and are exposed to combat stress. Men are exposed to more acts of random physical violence. The kinds of interpersonal violence that women are exposed to tend to be in domestic situations, by, unfortunately, parents or other family members, and they tend not to be one-shot deals. The wear-and-tear that comes from these longer relationships can be quite devastating."

Adeline Alvarez married at 18 and gave birth to a son, but was determined to finish college. "I struggled a lot to get the college degree. I was living in so much frustration that that was my escape, to go to school, and get ahead and do better." Later, her marriage ended and she became a single mother. "It's the hardest thing to take care of a teenager, have a job, pay the rent, pay the car payment, and pay the debt. I lived from paycheck to paycheck."

Not everyone experiences the kinds of severe chronic stresses Alvarez describes. But most women today are coping with a lot of obligations, with few breaks, and feeling the strain. Alvarez's experience demonstrates the importance of finding ways to diffuse stress before it threatens your health and your ability to function.

21. Which of the following is true according to the first two paragraphs?

    A. Women are biologically more vulnerable to stress.

    B. Women are still suffering much stress caused by men.

    C. Women are more experienced than men in coping with stress.

    D. Men and women show different inclinations when faced with stress.

22. Dr. Yehuda's research suggests that women _____.

    A. need extra doses of chemicals to handle stress

    B. have limited capacity for tolerating stress

    C. are more capable of avoiding stress

    D. are exposed to more stress

23. According to Paragraph 4, the stress women confront tends to be _____.

    A. domestic and temporary

    B. irregular and violent

    C. durable and frequent

    D. trivial and random

24. The sentence "I lived from paycheck to paycheck." (Line 5, Paragraph 5) shows that

_____.

    A. Alvarez cared about nothing but making money

    B. Alvarez's salary barely covered her household expenses

    C. Alvarez got paychecks from different jobs

    D. Alvarez paid practically everything by check

25. Which of the following would be the best title for the text?

    A. Strain of Stress: No Way Out?

    B. Responses to Stress: Gender Difference.

    C. Stress Analysis: What Chemicals Say.

    D. Gender Inequality: Women Under Stress.

Text 2

It used to be so straightforward. A team of researchers working together in the laboratory would submit the results of their research to a journal. A journal editor would then remove the authors' names and affiliations from the paper and send it to their peers for review. Depending on the comments received, the editor would accept the paper for publication or decline it. Copyright rested with the journal publisher, and researchers seeking knowledge of the results would have to subscribe to the journal.

No longer. The Internet — and pressure from funding agencies, who are questioning why commercial publishers are making money from government-funded research by restricting access to it — is making access to scientific results a reality. The Organization for Economic Cooperation and Development (OECD) has just issued a report describing the farreaching consequences of this. The report, by John Houghton of Victoria University in Australia and Graham Vickery of the OECD, makes heavy reading for publishers who have, so far, made handsome profits. But it goes further than that. It signals a change in what has, until now, been a key element of scientific endeavor.

The value of knowledge and the return on the public investment in research depends, in part, upon wide distribution and ready access. It is big business. In America, the core scientific publishing market is estimated at between $ 7 billion and $ 11 billion. The International Association of Scientific, Technical and Medical Publishers says that there are more than 2,000 publishers worldwide specializing in these subjects. They publish more than 1.2 million articles each year in some 16,000 journals.

This is now changing. According to the OECD report, some 75% of scholarly journals are now online. Entirely new business models are emerging; three main ones were identified by the report's authors. There is the so-called big deal, where institutional subscribers pay for access to a collection of online journal titles through site-licensing agreements. There is open-access publishing, typically supported by asking the author (or his employer) to pay for the paper to be published. Finally, there are open-access archives, where organizations such as universities or international laboratories support institutional repositories. Other models exist that are hybrids of these three, such as delayed open-access, where journals allow only subscribers to read a paper for the first six months, before making it freely available to everyone who wishes to see it. All this could change the traditional form of the peer-review process, at least for the publication of papers.

26. In the first paragraph, the author discusses _____ .

    A. the background information of journal editing

    B. the publication routine of laboratory reports

    C. the relations of authors with journal publishers

    D. the traditional process of journal publication

27. Which of the following is true of the OECD report?

    A. It criticizes government-funded research.

    B. It introduces an effective means of publication.

    C. It upsets profit-making journal publishers.

D. It benefits scientific research considerably.

28. According to the text, online publication is significant in that _____.

    A. it provides an easier access to scientific results

    B. it brings huge profits to scientific researchers

    C. it emphasizes the crucial role of scientific knowledge

    D. it facilitates public investment in scientific research

29. With the open-access publishing model, the author of a paper is required to _____.

    A. cover the cost of its publication

    B. subscribe to the journal publishing it

    C. allow other online journals to use it freely

    D. complete the peer-review before submission

30. Which of the following best summarizes the main idea of the text?

    A. The Internet is posing a threat to publishers.

    B. A new mode of publication is emerging.

    C. Authors welcome the new channel for publication.

    D. Publication is rendered easier by online service.

Text 3

In the early 1960s Wilt Chamberlain was one of only three players in the National Basketball Association(NBA) listed at over seven feet. If he had played last season, however, he would have been one of 42. The bodies playing major professional sports have changed dramatically over the years, and managers have been more than willing to adjust team uniforms to fit the growing numbers of bigger, longer frames.

The trend in sports, though, may be obscuring an unrecognized reality: Americans have generally stopped growing. Though typically about two inches taller now than 140 years ago, today's people — especially those born to families who have lived in the U.S. for many generations — apparently reached their limit in the early 1960s. And they aren't likely to get any taller. "In the general population today, at this genetic, environmental level, we've pretty much gone as far as we can go," says anthropologist William Cameron Chumlea of Wright State University. In the case of NBA players, their increase in height appears to result from the increasingly common practice of recruiting players from all over the world.

Growth, which rarely continues beyond the age of 20, demands calories and nutrients—notably, protein — to feed expanding tissues. At the start of the 20th century, under-nutrition and childhood infections got in the way. But as diet and health improved, children and adolescents have, on average, increased in height by about an inch and a half every 20 years, a pattern known as the secular trend in height. Yet according to the Centers for Disease Control and Prevention, average height—5′9″ for men, 5′4″ for women — hasn't really changed since 1960.

Genetically speaking, there are advantages to avoiding substantial height. During childbirth, larger babies have more difficulty passing through the birth canal. Moreover, even though humans have been upright for millions of years, our feet and back continue to struggle with bipedal posture and cannot easily withstand repeated strain imposed by oversize limbs. "There are some real constraints that are set by the genetic architecture of the individual organism," says anthropologist William Leonard of Northwestern University.

Genetic maximums can change, but don't expect this to happen soon. Claire C. Gordon, senior anthropologist at the Army Research Center in Natick, Mass., ensures that 90 percent of the uniforms and workstations fit recruits without alteration. She says that, unlike those for basketball, the length of military uniforms has not changed for some time. And if you need to predict human height in the near future to design a piece of equipment, Gordon says that by and large, "you could use today's data and feel fairly confident."

31. Wilt Chamberlain is cited as an example to _____.

    A. illustrate the change of height of NBA players

    B. show the popularity of NBA players in the U.S.

    C. compare different generations of NBA players

    D. assess the achievements of famous NBA players

32. Which of the following plays a key role in body growth according to the text?

    A. Genetic modification.   B. Natural environment.

    C. Living standards.   D. Daily exercise.

33. On which of the following statements would the author most probably agree?

    A. Non-Americans add to the average height of the nation.

    B. Human height is conditioned by the upright posture.

    C. Americans are the tallest on average in the world.

    D. Larger babies tend to become taller in adulthood.

34. We learn from the last paragraph that in the near future _____.

    A. the garment industry will reconsider the uniform size

    B. the design of military uniforms will remain unchanged

    C. genetic testing will be employed in selecting sportsmen

    D. the existing data of human height will still be applicable

35. The text intends to tell us that _____.

    A. the change of human height follows a cyclic pattern

    B. human height is becoming even more predictable

    C. Americans have reached their genetic growth limit

    D. the genetic pattern of Americans has altered

Text 4

In 1784, five years before he became president of the United States, George Washington, 52, was nearly toothless. So he hired a dentist to transplant nine teeth into his jaw — having extracted them from the mouths of his slaves.

That's a far different image from the cherry-tree-chopping George most people remember from their history books. But recently, many historians have begun to focus on the roles slavery played in the lives of the founding generation. They have been spurred in part by DNA evidence made available in 1998, which almost certainly proved Thomas Jefferson had fathered at least one child with his slave Sally Hemings. And only over the past 30 years have scholars examined history from the bottom up. Works of several historians reveal the moral compromises made by the nation's early leaders and the fragile nature of the country's infancy. More significantly, they argue that many of the Founding Fathers knew slavery was wrong — and yet most did little to fight it.

More than anything, the historians say, the founders were hampered by the culture of their time. While Washington and Jefferson privately expressed distaste for slavery, they also understood that it was part of the political and economic bedrock of the country they helped to create.

For one thing, the South could not afford to part with its slaves. Owning slaves was "like having a large bank account," says Wiencek, author of *An Imperfect God: George Washington, His Slaves, and the Creation of America*. The southern states would not have signed the Constitution without protections for the "peculiar institution", including a clause that counted a slave as three fifths of a man for purposes of congressional representation.

And the statesmen's political lives depended on slavery. The three-fifths formula handed Jefferson his narrow victory in the presidential election of 1800 by inflating the votes of the southern states in the Electoral College. Once in office, Jefferson extended slavery with the *Louisiana Purchase* in 1803; the new land was carved into 13 states, including three slave states.

Still, Jefferson freed Hemings' children — though not Hemings herself or his approximately 150 other slaves. Washington, who had begun to believe that all men were created equal after observing the bravery of the black soldiers during the Revolutionary War, overcame the strong opposition of his relatives to grant his slaves their freedom in his will. Only a decade earlier, such an act would have required legislative approval in Virginia.

36. George Washington's dental surgery is mentioned to _____.

    A. show the primitive medical practice in the past

    B. demonstrate the cruelty of slavery in his days

    C. stress the role of slaves in the U.S. history

    D. reveal some unknown aspect of his life

37. We may infer from the second paragraph that _____.

 A. DNA technology has been widely applied to history research

 B. in its early days the U.S. was confronted with delicate situations

 C. historians deliberately made up some stories of Jefferson's life

 D. political compromises are easily found throughout the U.S. history

38. What do we learn about Thomas Jefferson?

 A. His political view changed his attitude towards slavery.

 B. His status as a father made him free the child slaves.

 C. His attitude towards slavery was complex.

 D. His affair with a slave stained his prestige.

39. Which of the following is true according to the text?

 A. Some Founding Fathers benefit politically from slavery.

 B. Slaves in the old days did not have the right to vote.

 C. Slave owners usually had large savings accounts.

 D. Slavery was regarded as a peculiar institution.

40. Washington's decision to free slaves originated from his _____.

 A. moral considerations   B. military experience

 C. financial conditions   D. political stand

Part B

Directions:

*In the following article, some sentences have been removed. For Questions 41—45, choose the most suitable one from the list A—G to fit into each of the numbered blanks. There are two extra choices, which do not fit in any of the blanks. Mark your answers on **ANSWER SHEET 1**.*

The time for sharpening pencils, arranging your desk, and doing almost anything else instead of writing has ended. The first draft will appear on the page only if you stop avoiding the inevitable and sit, stand up, or lie down to write. (41) _____

Be flexible. Your outline should smoothly conduct you from one point to the next, but do not permit it to railroad you. If a relevant and important idea occurs to you now, work it into the draft. (42) _____ Grammar, punctuation, and spelling can wait until you revise. Concentrate on what you are saying. Good writing most often occurs when you are in hot pursuit of an idea rather than in a nervous search for errors.

(43) _____ Your pages will be easier to keep track of that way, and, if you have to clip a paragraph to place it elsewhere, you will not lose any writing on the other side.

If you are working on a word processor, you can take advantage of its capacity to make additions and deletions as well as move entire paragraphs by making just a few simple keyboard commands. Some software programs can also check spelling and certain grammatical elements in your writing. (44) _____ These printouts are also easier to read than the screen when you work on revisions.

Once you have a first draft on paper, you can delete material that is unrelated to your thesis and add material necessary to illustrate your points and make your paper convincing. The student who wrote "The A & P as a State of Mind" wisely dropped a paragraph that questioned whether Sammy displays chauvinistic attitudes toward women. (45)_____

Remember that your initial draft is only that. You should go through the paper many times — and then again — working to substantiate and clarify your ideas. You may even end up with several entire versions of the paper. Rewrite. The sentences within each paragraph should be related to a single topic. Transitions should connect one paragraph to the next so that there are no abrupt or confusing shifts. Awkward or wordy phrasing or unclear sentences and paragraphs should be mercilessly poked and prodded into shape.

[A] To make revising easier, leave wide margins and extra space between lines so that you can easily add words, sentences, and corrections. Write on only one side of the paper.

[B] After you have clearly and adequately developed the body of your paper, pay particular attention to the introductory and concluding paragraphs. It's probably best to write the introduction last, after you know precisely what you are introducing. Concluding paragraphs demand equal attention because they leave the reader with a final impression.

[C] It's worth remembering, however, that though a clean copy fresh off a printer may look terrific, it will read only as well as the thinking and writing that have gone into it. Many writers prudently store their data on disks and print their pages each time they finish a draft to avoid losing any material because of power failures or other problems.

[D] It makes no difference how you write, just so you do. Now that you have developed a topic into a tentative thesis, you can assemble your notes and begin to flesh out whatever outline you have made.

[E] Although this is an interesting issue, it has nothing to do with the thesis, which explains how the setting influences Sammy's decision to quit his job. Instead of including that paragraph, she added one that described Lengel's crabbed response to the girls so that she could lead up to the A & P "policy" he enforces.

[F] In the final paragraph about the significance of the setting in "A & P", the student brings together the reasons Sammy quit his job by referring to his refusal to accept Lengel's store policies.

[G] By using the first draft as a means of thinking about what you want to say, you will very likely discover more than your notes originally suggested. Plenty of good writers don't use outlines at all but discover ordering principles as they write. Do not attempt to compose a perfectly correct draft the first time around.

Part C

Directions:

Read the following text carefully and then translate the underlined segments into Chinese. Your translation should be written clearly on **ANSWER SHEET 2.**

In his autobiography, Darwin himself speaks of his intellectual powers with extraordinary modesty. He points out that he always experienced much difficulty in expressing himself clearly and concisely, but (46) he believes that this very difficulty may have had the compensating advantage of forcing him to think long and intently about every sentence, and thus enabling him to detect errors in reasoning and in his own observations. He disclaimed the possession of any great quickness of apprehension or wit, such as distinguished Huxley. (47) He asserted, also, that his power to follow a long and purely abstract train of thought was very limited, for which reason he felt certain that he never could have succeeded with mathematics. His memory, too, he described as extensive, but hazy. So poor in one sense was it that he never could remember for more than a few days a single date or a line of poetry. (48) On the other hand, he did not accept as well founded the charge made by some of his critics that, while he was a good observer, he had no power of reasoning. This, he thought, could not be true, because the "Origin of Species" is one long argument from the beginning to the end, and has convinced many able men. No one, he submits, could have written it without possessing some power of reasoning. He was willing to assert that "I have a fair share of invention, and of common sense or judgment, such as every fairly successful lawyer or doctor must have, but not, I believe, in any higher degree." (49) He adds humbly that perhaps he was "superior to the common run of men in noticing things which easily escape attention, and in observing them carefully."

Writing in the last year of his life, he expressed the opinion that in two or three respects his mind had changed during the preceding twenty or thirty years. Up to the age of thirty or beyond it poetry of many kinds gave him great pleasure. Formerly, too, pictures had given him considerable, and music very great, delight. In 1881, however, he said: "Now for many years I cannot endure to read a line of poetry. I have also almost lost my taste for pictures or music." (50) Darwin was convinced that the loss of these tastes was not only a loss of happiness, but might possibly be injurious to the intellect, and more probably to the moral character.

2008年 考研英语全真试题
（阅读理解部分）解析

Part A

Text 1

长难句分析

1. Studies of both animals and humans have shown that sex hormones somehow affect the stress response, causing females under stress to produce more of the trigger chemicals than do males under the same conditions.

❖**结构分析** 本句逗号之前的部分比较容易理解。非谓语动词 causing 的逻辑主语是前面 that 所引导的宾语从句,即"性激素会在某种程度上影响到对压力的反应",这种情况导致 female under stress(压力之下的雌性)产生更多的可触发不良反应的化学物质。

2. I think that the kinds of things that women are exposed to tend to be in more of a chronic or repeated nature.

❖**结构分析** I think 之后的句子主语为 the kinds of things,谓语为 tend to be,意为"往往是…",中间是定语从句修饰 things, 意为"那些女性所面对的事情"。

试题分析

21. ［A］细节题。根据前两段的内容,先排除明显和文章无关的 B"女性仍然在遭受男性所带来的压力";女性压力比男性多,但文章也没有说"经验"问题和面对压力时的倾向问题,因此 C"在处理压力方面,女性比男性更有经验"和 D"面对压力时,女性和男性表现出不同的倾向"也不对;第一段说女性在面对压力时更易患抑郁病,第二段又说雌性在同等压力条件下分泌更多化学物质,可见 A"从生物角度看,女性更易受到压力的影响"为正确答案。

22. ［D］推断题。先排除答案 A,约胡达的研究没有提到药剂量的事;B "抵抗压力的能力有限" 与第三段 "女性承受压力的能力甚至比男性还要强"不符;C"更会避免压力"也不准确;答案为 D"压力更多",这在第一段和第三段都有所体现。

23. ［C］细节题。根据 I think that the kinds of things that women are exposed to tend to be in more of a chronic or repeated nature. chronic 对应 durable, repeated 对应 frequent。因此答

案为 C"长久的和经常的"。

24. [B] 句意题。这种题和词汇题一样,一方面要认真理解字面意思,另一方面则要根据上下文进行判断。阿尔瓦雷斯生活比较窘迫,需要努力工作赚钱养家;A"阿尔瓦雷斯只关心赚钱"和 D"阿尔瓦雷斯用支票支付所有费用"可以排除;C 和文章相关,但不符合 I lived from paycheck to paycheck. (从薪水到薪水)的字面意思;答案为 B"阿尔瓦雷斯的薪水几乎不能维持家庭开支",这也可以从上下文得到印证。

25. [D] 主旨大意题。综合全文才能进行选择,不能仅限于某个部分。A 和 C 由于没有提到性别问题,均可排除;B 只说性别差异,而没有提到社会问题,属于以偏盖全;D"性别不平等:压力下的女性"为最佳答案。

参考译文

尽管在现代生活中,女性在某些方面仍然在追赶男性,但她们似乎在一个不受欢迎的方面领先于男性。纽约退伍军人管理医院精神科主任约胡达医生认为:"与男性相比,女性在面对压力时更容易患上抑郁症和焦虑症。"

对动物和人的研究都表明,性激素会在某种程度上影响到对压力的反应,使处于压力之下的雌性在同等条件下比雄性分泌更多能触发不良反应的化学物质。一些研究表明,如果切除掉处于压力极限的雌鼠的卵巢(雌性生殖器官),它们的化学反应就会降低到和雄鼠一样的水平。

女性承受压力的机会越来越多,这使她们因压力而产生更多的化学物质。约胡达医生认为,"这不是因为女性无法调节压力,而是因为她们所要处理的压力太多。她们对压力的承受能力甚至比男性还要强,但是由于她们要面对的事情如此之多,以致于她们更易疲劳,也更明显。"

约胡达医生注意到两性之间的另一种差异。"我认为女性所要面对的事情往往具有长期性和反复性。男人去打仗,要承受战斗的压力。他们所承受的更多的是偶然性的身体暴力行为。而女性所承受的却往往是家庭内部暴力,很不幸的是,这些暴力来自父母或其他家庭成员,并且它们要不只一次地发生。这种来自长期人际关系的摩擦可能会产生巨大的破坏性。"

阿德琳·阿尔瓦雷斯十八岁时结婚并生了一个儿子,但是她去决心完成大学学业。"为了获是大学文凭,我费尽心力。我的生活真是一团糟,上学、进步、做得更好是我逃避生活困境的途径。"后来她的婚姻破裂了,成了一位单亲妈妈。"同时要照顾孩子、工作,支付房租、车款、还债,对我来说真是一件十分辛苦的事。我的生活就是不停地赚钱。"

并不是每个人都像阿尔瓦雷斯那样要经历这样长期的压力。但是,现在几乎所有的妇女都要承担很多义务,没有时间休息,感到疲劳。阿尔瓦雷斯的经历说明,在压力威胁到身体健康和生活能力之前找到减轻它们的办法是非常重要的。

Text 2

长难句分析

1. The Internet — and pressure from funding agencies, who are questioning why commercial publishers are making money from government — funded research by restricting access to it — is making access to scientific results a reality.

❖结构分析　句子主干为 The Internet is making access to scientific results a reality. 但pressure 是和 Internet 并列的主语,即"互联网和来自基金会的压力使得到科研成果成为现实",who 引导的非限制性定语从句对 funding agencies 进行补充说明:这些基金会质疑,为什么商业出版者通过限制对研究成果的使用而从由政府资助的研究中获利。

2. Other models exist that are hybrids of these three, such as delayed open-access, where journals allow only subscribers to read a paper for the first six months, before making it freely available to everyone who wishes to see it.

❖结构分析　such as 后面是一个例子,where 引导的非限制性定语从句说明这种"延迟开放存取"模式是什么样子的,before making it freely available to everyone 指的是"在让所有人都能得到之前",后面的 who 是简单的定语从句,修饰 everyone,即说明是什么样的人。

试题分析

26. [D] 归纳题。考生要对第一段进行归纳理解。答案为 D"期刊出版的传统流程";B"实验报告的出版流程"不确切,因为实验报告不是期刊出版的唯一内容。

27. [C] 细节题。可根据第二段相关内容找到答案。A"它批评政府资助的研究"没有被提及;B"它介绍了一种有效的出版方式"的判断不符合原意,报告并未对新的出版方式进行评价;D"它对科学研究大有裨益"不正确,是因为原文说的是改变了某些因素,也没有进行评价;答案是 C"它使以赢利为目的的出版商感到不安",因为 The report... makes heavy reading for publishers who have, so far, made handsome profits.

28. [A] 细节题。文章在第二段讲到,在互联网时代对科研成果的免费使用正成为现实,最后段又讲到现在完全不同的商业模式正在出现, 主要是可以为读者提供在线阅读,比以前更方便地阅读到科研成果。只有 A"它使读者更方便地了解科研成果"符合文意;B"它为科研人员带来巨额利润"显然和原文意思相反;C"它强调了科学研究的关键作用"没有被提到;也没有说在线出版和政府投资的关系,故 D"它便于政府对科技进行投资"也可排除。

29. [A] 细节题。确定答案所在位置,进行仔细阅读,可知 open-access publishing model 是 asking the author (or his employer) to pay for the paper to be published,答案为 A"支付出版费用"。

30. [B] 主旨大意题。逐一排除。A"互联网对出版商构成了威胁"以偏概全,显然不能成为本文主题。C"作者们欢迎新的出版渠道"和原文叙述不符,因为有的新型出版渠道需要作者付费。D"在线服务使出版更容易"曲解了原文的意思,因为在线服务是为读者带来方便,而不是使出版更容易。只有 B"新型出版模式的兴起"符合文意。

参考译文

在过去这曾经是直截了当的一件事。在同一实验室的研究小组会把他们的研究结果提供给专业期刊。一位杂志编辑就会把作者的名字和所属机构隐去,并把它送给同行专家们进行审阅,然后他会根据收到的意见决定是否要发表。版权归该期刊所有,那些需要阅读这些研究结果的研究者要订阅该期刊。

而现在情况不同了。许多基金会质疑,为什么商业出版者通过限制对研究成果的使用而从由政府资助的研究中获利,这种质疑所带来的压力和互联网的发展正日益使对科研成果的免费使用成为现实。经济发展与合作组织(OECD)刚刚发表的一份报告描述了这种产业化所带来的深远影响。该报告由来自澳大利亚维多利亚大学的约翰·霍顿和来自经合组织的格雷厄姆·维克思共同撰写,它让那些到目前为止获得巨额利润的出版商们读起来心情沉重。但事情却远非仅止于此,它还表明,目前科学研究中一个关键的因素发生了变化。

知识的价值和公共科研投资的回报在某种程度上依靠科技成果的广泛传播和对它们方便的获取。这是个大产业。在美国,科学核心期刊的市场价值据估算在 70 亿到 110 亿之间。国际科技与医学出版协会称,全球有 2,000 多家出版社专门出版此类书籍,它们每年都在 16,000 左右的期刊上发表超过 120 万篇的文章。

现在情况正在发生改变。据经合组织的报告,现在大约有 75% 的学术期刊都可以在线阅读。完全不同的商业模式正在出现,报告的作者认为其中有三种主要模式。首先是所谓的"大交易",机构订户通过许可协议购买而阅读在线期刊。其次是开放存取式出版,主要是依靠作者(或其雇主)为其论文的出版支付费用。最后是开放存取式归档,是由大学或国际实验室等组织所支持的储存库。其他还有一些模式混合了前面提到的这三种,比如延迟开放存取,期刊在出版后的前六个月只允许订阅者阅读,然后才让所有希望阅读该期刊的读者能免费得到。所有这些形式都能改变传统的同行评议程序,至少,对于论文的出版而言是这样的。

Text 3

长难句分析

1. **Though typically about two inches taller now than 140 years ago, today's people — especially those born to families who have lived in the U.S. for many generations — apparently reached their limit in the early 1960s.**

◆结构分析 主句是 Today's people apparently reached their limit in the early 1960s...破折号中的插入语 those born to families 指的是那些出生在什么样家庭的人，who所引导的定语从句修饰"在美国生活了很多年的家庭"。前面是一个表示让步的成分。

2. Moreover, even though humans have been upright for millions of years, our feet and back continue to struggle with bipedal posture and cannot easily withstand repeated strain imposed by oversize limbs.

◆结构分析 主句中有两个由 and 连接的动宾结构，一个是 continue to struggle with bipedal posture，字面意思是"仍在为双足行走的姿势而挣扎"，另一个是 cannot easily withstand repeated strain imposed by oversize limbs，字面意思为"不能轻易承受由于四肢过大而施加的重复的压力"。

试题分析

31. [A] 推断题。根据本文的主题，与身高相关的选项才能成为答案，把张伯伦当做例子很显然是为了"说明 NBA 球员身高的变化"，故选 A。

32. [C] 细节题。第三段一开始就说到了"营养"和"热量"在成长过程中所起到的重要作用，后来又说 as diet and health improved，随着饮食的改善和健康的提高，人的身高才增长了。因此答案为 C"生活条件"。

33. [B] 推断题。要仔细找到相关部分，逐一验证。A"外来人口使美国平均身高增加"不正确，因为外来人口使身高增加只是 NBA 存在的现象，其他领域作者没说；C"美国人的平均身高世界第一"没提到；D"体形较大的婴儿长大后个子较高"也不正确，因为作者只是说体形较大的婴儿出生时困难较大，没提及和后来的身高的关系；故答案为 B"人类身高受到直立行走的限制"，参见长难句分析 2。

34. [D] 推断题。先排除 B"军服的设计将保持不变"，这个干扰项和身高没有关系；A"服装业将重新考虑制服的尺寸"和原文意思相反，因为作者认为人的身高已经达到了极限；C"选择运动员时将使用基因检测"没有被提及；文章明确说："You could use today's data and feel fairly confident."故答案为 D"现有的人类身高数据仍将适用"。

35. [C] 主旨大意题。本文所讨论的主要是身高极限的问题，A"人类身高的变化有循环周期"和 D"美国人的基因类型已经发生改变"可排除，因为这两点显然和作者的意思不符；由于作者认为人类身高可能不会再发生改变，B"人类身高变得更易预测"也不正确；只有 C"美国人已达到身高的基因极限"符合本文主旨。

参考译文

在 1960 年代初期，威尔特·张伯伦是仅有的身高超过 7 英尺的 NBA 三名球员之一。如果他上个赛季还在打球的话，他只是 42 个拥有这样身高的球员中的一个了。过去数年时间内,参加主要职业赛事的运动员的身材发生了巨大变化,那些球队经理们也非常乐意调整他们的队服大小,以适应那些身材高大的运动员在数量上的不断增长。

　　但是运动界这种趋势可能会掩盖一个还未被认识到的事实:总体来说美国人身高已经停止了增长。尽管美国人现在比 140 年前平均高了约两英寸,现在的美国人——尤其是那些出生并已经在美国生活了好几代的家庭里的人——在 60 年代早期就已经达到了身高的极限,并且他们也不可能长得更高了。莱特州立大学人类学家威廉·卡梅伦认为,"目前,在现在的环境和基因水平下,人口的总体身高已经达到了极限。"就 NBA 球员而言,他们不断增长的身高似乎是由于从世界各地招募来的球员越来越多。

　　很少有人在 20 岁之后还在长高,长高需要热量和营养(特别是蛋白质)给身体组织的增长提供能量。在 20 世纪之初,营养不良和儿童传染病妨碍人的身高增长。但是随着饮食和健康水平的提高,少年儿童的身高平均每 20 年增长约 1.5 英寸,人们称之为身高增长长期模式。然而,疾病控制与防治中心的数据表明,自 60 年代后,人的平均身高(男性 5.9 英尺,女性 5.4 英尺)并没有改变过。

　　从基因的角度来说,避免个头过高是有好处的。在分娩过程中,体形较大的婴儿更难以通过产道。此外,尽管人类直立行走已经有了几百万年的历史,但是我们的双脚和背部仍然在努力适应两足行走的姿势,难以承受由肢体过长而带来的不间断的压力。西北大学人类学家威廉·莱昂纳德认为,"个体有机体的基因结构真正限制了人的身高"。

　　基因身高的最大值可能会改变,但是不要期望这会很快就发生。马萨诸塞州内蒂克陆军研究中心的资深人类学家克莱尔·C. 戈登确信,90%的制服和工作间适合新兵使用,无须改动。她还说,与篮球运动员的球衣不同,军队制服的尺寸已经有段时间没有改动了。如果你要预测不久的将来人的身高以设计某种装备的话,你基本上"能使用目前的数据,并且你要为此充满信心"。

Text 4

长难句分析

1. **The southern states would not have signed the Constitution without protections for the "peculiar institution", including a clause that counted a slave as three fifths of a man for purposes of congressional representation.**

　　❖ 结构分析　主句是个虚拟语气,would not have signed 是对过去事实的一种假设,意即"南方各州不会签署宪法",后面是条件,即"如果没有保护性条款的话,他们就不会签。"including 是伴随状语,意为"包括…",counted a slave as three fifths of a man 意为"把一个奴隶按 3/5 个人来计算",for purpose of 意为"以…为目的"。

2. **Washington, who had begun to believe that all men were created equal after observing the bravery of the black soldiers during the Revolutionary War, overcame the strong opposition of his relatives to grant his slaves their freedom in his will.**

❖结构分析　句子主干为 Washington overcame the strong opposition of his relatives.后面的
不定式 to grant 是结果状语。插入部分是由 who 引导的非限制性定语从句，
说明华盛顿"在看到黑人士兵的英勇无畏后开始相信人生而平等"。

试 题 分 析

36. [D] 结构推断题。这道题难度很大,容易引起争论。要从全文出发,不能仅从某个段落入
手。可以先把 A"过去原始的医疗手段"排除掉,因为这和文章没多大关系;C"强调奴
隶在美国历史中的重要作用"也可排除,因为这个故事不能体现出奴隶的价值;锁定
在 B"表明他那个时代奴隶制的残酷"和 D"揭示他生活中不为人知的方面"中间选
择一个最佳答案。这里的关键是作者怎么看待奴隶制的问题,他有没有进行道德上
的评判。从文章可以看出,他客观地讲述了那些开国元勋对待奴隶制的困境而没有
批判奴隶制。华盛顿和杰弗逊的故事都在告诉我们这些人物不为人知的一面,比较
之下 D 更准确。

37. [B] 归纳判断题。A"DNA 技术已经被广泛应用到历史研究"夸大了文章所讲的事实,
DNA 技术只是被当做一个例子,没有说它被广泛应用;C"历史学家有意编造了杰弗
逊的故事"显然和原意不符,杰弗逊的故事不是编造的,而是有根据的;D"美国历史
中经常出现政治妥协"也无法从文中推断出来,因为对奴隶制的妥协不能说明是"经
常发生"妥协;答案是 B"美国早期曾经遇到过微妙而棘手的局势",在美国历史早
期,关于奴隶制的问题那些开国元勋们一方面认识到其不好的方面,另一方面为了
政治利益又不得不进行妥协,局势比较微妙。同时 delicate 一词还有"棘手"的意思。

38. [C] 细节题。文章说,杰弗逊憎恶奴隶制,但为了政治却又不得不妥协,在他大选获胜后
还把奴隶制推广到更多的州,可见 C"他对奴隶制的态度是复杂的"为正确答案;A
"他的政治见解改变了他对奴隶制的态度"是错的,文章没有提到他对奴隶制态度的
改变;B"他作为父亲的身份使他解放那些儿童奴隶"也不正确,因为文章只说他释放
了孩子,但并没说因为他是一个父亲;D"他和奴隶的暧昧关系影响了他的声望"在文
章中没有被提及。

39. [A] 细节题。倒数第二段杰弗逊的例子说明,他从对奴隶制的妥协中获得了政治利益,当
选为总统。故 A"有些开国元勋从奴隶制中获取政治利益"为正确答案;B"过去奴隶
没有投票权"不正确,是因为一个奴隶拥有 3/5 个投票权;C"奴隶主经常有大笔存
款"误解了原文的意思,大笔存款只是对奴隶的比喻性说法;D"奴隶制过去被认为是
特殊制度"没有被提及。

40. [B] 细节题。最后一段说,华盛顿因为独立战争中看到黑人奴隶的英勇表现,才确信人是
生而平等的,因此才在遗嘱中解放了自己的奴隶。因此答案是 B"军队经历"。

参考译文

1748 年,在乔治·华盛顿当选美国总统前 5 年,他 52 岁,牙齿几乎全都掉光了。因此他请了一名牙医往自己的嘴里移植了 9 颗牙齿——这些牙都是从他的奴隶口中拔出来的。

华盛顿的这一形象与大多数人从历史课本里得到的砍倒樱桃树的华盛顿的形象全然不同。但是最近,许多历史学家开始关注奴隶在那些开国元勋的生活中所扮演的角色问题。他们的兴趣部分来自 1998 年的 DNA 证据,它几乎确认托马斯·杰弗逊与他的奴隶萨莉·赫明斯生了至少一个孩子。并且,只是在过去三十年里学者们才从底层开始研究历史。几位历史学家的著作揭示了美国早期领导人的道德妥协及新生国家的脆弱性。更有意思的是,他们认为很多开国元勋明明知道奴隶制是错的,但他们中的大多数却没有试图去推翻它。

历史学家们认为,最重要的事情是这些元勋们受到他们时代文化的限制。尽管华盛顿和杰弗逊在私下里表达过对奴隶制的憎恶,他们同时也明白,这是他们要创造的国家的政治和经济基础的一部分。

一方面,南方不能失去奴隶。《并不完美的乔治·华盛顿:他的奴隶与美国的诞生》一书的作者 Wiencek 说,拥有奴隶"就像拥有一笔巨额存款"。如果没有对这种"特殊制度"的保护性条款——其中包括把一个奴隶当做 3/5 个人进行计算以保证国会代表权——那些南方各州是不会签署宪法的。

这些政治家们的政治生命也要取决于奴隶制。那项 3/5 的规定增加了南方各州选举团的票数,使他在 1800 年的总统选举中以微弱优势胜出。他一上台就在 1803 年颁布《路易斯安那购地条款》,扩大了奴隶制;这片新的土地被分成了 13 个州,其中有 3 个是实行奴隶制的。

但是,杰弗逊赋予赫明斯的孩子以自由——虽然赫明斯本人或其他大约 150 名奴隶没有获得自由。华盛顿在目睹了黑人士兵在独立战争中的英勇表现之后开始相信所有人都是生而平等的,他不顾亲戚们的强烈反对,在遗嘱中赋予他的奴隶以自由。仅仅在十年前,这样的行为在弗吉尼亚还需要得到立法机关的批准才行。

Part B

试 题 分 析

[说明]本文是对写作过程的一些建议,是说明性的文章。但是,由于作者所使用的不是完全描述性的客观式语言,可能会给我们的理解带来一定困难。另外一点需要注意的是,这种题型考查的大多都是上下文之间的逻辑关系,因此找到相应的关键词或线索对解决这部分问题就至关重要。

41. [D] 文章开头部分是说,写作准备工作完成之后就要面对写作本身,而不要回避,所以说"你怎么去写无所谓,只要去写就行了"。因此,我们可以判断接下来的话应该是写作的一个初步环节了。从备选答案来看,A 与文章的修改有关,故应该与后面谈到

revision 时有关;B 从文章开头的写作到结尾的写作都谈到了,显然不符合文章的逻辑结构,那样的话文章到这里就可以结束了;C 谈到了电脑、打印出来的草稿等,是交待我们在写作时的一些注意事项,故也不能选;D 最符合此处的语境:在开始的时候,别管怎么样,准备工作完成以后就不要再拖拖拉拉,直奔主题:写作。上下文衔接自然,是正确答案;E 的转折是围绕 issue 一词来说的,这里显然没有上文的支持,不能选择;F 谈的是文章结尾,放在这里显然不合适;G 讲的是如何在初稿中增加新的内容,也不合适。此题较难,必须耐心一点,逐个分析、排除。

42. [G] 这一段是接着上一段讲的,关注的对象是提纲和草稿,因此从写作环节和文章的结构来看选项应该和初稿或提纲有关。而与此有关的只有 G,讲的是如何在初稿中添加新的内容。

43. [A] 这段的后半部分说,Your pages will be easier to keep track of that way... 意即"这样做有助于你更易于整理所写的内容",根据这一线索,要找到相关选项进行分析排除。A 意为"为了便于修改,应该把边距和行距留得大一点"。所以根据前后文的逻辑关系,答案非 A 莫属。

44. [C] 本题空白之前是说电脑的方便之处,但空白之后说,在修改过程中,读打印出来的材料比看电脑屏幕更容易,空白处填入的内容应与电脑、打印出来的材料相关。答案 C 中的转折词 however 是一个标志,把论述点从电脑的优势转到打印稿上来。把稿件打印出来以便于阅读,还说有些谨慎的作家会把每次修改的内容都打印一遍,以防遗失,正好和下文能对接起来。

45. [E] 本题的干扰项为 F,因为关键词 R&P 和 Sammy 都出现了。但 F 的内容与上下文没有什么关系。本段第一句提到在写作中要删去与主题不相关的素材,而 F 选项却没有接着这一点往下说,而 E 则与此相关,故选 E 而不选 F。

参考译文

削铅笔、整理书桌和其他任何与写作无关的事情所需要的时间结束了。不要回避那件无法回避的事情,无论你是坐着、站着或躺着去写作,初稿都会跃然纸上。(41)你怎么去写都无所谓,只要去写就行了。既然你已经把某个话题提炼为一个初步的论题,你就可以整合你的论点,并开始充实你所拟订的任何提纲了。

要灵活一点。你的提纲应该能指导你顺利地从一个论点过渡到下一个论点,但是别让它牵着你的鼻子走。如果你想到了某个相关的重要论点,就把它写进草稿。(42)如果你把第一稿当做工具来思考你要说的话时,你就可能发现比你最初能想到的更多的东西。很多杰出的作家并不列提纲,而是在他们写作的时候才去发现写作的顺序。不要试图让你的初稿就完善无缺。语法、标点和拼写可以留待修改时再去考虑。把精力集中在你要说的内容上。只有当你热烈地捕捉某个观点而不是紧张地寻找错误时,你才能写出好文章来。

(43)为了便于修改,应该把边距和行距留得大一点,这样你就能更容易地添词加句或写上修改意见。只能在纸的一面写字。这样做能使你更易于整理所写的内容,而且,当你想把某个段落剪切到某个别的地方时,你也不会失去写在纸张背面的内容。

如果你使用文字处理软件,你就可以利用它的功能,仅用几个简单的键盘指令就可以添加、删除或者移动整个段落。有些软件还能做拼写检查和某些语法项目的检查。(44)然而,要注意,尽管一份刚打印出来的稿子看起来很糟糕,但它读起来就像自己的思想和写作刚刚跑进稿纸上一样。许多作家每完成一稿时都谨慎地把数据存到磁盘里,然后再打印一份,以防由于停电或其他原因导致文件的遗失。修改打印出来的文本比在电脑屏幕上修改方便多了。

你的观点的必要材料,使你的稿子更让人信服。一名写关于"A&P 作为精神状态"的学生就很明智地删除了质疑萨米对女性有大沙文主义倾向的段落。(45)尽管这是一个很有趣的问题,但这和她的论题无关,即解释环境如何影响萨米并使他辞职的。于是她就用另一段来代替,描述伦格尔对女性的恶劣态度,从而引出他所执行的 A&P"政策"这一内容。

Part C

试题分析

46. 全句译文:他认为,正是这种困难起了补偿作用,可以使他长时间专注地思考每个句子,从而能发现自己在推理和亲自观察中出现的错误,这反而成了他的优势。

翻译提示:that 引导的宾语从句中,主干为 This very difficulty may have had the compensating advantage. of forcing him to think long and intently about every sentence 修饰 advantage,即"强迫他长时间专注地思考每个句子的优势"。 and thus enabling him to detect errors 作伴随状语,in reasoning and in his own observations 意为"在推理和观察方面"。

47. 全句译文:他还声称自己长时间进行纯抽象思维的能力非常有限;因此,他曾深信自己在数学方面本来就不该有什么成就。

翻译提示:he asserted 后面是宾语从句, 其主干为 His power was very limited. to follow a long and purely abstract train of thought 是说明什么样的能力,即"长时间进行纯抽象思维的能力",train of thought 意为"思路,一连串的思想"。for which reason 意为"由于这个原因,因此"。he never could have succeeded with mathematics 是虚拟语气,表示对过去所发生的事情的假设:"他本不该在数学方面有任何成就"。

48. 全句译文:另一方面,一些批评者指责说,尽管他善于观察,但却不能推理,他对此既不接受也认为这样的指责毫无根据。

翻译提示:he didn't accept as well founded the charge 的正常语序为 he didn't accept the charge as well founded, 字面意思为"他不能把这些指责当做是有根据的而接受",意为"他认为这些指责没有根据。" 在英语中如果某个句子成分过长的话, 往往会将其位置进行后调。此处 charge 后面又加了一个定语 made by some of his critics, 由他的批评者所做出的指责。...that, while he was a good observer, he had no power of reasoning 是 charge 的同位语,说明什么样的指责。

49. 全句译文:他还谦虚地补充说,或许他"和普通人相比,更能注意到他们容易忽略的细节,更能对这些细节进行仔细观察。

翻译提示:add 此处的意思是"补充说",be superior to 意为"比⋯有优势",in noticing things... and in observing them carefully 意为"在观察事物和仔细对它们进行观察方面",which easily escape attention 修饰 things, 意为"那些不易引人注意的事物"。

50. 全句译文:达尔文确信,失去这些爱好不仅仅是少了乐趣,而且会损害一个人的智力,更有可能败坏人的道德品质。

翻译提示:be convinced that 意为"确信⋯",后面的 that 从句中主干为 the loss of these tastes was not only... but...。be injurious to the intellect, and more probably to the moral character 中的结构是 be injurious to the intellect and the moral character, 加上 more probably 是强调后者"更有可能"。

参考译文

　　达尔文在其自传中谈及自己的智力时极其谦虚。他说自己常常感到清楚简明地表达自己观点很困难,但(46)他认为,正是这种困难起了补偿作用,可以使他长时间专注地思考每个句子,从而能发现自己在推理和亲自观察中出现的错误,这反而成了他的优势。他不承认自己拥有像赫胥黎那样敏锐的理解力和智慧。(47)他还声称自己长时间进行纯抽象思维的能力非常有限;因此,他曾深信自己在数学方面本来就不该有什么成就。他经常描述自己的记忆力也博而不精。从某种意义上讲,他的记忆力非常糟糕,他对某个日期或一行诗句的记忆从来就超不过几天。(48)另一方面,一些批评者指责说,尽管他善于观察,但却不能推理,他对此既不接受也认为这样的指责毫无根据。他认为,事实并非如此,因为"物种起源"从头至尾是一个长篇的论证,使许多有能力的人感到信服。他指出,如果没有推理能力,任何人都不可能写出一部这样的书。他欣然承认,"像那些成功的律师或医生一样,我拥有创造能力、常识和判断力,但并不比他们更强。"(49)他还谦虚地补充说,或许他"和普通人相比,更能注意到他们容易忽略的细节,更能对这些细节进行仔细观察"。

　　在他生命的最后一年,他同样表达了这样的观点,即在过去的二三十年里,他的观点至少在两三个方面发生了变化。在 30 岁左右,诗歌给了他很多享受。在此之前,绘画给他带来过巨大快乐,而音乐带来的愉悦更大。然而,在 1881 年,他写道:"我已经很多年都没耐心阅读一句诗了。我失去了对绘画和音乐的兴趣。"(50)达尔文确信,失去这些爱好不仅仅是少了乐趣,而且会损害一个人的智力,更有可能败坏人的道德品质。

2009 年 考研英语全真试题
（阅读理解部分）

Part A

Directions:

*Read the following four texts. Answer the questions below each text by choosing A, B, C or D. Mark your answers on **ANSWER SHEET 1**.*

Text 1

Habits are a funny thing. We reach for them mindlessly, setting our brains on auto-pilot and relaxing into the unconscious comfort of familiar routine. "Not choice, but habit rules the unreflecting herd," William Wordsworth said in the 19th century. In the ever-changing 21st century, even the word "habit" carries a negative connotation.

So it seems antithetical to talk about habits in the same context as creativity and innovation. But brain researchers have discovered that when we consciously develop new habits, we create parallel synaptic paths, and even entirely new brain cells, that can jump our trains of thought onto new, innovative tracks.

Rather than dismissing ourselves as unchangeable creatures of habit, we can instead direct our own change by consciously developing new habits. In fact, the more new things we try — the more we step outside our comfort zone — the more inherently creative we become, both in the workplace and in our personal lives.

But don't bother trying to kill off old habits; once those ruts of procedure are worn into the brain, they're there to stay. Instead, the new habits we deliberately press into ourselves create parallel pathways that can bypass those old roads.

"The first thing needed for innovation is a fascination with wonder," says Dawna Markova, author of *The Open Mind* and an executive change consultant for *Professional Thinking Partners*. "But we are taught instead to 'decide', just as our president calls himself 'the Decider'." She adds, however, that "to decide is to kill off all possibilities but one. A good innovational thinker is always exploring the many other possibilities."

All of us work through problems in ways of which we're unaware, she says. Researchers in the late 1960s discovered that humans are born with the capacity to approach challenges in four primary ways: analytically, procedurally, relationally (or collaboratively) and innovatively. At the end of puberty, however, the brain shuts down half of that capacity, preserving only those modes of thought that have seemed most valuable during the first decade or so of life.

The current emphasis on standardized testing highlights analysis and procedure, meaning that few of us inherently use our innovative and collaborative modes of thought. "This breaks the major rule in the American belief system — that anyone can do anything," explains M. J. Ryan, author of the 2006 book *This Year I Will...* and Ms. Markova's business partner. "That's a lie that we have perpetuated, and it fosters commonness. Knowing what you're good at and doing even more of it creates excellence." This is where developing new habits comes in.

21. The view of Wordsworth habit is claimed by being _____.

    A. casual   B. familiar   C. mechanical   D. changeable

22. The researchers have discovered that the formation of habit can be _____.

    A. predicted   B. regulated   C. traced   D. guided

23. "ruts"(Line 1, Paragraph 4) has closest meaning to _____.

    A. tracks   B. series   C. characteristics   D. connections

24. Ms. Markova's comments suggest that the practice of standard testing?

    A. Prevents new habits form being formed.

    B. No longer emphasizes commonness.

    C. Maintains the inherent American thinking model.

    D. Complies with the American belief system.

25. Ryan most probably agree that _____.

    A. ideas are born of a relaxing mind

    B. innovativeness could be taught

    C. decisiveness derives from fantastic ideas

    D. curiosity activates creative minds

Text 2

It is a wise father that knows his own child, but today a man can boost his paternal (fatherly) wisdom — or at least confirm that he's the kid's dad. All he needs to do is shell our $30 for paternity testing kit (PTK) at his local drugstore — and another $120 to get the results.

More than 60,000 people have purchased the PTKs since they first become available without prescriptions last years, according to Doug Fog, chief operating officer of Identigene, which makes the over-the-counter kits. "More than two dozen companies sell DNA tests directly to the public, ranging in price from a few hundred dollars to more than $2,500.

Among the most popular: paternity and kinship testing, which adopted children can use to find their biological relatives and families can use to track down kids put up for adoption. DNA testing is also the latest rage among many passionate genealogists — and supports businesses that offer to search for a family's geographic roots.

Most tests require collecting cells by webbing saliva in the mouth and sending it to the company for testing. All tests require a potential candidate with whom to compare DNA.

But some observers are skeptical, "There is a kind of false precision being hawked by people claiming they are doing ancestry testing," says Trey Duster, a New York University sociologist. He notes that each individual has many ancestors — numbering in the hundreds just a few centuries back. Yet most ancestry testing only considers a single lineage, either the Y chromosome inherited through men in a father's line or mitochondrial DNA, which a passed down only from mothers. This DNA can reveal genetic information about only one or two ancestors, even though, for example, just three generations back people also have six other great-grandparents or, four generations back, 14 other great-great-grandparents.

Critics also argue that commercial genetic testing is only as good as the reference collections to which a sample is compared. Databases used by some companies don't rely on data collected systematically but rather lump together information from different research projects. This means that a DNA database may differ depending on the company that processes the results. In addition, the computer programs a company uses to estimate relationships may be patented and not subject to peer review or outside evaluation.

26. In paragraphs 1 and 2 , the text shows PTK's _____.

    A. easy availability   B. flexibility in pricing

    C. successful promotion   D. popularity with households

27. PTK is used to _____.

    A. locate one's birth place   B. promote genetic research

    C. identify parent-child kinship   D. choose children for adoption

28. Skeptical observers believe that ancestry testing fails to _____.

    A. trace distant ancestors   B. rebuild reliable bloodlines

    C. fully use genetic information   D. achieve the claimed accuracy

29. In the last paragraph ,a problem commercial genetic testing faces is _____.

    A. disorganized data collection   B. overlapping database building

    C. excessive sample comparison   D. lack of patent evaluation

30. An appropriate title for the text is most likely to be _____.

    A. Fors and Againsts of DNA Testing   B. DNA Testing and Its Problems

    C. DNA Testing outside the Lab   D. Lies behind DNA Testing

Text 3

The relationship between formal education and economic growth in poor countries is widely misunderstood by economists and politicians alike. Progress in both area is undoubtedly necessary for the social, political and intellectual development of these and all other societies; however, the conventional view that education should be one of the very highest priorities for promoting rapid economic development in poor countries is wrong. We are fortunate that is it, because building new educational systems there and putting enough people through them to improve economic performance would require two or three generations. The findings of a research institution have consistently shown that workers in all countries can be trained on the job to achieve radical higher productivity and, as a result, radically higher standards of living.

Ironically, the first evidence for this idea appeared in the United States. Not long ago, with the country entering a recessing and Japan at its pre-bubble peak, the U.S. workforce was derided as poorly educated and one of primary cause of the poor U.S. economic performance. Japan was, and remains, the global leader in automotive-assembly productivity. Yet the research revealed that the U.S. factories of Honda, Nissan, and Toyota achieved about 95 percent of the productivity of their Japanese counterparts — a result of the training that U.S. workers received on the job.

More recently, while examining housing construction, the researchers discovered that illiterate, non-English-speaking Mexican workers in Houston, Texas, consistently met best-practice labor productivity standards despite the complexity of the building industry's work.

What is the real relationship between education and economic development?　We have to suspect that continuing economic growth promotes the development of education even when governments don't force it. After all, that's how education got started. When our ancestors were hunters and gatherers 10,000 years ago, they didn't have time to wonder much about anything besides finding food. Only when humanity began to get its food in a more productive way was there time for other things.

As education improved, humanity's productivity potential increased as well. When the competitive environment pushed our ancestors to achieve that potential, they could in turn afford more education. This increasingly high level of education is probably a necessary, but not a sufficient, condition for the complex political systems required by advanced economic performance. Thus poor countries might not be able to escape their poverty traps without political changes that may be possible only with broader formal education. A lack of formal education, however, doesn't constrain the ability of the developing world's workforce to substantially improve productivity for the foreseeable future. On the contrary, constraints on improving productivity explain why education isn't developing more quickly there than it is.

31. The author holds in paragraph 1 that the important of education in poor countries _____.

    A. is subject groundless doubts   B. has fallen victim of bias

    C. is conventional downgraded   D. has been overestimated

32. It is stated in paragraph 1 that construction of a new education system _____.

    A. challenges economists and politicians

    B. takes efforts of generations

    C. demands priority from the government

    D. requires sufficient labor force

33. A major difference between the Japanese and U.S. workforces is that _____.

    A. the Japanese workforce is better disciplined

    B. the Japanese workforce is more productive

C. the U.S. workforce has a better education

D. the U.S. workforce is more organize

34. The author quotes the example of our ancestors to show that education emerged _____.

    A. when people had enough time   B. prior to better ways of finding food

    C. when people on longer went hung   D. as a result of pressure on government

35. According to the last paragraph, development of education _____.

    A. results directly from competitive environments

    B. does not depend on economic performance

    C. follows improved productivity

    D. cannot afford political changes

Text 4

The most thoroughly studied in the history of the new world are the ministers and political leaders of seventeenth-century New England. According to the standard history of American philosophy, nowhere else in colonial America was "so much important attached to intellectual pursuits." According to many books and articles, New England's leaders established the basic themes and preoccupations of an unfolding, dominant Puritan tradition in American intellectual life.

To take this approach to the New Englanders normally mean to start with the Puritans' theological innovations and their distinctive ideas about the church — important subjects that we may not neglect. But in keeping with our examination of southern intellectual life, we may consider the original Puritans as carriers of European culture adjusting to New world circumstances. The New England colonies were the scenes of important episodes in the pursuit of widely understood ideals of civility and virtuosity.

The early settlers of Massachusetts Bay included men of impressive education and influence in England. Besides the ninety or so learned ministers who came to Massachusetts church in the decade after 1629, there were political leaders like John Winthrop, an educated gentleman, lawyer, and official of the Crown before he journeyed to Boston. These men wrote and published extensively, reaching both New World and Old World audiences, and giving New England an atmosphere of intellectual earnestness.

We should not forget, however, that most New Englanders were less well educated. While few crafts men or farmers, let alone dependents and servants, left literary compositions to be analyzed. Their thinking often had a traditional superstitions quality. A tailor named John Dane, who emigrated in the late 1630s, left an account of his reasons for leaving England that is filled with signs. Sexual confusion, economic frustrations, and religious hope — all name together in a decisive moment when he opened the Bible, told his father the first line he saw would settle his fate, and read the magical words:"come out from among them, touch no unclean thing, and I will be your God and you shall be my people." One wonders what Dane thought of the careful sermons explaining the Bible that he heard in puritan churched.

Meanwhile , many settles had slighter religious commitments than Dane's, as one clergyman learned in confronting folk along the coast who mocked that they had not come to the New world for religion . "Our main end was to catch fish. "

36. The author notes that in the seventeenth-century New England _____ .

　　A. Puritan tradition dominated political life

　　B. intellectual interests were encouraged

　　C. Politics benefited much from intellectual endeavors

　　D. intellectual pursuits enjoyed a liberal environment

37. It is suggested in paragraph 2 that New Englanders _____ .

　　A. experienced a comparatively peaceful early history

　　B. brought with them the culture of the Old World

　　C. paid little attention to southern intellectual life

　　D. were obsessed with religious innovations

38. The early ministers and political leaders in Massachusetts Bay _____ .

　　A. were famous in the New World for their writings

　　B. gained increasing importance in religious affairs

　　C. abandoned high positions before coming to the New World

　　D. created a new intellectual atmosphere in New England

39. The story of John Dane shows that less well-educated New Englanders were often ____

　　____ .

　　A. influenced by superstitions　　　　B. troubled with religious beliefs

　　C. puzzled by church sermons　　　　D. frustrated with family earnings

40. The text suggests that early settlers in New England _____ .

　　A. were mostly engaged in political activities

　　B. were motivated by an illusory prospect

　　C. came from different backgrounds

　　D. left few formal records for later reference

Part B

Directions:

*In the following text, some sentences have been removed. For Questions 41—45, choose the most suitable one from the list A—G to fit into each of the numbered blank. There are two extra choices, which do not fit in any of the gaps. Mark your answers on **ANSWER SHEET 1**.*

Coinciding with the groundbreaking theory of biological evolution proposed by British naturalist Charles Darwin in the 1860s, British social philosopher Herbert Spencer put forward his own theory of biological and cultural evolution. Spencer argued that all worldly phenomena, including human societies, changed over time, advancing toward perfection. (41) _____

American social scientist Lewis Henry Morgan introduced another theory of cultural evolution in the late 1800s. Morgan, along with Tylor, was one of the founders of modern anthropology. In his work, he attempted to show how all aspects of culture changed together in the evolution of societies (42) _____

In the early 1900s in North America, German-born American anthropologist Franz Boas developed a new theory of culture known as historical particularism. Historical particularism, which emphasized the uniqueness of all cultures, gave new direction to anthropology. (43) _____

_____

Boas felt that the culture of any society must be understood as the result of a unique history and not as one of many cultures belonging to a broader evolutionary stage or type of culture (44) _____

Historical particularism became a dominant approach to the study of culture in American anthropology, largely through the influence of many students of Boas. But a number of anthropologists in the early 1900s also rejected the particularist theory of culture in favor of diffusionism. Some attributed virtually every important cultural achievement to the inventions of a few, especially gifted peoples that, according to diffusionists, then spread to other cultures. (45) _____

Also in the early 1900s, French sociologistÉ mile Durkheim developed a theory of culture that would greatly influence anthropology. Durkheim proposed that religious beliefs functioned to reinforce social solidarity. An interest in the relationship between the function of society and culture — known as functionalism — became a major theme in European, and especially British, anthropology.

[A] Other anthropologists believed that cultural innovations, such as inventions, had a single origin and passed from society to society. This theory was known as diffusionism.

[B] In order to study particular cultures as completely as possible, Boas became skilled in linguistics, the study of languages, and in physical anthropology, the study of human biology and anatomy.

[C] He argued that human evolution was characterized by a struggle he called the "survival of the fittest," in which weaker races and societies must eventually be replaced by stronger, more advanced races and societies.

[D] They also focused on important rituals that appeared to preserve a people's social structure, such as initiation ceremonies that formally signify children's entrance into adulthood.

[E] Thus, in his view, diverse aspects of culture, such as the structure of families, forms of marriage, categories of kinship, ownership of property, forms of government, technology, and systems of food production, all changed as societies evolved.

[F] Supporters of the theory viewed as a collection of integrated parts that work together to keep a society functioning.

[G] For example, British anthropologists Grafton Elliot Smith W. J. Perry incorrectly suggested, on the basis of inadequate information, that farming, pottery making, andmetallurgy all originated in ancient Egypt and diffused throughout the world. In fact, all of these cultural developments occurred separately at different times in many parts of the world.

Part C

Directions:

*Read the following text carefully and then translate the underlined segments into Chinese. Your translation should be written carefully on **ANSWER SHEET 2**.*

There is a marked difference between the education which every one gets from living with others, and the deliberate educating of the young. In the former case the education is incidental; it is natural and important, but it is not the express reason of the association. (46)It may be said that the measure of the worth of any social institution is its effect in enlarging and improving experience; but this effect is not a part of its original motive. Religious associations began, for example, in the desire to secure the favor of overruling powers and to ward off evil influences; family life in the desire to gratify appetites and secure family perpetuity; systematic labor, for the most part, because of enslavement to others, etc. (47)Only gradually was the by-product of the institution noted, and only more gradually still was this effect considered as a directive factor in the conduct of the institution. Even today, in our industrial life, apart from certain values of industriousness and thrift, the intellectual and emotional reaction of the forms of human association under which the world's work is carried on receives little attention as compared with physical output.

But in dealing with the young, the fact of association itself as an immediate human fact, gains in importance. (48) While it is easy to ignore in our contact with them the effect of our acts upon their disposition, it is not so easy as in dealing with adults. The need of training is too evident; the pressure to accomplish a change in their attitude and habits is too urgent to leave these consequences wholly out of account. (49) Since our chief business with them is to enable them to share in a common life we cannot help considering whether or not we are forming the powers which will secure this ability. If humanity has made some headway in realizing that the ultimate value of every institution is its distinctively human effect we may well believe that this lesson has been learned largely through dealings with the young.

(50) We are thus led to distinguish, within the broad educational process which we have been so far considering, a more formal kind of education — that of direct tuition or schooling. In undeveloped social groups, we find very little formal teaching and training. These groups mainly rely for instilling needed dispositions into the young upon the same sort of association which keeps the adults loyal to their group.

2009 年 考研英语全真试题
(阅读理解部分)解析

Part A

Text 1

长难句分析

1. But brain researchers have discovered that when we consciously develop new habits, we create parallel synaptic paths, and even entirely new brain cells, that can jump our trains of thought onto new, innovative tracks.

❖ **结构分析** 句子主干为 brain researchers have discovered that... 重点分析后面的宾语从句。其主句为 we create parallel synaptic paths, and even entirely new brain cells, 后面是定语从句 that can jump our trains of thought onto new, innovative tracks, 修饰 paths 和 cells, 意为"能使我们的大脑跳跃到新的、创新性的轨道上来（的路径和脑细胞）"，前面是一个时间状语从句 when we consciously develop new habits。

2. At the end of puberty, however, the brain shuts down half of that capacity, preserving only those modes of thought that have seemed most valuable during the first decade or so of life.

❖ **结构分析** preserving 是作伴随状语的非谓语动词，其逻辑主语是句子的主语 the brain, preserving only those modes of thought 意为是"保留那些有价值的思维模式"，后面 that 引导定语从句, 修饰"思维模式", 意为"在生命的前十年左右似乎有价值的(思维方式)"。

3. The current emphasis on standardized testing highlights analysis and procedure, meaning that few of us inherently use our innovative and collaborative modes of thought.

❖ **结构分析** 句子主干为 The current emphasis... highlights analysis and procedure... 非谓语动词 meaning 在这里作状语, 后面跟一个宾语从句。

试 题 分 析

21. [C] 细节推断题。关键确定华兹华斯的话, 他说"不是'选择'而是'习惯'统治着不会思考的人们。"文章的主题思想是习惯并不完全是束缚人的, 也具有创新性, 应该和华兹华斯的看法相反。A"偶然的"和整篇文章都没有关系,故先排除;B"熟悉的"不能算是"习惯"的特征;D"可变的"则显然和华兹华斯的意思相反。因此答案应该为C"机械的",和现代变为习惯的"创造性"相反。这样的题要使用排除法。

22. [D] 细节题。先确定答案在文章中的位置,然后仔细阅读,对比四个选项进行排除和选择。参阅长难句分析1。习惯可被"有意识地培养"从而具有"创新性",因此要排除掉A"预测"和C"调节,调整",因为它们和"培养习惯"无关;B"追踪"有迷惑性,但是"培养"新的习惯并不是对旧习惯的改变,因此也不正确;D"引导"和"有意识地培养"相契合,故为正确答案。

23. [A] 词义猜测题。这种题型一定要靠上下文推断,尤其是一些指代关系要搞清楚。once those ruts of procedure 这个短语中,those 一词的存在就已经说明前文已经提到过,它指的是old habits,后文又用 pathways 和 old 来形容 habits,因此 ruts 一词的意思应当和 way, road 相关。答案为 A"轨道"。

24. [D] 细节题。答案在第五段第一句话"创新的第一要素是对于新奇事物的着迷"。对应答案 D"好奇心激发创造性思维"。C"决断能力来自奇异的观念"为迷惑项,虽然这句话提到了"决定"这个词,但实际上作者认为这和创新关系不大,从而也没有对其进行更深一步的论述。

25. [A] 推理判断题。瑞安所说话的意思很明确,标准化考试使人们不再使用大脑中的创新能力和合作能力,答案只能是 A"阻止新习惯的形成",其他三项和文章无关。

参考译文

习惯是件有趣的事。我们会不知不觉地形成习惯,使我们的大脑进入自动驾驶模式,也使其放松,进入到所熟悉常规的无意识舒适状态。威廉·华兹华斯在 19 世纪的时候就说过:"不是'选择'而是'习惯'统治着不会思考的人们。"在变幻莫测的 21 世纪,即使"习惯"这个词本身也带上了消极的含义。

因此,在与创造性和创新相同的语境下谈论习惯似乎是背道而驰的。但是大脑研究人员已发现,当我们有意识地开始培养新习惯时,我们会同时产生相关路径甚至新的脑细胞,它们能使我们的大脑跳跃到新的、创新性的轨道上来。

我们不要把自己看成是无法改变自己习惯的动物,相反,我们可以通过有意识地培养新习惯而改变自己。事实上,我们尝试的事情越多——我们越是能跨出自己习惯的领域——我们就会变得越有创造性,无论在工作还是生活中都是如此。

但是不要试图去摆脱旧习惯;一旦这些程序式的惯例进入大脑,它们就是住在那里。相反,我们有意建立起来的新习惯也会创造出一些平行路径,能够避开旧路径。

《开放的思考》一书的作者多娜·马尔科娜也是《职业思想伴侣》杂志的执行顾问,她说:"创新的第一要素是对于新奇事物的着迷。但是有人却教我们如何做出'决定',就像我们的老板称自己为'决策者'一样。"她还补充说,"做决定就是排除所有可能性而只保留一个。一个优秀的有创新能力的思考者会一直探寻其他更多的可能性。"

她说,我们都以自己没有意识到的方式解决问题。在 20 世纪 60 年代后期,研究者发现人生来就具有用四种基本的方式来应对挑战的能力:分析、程序化、联系(或叫合作)与创新。但是在青春期后期,大脑就关闭了其中一半的能力,只保留着那些在生命的前十年左右似乎有价值的思维方式。

目前对于标准化测试的重视更强调分析和程序化,这就意味着很少有人用到思维方式中的创新和合作。2006 年《今年我将…》的作者 M. J. 瑞安,同时也是马尔科娃女士的商业伙伴,她解释道:"这打破了美国信仰体系中的主要原则,即任何人都可做任何事。这是一句被我们弄得永垂不朽的谎言,并且它也造就了平庸之士。要了解你擅长的是什么并重复去做就会创造辉煌。"就是在这里,新的习惯养成了。

Text 2

长难句分析

1. **More than 60,000 people have purchased the PTKs since they first become available without prescriptions last years, according to Doug Fog, chief operating officer of Identigene, which makes the over-the-counter kits.**

   ❖ 结构分析 句子主干为 More than 60,000 people have purchased the PTKs... 后面是时间状语从句,即"自从可以不用处方就能得到它们以来",后面的 according to 是根据某人的说法,里面的人名和称号可以不用考虑,which 引导的非限制性定语从句修饰 Identigene,说明它的性质是"直接向公众出售这套检测的"。

2. **Databases used by some companies don't rely on data collected systematically but rather lump together information from different research projects.**

   ❖ 结构分析 这句话中的 used 和 collected 都是作定语的过去分词,意思分别是"被使用的"和"被收集的"。not... but rather 是一个并列结果,意思是"不是…而是…"。

3. **In addition, the computer programs a company uses to estimate relationships may be patented and not subject to peer review or outside evaluation.**

   ❖ 结构分析 注意 the computer programs 后面是个定语从句,省略了连词 that 或 which,意为"某家公司所使用的电脑程序",后面的 may be patented and not subject to 是谓语,意为"可能拥有专利,可能不接受…"。

试 题 分 析

26. [A] 细节题。根据前两段内容,只花 30 美元就能得到 PTK,并且无需处方,都说明答案应为 A"容易获得"。B、C 和 D 都没有被提到。

27. [C] 细节题。第三段开始就说:"在各种 DNA 测试中最流行的是父系和血缘关系测试,它们可为被收养的孩子找到有血亲关系的亲属,一些家庭也可以用它们寻找丢失的孩子。"可见答案为 C"确认亲子关系",而不是迷惑项 D"挑选要收养的孩子"。

28. [D] 细节题。第五段明确指出 There is a kind of false precision being hawked by people claiming they are doing ancestry testing, 这句话主谓很清楚，就是"存在某种不精确性"，后面的 being... by people claiming they are... 包括两个作定语的非谓语动词，claiming... 修饰 people，即那些做祖先鉴定的人，前面的 being hawked by 表示被动，修饰 false precision，即这些虚假的精确性是被谁散布出来的。因此，答案很明显是 D "达到所声称的精确性"。

29. [A] 细节题。最后一段第二句话明确说："某些公司所使用的数据库中的数据并没得到系统收集，而是把从不同实验项目中得到的信息混合在一起。"因此 A "混乱的数据收集"是正确答案。

30. [B] 主旨大意题。要根据全文提供的各种信息进行综合判断，这种题也可以从排除入手，先把明显错误的排除。这里 C "试验室之外的 DNA 测试"被排除，它基本和文章无关；然后排除掉 D "DNA 测试背后的谎言"，因为文章显然不只是谈到对 DNA 测试精确性的怀疑，还谈到了其他问题，这个答案有些以偏概全了；A "对 DNA 测试的支持与反对"具有一定迷惑性，但仔细判断，文章提到有人怀疑 DNA 测试，但并没有"反对"；因此答案是 B "DNA 测试及其问题"比较符合文意。

参考译文

　　了解自己孩子的父亲是明智的。可是如今却有人能够把这种明智再推进一步——或至少知道他是孩子的父亲。需要他做的事情仅仅是花 30 美元在当地药店做一套父系血缘测试，然后再花 120 美元取回结果。

　　根据某基因鉴定公司(该公司直接向公众出售这套测试)首席操作员道格·福格的话，自从这套测试在去年可以无需处方而被购买以来，有 6 万多人购买了 PTK。目前直接向公众出售 DNA 检测的公司超过了 24 家，价格从几百美元到 2,500 多美元不等。

　　在各种 DNA 测试中最流行的是父系和血缘关系测试，它们可为被收养的孩子找到有血亲关系的亲属，一些家庭也可以用它们寻找丢失的孩子。DNA 测试也使许多热情的谱系专家欣喜若狂，同时也给那些帮助人们寻找祖籍的公司带来了生意。

　　多数测试要通过收集测试者口中的唾液采集细胞，并送到公司进行检测。所有的测试都需要一个有可能匹配的候选者的 DNA 以进行比较。

　　但是有些观察者对此持怀疑态度。纽约大学社会学家特雷·迪斯特说："那些声称可以做祖先鉴定的人在散播一种虚假的精确性。"他注意到，每个人都会有许多祖先，只要上溯几百年，这个数字就会达到数百。然而大多数祖先鉴定只考虑某一个世系，要么是由父系遗传下来的 Y 染色体，要么是由母系遗传下来的有些分裂软骨素 DNA，这种 DNA 也仅能反映一到两个祖先的信息，比如回溯三代人也有 6 位检测之外的曾祖父母，追溯四代则会有 14 位。

　　批评者们认为，商业基因测试实际上相当于用来与样品进行比较的参考基因库。某些公司所使用的数据库中的数据并没得到系统收集，而是把从不同实验项目中得到的信息混合在一起。这就意味着一个 DNA 的数据库会因为依据的公司实验结果的不同而有所差异。此外,某个公司为了判断血缘关系而使用的电脑程序可能拥有专利,因此不会接受同类公司或外部机构的评估。

Text 3

长难句分析

1. however, the conventional view that education should be one of the very highest priorities for promoting rapid economic development in poor countries is wrong.

❖结构分析 句子主干是 The conventional view is wrong. view 后有一个同位语从句,说明它的内容:"教育是促进贫困国家经济快速发展的最重要因素"。

2. We are fortunate that is it, because building new educational systems there and putting enough people through them to improve economic performance would require two or three generations.

❖结构分析 because 后面从句的主干是 Building new educational systems and putting enough people through them would require two or three generations. 中间插入的是作目的状语的不定式。

3. More recently, while examining housing construction, the researchers discovered that illiterate, non-English-speaking Mexican workers in Houston, Texas, consistently met best-practice labor productivity standards despite the complexity of the building industry's work.

❖结构分析 句子主干为 The researchers discovered that workers in Houston... met bestpractice labor productivity. 在理解时可把其他成分先丢掉,其后的 despite 表示让步,意为"尽管…"。前面是一个时间状语短语,examining 是非谓语动词,其主语是句子主语 the researchers。

4. A lack of formal education, however, doesn't constrain the ability of the developing world's workforce to substantially improve productivity for the foreseeable future.

❖结构分析 这句话是个简单句,谓语动词结构为 doesn't constrain... to improve...意为"没有限制…的发展"。

试题分析

31. [D] 细节推断题。第一段说得很明确,"那种认为教育是促进贫困国家经济快速发展的最重要因素的观点是错误的"。因此答案应为 D"被高估了"。

32. [B] 细节题。第一段倒数第二句话"需要两三代人努力才能建立新的教育体系并使足够多的人接受它的教育,从而推进经济发展,因此,我们这一代是很幸运的。"可知答案为 B"需要几代人的努力"。

33. [B] 推断题。我们根据第二段的内容可以先行排除掉 C"美国劳动力教育程度更高"和 D "美国劳动力组织性更强",因为和日本劳动力相比,美国劳动力受教育程度不高,也没有提到组织的问题;而 A"日本劳动力纪律性更强"所提到的纪律性也没有被谈及;因此答案只能是 B"日本劳动力生产率更高"。这一点也可从第三句话判断出来:"日本曾经以及现在也是全球自动化生产线效率最高的国家。"后文虽有转折,但美国劳动力的生产率是日本的95%,不能推翻这一判断。

34. [C] 细节题。我们根据第四段可以先把 B"在人们有更好的寻找食物的方法之前"和 D"政府压力的结果"排除掉,它们都和原文的意思相反;A"当人们有足够时间时"和 C 之间要有一个最佳答案,需要仔细区别。作者说,教育的出现源于经济的不停发展,后面又讲"只有当人类开始以更有效的方式获取食物时,他们才有时间考虑其他事情。"所以问题的根本还在于食物。答案应该为 C"当人们不再挨饿时"。

35. [C] 综合判断题。先看答案 A"是竞争环境的直接产物",而文中说,"当充满竞争的环境迫使我们的祖先达到这种生产潜能的时候,他们才能够提供更多的教育。"可见教育的发展不是环境的直接产物,A 排除;B"不依赖经济表现"可直接排除,可参见对上题的分析;D"不能带来政治变革"也和原文意思相悖;答案是 C"跟随生产力的提高而提高",最后两句话说明不是教育提高生产力,而是生产力限制教育的发展。

参考译文

在贫困国家中正规教育与经济增长之间的关系遭到经济学家和政治家们的普遍误解。无疑,这两个领域的发展对这些国家和其他所有国家的社会、政治和知识水平的发展是不可或缺的。然而,那种认为教育是促进贫困国家经济快速发展最重要因素的观点是错误的。需要两三代人努力才能建立新的教育体系并使足够多的人接受它的教育,从而推进经济发展,因此,我们这一代是很幸运的。一家研究机构的调查结论已经多次证明,在所有国家工人可通过职业培训而达到极高的生产能力,其结果是达到极高的生活水平。

具有讽刺意味的是,正是在美国初次出现了对这一观念的证据。前不久,美国进入了经济衰退期,同时日本处于前泡沫经济的顶峰时期。美国的劳力受教育程度较低,因此而受到嘲笑,这也被认为是美国糟糕的经济表现的一个主要原因。日本曾经以及现在也是全球自动化生产线效率最高的国家。然而,研究证明本田、日产和丰田三家公司在美国的工厂达到了日本本土工厂生活效率的95%——这是美国工人接受工作培训的结果。

最近,研究人员在住宅建设进行调查时发现,在休斯敦和得克萨斯,不识字、不会讲英语的墨西哥工人却达到了最佳的劳动生产力标准,尽管建筑工作很复杂。

教育和经济发展之间究竟有什么关系呢?我们不得不怀疑经济的不停增长会促使教育的发展,却无需政府的强制措施,毕竟,教育就是这样开始的。当一万年前我们的祖先还在狩猎和采集的时候,他们没有时间考虑寻找食物之外的任何事情。只有当人类开始以更有效的方式获取食物时,他们才有时间考虑其他事情。

随着教育的发展,人类的生产潜能也提高了,当充满竞争的环境迫使我们的祖先达到这种生产潜能的时候,他们才能够提供更多的教育。这种水平不断提高的教育可能是高级经济表现所需要的复杂政治体系的必要条件,但却不是充分条件。这样,只有广泛的正规教育才有可能会带来政治变革,没有这种政治变革,那些贫穷国家是无法摆脱贫困的。然而,在可以预见的未来,缺乏正规教育并不能限制发展中国家的劳动能力的发展,使他们无法从根本上在可预知的未来提高生产力。相反,对生产力的束缚说明了什么教育没有以更快的速度发展。

Text 4

长难句分析

1. The most thoroughly studied in the history of the new world are the ministers and political leaders of seventeenth-century New England.

❖结构分析 主干是 The most thoroughly studied are the ministers and political leaders. the most studied 相当于说 the subjects that are most thoroughly studied, 意思是"被最彻底地研究的课题"。

2. To take this approach to the New Englanders normally mean to start with the Puritans' theological innovations and their distinctive ideas about the church — important subjects that we may not neglect.

❖结构分析 这句话的主语是不定式 to take this approach to...,谓语是 mean。这种句式就是以非谓语动词作主语,在英语中很常见。

3. Sexual confusion, economic frustrations, and religious hope — all name together in a decisive moment when he opened the Bible, told his father the first line he saw would settle his fate, and read the magical words: "come out from among them, touch no unclean thing, and I will be your God and you shall be my people."

❖结构分析 这个句子表面上看很复杂,但实际上主干很短: All name together in a decisive moment. 破折号前面就是 all 所包含的内容。when 后面的成分是修饰 moment, 这一时刻是什么样的。told his father the first line he saw would... 这一部分中 the first line he saw 意指他看到的第一行字,he saw 是插入的定语从句。

试 题 分 析

36. [B] 细节推断题。答案对应于第一段第二句话 According to the standard history of American philosophy, nowhere else in colonial America was "So much important attached to intellectual pursuits. 因此答案应为 B"鼓励对知识的兴趣"。

37. [B] 细节题。先排除答案 A"在早期经历了一段相对和平的时期"和 C"对南方知识生活漠不关心",前者未被提及,C 中的南方知识生活指的就是新英格兰人,因此意思相反;D"痴迷于宗教革新"引申过多,文中只是提到新英格兰人的"宗教革新",并没有提供更多信息;因此答案应为B"带来了旧世界的文化"。

38. [D] 细节题。答案在第三段。A具有一定迷惑性,但却过于夸张,因为原文说的是他们的写作"reaching both New World and Old World audiences",没有说著名;B"在宗教事物中的重要性越来越强"和C"在来到新英格兰之前放弃了高位"均没有被提及;D"在新英格兰开创了新的知识氛围"为正确答案,依据是最后的说法:giving New England an atmosphere of intellectual earnestness.

39. [A] 细节推断题。文章在举约翰·达内的例子之前有一句话,可说明为什么要以他为例。Their thinking often had a traditional superstitions quality,这里提到的正是"迷信色彩",答案确定为A"受迷信的影响"。

40. [C] 推断题。先排除掉B"受到虚幻的美好前景的激励"和D"几乎没留下正式记录供后人参考",它们显然不符合文章的意思;A"大多数投身于政治活动"也不正确,因为新英格兰的早期定居者不仅包括那些政治家,还有许多"没有受到过良好教育的人",他们对政治的态度不得而知;C"来自不同的知识背景"才符合这个意思。

参考译文

在对新大陆的历史研究中,对17世纪英格兰的牧师及政治领袖的研究是最为彻底的。根据标准美国哲学史,在美洲殖民地,没有哪个地方像英格兰那样"更重视学术追求"。根据许多书籍和文章的记载,新英格兰的领袖们为美国知识生活中正在形成的、主流的清教徒传统设立了基本主题和关注对象。

通过这种途径来了解新英格兰人就意味着首先要了解清教徒在神学上的革新和他们关于教会的独特看法,这些主题不可忽视。但是为了和我们对南部知识生活的研究保持一致,我们要把清教徒看做是适应了新大陆环境的欧洲文化传播者。在追求被广泛认同的文化艺术理想过程中,新英格兰殖民地是许多重要事件发生的场所。

早期马萨诸塞湾的居民包括一些受到过良好教育并在英格兰具有影响力的人物。有大约90位学识渊博的教士在1629年之后的十年间来到马萨诸塞教堂,除此之外,还有许多政治领袖,比如约翰·温思罗普,一位有教养的绅士、律师,在到达波士顿之前他还是皇家官员。这些人创作并出版了大量著作,新旧世界的读者都可读到他们,这带给新英格兰一种渴望知识的氛围。

但是我们不要忘记,大多数新英格兰人没有受到过良好教育。几乎没有工匠或农民给我们留下文学作品以供分析,更不用说其家人和仆人了。他们的思想经常带有传统的迷信色彩。一们名叫约翰·达内的裁缝在17世纪30年代后期移民到新大陆,他留下的记录描述了他离开英格兰的原因,其中充满了各种符号征兆。对于性的困惑、经济的失败及对于宗教的希望——这些都在一个决定性的时刻:即当他打开圣经,告诉他父亲他看到的第一行字将决定他的命运的时候,汇集在一起。他读到了如下神奇的文字:"你们务必从他们中间出来,不要沾不洁净的东西,我就会成为你们的神,你们将成为我的子民。"人们会很好奇,达内当年在清教徒教堂里听到了对这句话的详细解释时在想什么。

同时,许多居民并不像达内那样对宗教如此虔诚,就像一位牧师在海边遇到了一些人所了解到的那样。这些人以嘲笑的口吻说他们并非是为了宗教才来到这个新世界的。"我们主要的目的是捕鱼"。

Part B

试 题 分 析

[说明]本文是一篇典型的以时间为顺序的说明文,讲述文化理论的发展过程及各种不同的文化理论,逻辑比较清楚,内容归属也比较明白。从设空的位置来看,都在段落的后半部分,因此从推理上看偏于归纳概括或因果关系。因此要偏重于每一段落内部的逻辑关系。

41. [C] 空白处实际上是对前面内容的概括。前面提到,斯宾塞提出的进化论认为世界上的一切现象,包括人类社会在内,都随着时间而不断变化,并越来越完善。因此,C "适者生存"是对他的社会理论的一种概括。

42. [E] 这一段讲美国社会学家刘易斯·享利摩根的"文化进化理论"。他试图证明文化的方方面面是如何随着社会的进化而改变的。因此,E 的主语 diverse aspects of culture 正是接着这个话题而说的。

43. [A] 这一段先介绍了"历史特殊论",但选项中没有哪一个与此相关,所以还要看下面的文字以理清这种逻辑关系。下面的一段谈论博厄斯的"历史特殊论",倒数第二段则又说,到了 20 世纪早期许多理论家更倾向于传播理论。因此,答案应该是 A,即和"历史特殊论"相对的"文化传播论"。这里关键的问题是要明白这一段和后面几段的逻辑关系。

44. [B] 此题比较容易辨别,因为博厄斯持"历史特殊论"的观点,为了研究特殊文化而精通语言学和机体人类学。

45. [G] 此题与上文提到的"文化传播论"存在前后的逻辑关系。"文化传播论"实际上将每一种重要的文化成果都归结于少数人的创造,然后又传播到其他地方。根据上下文,空白处应该是与这一理论相关的内容。G 是以举例的方式对这一理论内容进行说明。故选 G。

参考译文

英国自然科学家达尔文在 19 世纪 60 年代提出的生物进化论可谓石破天惊,与此同时,英国社会学家斯宾塞提出其生物和文化进化论。斯宾塞认为,世界上的一切现象,包括人类社会在内,都随着时间而不断变化,并越来越完善。(41)他认为人类的进化特征是一种斗争,他称之为"适者生存",在其中较弱的种族和社会最终将会较强的、更先进的种族和社会所取代。

美国社会学家刘斯易·享利摩根在19世纪第一个十年晚期又提出一种"文化进化理论"。和泰勒一样摩根也是现代人类学的奠基人之一。在他的著作中,他试图证明文化的方方面面是如何随着社会的进化而改变的。(42)以他之见,文化的各个方面,如家庭结构、婚姻形式、亲属关系类型、财产所有制度、政府形式、技术和食物生产体系等等都随着社会的进化而改变。

在12世纪初,德国出生的美国人类学家弗朗茨·博厄斯提出了新的文化理论,以"历史特殊论"而为人所知。历史特殊论强调一切文化的特殊性,为人类学的发展指出了新方向。(43)其他人类学家相信文化创新,比如发明,具有单一起源并会从一个社会被传递到另一个社会。这种理论被称为文化传播论。

博厄斯感到任何社会的文化都可被理解为由其特定历史所造成的结果,而不是属于更广阔的进化阶段或文化类型的文化的一种。(44)为了尽可能完整地研究个别的文化,博厄斯精通语言学和机体人类学(人类生物学和解剖学)。

历史特殊论之所以后来在美国人类学界成为研究文化的主流方法,主要还是由于博厄斯许多学生的影响。但是在20世纪早期许多人类学家拒绝文化理论的特殊论,更倾向于传播论。有些人类学家根据传播论,实际上把所有重要的文化成就都归功于某些民族,尤其是具备天才能力的民族,然后才流传到其他文化。(45)比如,英语人类学家格拉夫顿·艾略特·史密斯和W.J.佩里就以不恰当的信息为基础,错误地认为农业、陶器制作和冶金术都起源于古埃及,然后传播到全世界。事实上,所有这些文化都在不同时间,在世界上许多地方得到发展。

仍然是在20世纪早期,法国社会学家埃米尔·迪尔凯姆提出了一种对人类学影响巨大的文化理论。迪尔凯姆指出,宗教信仰的功能是加强社会团结。在欧洲,人们对社会功能和文化的关系的兴趣——被称为功能主义——成为研究主题,尤其是对英国的人类学来说,更是如此。

Part C

试题分析

46. **全句译文**:虽然可以说,衡量任何社会制度价值的标准就在于它对丰富和改善人类经验所起的作用,但是这种作用并不是它最初动机的组成部分。

　　翻译提示:but 前后是两个并列句,后面的句子比较简单,因此关键是前面的长句。前面一句话又分两个部分,it may be said that 是主句,比较好理解,后面由 that 引导从句的主干是 the measure is its effect,即"衡量的标准是效果"。翻译时把其他的修饰成分加上,句意就完整了。

47. **全句译文**:人们逐渐地才注意到制度的这一副产品,而认识到这种作用是制度运作中的指导性因素这一点,则需要更缓慢的过程。

　　翻译提示:and 前后是两个句子,第一个句子是倒装句,句子主干为 The by-product of the institution was only gradually noted. and 后面的句子也是倒装句,其主干是

This effect was considered as a directive factor in the conduct of the institution. and only more gradual still 是接着上面一句话说的,译为"更为缓慢的是"。

48. 全句译文:虽然在和年轻人打交道时我们很容易忽视自己行为对他们性情的影响,但在和成年人打交道时就不那么容易忽视这一点。

翻译提示:while 引导让步状语从句,其主干为 it is easy to ignore the effect,前半句的意思为:"虽然在和年轻人打交道时我们很容易忽视自己行为对他们性情的影响",主句中的 it is not so easy 意为"没那么容易",是接着上面的话题说的,即"没那么容易忽视这种影响"。

49. 全句译文:由于我们对年轻人所做的首要工作是使他们参与到日常生活,我们就禁不住要考虑是否正在形成让他们获得这种能力的力量。

翻译提示:since 引导原因状语从句,主语为 our chief business, enable sb. to do sth. 意为"使某人能做某事",因此这一部分的意思为:"由于我们对年轻人所做的首要工作是使他们参与到日常生活"。主句主干为 we cannot help considering,后面接 considering 的宾语从句 we are forming the powers,其后是一个定语从句,意为"我们能保证这种能力的力量"。

50. 全句译文:这就使得我们能够在我们一直讨论的广义的教育过程中区分出一种更正式的教育,即直接教导或叫学校教育。

翻译提示:句子主干是 we are thus let to distinguish a more formal kind of education. within the broad educational process 是插入的状语,后面的 which 引导的是定语从句。...that of direct tuition or schooling 是对前面 a more formal kind of education 的解释说明。

参考译文

在人与人的相处中受到的教育与对年轻人专门进行教育之间存在着极大不同。对前者而言教育具有偶然性,自然而又重要,但这并不能表达人们相互合作的原因。(46)虽然可以说,衡量任何社会制度价值的标准就在于它对丰富和改善人类经验所起的作用,但是这种作用并不是它最初动机的组成部分。比如说,宗教上相互协作开始于人们确保支配权力的需要,并且避免邪恶的影响;家庭中的协作是为了满足生活需求并保证家庭永恒;在多数情况下,系统性劳动是要征服其他劳动者等。(47)人们逐渐地才注意到制度的这一副产品,而认识到这种作用是制度运作中的指导性因素这一点,则需要更缓慢的过程。甚至到现在,在工业生活中,除去勤劳和节俭等既定价值之外,人们更关注的是协作形式所引起的物质上的结果,而不是它所带来的对知识和情感的影响,而正是这后一种协作才使世界得以运转。

但是,在对待年轻人时,协作作为一种存在的现实是非常重要的。(48)在和年轻人打交道时我们很容易忽视自己行为对他们性情的影响,但在和成年人打交道时就不那么容易忽视这一点。显然需要对他们进行培训;要改变他们的态度和习惯,这一任务所带来的压力非常紧迫,从而不能对它所带来的后果完全不予考虑。(49)由于我们对年轻人所做的首要工作是使他们参与到日常生活,我们就不禁要考虑是否正在形成让他们获得这种能力的力量。如果人类能够进一步认识到,各种制度的最终价值都在于它对人能产生明显影响的话,我们也许会相信我们主要是通过与年轻人打交道而学习到这一点的。

(50)这就使得我们能够在我们一直讨论的广义的教育过程中区分出一种更正式的教育,即直接教导或叫学校教育。在不发达的社会群体中,正式教育或培训基本上不存在。这些群体给年轻人逐渐灌输所需素质的方法主要依靠的是相互协作,这与使成年人忠诚于其群体的协作属于同一类型。

2010年 考研英语(一)全真试题

（阅读理解部分）

Part A

Directions:

Read the following four texts. Answer the questions below each text by choosing A, B, C or D.
Mark your answers on ANSWER SHEET 1.

Text 1

Of all the changes that have taken Place in English-language newspapers during the past quarter-century, perhaps the far-reaching has been the inexorable decline in the scope and seriousness of their arts coverage.

It is difficult to the point of impossibility for the average reader under the age of forty to imagine a time when high-quality arts criticism could be found in most big-city newspapers. Yet a considerable number of the most significant collections of criticism published in the 20th century consisted in large part of newspaper reviews. To read such books today is to marvel at the fact that their learned contents were once deemed suitable for publication in general-circulation dailies.

We are even farther removed from the unfocused newspaper reviews published in England between the turn of the 20th Century and the eve of World War Ⅱ, at a time when newsprint was dirt-cheap and stylish arts criticism was considered an ornament to the publications in which it appeared. In those far-off days, it was taken for granted that the critics of major papers would write in detail and at length about the events they covered. Theirs was a serious business, and even those reviewers who wore their learning lightly, like George Bernard Shaw and Ernest Newman, could be trusted to know what they were about. These men believe in journalism as a calling, and were proud to be published in the daily press."So few authors have brains enough or literary gift enough to keep their own end up in journalism," Newman wrote,"that I am tempted to define 'journalism' as 'a term of contempt applied by writers who are not read to writers who are'."

Unfortunately, these critics are virtually forgotten. Neville Cardus, who wrote for the Manchester Guardian from 1917 until shortly before his death in 1975, is now known solely as a writer of essays on the game of cricket. During his lifetime, though, he was also one of England's foremost classical-music critics, and a stylist so widely admired that his *Autobiography* (1947) became a bestseller. He was knighted in 1967, the first music critic to be so honored. Yet only one of his books is now in print, and his vast body of writings on music is unknown save to specialists.

Is there any chance that Cardus's? criticism will enjoy a revival? The prospect seems remote. Journalistic tastes had changed long before his death, and postmodern readers have little use for the richly upholstered Vicwardian prose in which he specialized. Moreover, the amateur tradition in music criticism has been in headlong retreat.

21. It is indicated in Paragraphs 1 and 2 that _____.

　　A. arts criticism has disappeared from big-city newspapers

　　B. English-language newspapers used to carry more arts reviews

　　C. high-quality newspapers retain a large body of readers

　　D. young readers doubt the suitability of criticism on dailies

22. Newspaper reviews in England before World War Ⅱ were characterized by _____.

　　A. free themes　　　B. casual style　　　C. elaborate layout　　　D. radical viewpoints

23. Which of the following would Shaw and Newman most probably agree on?

　　A. It is writers' duty to fulfill journalistic goals.

　　B. It is contemptible for writers to be journalists.

　　C. Writers are likely to be tempted into journalism.

　　D. Not all writers are capable of journalistic writing.

24. What can be learned about Cardus according to the last two paragraphs?

　　A. His music criticism may not appeal to readers today.

　　B. His reputation as music critic has long been in dispute.

　　C. His style caters largely to modern specialists.

　　D. His writings fail to follow the amateur tradition.

25. What would be the best title for the text?

　　A. Newspapers of the good Old Days　　　B. The Lost Horizon in Newspapers

　　C. Mournful Decline of Journalism　　　D. Prominent Critics in Memory

Text 2

Over the past decade, thousands of patents have been granted for what are called business methods. Amazon. com received one for its "one-click" online payment system. Merrill Lynch got legal protection for an asset allocation strategy. One inventor patented a technique for lifting a box.

Now the nation's top patent court appears completely ready to scale back on business-method patents, which have been controversial ever since they were first authorized 10 years ago. In a move that has intellectual-property lawyers abuzz, the U.S. Court of Appeals for the Federal Circuit said it would use a particular case to conduct a broad review of business-method patents. *In re Bilski*, as the case is known, is "a very big deal", says Dennis D. Crouch of the University of Missouri School of law. It "has the potential to eliminate an entire class of patents."

Curbs on business-method claims would be a dramatic about-face, because it was the federal circuit itself that introduced such patents with its 1998 decision in the so-called state Street Bank case, approving a patent on a way of pooling mutual-fund assets. That ruling produced an explosion in business-method patent filings, initially by emerging internet companies trying to stake out exclusive rights to specific types of online transactions. Later, more established companies raced to add such patents to their files, if only as a defensive move against rivals that might bent them to the punch. In 2005, IBM noted in a court filing that it had been issued more than 300 business-method patents despite the fact that it questioned the legal basis for granting them. Similarly, some Wall Street investment firms armed themselves with patents for financial products, even as they took positions in court cases opposing the practice.

The Bilski case involves a claimed patent on a method for hedging risk in the energy market. The Federal circuit issued an unusual order stating that the case would be heard by all 12 of the court's judges, rather than a typical panel of three, and that one issue it wants to evaluate is whether it should "reconsider" its state street Bank ruling.

The Federal Circuit's action comes in the wake of a series of recent decisions by the Supreme Court that has narrowed the scope of protections for patent holders. Last April, for example the justices signaled that too many patents were being upheld for "inventions" that are obvious. The judges on the Federal circuit are "reacting to the anti-patent trend at the supreme court", says Harold C. Wegner, a patent attorney and professor at George Washington University Law School.

26. Business-method patents have recently aroused concern because of _____.

    A. their limited value to businesses

    B. their connection with asset allocation

    C. the possible restriction on their granting

    D. the controversy over authorization

27. Which of the following is true of the Bilski case?

    A. Its ruling complies with the court decisions.

    B. It involves a very big business transaction.

    C. It has been dismissed by the Federal Circuit.

    D. It may change the legal practices in the U.S.

28. The word "about-face"(Line 1, Para. 3)most probably means _____.

    A. loss of good will   B. increase of hostility

C. change of attitude　　　D. enhancement of dignity

29. We learn from the last two paragraphs that business-method patents _____.

A. are important to legal challenges　　B. are often unnecessarily issued

C. lower the esteem for patent holders　　D. increase the incidence of risks

30. Which of the following would be the subject of the text?

A. A looming threat to business-method patents.

B. Protection for business-method patent holders.

C. A legal case regarding business-method patents.

D. A prevailing trend against business-method patents.

Text 3

In his book *The Tipping Point*, Malcolm Gladwell argues that "social epidemics" are driven in large part by the actions of a tiny minority of special individuals, often called influentials, who are unusually informed, persuasive, or well connected. The idea is intuitively compelling, but it doesn't explain how ideas actually spread.

The supposed importance of influentials derives from a plausible-sounding but largely untested theory called the "two-step flow of communication": Information flows from the media to the influentials and from them to everyone else. Marketers have embraced the two-step flow because it suggests that if they can just find and influence the influentials, those select people will do most of the work for them. The theory also seems to explain the sudden and unexpected popularity of certain looks, brands, or neighborhoods. In many such cases, a cursory search for causes finds that some small group of people was wearing, promoting, or developing whatever it is before anyone else paid attention. Anecdotal evidence of this kind fits nicely with the idea that only certain special people can drive trends?

In their recent work, however, some researchers have come up with the finding that influentials have far less impact on social epidemics than is generally supposed. In fact, they don't seem to be required of all.

The researchers' argument stems from a simple observation about social influence, with the exception of a few celebrities like Oprah Winfrey — whose outsize presence is primarily a function of media, not interpersonal, influence — even the most influential members of a population simply don't interact with that many others. Yet it is precisely these non-celebrity influentials who, according to the two-step-flow theory, are supposed to drive social epidemics by influencing their friends and colleagues directly. For a social epidemic to occur, however, each person so affected, must then influence his or her own acquaintances, who must in turn influence theirs, and so on; and just how many others pay attention to each of these people has little to do with the initial influential. If people in the network just two degrees removed from the initial influential prove resistant, for example, the cascade of change won't propagate very far or affect many people.

Building on the basic truth about interpersonal influence, the researchers studied the dynamics of social contagion by conducting thousands of computer simulations of populations, manipulating a number of variables relating to people's ability to influence others and their tendency to be influenced. They found that the principal requirement for what is called "global cascades" — the widespread propagation of influence through networks — is the presence not of a few influentials but, rather, of a critical mass of easily influenced people.

31. By citing the book *The Tipping Point*, the author intends to _____.

A. analyze the consequences of social epidemics

B. discuss influentials' function in spreading ideas

C. exemplify people's intuitive response to social epidemics

D. describe the essential characteristics of influentials

32. The author suggests that the "two-step flow theory" _____.

A. serves as a solution to marketing problems

B. has helped explain certain prevalent trends

C. has won support from influentials

D. requires solid evidence for its validity

33. What the researchers have observed recently shows that _____.

A. the power of influence goes with social interactions.

B. interpersonal links can be enhanced through the media.

C. influentials have more channels to reach the public.

D. most celebrities enjoy wide media attention.

34. The underlined phrase "these people" in paragraph 4 refers to the ones who _____.

A. stay outside the network of social influence

B. have little contact with the source of influence

C. are influenced and then influence others

D. are influenced by the initial influential

35. What is the essential element in the dynamics of social influence?

A. The eagerness to be accepted.

B. The impulse to influence others.

C. The readiness to be influenced.

D. The inclination to rely on others.

Text 4

Bankers have been blaming themselves for their troubles in public. Behind the scenes, they have been taking aim at someone else: the accounting standard-setters. Their rules, moan the banks, have forced them to report enormous losses, and it's just not fair. These rules say they must value some assets at the price a third party would pay, not the price managers and regulators would like them to fetch.

Unfortunately, banks' lobbying now seems to be working. The details may be unknowable, but the independence of standard-setters, essential to the proper functioning of capital markets, is being compromised. And, unless banks carry toxic assets at prices that attract buyers, reviving the banking system will be difficult.

After a bruising encounter with Congress, America's Financial Accounting Standards Board (FASB)rushed through rule changes. These gave banks more freedom to use models to value illiquid assets and more flexibility in recognizing losses on long-term assets in their income statement. Bob Herz, the FASB's chairman, cried out against those who "question our motives." Yet bank shares rose and the changes enhance what one lobby group politely calls "the use of judgment by management."

European ministers instantly demanded that the International Accounting Standards Board (IASB)do likewise. The IASB says it does not want to act without overall planning, but the pressure to fold when it completes its reconstruction of rules later this year is strong. Charlie McCreevy, a European commissioner, warned the IASB that it did"not live in a political vacuum" but "in the real word" and that Europe could yet develop different rules.

It was banks that were on the wrong planet, with accounts that vastly overvalued assets. Today they argue that market prices overstate losses, because they largely reflect the temporary illiquidity of markets, not the likely extent of bad debts. The truth will not be known for years. But bank's shares trade below their book value, suggesting that investors are skeptical. And dead markets partly reflect the paralysis of banks which will not sell assets for fear of booking losses, yet are reluctant to buy all those supposed bargains.

To get the system working again, losses must be recognized and dealt with. America's new plan to buy up toxic assets will not work unless banks mark assets to levels which buyers find attractive. Successful markets require independent and even combative standard-setters. The FASB and IASB have been exactly that, cleaning up rules on stock options and pensions, for example, against hostility from special interests. But by giving in to critics now they are inviting pressure to make more concessions.

36. Bankers complained that they were forced to _____.

    A. follow unfavorable asset evaluation rules

    B. collect payments from third parties

    C. cooperate with the price managers

    D. reevaluate some of their assets.

37. According to the author, the rule changes of the FASB may result in _____.

    A. the diminishing role of management

    B. the revival of the banking system

    C. the banks' long-term asset losses

D. the weakening of its independence

38. According to Paragraph 4, McCreevy objects to the IASB's attempt to _____.

    A. keep away from political influences

    B. evade the pressure from their peers

    C. act on their own in rule-setting

    D. take gradual measures in reform

39. The author thinks the banks were "on the wrong planet" in that they _____.

    A. misinterpreted market price indicators

    B. exaggerated the real value of their assets

    C. neglected the likely existence of bad debts

    D. denied booking losses in their sale of assets

40. The author's attitude towards standard-setters is one of _____.

    A. satisfaction   B. skepticism   C. objectiveness   D. sympathy

Part B

Directions:

For Questions 41 — 45, choose the most suitable paragraphs from the first A—G and fill them into the numbered boxes to from a coherent text. **Paragraph E has been correctly placed.** *There is one paragraph which does not fit in with the text. Mark your answers on* **ANSWER SHEET 1.**

[A] The first and more important is the consumer's growing preference for eating out; the consumption of food and drink in places other than homes has risen from about 32 percent of total consumption in 1995 to 35 percent in 2000 and is expected to approach 38 percent by 2005. This development is boosting wholesale demand from the food service segment by 4 to 5 percent a year across Europe ,compared with growth in retail demand of 1 to 2 percent. Meanwhile, as the recession is looming large, people are getting anxious. They tend to keep a tighter hold on their purse and consider eating at home a realistic alternative.

[B] Retail sales of food and drink in Europe's largest markets are at a standstill, leaving European grocery retailers hungry for opportunities to grow. Most leading retailers have already tried e-commerce, with limit success, and expansion abroad. But almost all have ignored the big profitable opportunity in their own backyard: the wholesale food and drink trade, which appears to be just the kind of market retailers need.

[C] Will such variations bring about a change in the overall structure of the food and drink market? Definitely not. The functioning of the market is based on flexible trends dominated by potential buyers. In other words it is up to the buyer rather than the seller to decide what to buy. At any rate this change will ultimately be acclaimed by an ever-growing number of both domestic and international consumers regardless of how long the current consumer pattern will take hold.

[D] All in all, this clearly seems to be a market in which big retailers could profitably apply their gigantic scale, existing infrastructure, and proven skills in the management of product ranges, logistics, and marketing intelligence. Retailers that master the intricacies of wholesaling in Europe may well expect to rake in substantial profits thereby. At least, that is how it looks as a whole. Closer inspection reveals important differences among the biggest national markets, especially in their customer segments and wholesale structures, as well as the competitive dynamics of individual food and drink categories. Big retailers must understand these differences before they can identify the segments of European wholesaling in which their particular abilities might unseat smaller but entrenched competitors. New skills and unfamiliar business models are needed too.

[E] Despite variations in detail, wholesale markets in the countries that have been closely examined — France, Germany, Italy, and Spain — are made out of same building blocks. Demand comes mainly from two sources: independent mom-and-pop grocery stores which, unlike large retail chains, are too small to buy straight from producers, and food service operators range from snack machines to large institutional catering ventures, but most of these businesses are known in the trade as "horeca": hotels, restaurants, and cafes. Overall, Europe's wholesale market for food and drink is growing at the same sluggish pace as the retail market, but the figures, when added together, mask two opposing trends

[F] For example, wholesale food and drink sales come to $268 billion in France, Germany, Italy, Spain and the United Kingdom in 2000 — more than 40 percent of retail sales. Moreover, average overall margins are higher in wholesale than in retail; wholesale demand from the food service sector is growing quickly as more Europeans eat out more often; and changes in the competitive dynamics of this fragmented industry are at last making it feasible for wholesalers to consolidate.

[G] However, none of these requirements should deter large retails and even some large good producers and existing wholesalers from trying their hand, for those that master the intricacies of wholesaling in Europe stand to reap considerable gains.

41. → 42. → 43. → 44. → E → 45.

Part C

Directions:

Read the following text carefully and then translate the underlined segments into Chinese. Your translation should be written carefully on ANSWER SHEET 2.

One basic weakness in a conservation system based wholly one economic motives is that most members of the land community have no economic value. Yet these creatures are members of the biotic community and, if its stability depends on its integrity, they are entitled to continuance.

When one of these noneconomic categories is threatened and, if we happen to love it, we invent excuses to give it economic importance. At the beginning of the century, songbirds were supposed to be disappearing. (46)Scientists jumped to the rescue with some distinctly shaky evidence to the effect that insects would eat us up if birds failed to control them. The evidence had to be economic in order to be valid.

It is painful to read these roundabout accounts today. We have no land ethic yet, (47)but we have at least drawn nearer the point of admitting that birds should continue as a matter of intrinsic right, regardless of the presence or absence of economic advantage to us.

A parallel situation exists in respect of predatory mammals and fish-eating birds. (48)Time was when biologists somewhat overworked the evidence that these creatures preserve the health of game by killing the physically weak, or that they prey only on "worthless species". Here again, the evidence had to be economic in order to be valid. It is only in recent years that we hear the more honest argument that predators are members of the community, and that no special interest has the right to exterminate them for the sake of a benefit, real or fancied, to itself.

Some species of trees have been "read out of the party" by economic-minded foresters they grow too slowly or have too low a sale value to pay as timber crops. (49)In Europe, where forestry is ecologically more advanced, the noncommercial tree species are recognized as members of the native forest community, to be preserved as such, within reason. Moreover, some have been found to have a valuable function in building up soil fertility. The interdependence of the forest and its constituent tree species. ground flora, and fauna is taken for granted.

To sum up: a system of conservation based solely on economic self-interest is hopelessly lopsided. (50)It tends to ignore, and thus eventually to eliminate, many elements in the land community that lack commercial value, but that are essential to its healthy functioning. It assumes, falsely, that the economic parts of the biotic clock will function without the uneconomic parts.

2010年 考研英语(一)全真试题
(阅读理解部分)解析

Part A

Text 1

长难句分析

1. **We are even farther removed from the unfocused newspaper reviews published in England between the turn of the 20th Century and the eve of World War Ⅱ, at a time when newsprint was dirt-cheap and stylish arts criticism was considered an ornament to the publications in which it appeared.**

   ❖结构分析 主句是 We are even farther removed from the unfocused newspaper reviews. 后面 published in... 是定语,修饰 newspaper reviews, at a time 及后面的从句是 the turn of the 20th Century and the eve of World War Ⅱ 的同位语,对这一时代进行更详细的说明。stylish arts criticism was considered an ornament to the publications in which it appeared 和前面的 newsprint was dirt-cheap 并列,对当时的情况补充说明。be considered (as/to sth.) 意为"被当成…"。an ornament to the publications 后面 in which it appeared 是定语从句,which 是连接代词,指的是前面出现的 publications, it 指代的是 arts criticism。

2. **During his lifetime, though, he was also one of England's foremost classical-music critics, and a stylist so widely admired that his Autobiography(1947)became a bestseller.**

   ❖结构分析 句子主干是一个简单的系表结构,he was... and...。and 后面的句子包括一个 so... that 复合结构,意为"如此…以至于…"。admired 修饰 stylist,意为"如此广受崇拜,以至他的自传成了当时的畅销书。"

试题分析

21. [B] 细节题。文章讲的是英语报纸在内容上的变化,主要和艺术评论相关。可以使用排除法把和文章关系不大的 C 和 D 排除掉。A 太过绝对,不是说现在没有了艺术评论,而是说内容少了,也没有以前那么严肃。因此 B 为最佳选择。

22. [A] 词义猜测题。第二段说 We are even farther removed from the unfocused newspaper reviews published in England between the turn of the 20th Century and the eve of World War Ⅱ. 关键是理解 unfocused 一词的意思为"不聚焦的",此处指的是自由散漫的评

论。D、C "排版精致"和 "激进的观点" 都和原文没关系,可排除。文章用 unfocused 一词说明内容的多样性,故答案应该为 A。

23. [D] 推断题。第三段提到题干里的这两个人,即肖伯纳和纽曼,他们都认为"报纸是严肃的事业",并且后面还引用了纽曼的一段话:"鲜有作者具备足够的头脑及文学知识,从而能够在新闻业终老一生,这诱使我把'新闻'解释为'那些读者寥寥、胸无点墨的作者用来贬低读者众多、学识渊博的作者时所使用的贬义词'"。看来,这些作家们认为并不是人人都可以从事新闻业的,故答案应该为 D。

24. [A] 推断题。此题可用排除法,首先是 C 不可能正确,因为显然卡达斯的评论不会是"迎合当代的批评家",文中只是说现在只有批评家们才关注他写的艺术评论。D "他的批评没有遵循业余传统"也无从说起,文章最后一句"业余传统也迅速衰退"应该是现在的事情,而卡达斯那个时候并不存在这一问题。选项 B "他的名声一直饱受争议"与事实不符,现在他的作品是被人"遗忘"了,而不是争议。因此答案为 A。文中说明,卡达斯作为音乐批评家的身份被人遗忘,由此可知,他的批评失去了"吸引现在读者"的能力。

25. [B] 归纳题。先排除明显不对的 C "新闻业令人悲哀的衰退",其中"新闻业"一词显然范围太广,衰退的实际上是新闻报纸上的文艺批评。D 意为"记忆中杰出的评论家"似乎有理,但这一题目和文章的中心内容"报纸"没有什么关系,故排除。同样,A "过去好时代的报纸"和"文艺批评"没有联系。这两项都没有做到两者兼顾。正确答案为 B "报纸中失去的风景线",此处"风景线"指过去曾经有的那种高质量的文艺批评。这既符合文章主旨大意,又兼顾"报纸"和"文艺批评"二者,故为最佳选择。

参考译文

过去的四分之一个世纪中,英语报纸的变化良多,其中最大一点是对艺术报道的范围在无情地缩小,其严肃性也大打折扣。

四十岁以下的读者很难想象那样一个时代:大多数都市报纸上会刊登高质量的艺术批评。然而在 20 世纪所出版的最重要的批评文集中,有相当数量的文章选自报纸。今天阅读这些书时会感到非常惊奇:普通的日报竟一度是发表这些内容渊博文章的合适载体!

在 20 世纪之初和二战前夕发表在英格兰报纸上的散漫评论更是远离我们而去,当时印刷用纸贱如粪土,流行艺术评论被刊登在报纸上当做点缀。在那些远去的日子里,人们理所当然地认为报纸的内容应该详细。这是严肃的事业,即使是像肖伯纳和欧内斯特·纽曼这样不怎么卖弄学问的评论家也都因为明白报纸的主旨而获得信任。这些人相信新闻是一项事业,作家们为发表在报纸上的文章而感到自豪。纽曼曾写道:"鲜有作者具备足够的头脑及文学知识,从而能够在新闻业终老一生,这诱使我把'新闻'解释为'那些读者寥寥、胸无点墨的作者用来贬低读者众多、学识渊博的作者时所使用的贬义词'"。

不幸的是,这些批评家已被遗忘。内维克·卡达斯从 1917 年开始直到 1975 年去世,一直在为《曼彻斯特卫报》撰稿,现在他仅以板球评论而知名。然而,究其一生,他还是英格兰最重要的古典音乐评论家和文体家,当时深受崇拜,以至于其自传(1947)成了当时的畅销书。他于 1967 年受爵,是首位获此殊荣的音乐评论家。然而他仅有一部著作现在尚刊行于世,除了少数专家,他在音乐方面的著作已经无人知晓。

卡达斯那样的批评还有复兴的机会吗?前景似乎很渺茫。在他去世之前新闻业的品味就业已发生变化,而后现代的读者们在他那种词藻华丽的散文面前也会感到无能为力。此外,音乐批评中的业余传统也已迅速衰退。

Text 2

长难句分析

1. In a move that has intellectual-property lawyers abuzz, the U.S. Court of Appeals for the Federal Circuit said it would use a particular case to conduct a broad review of business-method patents.

❖结构分析 主句是 The U.S. Court of Appeals for the Federal Circuit said... 后面是宾语从句,前面 in a move 是状语。in a move 后面由 that 引导的定语从句修饰,have sb. abuzz 是一个复合结构,意为"使某人嗡嗡作响",引申为喋喋不休的争论。

2. Curbs on business-method claims would be a dramatic about-face, because it was the federal circuit itself that introduced such patents with its 1998 decision in the so-called state Street Bank case, approving a patent on a way of pooling mutual-fund assets.

❖结构分析 主句是逗号前的部分,主语是 curbs on business-method claims. about-face 是指态度转变。because 从句中包含一个强调句型 it was... that,其后的 with its 1998 decision in the... case 意思是"随着 1998 年在某案件的决议,联邦法院引进了这种专利"。approving 是伴随状语,说明当时出现的情况,approving a patent on... 意为"批准了关于…的专利"。

3. In 2005, IBM noted in a court filing that it had been issued more than 300 business-method patents despite the fact that it questioned the legal basis for granting them.

❖结构分析 句子主干为 IBM noted that... 后面是宾语从句。despite the fact that...引导让步状语从句,意为"尽管事实上…"。question the legal basis for granting them 中的 them 指的是 business-method patents,即授予这些专利的法律基础。

试题分析

26. [C] 细节题。首先排除掉 A 和 B,这两个答案是无中生有,和文章基本上没有关系。第二段的第一句话 Now the nation's top patent court appears poised to scale back on business-method patents, which have been controversial ever since they were first authorized 10 years ago. 中 controversial 一词对应题干里的 concern,似乎 D"对授权

的争议"为正确答案,但要注意题干里有 recently 一词,而 which 引导的定语从句明确告诉我们,这类专利从十年前取得合法地位之日起就饱受争议,因此 D 也可排除。答案应该为 C"对他们授权可能的限制",其中 appear 表示"看起来,似乎",替换选项中的 possible(可能的);scale back(缩减)替换 restriction。

27.[D] 细节题。首先排除到 A 和 C,它们和文章没有任何关系,属于明显可排除的干扰项。文章第二段倒数第二句话 In re Bilski, as the case is known, is "a very big deal," says Dennis D. Crouch of the University of Missouri School of Law.似乎和 A 契合,因为我们都知道 big deal 有"大买卖"的意思,但后面还有一句话 It "has the potential to eliminate an entire class of patents."可见,big deal 此处的意思是"这是一件大案子",和里面有没有有重要交易没有关系。D 和上面引用的话一致,语气也一致,potential 和选项里的 may 对应,表示"有可能"。

28.[C] 词义猜测题。从前两段主要内容和第三段开头,不难看出原来 the Federal Circuit 鼓励专利申请,现在要抑制,约束(即三段第一个单词 curbs),那就是说态度发生了重要变化。

29.[B] 推断题。此题难度不大,可以直接从文章最后一段找到依据:Last April, for example the justices signaled that too many patents were being upheld for "inventions" that are obvious.这正与 B 契合。另外这也和文章全文的主旨一致,即讨论所谓的商业方法专利问题。

30.[A] 主旨大意题。先排除掉 B 和 C,B 与文章表达的意思相反,而 C 主次颠倒,因为虽然文章提到了 Bilski 一案,但只是作为例证,并非以它为主要内容。Now the nation's top patent court appears poised to scale back on business-method patents. 从中可以看出这都是对 business-method patents 的一种潜在的威胁。因此应选 A"对商业方法专利是一种潜在的威胁",a looming threat 和 potential 可以看成是同义替换。

参考译文

过去十年,成千上万所谓的"商业方法"专利获得批准。Amazon.com 的"一键支付系统"获得专利。美林证券的资产分配方法获取了法律保护。一位发明家为其抬箱子的方法申请了专利。

国家最高专利法庭似乎准备要缩减商业方法专利,而这类专利从十年前取得合法地位之日起就饱受争议。在一件使知识产权律师争论不休的行动中,美国联邦巡回上诉法院表示将利用某个案例,即 Bilski 案,对商业专利进行广泛调研。密苏里大学法法院的丹尼斯·D.克劳奇说,"这是一个大案子",它"有可能把整个一类专利彻底清除"。

抑制商业方法专利标志着联邦法院对此态度大变,因为 1998 年所谓的"美国道富银行案"的决议中,正是联邦法院本身同意授予一种合并共有资金财产的方法以专利权,这是该种专利首次获准通过。这一裁决造成了商业方法专利申请的快速膨胀,起初新兴的互联网公司试图要为某些在线交易的特殊类型寻求专营权,后来作为提防竞争对手攻击的防护措施,更多普通公司也竞相把此种专利纳入到自己的计划之中。在 2005 年,IBM 公司在一份诉讼记录中注意到其曾申请过 300 多项商业方法专利,尽管它质疑批准这些专利的法律基础。与此相似,尽管一些华尔街投资公司在法庭上也反对这种做法,却也用专利作为保护自己金融产品的武器。

在 Biliski 案件中,其当事人声称自己拥有一项专利,这是一套在能源市场上降低风险的方法。联邦法院为此发表了一项不同寻常的声明,说这件案子将由法院的所有 12 名法官审理,而不是通常的三人组合,并且它要评估是否应该"重新考虑"关于美国道富银行的决议。

最高法院最近的几项决议已经缩小了对专利持有者的保护范围,联邦法院的决议紧随其后。比如去年 4 月的法律案件表明有过多的专利被作为显而易见的"发明"而被通过。哈罗德·C.韦格纳是华盛顿大学法学院的专利律师与教授,他说联邦法院的法官们已经"在最高法院对反专利潮流做出反应"。

Text 3

长难句分析

1. In his book *The Tipping Point*, Malcolm Gladwell argues that "social epidemics" are driven in large part by the actions of a tiny minority of special individuals, often called influentials, who are unusually informed, persuasive, or well connected.

❖结构分析　句子主干为 Malcolm Aladuell argues that...后面是宾语从句。宾语从句的主干是一个被动语态,"social epidemics" are driven in large part by the actions of...individual 后面的修饰成份中,often called influentials 是定语,后面的 who 引导的非限制性定语从句修饰 influentials, be informed 意为"消息灵通",be well connected 是被动式,意思是"社会联系多"。

2. The researchers' argument stems from a simple observation about social influence, with the exception of a few celebrities like Oprah Winfrey — whose outsize presence is primarily a function of media, not interpersonal, influence — even the most influential members of a population simply don't interact with that many others.

❖结构分析　句子主干为开头部分: The researchers' argument stems from a simple observation about social influence... 后面紧接着的成份是对 argument 一词的解释,意为"甚至最具影响力的人物也不可能与那么多'其他人'进行交往"。中间是插入的成份 with the exception of a few celebrities 破折号之间的句子是修饰这个人名的非限制性定语从句,意为"她巨大的影响力来自媒体的作用而不是人际交往。"

试 题 分 析

31. [B] 细节题。首先排除 A,因为文章并没有探讨社会风潮的后果,而是对其产生及流行的原因进行说明,而该书作者的观点是"社会风潮"是由"影响者"所驱动的。C 与 D 文章中也没有提到。答案为 B,即讨论影响者的功能,他们与社会风潮的关系问题。

32. [D] 推断题。关于"two-step-flow theory",即两级传播理论,作者在第二段开始时说,The supposed importance of influentials derives from a plausible-sounding but largely untested theory called the "two-step flow of communication... 意思是说这种理论听起来似乎有道理,其实却"未经证实",因此答案 D"需要切实的证据"就是对这句话的解释。

33. [A] 推断题。由题干"最近研究人员发现"可知此题应该是针对第四段而设。这一段说:The researchers' argument stems from a simple observation about social influence... even the most influential members of a population simply don't interact with that many others. A 与该句意思对应,其中 influence 对应 influential,social interactions 对应 interact with that many others。B 之所以不对是因为虽然这句话提到了媒体,但是作为人际交往的反面而被提及的。C 和 D 本身的判断是正确的,但和文章关系不大,因此可以排除。答案应该是 A。

34. [C] 细节题。首先确定 these people 所在的语境。根据这句话的前一句话"每个人是如何影响他(她)们的熟人,然后这些熟人又是如何接着去影响他们的熟人;这些人和最初的名人是没有关系的。"所以这些人指的是互相影响的人们。所以 C 恰是对这一点的正确表述。A 和 B 显然有悖于文章内容,D 项忽视了这些人对其他人的影响。

35. [C] 细节题。根据题干的关键词"dynamics"可以把答案出现的范围定在最后一段,研究者们发现对人的影响力或受影响的倾向相关的某些变量进行运算,研究了信息的社会传播的动态机制。据此可把答案锁定在 B 和 C 之间。文章接着说 they found that the principal requirement... is the presence not of a few influentials but, rather, of a critical mass of easily influenced people, not... rather 结构意为"与其说…还不如说…",明显是侧重于"easily influenced people",即易受影响的人们。所以答案为 C。

参考译文

马克科姆·格拉德韦尔在《引爆流行》一书中认为,"社会风潮"在很大程度上是由一小部分特殊人群的行为所驱动的,就是人们常说的"影响者",他们消息灵通、能言善辩、人脉广泛。这种观点引人注目,但并无法解释观念实际的传播过程。

人们之所以认为"影响者"很重要,是受到了一种貌似合理但却未经验证的理论的影响,即"两级传播理论":信息从媒体流向"影响者",然后从"影响者"再流向其他人。营销人员拥抱两级传播理论,因为它暗示如果能够找到并影响"影响者",这些人就会为他们完成大部分营销工作。这种理论也似乎能解释为什么某种装扮、品牌或地段会出人意料地突然流行。如果对这些事例的原因进行走马观花式的调查,会发现一小部分人在大多数人尚未注意之前就已经率先穿上某种衣服或推动、发展什么新事物了。这类表面证据与影响者理论极为吻合——只有某些特殊人群才能带动潮流。

某些研究者最近发现,"影响者"其实对社会风潮的影响力比人们所认为的程度要小得多。事实上,他们似乎根本就无足轻重。

这些研究者的观点来自于对社会影响力的简单观测:除了像奥普拉·温弗里这样的少数人之外——她无所不在的影响力并不是依靠人际交往,而是借助媒体的影响——甚至最具影响力的人物也不可能与那么多"其他人"进行交往。然而,两级交往理论认为,正是那些并非名人的"影响者"直接影响了自己的朋友、同事,从而推动了社会风潮。然而,要想最终形成社会风潮,受到影响的个人一定会再影响到自己的熟人,而他的熟人又影响其他人,以此类推;但是后面这些熟人中的每个人又会受到多少人的关注,与最初的影响者几乎没有关系。在人际影响网络中,假如距离第一个影响者仅两个层级的人采取了抵制态度,那么影响的范围就不会继续扩大或者影响许多人。

这些学者以人际交往的基本事实为依据,对数千人口进行计算机模拟,对人的影响力或受影响的倾向相关的某些变量进行运算,研究了信息的社会传播的动态机制。他们发现了"全球连锁反应",即影响力通过人际网络而广泛传播,所要求的条件并不是存在着几个影响者,而主要取决于易受影响者是否达到了临界数量。

Text 4

长难句分析

1. **The details may be unknowable, but the independence of standard-setters, essential to the proper functioning of capital markets, is being compromised.**

   ❖结构分析　这是由 but 连接的两个并列句,前面的句子很明了,后面句子的主干为 The independence of standard-setters is being compromised.essential to the proper functioning of capital markets 相当于一个非限制性的定语从句,是对前面"独立性"的进一步说明,意思是"这种独立性对资产市场的正常运行是必不可少的(是关键的)"。

2. **And dead markets partly reflect the paralysis of banks which will not sell assets for fear of booking losses, yet are reluctant to buy all those supposed bargains.**

   ❖结构分析　主句是 Dead markets partly reflect the paralysis of banks. which 引导的定语从句修饰 banks, yet 是连接并列定语从句,意为"这些银行还不愿意购买这些被认为是便宜货的资产。"

试题分析

[说明]本文是一篇经济类文章,讲的是银行处理不良资产的会计准则问题。

36. [A] 细节题。本题题干提到了"银行家的抱怨",因此可把答案范围锁定在第一段。银行业抱怨会计规则强迫他们报告遭受的巨大损失,认为这并不公平。因此 A 正确。B 错误理解了原文,第三方愿意付出的价格当然不是"collect payments"。C 没有被提到,更没有强调与 price managers 合作的概念。D 错误是因为文章没有强调要他们重新评估,而是强调必须按照 rules 办事,不能自己随意估计资产价格,要以第三方出价的方式来估计资产。

37. [D] 推断题。首先第三段讲 FASB 匆忙改变规则(rushed through rule changes)的例子是为了证明第二段中的 the independence of standard-setters,... is being compromised. 而 D 就是对此的替换表述。FASB= standard-setter。其次,第三段中交代的规则的变化就是在银行游说奏效下,银行获得更多的自由和灵活性,而这也正说明 FASB 独立地位的削弱。A 迷惑性较大,是主观推导项。文章强调 FASB 的独立性现在受国会和银行家的胁迫妥协了,这对于金融市场的正确运行是不利的。

38. [C] 细节题。第四段说麦克里维警告说 IASB 并没有活在政治真空里,只是提醒它政治的影响无处不在,并无法说明它要摆脱政治影响,只是不想让它像 FASB 那样修改规则。故 A"摆脱政治影响"不正确。B 的 peers 显然指的是 FASB,文中并没有说 FASB 给 IASB 施压,故 B 也不能选。D 项也没有被提及。

39. [B] 细节题。文章说 It was banks that were on the wrong planet, with accounts that vastly overvalued assets,B 中 exaggerate 替换了 overvalue。因此 B 是正确的。选项 C 似乎与文章中的 Today they argue that market prices overstate losses, because they largely reflect the temporary illiquidity of markets, not the likely extent of bad debts.相符,但很显然并没有"忽视"什么,文章用的是"reflect",不要混淆。

40. [D] 推断题。本文作者一直支持会计准则必须独立,标准制定者要捍卫准则,政客和银行家的阴谋是不应该得逞的。文章的主题,就是反对银行的观点,强调保持会计准则制定机构的独立性,对他们在压力面前做出的一些让步表示无奈。也就是站在他们的角度,作者反对银行;而会计准则制定机构也受到了来自银行等方面的压力,FASB 受到了国会的压力,不得不匆忙更改规则,IASB 也正面临 European ministers 方面的压力,面临贞节不保的窘境。所以作者支持同情标准制定者,站在他们一边。

参考译文

银行家们会当众将他们的问题归咎于自身,但在私底下,他们却一直把目标对准别人:会计标准制定者。银行业抱怨会计规则强迫他们报告遭受的巨大损失,认为这并不公平。这些规则规定他们必须以第三方愿意付出的价格来评估部分资产的价值, 而并不是按照管理者和监管者期望该资产能够获得的价格。

不幸的是,银行的游说似乎已经生效。我们可能无法获知其中细节,但是准则制定者在独立性方面(这正是资产市场正常运行的关键)已经做出妥协了。银行如果不能够以吸引买家的价格转移不良资产,银行系统的复兴将会非常困难。

美国 FASB(财务会计准则委员会)在与国会发生激烈摩擦之后匆匆通过了规则的修改。这些修改使得银行有更大的自由选择使用不同模型评估非流动资产,同时能更灵活地确定收益表中长期的资产损失。FASB 主席鲍勃·赫茨大声疾呼,反对那些"怀疑我们的动机"的人。然而银行股票上涨了,这些修改强化了一个游说团的客气之言,即"管理层使用理性判断"。

欧洲的部长们马上敦促国际会计准则委员会(IASB)效仿此法。IASB表示，不能没有全盘计划就贸然行事，但它在今年下半年完成规则修订时可能会屈服于巨大的压力。4月1日，欧洲委员会委员查理·麦克里维警告IASB说，它并没有"处在政治真空中"而是"在现实世界里"，并表示欧洲可能最终会提出不同的会计规则。

是这些银行住在了错误的星球上，估值过高的资产充斥着它们的账户。现在他们认为市场价格主要反映了市场的暂时性流动性不足，而不是坏账的可能范围，因此市价高估了银行的损失。数年之内将无人会了解真相。但是，银行股票以低于账面价值的价格交易却反映出了投资者们的疑虑。死气沉沉的市场在一定程度上反映了瘫痪的银行既不希望承受账面损失而出售资产，也不愿意去购买这些被认为是便宜货的资产。

为了使银行系统重新运转，必须要确认和处理流失的资产。只有当银行的资产价格水平足够吸引买家时，美国收购不良资产的新计划才会有效。成功的市场需要独立甚至是好斗的标准制定者。FASB和IASB以往正是这样对抗特殊利益集团的敌意的，例如改进股权和退休金的相关规则。然而此次为了缓和危机，他们给自己带来了做出更多妥协的压力。

Part B

试题分析

[说明]这是今年首次出现的考题形式，与以往选标题或空缺段落相比，难度有所增加，以至于使许多考生感到无所适从。但实际上该题还是和前几年的B节相似，考查的是辨别文章语篇结构的能力。首先要先了解文章大意。我们可以从各个段落中看出这里讲的大致意思是欧洲的饮食市场问题，即要面临从零售到批发这样的转型。在做题时一定要从全文整体着眼，不能就题论题。

41. [B] 英语文章的首段往往是提出问题的总论，因此不应该包括与上文衔接的关系词。从这个角度来看，只有B符合这个条件。有的同学认为A中提到the first and more important...，所以先了A，就犯了一个错误，即一般来说不会有这么明显的提示词，并且，the first是讲其中的一个问题，因而不可能是文章的开头。故B为正确答案。

42. [F] 先排除掉A，因为the first and more important没有可与上文衔接的内容。C讲"变化"可能带来的后果，也可排除。而D的all in all显然是总结句式，放在这里也不合适。G项的however是转折，根据其内容分析也不可能正确。第一段最后一句话进行判断，but后指出了虽然食品零售商面临着"at a standstill(几乎停止发展)"的问题，他们却忽略了。而F首句便举例说明法国、德国、意大利等国家的食品批发产业的市场规模比食品零售产业要大40%。而且在moreover后又进一步说明批发的利润比零售大很多。因此可以判断此选项是对第一段的例证说明。其中for example是明显的信息提示词。

43. [D] 上段介绍了食品批发商的优势，排除A和C。G是转折，"然而，这些要求都不能阻止大型的零售业甚至某些供货商和现有的批发商一试身手"，显然前文还没有提到什么能阻止零售商的"困难"，因此也可排除。而D选项第一句All in all, this clearly seems to be a market in which...则对上文的内容进行总结，其中all in all是较明显的信息提示词，即上文中提到的食品批发的优势推出这是明显对于 big retailers that master the intricacies of wholesaling 是一个"market"。因此 D 为正确答案。

44.[G] 上段最后一句提出的 particular abilities 以及 new skills and unfamiliar business models are needed，即零售商需要新的技能及不熟悉的商业模式。而 G 选项第一句提到的"these requirements(这些要求)"正是指上文所提到的技能。排除 A 和 C 即可。

45. [A] 剩下的选项只有 A 和 C，此题前文的已知段落 E 选项中最后一句中"two opposing trends"在 A 中得到了体现，即一方面由于人们选择在外就餐而扩大了食品批发的需求，而另一方面人们又开始感到"anxious(焦虑)"。而 C 第一句提到的"such variations"在上文中并没有得到体现，因此可以断定 A 为正确答案。

参考译文

欧洲最大的饮食批发零售市场陷于停滞，这使欧洲的食品零售商对增长销售的机会如饥似渴。许多重要的零售商业已尝试电子商务或拓展海外业务,但都不太成功。但是几乎所有零售商都忽视了他们自己后院的巨大商机:食品和饮料的批发业务,这似乎正是零售业所需要的市场。

比如,饮食批发销售在法国、德国、意大利、西班牙与英国在2000年达到了2,680亿美元,超过零售业的40%。还有,批发业的平均总体利润比零售业更高;由于更多欧洲人外出就餐,来自于饮食服务业的批发需求增长迅速;并且批发业的动态竞争最终会使批发商有适当机会相互合并。

总之,在这个市场中,大零售商们可以在产品种类、后勤保障和营销智慧方面利用其巨大的规模、现有的基础设施和历经锤炼的技术,赚取利润。因此,掌控欧洲批发业复杂事务的零售商可能会期待快速营利。至少,总体看起来它就是这样子的。进一步的调查可发现,全国最大的市场之间, 尤其是在顾客构成和批发体系及个体饮食类别之间存在的动态竞争这些方面存在重要差异。在欧洲批发市场中这些大零售商的特殊能力也许会把那些规模较小但却强硬的竞争对手赶出市场,因此在他们认同欧洲批发市场时要首先认识到这些差异。也需要新的技术或陌生的商业模式。

然而,这些要求都不能阻止大型的零售业甚至某些供货商和现有的批发商一试身手,因为那些控制欧洲批发业的商家一定会收获丰硕的利润。

尽管存在着细微差别, 在我们所仔细研究过的国家——法国、德国、意大利和西班牙——的批发市场都由同样的建筑区组成。主要有两个需求来源:首先是独立的夫妻杂货店,和大零售销售链不同,它们都规模太小,不能直接从制造商那里购买产品;其次包括从快餐机到大型公共饮食机构在内的食品服务经营者,但是大多数这类生意都可被称作 horeca,即:hotels(酒店)、restaurants(饭店)和 cafes(小餐馆)。总体来说,欧洲的饮食批发市场与零售市场一样都增长缓慢,但是这些数字加在一起的话就掩盖了两个相反的趋势。

首先,也更重要的是消费者越来越喜欢出去就餐;在家庭之外的场所消费的食品和饮料在 1995 年占总消费量的 32%,这一数字在 2000 年增长到 35%,到 2005 年有望增长到38%。这种发展推动了饮食业的批发业务,使其在欧洲一年之内增长了 4%—5%,而相比之下零售业的需求则只增长了 1%—2%。与此同时,由于经济衰退愈加明显,人们也愈加焦虑。他们更倾向于捂紧自己的钱袋,认为在家就餐是更现实的选择。

Part C

试题分析

46. **全句译文**：科学家们急忙介入,但提出的证据显然站不住脚,其大意是,如果鸟类不能控制昆虫的数量,昆虫便会吞噬我们人类。

    翻译提示：主句很简单,Scientists jumped to the rescue. with 后面是介词短语,即"用…来营救",根据上下文的意思,可译为"科学家们急忙介入"。 to the effect 意为"大意是说", 是插入到 evidence 和 that insects... 从句之间的成份。that 是 evidence 的同位语,是对"evidence"的说明,证据的内容是什么。

47. **全句译文**：但是我们至少几近承认,无论鸟类能否带给我们经济价值,它们自有生存下去的权利。

    翻译提示：主干是 We have drawn nearer the point of...我们已经接近什么观点,我们近乎承认。 admitting 后面是宾主从句,说明承认的对象是"鸟儿的生存是它们的固有权利",continue 在此处的意思是"继续生存"。regardless of 意为"不管…",economic advantage 意为"经济利益"。

48. **全句译文**：曾经有段时间,生物学家或多或少滥用了一种证据,即这些生物通过杀死体弱者来保持种群的健康,或者说它们仅仅捕食没有价值的物种。

    翻译提示：time was when 是实际上的主语,"曾经有…的时代/时间", 关键是理解后面的 evidence 及其 that 引导的同位语从句,overwork 意为"过度使用",by killing...意为"通过捕杀…"。后面的 or that 是并列的同位语从句。

49. **全句译文**：在林业生态更为发达的欧洲,没有商业价值的树种被合理地看成是当地森林群落的成员,并得到相应的保护。

    翻译提示：句子的主干是 The noncommercial tree species are recognized as.... to be preserved as such 也是和 be recognized 连用,be recognized to be 意思也是"被认为…",即"非商业用途的树种被当做原始森林群落的成员, 同样应得到保护"。within reason 意为"合理的,有节制的"。 where forestry is ecologically more advanced 是修饰 Europe 的非限制性定语从句。

50. **全句译文**：这种保护系统往往忽视陆地群落中诸多缺乏商业价值,但对其健康运行至关重要的物种,而最终导致它们的灭绝。

    翻译提示：句子主干为 It tends to ignore and to eliminate many elements.后面的两个 that 引导的定语从句修饰 elements,意为"那些没有商业价值但对陆地生物群落的健康运行至关重要的物种"。

参考译文

在一个完全以经济目的为基础的守恒系统中存在一个基本缺点，即陆地上大多数生物群落没有什么经济保监会。然而这些生物是生物群落的成员，如果其稳定性依赖生物群落的完整性，它们就有权利生存下去。

当其中某个没有经济价值的种类面临威胁时，如果我们碰巧喜欢这种生物的话，我们就找借口并赋予它经济价值。本世纪之初，燕雀被认为将面临灭绝。(46)科学家们急忙介入，但提出的证据显然站不住脚，其大意是，如果鸟类不能控制昆虫的数量，昆虫便会吞噬我们人类。为了让证据发挥作用，就必须与经济挂上钩。

现在再来读这些转弯抹角的解释会让人感到痛苦，(47)"但是我们至少几近承认，无论鸟类能否带给我们经济价值，它们自有生存下去的权利。"

肉食哺乳动物和以鱼类为食的鸟类也面临同样情况。(48)曾经有段时间，生物学家或多或少滥用了一种证据，即这些生物通过杀死体弱者来保持种群的健康，或者说它们仅仅捕食没有价值的物种。和前面提到的情况一样，为了让证据发挥作用，必须与经济挂上钩。只在最近几年我们才听到了更诚实的观点：肉食动物也是生物群落的成员，任何特殊的利益集团都没有权利为了自己或真或假的好处而使它们灭绝。

某些树种也被用满脑子都是经济学的林务官排除在外，因为它们生长缓慢或作为木料的卖价太低。(49)在林业生态更为发达的欧洲，没有商业价值的树种被合理地看成是当地森林群落的成员，并得到相应的保护。此外，人们发现某些树种具有提高土壤肥沃度的重要功能。森林与其组成树种之间、与地表植物和动物群落之间的相互依赖的关系是不证自明的。

总而言之，仅建立在经济学基础上的守恒系统太过偏颇。(50)"这种保护系统往往忽视陆地群落中诸多缺乏商业价值，但对其健康运行至关重要的物种，而最终导致它们的灭绝。"它错误地认为，没有那些非经济性物种的存在，生物界也会正常运转。